"WAS I SUPPOSED TO LET YOU BLEED TO DEATH, SYREENA?"

he asked quietly, trying to take back the pain he had caused her with the balm of his words. "Why are you so eager to value my life above your own?"

"Because I am not so special that an entire people should be deprived of their monarch for my sake!"

"Lucky for you, I disagree with that assessment."

Damien understood, however, that there was baggage beyond her statement other than the immediate disagreement. Still, it did not measure up for him. She had never struck him as the type who devalued herself.

She looked at him as if he were completely insane for a long moment, her confused eyes searching over him for an answer and a logic that just was not within grasp. Then, without knowing why, she leaned in and kissed him.

BOOK YOUR PLACE ON OUR WEBSITE AND MAKE THE READING CONNECTION!

We've created a customized website just for our very special readers, where you can get the inside scoop on everything that's going on with Zebra, Pinnacle and Kensington books.

When you come online, you'll have the exciting opportunity to:

- View covers of upcoming books
- Read sample chapters
- Learn about our future publishing schedule (listed by publication month *and author*)
- Find out when your favorite authors will be visiting a city near you
- Search for and order backlist books from our online catalog
- Check out author bios and background information
- Send e-mail to your favorite authors
- Meet the Kensington staff online
- Join us in weekly chats with authors, readers and other guests
- Get writing guidelines
- AND MUCH MORE!

**Visit our website at
http://www.kensingtonbooks.com**

DAMIEN

THE NIGHTWALKERS

JACQUELYN FRANK

ZEBRA BOOKS
KENSINGTON PUBLISHING CORP.
www.kensingtonbooks.com

ZEBRA BOOKS are published by

Kensington Publishing Corp.
850 Third Avenue
New York, NY 10022

All Kensington titles, imprints, and distributed lines are available at special quantity discounts for bulk purchases for sales promotion, premiums, fund-raising, educational, or institutional use.

Special book excerpts or customized printings can also be created to fit specific needs. For details, write or phone the office of the Kensington Special Sales Manager: Attn. Special Sales Department. Kensington Publishing Corp., 850 Third Avenue, New York, NY 10022. Phone: 1-800-221-2647.

Zebra and the Z logo Reg. U.S. Pat. & TM Off.

ISBN-13: 978-0-8217-8068-8
ISBN-10: 0-8217-8068-9

First Printing: June 2008
10 9 8 7 6 5 4 3 2 1

Printed in the United States of America

Prologue

England: The Year 1562

Elizabeth laughed aloud, the sound carrying well into the enormously vaulted ceilings of the ballroom in spite of her obvious breathless state. She was pressing a hand into the curve of her waist, at just the point where her corset always tended to bite at her lung capacity. However, only those in her strictest confidence would be aware of that amusing bit of trivia. To anyone else in the court, young Queen Bess was simply striking an elegant figure as she danced.

Her partner was merciless, grasping her fingers firmly and leading her into turn after turn of the intricate dance. There were few people in Queen Elizabeth's court who could keep up with the monarch's passion and stamina for the dance. Apparently, the Romanian Prince who had Bess by the hand was well able to keep up with her, and even push her past her extraordinary limits.

Robert Dudley watched the debacle with dark, avaricious eyes and a tic that jumped tellingly in his jaw. Cecil, Lord

Burghley, could not resist the opportunity to taunt the Queen's neglected favorite. "It would seem, Dudley, that our Good Bess is quite taken with Prince Damien. I do not believe I have ever seen her make such fast friends with a visiting dignitary before."

Dudley did not respond immediately. He had been forced to watch suitors from a variety of countries come and court his Bess, but this Romanian prince would have just as little success as they'd had if he thought to propose to the notoriously capricious Queen of England.

Her heart is mine, he thought fiercely.

No matter how many handsome dignitaries Cecil thought to parade before her as potential fodder for matrimony, Bess would never betray her heart . . . or his.

Damien finally pulled Elizabeth into the final turn of the dance, smiling at her with gleaming mischief in his stunning midnight blue eyes.

"You best me tonight!" the English Queen declared breathlessly, taking his offered arm and letting her guest escort her back to her throne. She sat down with little regard for ladylike grace, kicking out her voluminous skirts as she swept a cup of wine out of the hands offering it up to her. "My lord, you will tell me how you ever learned to dance our latest dances with such skill and stamina!"

The Prince gave her a wickedly charming grin, reaching to stroke his closely barbered beard as if giving the matter considerable thought.

"I suspect it was because I heard that the one true way of gaining the attention of the English sovereign is to dance circles all about her." He exhaled a dramatic sigh. "And now my machinations are discovered and I think you will send me away, never to set foot on the soil of your beautiful homeland again."

"That all depends," she countered slyly, "on why one wishes to gain Our attention."

"I shall concoct a devious ulterior motive if you wish. Otherwise I must confess it was nothing but sheer curiosity that compelled me."

Elizabeth threw back her head and laughed. His charm and forthright humor were scandalous to the suspicious eyes of England's native court, but it was clear Prince Damien could not care less. Elizabeth liked that. She had been delighted by Damien from the moment he had greeted her four days ago. He had done so with the irreverent observation that he was not there to court or woo her, that she could expect no offer of marriage from him whatsoever, because he knew without a doubt that she was too good for him and would be far better off without him underfoot.

It had been an outrageous way of breaking the ice, quickly reassuring the tickled monarch that her guest was merely there to enjoy himself, not to play a matrimonial chess match with her as so many visitors from foreign principalities seemed to be doing. They had been thick as thieves ever since. Elizabeth saw in Damien an equal, perhaps a potential confidant who could understand her unique position in the workings of the world.

"Come, walk with Us, Damien," she said, standing up now that she had caught her breath and taking his ready arm once more.

Elizabeth led Damien into the recesses of the grand London palace. They were being followed, of course, by the small clutch of women who served as Elizabeth's ladies-in-wait, but both sovereigns easily disregarded their presence.

"Witticisms and charm aside, Damien," she said casually, "what is your purpose here, really?"

"I have no purpose. I am simply traveling and seeing the world at present."

"And what of your people? Your homeland? Do they not need their prince?"

"Of course they do," he responded easily. "But my principality is not like yours. My culture . . . well, it is very different from yours. It can bear my absence now and then."

"You are very lucky, then," she remarked, trying not to sound as envious as he knew she was.

Damien looked down at the Queen from his considerable height, a small smile curling at one corner of his mouth. He did not often mingle with this culture, but sometimes he heard interesting bits of information about the doings of the world and felt compelled to investigate for himself.

The young English Queen was one of a kind. Her future held a promise and potential that could very well outshine even her own expectations. It would be a shame to let her existence pass him by without getting a close-up perspective of the woman. Also, he had not been lying when he had claimed the need for amusement. Boredom could sometimes be far too easy to come by. This little niche of the world had its intriguing delights. The shadowy machinations of English court politics alone was enough to keep one on one's toes. There were so many sublayers of scheming and plotting that it was a mental exercise just to keep track of it all.

Damien had always enjoyed a good intrigue, and it was always a good joke to try and determine what the outcome of it all would be. Sometimes it was an even better joke to alter the outcome himself if he could.

"Well, my lady, I fear I must beg you to excuse me," he said, his dark eyes and lips both smiling with clever magnetism.

Elizabeth had to admit the man was nothing short of beautiful. In the way a woman could be called handsome, he was definitely beautiful. He was tall, certainly over six feet if he was an inch, black haired, and an even, pale-skin tone that needed no help of make-up or powders to achieve the near translucence that was so trendily desirable. He wore no grease in his beard or his mustache; neither did he grow them long and twist them into the points that were the fashion. Instead, they were as excessively clean as his hair, which was caught back at the nape of his neck in a simple queue, tied with a soft blue ribbon that matched the blue-black sheen of the captured strands.

Whatever his position in his world, he apparently was not a monarch who lazed about on his throne. His body was honed like that of a fighter quite experienced with a heavy sword. His upper-body strength was not one anyone could come by naturally, and his wide shoulders could potentially hold the balance of the world. This all narrowed into a tight and trim waistline, no languorous fat anywhere in sight, and long, graceful ropes of muscles clearly evident beneath the fit of the rich material of his breeches. It was enough to make even a queen lick her lips in thoughtful appreciation and contemplation. Elizabeth laughed at herself, very grateful that the man beside her could not read her mind.

"I forbid you to leave," she heard herself insisting, loath to be deprived of the company of the one man in all of England who expected nothing from her but the enjoyment of her company. It was a spoiling luxury, she had to confess, but she was Queen, and she could have any luxury she desired.

Unfortunately, she was not *his* queen.

"Normally, sweet lady, I would forbid myself to leave. However, I must deprive myself of Her Majesty's company this evening in order to, as luck would have it, attend to matters of state. My humblest apologies."

"No, Damien, there is no need for that. We princes are often more slaves to our people than we are leaders. Go. But I will secure your promise to return tomorrow evening. We have a performance scheduled for Our amusement that We think will delight you."

"No doubt. Your taste in these matters has proven to be flawless."

Damien swept her beringed hand up to his lips and kissed the pale skin over the rapid little pulse beating against the inside of her wrist, while giving her a shockingly naughty wink. He then turned on his heel, walking away from her with a grin on his lips, bowing slightly as he passed the appreciative eyes and whispers of the Queen's ladies.

"Damien," Dawn greeted him the moment he entered the castle they were using as a den well outside of London.

Acute as their senses were, Vampires despised living in the city proper. Humans had appalling hygiene and refuse disposal habits. The streets smelled like sewers, the odor of the Thames an unbearable putrefaction, and no amount of French perfume could cover the fact that the practice of bathing had failed to escape human superstitions. They believed it would make them ill, when of course the opposite was true.

"Sweet," Damien greeted in return, a soft growl of appreciation escaping him as the young female Vampire, whose auburn hair was as fiery as the colors of her namesake, leaned into him with a sinuous little wriggle. She feinted for his neck and he laughed as her tongue flicked against his artery with a single-minded and slow lick.

"Mmm," she purred naughtily beneath his ear.

"Fresh little bit," he accused her as he dodged the playful prick of her needle-sharp fangs. He turned her around by her shoulders, sending her away with a slap on her bottom. "I have things to do before dealing with your appetites."

The insolent redhead glanced at him over her shoulder as she was propelled into a forward motion by his spank. It was clear by the hunger in her eyes that she would not be placated for very long. Still, if she needed tending that badly, Dawn would not hesitate to find another ready volunteer. He had no hold on her, and she none on him, save their mutual appetites.

Damien pulled off his gloves and disarmed himself of the sword about his waist and the dagger hidden in his boot.

He handed these to Racine, who was at the ready, as usual. He tweaked one of the long curls of her dust-colored hair in affection before leaving her to the task of clearing away his things.

He walked through the foyer, across the foremost common room, and into the main salon. There, sprawled across the furniture in a cozy circle that ran the entire circumference of the room, were the members of his court who had followed him to England. Simone had lit a fire, completely addicted to that particular creature comfort and making it easy for him to divine that it had been her doing. That and the fact that she was lounging in a chaise just across from the blaze.

"Damien," she said, her voice petulant enough to warn him of a coming complaint. "It is ever so dull here. When will we move on?"

"We only just got here, pet," he reminded her.

"Well, it's boring," she argued, sitting up. "These people are so . . . smelly. And dreadfully dull. Can we not go back to Byzantium?"

"You always want to go back to Byzantium," Lind remarked dryly, lifting his fair head from the ample charms of Jessica's breasts, which he had been dozing lightly upon.

Damien tuned out the bantering arguments and complaints for a moment, looking around at the ten adults who considered themselves his closest friends. Walking out of Elizabeth Tudor's court and into this den of women and men who dressed themselves only as an afterthought always took a moment of adjustment.

Unlike the humans of this decade who layered themselves in corsets and petticoats and layer upon layer of needless clothing, the Vampires of his immediate circle wore as little as possible. Some of the women wore breeches, some of the men kilts. It was all a matter of anachronistic taste. Though his kind normally originated in their Romanian homeland, each had been born in a different century and location, Damien accumulating their friendship like another might collect a variety of vintage wines. Their mode of dress tended to reflect the time and culture they had been born to, or a simplistic combination of whatever made them most comfortable.

It was not that Damien cared what his followers looked like. He hardly even cared what they did, so long as it was not against their laws and did not get any of them killed. Still, it was a little dose of culture shock to move between the human realm and the Vampire world.

He glanced over to the one person who was not lying about as if she were bored out of her mind. Instead, Jasmine was standing in an attentive position, looking out of the window, her legs braced apart so that the muscles were flexed, accented by the tight fit of her breeches and boots. He approached her, stepping over a couple of pairs of legs in his journey to reach her.

"Jas," he greeted her, coming up close to her back so he could push past the tangled cloud of her black hair and follow her gaze to see what she was looking at. He inhaled the aloe and persimmon scent of her shampoo as an additive to his greeting.

"My lord," she greeted him back, her nose twitching as she took in his scent as well. "You need a bath," she remarked.

"Why bother until after tonight's hunt?" he pointed out.

"A fair point," she said absently.

"What are we staring at tonight, Jasmine?"

"Besides sloth, lust, and a variety of other deadly sins?" she asked, cocking both her head and an amused brow back toward the other occupants of the room.

"You are facing in the wrong direction for that, in any event," he taunted her, knowing very well that Jasmine did not express her boredom in the usual ways of their people. She was a thinker. She was always contemplating far deeper issues than immediate gratification. Just like her brother Horatio, by whom she had been raised. He had declined the invitation to accompany them to England. In fact, it had surprised Damien when Jasmine had accepted in his stead.

"I am looking into the future, Damien," she said softly, her tone giving him a chill as it joined her distant gaze out of the window. "And it occurs to me that I know why some of us go to sleep for decades at a time."

"Why, Jasmine?" he asked, though he had lived long enough to discover the answer himself after four hundred or so years.

"To keep ourselves from going mad, I believe. Either from boredom or because the turmoil of all the species mixing about on this planet can be so complicated. It exhausts me and makes me want to sleep just thinking about it."

"Puss, you are only fifty-four. A mere child, if you will not take that as an insult. Too young to be thinking about the hunger for entertainment in your old age, and far too young to worry about the fates of all the species crammed onto this planet." He reached to pull back her hair, kissing her baby-soft cheek fondly and stroking an affectionate finger down the side of the flawless, youthful skin of her face. Like all Vampires, she had not aged a day beyond her full sexual maturity in her twenties. "If it makes you feel more content, however, I think I can promise to give you a good entertainment should you ever need one. All you have to do is ask."

"Watching that ugly, freckled woman dodge men and assassins is not my idea of an amusement," she retorted wryly.

"Ah, but there is a method to my madness, sweet."

Damien smiled and turned to face the room. He cleared his throat and gained everyone's attention. A couple of them even sat up in hopeful expectation.

"My time in court has been rather fruitful. There is a bit of a religious uprising taking place in France. Protestants and Catholics and the usual nonsense."

"Oh! Are they sending young men?" Jessica asked excitedly.

"Is it an army or merely a pack of rebels?"

"Yes. You must quantify 'a bit,' Damien," Lind insisted.

"Let us just say it is enough of a bit to cover up our arrival and our hunting for a good while," he said with a chuckle. "We will leave in a week's time."

The next night, Damien arrived at the palace only to find out that Elizabeth was ill and would not be holding court that evening. The Prince was concerned. London, even in wintertime, was a breeding ground for terrible plagues and other treacherous diseases. Elizabeth Tudor did not strike him as the sort to get sick or the type to take to her bed even if she was. She was a feisty, stubborn thing; it was the very reason why Damien enjoyed her so very much.

The Prince took it upon himself to find another way into the Queen's household after Robert Dudley took a bit too much pleasure in turning him away. Damien could have easily influenced him to the contrary, but he was bored with Dudley's ideas of what constituted a play for power.

He made his way with unerring surety to the wing that housed Elizabeth's personal quarters. He came close enough to the worried whispers and scurrying going on around the Queen's chambers to listen for what information he could get, using both the perception of their speech and the divination of their thoughts to construct a full picture of the situation. Once he was certain Elizabeth's illness was minor and she would soon be well again, he would leave, gather his entourage, and head for the battlefields of France, where a number of new entertainments awaited them.

It only took him a moment to realize Elizabeth was not going to be all right at all. In fact, she was probably going to die before the night was over.

She had contracted the deadly smallpox.

Damn lethal nuisance of a disease, Damien thought angrily.

He left the wall he had been leaning against and quickly moved across the room. No one stopped him because no one was even aware of his presence. He walked right into Bess's bedroom and marched over to her bed, thrusting the curtains aside impatiently. He looked down on her, frowning with furious disgust. She looked weak, so deadly pale . . . almost as if she was not even the same woman who had laughed, danced, and flirted with him the night before.

There were two women sitting watch very close to the bed, and Damien turned to them. He held each by the chin for a brief moment, staring hard into their eyes until he had sufficiently manipulated their thoughts and perceptions. Then he turned back to Bess, kneeled on the bed with one knee, and scooped her up against the support of his chest. She lolled against him like a limp china doll as he shoved back the tangles of red curls covering her neck.

Then he reared back his head for a moment, fangs stretching and flexing out of his mouth with a wicked, sharp gleam for only a second before he drove them into the throat of the young English Queen.

The Vampire Prince felt her blood, superheated with fever, flowing over his tongue. He had not hunted earlier, so there was that sudden pleasure of the release of hunger that always came with the first infusion of prey blood.

Despite her illness and fever, Elizabeth reacted to his intrusion. She groaned softly, reaching blindly to grasp the arm banded tightly around her ribs beneath her breasts. He could not ignore the stroke of her fingers as they brushed over the fine hairs on his arm, and the twist of her body against his chest and thighs. The stimulation enhanced the pleasure of his feed, just as the act of nourishment always brought out the instinctual sensuality of the prey. The only thing that could have made it sweeter would have been fear or rage or anything that pumped a human full of the spice of adrenaline just before the skin was pierced.

She was already weak, so he did not take his fill. Nowhere near it. But he kept his mouth over the wound he had made. Her carotid pulse beat madly against his tongue, sweeping the effects of his second bite into her throat as his fangs injected her with the clotting agents that were stored within them, just as venom is delivered through the fangs of a snake.

But unlike venom, this would not harm Elizabeth in the least.

On the contrary. Somewhere, mixed in the chemistry of the coagulants that were quickly stopping the blood from escaping from the wound as he disengaged from her neck, was the antibody she would need to fight off the invader threatening her life.

There were few Vampires who were old enough or strong enough to take in an infection of the magnitude and complexity of smallpox. However, those like Damien who were powerful enough had the ability to divine and localize the pathogen, extracting it from disease-ravaged cells and forcing their own chemistry to produce the necessary antibody. It was no easy trick, and Vampires who were not up to the task could easily poison themselves with disease. Luckily, they could sense such things on their prey even before they caught up with it.

The reward for risking this conversion from disease to cure, however, was a pathological memory of the antibody that joined with hundreds of others and was added to the coagulant injected into prey at the end of a feed. Damien had preyed on a victim of smallpox before, and this had allowed his body to create the antibody whose benefit Elizabeth was now going to enjoy. He had not fed on her for the sake of hunger. That had been a small side bonus.

He had fed on her to help cure her.

Damien slid away from the Queen, laying her down gently into an abundance of feather-filled pillows. He caught an errant bead of blood on his thumb, pausing only long enough to lick the precious sweetness away.

His bite was not a miracle cure. It was merely a shortcut that would give her immune system a great advantage. Elizabeth was strong and a fighter. The combination would help her to recover. It would just take some time.

Damien would go to France, feast with his brethren on the battlefields, and return later, hopefully to find her alive and well and pleased to see him.

Chapter 1

Damien's head snapped up as he got the sudden sense that someone was very nearby. The sharp turn of his neck caused the braid at the base of his neck to snap like a whip against his throat.

It was nearly like pitch, the darkness around him was so black and so complete. There was no visible moon, leaving everything like a heavy blanket of suffocating velvet that those who considered themselves vulnerable might feel an urge to run away from. Even the glow of the streetlamps placed few and far between in the California suburb seemed helpless to penetrate this darkness.

However, the night did not bother Damien. Quite the opposite. It was his natural habitat, all of his senses equipped to work best within its folds. In spite of all that, something blew with alien chill down the back of his neck as this new presence crept within range of his perception.

He leaned back into the protective shadows of the foliage a little bit more as he realized it was not a human being that moved toward him with such near-perfect stealth. Normal humans were not capable of defying his senses so well that they could come this close before he became aware of them. So the Vampire Prince was left to wonder who, or what, it was that was following so stealthily in his footsteps.

He first had to determine if this was an accidental or purposeful tail. He exhaled, out of habit rather than a need to, shaking his head with momentary perturbation. All he had wanted to do that night was take part in a good hunt and then return to his holdings in peace. However, in order to have that sort of easy peace, he mused, one had to have no enemies.

Unfortunately, Vampires had a lot of enemies.

And the Prince of all Vampires usually had ten times the usual dose of them. Exterior politics and the number of annoying humans or troublemaking Nightwalkers aside, Vampires had an awful tendency to play King of the Mountain with one another. Though most knew better than to match skills with Damien, there were always a few who over-estimated their ability to unseat the royal Vampire from his throne. Theirs was a society where survival of the fittest was at the core of many of their motivations. In the case of the throne, it determined who would lead their entire species.

He should know, he thought with a sly half-smile that allowed the ivory of one anticipatory fang to glimmer in the darkness. Defeating the previous monarch was how Damien had come to be in his princely position several centuries ago.

But his predecessor had been something of a jackass, he mused as he waited idly for his stalker to catch up with him, and he had quite thoroughly earned his ritualistic beheading.

As he turned his senses to the task of making prey of his hunter, he was able to determine that it was not a Vampire that tracked him. All he needed to do to figure that out was flick into place the small nictitating membranes hidden in the anatomy of his eyes. That membrane added the ability to visualize a brightly fluoresced aura that varied with the amount of heat a body was giving off.

While Vampires did not have a natural circulation to speak of, they did retain the heat of the blood of their victims from one feeding to the next, able to maintain it well, provided they fed within twenty-four hours of the previous meal. However, the flaw to that system was that extremities like fingers and toes lost that artificial heat the quickest. So, in his visual perception, a Vampire who had not hunted yet would have a sort of bull's-eye effect at this young hour of the night. The heart and chest would be the hottest, flaring bright and white, but in eddying circles that white would fade to a circle of red, then orange, then pink, until the location of hands and feet were almost imperceptible to heat vision, blending in too well with the temperature around them.

A Vampire who had hunted already would be a uniform red, unlike a human, who was a changing series of white, red, and redder splashes of determining color. Human heat levels were always changing, with movement, effort, sickness, or arousal, and there was a perceptible time period before the human body compensated for those changes, evening them out somewhat. However, those with the sharpest of eyes and skills could easily determine the difference between a flushed Vampire and a mortal being after a century or two of practice.

The figure that tracked him was neither human nor Vampire, he determined. However, it was potentially a Nightwalker who could emulate any level of body temperature they wished, or it was a Demon. The Demon race was notorious for a body temperature several degrees cooler than most upright walking species on the planet. This was the case in the body that stood in shadow not too far away from him.

The Nightwalker species were the races that lived only in the night, hiding from a curious variance of negative effects the sun caused them. Of these species, Demons were the second least likely to cause grief or pose a danger for the Vampire Prince. Demons were infamously moral and reclusive, focusing within themselves and upon policing their own, and were very much less likely to venture out in order to cause trouble elsewhere.

Usually.

There had been a bit of trouble lately that made anything possible.

Of course, it could be a Shadowdweller. Those devious little tricksters were the masters of self-camouflage. They were the Nightwalker equivalent of chameleons. They were also an enormous pain in the posterior, Damien thought wryly. They had little to no political structure, wandering around in clans or religious clusters, quite often causing more than their fair share of mischief and trouble. They were like wild children, pestering other Nightwalkers, scrapping amongst themselves and with others, mucking with mortals like they were toys and dolls for playing with.

Not that Damien failed to see the appeal in that. He had mucked around with humans and others quite a bit in his youth.

Well, perhaps youth was being too liberal.

To be honest, he was still quite easily capable of toying with the workings of the races around him, if it suited his mood. He chuckled to himself at that. Gideon, an old Demon friend of his, had once accused him of being a cosmic busybody. It was not all that far from the truth.

Before Damien would allow himself the luxury of believing that this Demon was a friend, he needed to turn the hunt around and surprise his quarry. If he lollygagged in the bushes much longer, the person tagging after him would realize he had become aware of being followed.

Unexpectedly, the shadow suddenly broke from its surroundings and headed straight in his direction.

The direct approach.

That meant one of two things. Incredible stupidity, or immeasurable fearlessness. As he switched to normal vision and picked out the features of the approaching figure, he realized it was the latter.

"Noah," he said, breaking from the shadows himself to step up to the Demon King.

Noah smiled slightly, reaching out to take Damien's quickly offered hand and shaking it firmly. The two monarchs then settled their weight evenly on their feet and regarded one another with quick, skilled eyes.

"What brings you to my hunting grounds, so far from home?" Damien asked, cutting to the chase. Noah's holdings in England were a far cry from California, which was where Damien claimed his territory nowadays. It was not as though the King would be able to claim the likelihood of just passing by, since Demons were less frequently found in the United States. They were not enemies, though, which was clearly indicated by the fact that Damien asked his question first, rather than *after* trying to kill him.

Vampires were also very territorial.

"Call it a business matter," Noah returned congenially. "My apologies for invading your mealtime."

Damien waved the matter off with the flick of a long-fingered hand, the large ruby of the ring on his middle finger winking one of its facets at the Demon King.

"I had not acquired prey yet. It is no matter."

"I had measured as much," Noah returned.

The Demon King was a Fire Demon. Every Demon claimed a power and affinity with certain elements of the natural world around and within themselves. Fire was of course the most volatile and impressive of these elements. As such, Noah could sense energy patterns and, having lived over six centuries, had enough practice with them to know whether or not Damien had acquired a target for the night's feeding.

Noah had earned his throne much in the way Damien had, only he had been elected to it because of his unquestionable strength and ability to be a leader. The previous Demon

King had needed to die before that would happen. Of somewhat natural causes, too, because it was severely frowned on for Demons to battle or kill one another—though, being basically immortal, there was very little about the death of any member of either of their species that could be considered natural.

Usually it came down to some form of homicide. In that culture, however, it was unlikely a Demon would be elected King who had just murdered their predecessor. Demons took great affront to the murder of their monarchs.

Noah could also never be voted out of his office. Though the Great Council had elected him, they could not change their minds. His death would be the only way they could replace him with a successor. In less civilized times that had made it a very interesting prospect to be the King of Demons. Especially if the Great Council decided they had made a mistake and tried to assassinate the reigning monarch.

Then again, no Nightwalker race could ever be completely civilized. That was one of Damien's firmer beliefs.

"So what is your business?" Damien asked, indicating with that same ringed hand that the King should walk beside him. They were in a quaint little development in the San Jose suburbs, the rows of houses on either side of them sitting quiet and dark, set back from perfectly manicured lawns and neat little sidewalks.

"The Library."

Again, he cut right to the point of it. Damien liked that about Demons. They did not play social games, unless it suited some extraordinary purpose.

"Yes. The Library. I have not forgotten," the Prince said. "What is it you would like?"

"Scholars from your society, to be blunt. We have no intention of keeping the mysteries of this hidden Nightwalker Library to ourselves. It is clearly a universal collection of many Nightwalker histories. We have not reentered the place since our initial discovery of it in the caverns in Lycanthrope territory. Neither have any of Siena's people," Noah said, smiling slightly when he mentioned the name of the Lycanthrope Queen who had recently wed the commander of his own armed forces. Elijah, the Captain of the Demon warriors, was clearly looked on fondly by his ruler.

"We . . . that is, Siena and I decided it would only be fair to invite you to join us when we send our scholars in to begin to research what the significance of this place is. Since none of us have ever seen its like before and it is obviously compiled of the languages of all the Nightwalker species, all Nightwalkers should have a fair chance of having a crack at it. On equal terms."

"That is very fair of you. But I do not think I need to tell you that my people are not the scholarly type. Outside of our immediate political structure and my rather compact court, we are a nation of tribes. We run in small, independent packs, worry mostly about feeding, avoiding human hunters, and"—Damien gave Noah a feral grin—"seeking out sensuality. If we cannot consume it, kill it, or party with it, it does not interest us."

Noah laughed at that. That basically described almost every Nightwalker race there was. However, the Demon King knew that the Vampires were the epitome of that particular stereotype. Vampiric boredom was a frightening thing to behold. A Vampire tended to cause a great deal of upheaval when not distracted or amused. Still, Damien had his own way of policing his species. It did not get too far out of hand in this day and age, as it sometimes had in the past.

Of course, that could have something to do with the fact that Damien had matured and had stopped leading his people into the fray.

"If I send anyone to you who is interested," Damien said slowly, "they will no doubt have ulterior personal motives. Perhaps looking at this strange Library as a means of gaining power. There is nothing a Vampire enjoys more than gaining power. If I send someone who is not interested, the place will no doubt become a Vampire hangout until it loses its charm. They would only get in your way. No, it is best if we get any pertinent information from you and yours. Demon and Lycanthrope scholars are the best for this sort of task."

"I figured you would say that, but I thought I should ask in any event. I am surprised that you are showing no personal interest."

"On the contrary," Damien contradicted. "I am eaten up with curiosity. A joint Library with books in languages from so many of the Nightwalker species has intriguing implications. The one I find most curious is how we all managed to get in the same room long enough to even think of constructing such a place, never mind filling it as full as it was when we first saw it. It hints at curious histories so long past that even we who are so long-lived do not recall their origins. It flirts with the idea that we Nightwalkers may have more common origins than we would ever have suspected. It also opens the potential of pissing off a few of the elitist purists all of our races seem to have, arrogant, prejudiced bastards that we are. It is bound to cause trouble."

"And I know how much you enjoy trouble," Noah remarked wryly.

"I admit it, I do." Damien chuckled. "I am certain I will be seen snooping around your workers from time to time. Otherwise, I will instruct Horatio to attend your meetings and recaps of your discoveries. He will report back to me."

"Horatio?" This time Noah laughed. "Now there is an unlikely student. Diplomats make poor scholars. Sometimes history and recorded data is too factual for them. Too biased. They prefer to give too much the benefit of the doubt. Everything would be propaganda to Horatio."

"Just the same, he is already a fixture of your court. That will make it easier. There is also Kelsey. She is taking in the delights of Siena's court at the moment. Between them both and my occasional check-ins, I imagine I will get a fashionable form of the truth of the goings-on."

"Very well," Noah conceded. "But let me know if you change your mind."

"I rarely do."

"I realize this," Noah said. The other man stopped walking and they reached to shake hands once again. "Thank you for your time, Damien. I hope you will come to the naming celebration?"

"When is your sister due to give birth?"

"Within another month or two. Normally a Demon female would go a full thirteen months to term, but Gideon feels his son is very eager to make an appearance. Between that and Magdelegna's strong desire to finish this pregnancy, I have no doubt I will be an uncle again very shortly."

"Wish her well for me. I look forward to Horatio's news of the birth."

Noah gave him a nod, stepped back, and in a heartbeat became a twisting column of smoke that stayed in the shape of the tall, broad-shouldered man for several seconds before stretching out to the sky where it was lost to the night.

Damien followed the Demon King's retreat with his other senses for a moment before he turned his attention back to the task of seeking his supper.

Syreena hit the ground with a loud grunt, the impact of her body and the hard exhalation of her breath kicking up a cloud of dust that, upon her next breath, promptly entered her lungs. She coughed, spat blood from her mouth, and then twisted up onto her hands in order to glare at the person who had hit her.

Actually, she should say persons.

They were The Three.

And she had crossed them badly.

"Get up, child," the central robed figure commanded her.

She did so, drawing her slim legs beneath herself so she could push off from the dirt floor. She tossed back her hair, the two-toned tangles mixing iron gray and soft brown together for a moment before parting into uniform-colored sheets on either side of her head. They parted perfectly into a straight fall on one side and a feathered softness on the other. Her eyes flashed with anger. They were also one gray and one brown; however, they had the disconcerting position of being on the opposing sides of the hair color that would match them. The harlequin effect was always eerie, but in outrage it was downright disturbing.

"I am not a child," she snapped at them, defying the fear of The Three that had been instilled in her from a young age. "I will not apologize for my actions now or ever, even if you beat me to a pulp. So you may as well reconcile yourself to it."

"Your insubordination is untenable, Syreena. This is not how you were raised."

"I know how I was raised," she barked back, spitting once more before wiping the back of her hand across her lips. "I am no longer beholden to The Pride, Silas, and I have not been for fifteen years. If you recall, you are the ones who rejected me, who threw me out and into the Lycanthrope court so I could serve my sister."

"You were not rejected, Syreena. You were reassigned. Monks of The Pride serve dual relationships all of the time in the world. Why must it be one or the other with you? You are a Monk *and* you are the Queen's advisor."

"And I am a Princess," she reminded them. "A member of the royal family. Though my sister defers to your wisdom and protocols on occasion, she still holds reign over you as she does any member of the Lycanthrope race. That power is also mine now. You told me it was time to take up my mantle of royalty, and now you punish me for doing so!"

"We punish you," the figure on the left retorted, "because you attacked one of your brothers without cause."

"That pompous jackass dared question my sister's survival when she was on the edge of death. She was poisoned so badly by the sun, gasping as if every breath were her last, and he insults her, belittles her efforts toward a peace she was willing to sacrifice her life for! I would, and I *will* do it again if anyone—"

"No one puts their hands on a member of The Pride!" Silas barked at her, showing the first ruffle in his exterior calm since the entire incident between them had begun.

"Oh, you mean like you did not just lay hands on me?" she countered. "Do as I say, and not as I do? That may have worked when I was a child, but I am an adult now. A well-seasoned adult—I thank you, your training has done me well. I warn you, Silas, if you raise your hand to me one more time, you will learn what it is I have held in check through my teachings all of these years, just as Konini and Hendor did when they disrespectfully disparaged my family. You got your lick in. Be satisfied with it and move on. You will not drag me to heel this time. You never will again. Those days are past."

The Princess was not making an idle threat. Silas was well aware of what she was capable of, and just as aware of what he did *not* know she was capable of. No one would ever know that but Syreena herself, no matter that she had spent the past century under the tutelage of the best minds and members of The Pride.

Syreena was a Lycanthropic anomaly. The cure to a childhood illness had left her dramatically mutated. Once she had hit puberty, she had developed into a Lycanthrope without equal.

Every Lycanthrope could exist in three forms of themselves. The human aspect, the aspect of whatever animal it was that ran through their blood, and a human-shaped combination of the two called the Wereform.

Syreena had been given an additional two aspects, a split that took on the form and Wereform of an additional animal.

This gave her a position of precedence. No one truly knew where her abilities ended. No one but herself. While it intrigued everyone, even tempted them, none were all that willing to challenge her to her limits.

So even though The Three were the most feared and most powerful Monks of The Pride, Syreena was not surprised when they relented. It came in the form of Silas turning on his heel in displeased silence and marching out of the discipline room, the remaining two following silently in his wake.

Syreena exhaled in frustrated anger. She was not known for her temper, but it did not mean that she did not have one. In fact, she had been bred from temperamental stock. It was only her teachings and meditations that had allowed her to escape the infamy of the royal warlike tendencies. To be fair, her sister had escaped them as well. Siena was even renowned as a peacekeeper. Understandably, there was a distinct difference between Siena's politics and her personality. That was evident in the fact that she had chosen a diehard warrior for her husband.

Syreena remained in the dungeon room of the monastery, pacing the floor in an effort to spend some of her unburned emotional energy. To be honest, this attempt at reining her in had not been at all unexpected. After she had nearly strangled the two Monks who had dared to gainsay her and her sister's wishes, it was very much a given. Anyone who threatened a member of The Pride, even Siena herself, would face censure.

It did not follow that Siena would accept or allow the censure. She certainly would not have allowed Silas to strike her, had he been insane enough to do so. But Syreena was merely a younger Princess to them, heir to the throne only until Siena produced her first child. So, though it galled her until her stomach roiled with bile, they did not hold her in the same regard or esteem.

It did not even seem to matter to them that she had the potential to become one of The Three herself one day.

Though she never showed it outwardly, that really ticked her off.

She muttered a native curse, tossing her hair over so that only the brown side showed. She shook her head and body in a quick little shiver, sending the strands in a quick coating of her skin. Hair turned to feathers in a heartbeat, clothing dropping forgotten to the ground as a peregrine falcon took flight out of them.

Syreena flew through the closed caverns of the monastery dungeon quickly until she gained ground level. Then she winged quickly out of an entrance, leaving the cavern of The Pride behind her in a matter of minutes.

Siena turned her head when the sound of beating wings reached her ears. She watched from the corners of her eyes as the familiar falcon swooped into the chamber she used for prayer, transforming on the spot so that the Princess landed at a slight run of feet instead of talons. The Queen of the Lycanthropes rose from her meditative position on her knees, pausing briefly to shake the thin gown she wore into proper place.

Syreena stood in her nude human form, regarding her sister, whose long golden curls of hair hid the features of her luxuriant body far better than the sheer scrap of cloth she was using for a dress. Nudity meant nothing to either of them, nor any of their genus for that matter. A Lycanthrope could not change form in restrictive clothing, so they wore little to none of it. What they did wear was easily discarded either just before or during the change.

"How did it go?"

Syreena had not told Siena that The Pride had beckoned her, but neither was she surprised that her sister had found out. She was Queen, after all.

"Let's just say I won't be invited to tea anytime soon,"

Syreena responded glibly, giving her sister a half grin tha Siena could very much appreciate.

The sisters were as opposite as they could possibly be, a least in outward appearance. Where Siena was tall and carve out like a voluptuous Amazon, Syreena was petite, slim, an often referred to as willowy. Where Siena was golden-haire golden-skinned, and a seductive beauty, Syreena looked mor like a cunning calico cat with her bi-colored hair and oppo site-set harlequin eyes. Siena had grown up in the thick o court intrigues and the freedom to mesh with the other Night walker races. Syreena had grown up in the monastery, se cluded and sealed up from the real world from the momen everyone realized how different she was.

It was not that she had been shunned or outcast. Quite th opposite. She had been overtreasured. Lycanthropes loved good mutation, especially a powerful one like hers. She ha been sent to The Pride not only for training and education but to protect her from those who would use her as a weapo to gain power. More specifically, to gain the throne her fathe had held until only fifteen years earlier that, upon his deatb Siena had ascended to. Siena had demanded Syreena's re turn that very same day, extracting her from her shelteree existence in order for her to take her place as heir and to us her learning skills as a diplomat and chief advisor for Siena

They had been veritable strangers the day the Princes had come home, in spite of the constant exchange of letter. between them over their century apart. Though Syreena hac initially felt like an outsider, Siena had seemed to merely fli a mental switch that made her an immediately loving an doting elder sister.

Syreena had found it easy to love her, a fact that contin ued to baffle her to this day. Though the Monks had guidec and cared for her, they were not known for their overflow o affection or emotion. She had not realized she *could* love until Siena had taken her so easily into her heart.

"I hope they were not so foolish as to be too harsh with you," Siena said thoughtfully, crouching slightly to extinguish the incense she had been burning for her prayer.

"If you are referring to my rather bloated lip, I would not worry about it." Syreena touched the swollen area and shrugged matter-of-factly. "It makes for a tender beak when turning into a strong breeze or thermal, but otherwise causes no harm."

"I do not like the idea of anyone striking you," Siena responded, moving closer and inspecting her sister's otherwise unbruised body for a brief moment. "You should be afforded the same respect that they would show for me."

"I reminded them of that." Syreena chuckled, her harlequin eyes twinkling with triumphant mischief. "If The Three wore shorts under their robes, you can bet they would be in a mighty big twist at the moment."

The remark made Siena laugh out loud. Syreena was such a staid student, full of respect for her upbringing and all the lessons she had learned in the monastery, so this was a rare side of irreverence.

"Well, I am afraid to ask you this favor, then."

It was not like Siena to hedge, and Syreena narrowed her dual-colored eyes on her sister. "Ask anyway," she said.

"I would like you to join the scholars who are going into the Library. Most of them will, of course, be Monks of The Pride. However, since you have one foot in the monastery and one foot in the court, it makes you my best selection in bridging the gap between those two disparate interests. You will have the respect for study and religious tradition that so pleases The Pride, and you will balance that with your perspective of my interest, which I know is never too far from your heart."

"That sounds easy enough," Syreena said dryly, giving her eyes a dramatic roll.

"Ease, I suspect, will have very little to do with anything that is even remotely connected to the Nightwalker Library," the Queen noted, a curl furrowing through her brow. "There is one other reason I wish to send you."

"One I suspect has something to do with the fact that I can usually manage to end up on top in a fight," Syreena said helpfully.

"Every Monk of The Pride can fight, I realize, though they usually do so only to protect themselves and their own interests. I am not concerned with shielding them, for you all can do that for yourselves. I also take note of the fact that you personally are far more a pacifist than you are a warrior. I have learned that much about you these past fifteen years. Discounting, of course, your recent incident on my behalf."

"Of course," Syreena agreed, giving her sister a wicked smile.

"In spite of all these factors, I am forced to consider the fact that we were forced to destroy an encampment of necromancers, hunters, and the Demon traitors that was little more than one hundred feet above and away from the cavern the Library is located in. Then there is the additional fact that this is in our territory and we will be hosting other Nightwalkers in this expedition for knowledge. I need someone who has had at least some exposure to other Nightwalkers, someone who will take their safety and well-being into consideration. I cannot post military there. Not if there will be Demons about. The peace between Demons and Lycanthropes is far too young after so many centuries of war, and we Nightwalkers tend to have very long memories. Though the Demons will be scholars, there is still too much potential for a volatile outburst of some sort.

"Also, there is no way of knowing what information the Library will reveal. Issues may arise that could turn a scholarly debate deadly. There are just too many random, uncontained factors. You are the only one I know who will have the power and, clearly, the fearlessness it will take to stand up to members on all sides. You are not afraid of The Pride, which makes you unique among us. I admit even I cannot boast that bravery one hundred percent. You are not poisoned against Demons, and you are fully aware of my desire to maintain this peace with them. You have always defended and championed my political desires. Neither are you afraid of the Demons.

"What I am saying," she continued after taking a breath, "is that you are the next best thing to being there myself. I trust you and need you to do this."

"I understand," Syreena said, giving her sister a wry little smile. "I am Princess of this court, but I am queen of riding both sides of a fence."

"You say that as if your ability to care for multiple aspects of a situation is a bad thing," Siena countered, coming closer so she could study Syreena's features thoughtfully. "I have found it to be the most valuable thing about you."

"Yes, I know," Syreena agreed quietly.

What Siena did not realize was that this was true of everyone. Everyone found great value in Syreena and everyone coveted her dual-sided nature. The trouble was finding a point of reconciliation. Not with Siena, because Siena would care for her and respect her even if she grew twenty heads and twenty personalities to match. However, no one in their society, the Queen included, saw Syreena as a single being. She was always a singular one. They enjoyed one of her aspects or the other, but, other than the uniqueness of it, rarely both as a whole.

The court delighted in her mysteriousness. The Pride exploited the fact that they had discovered all of her inimitable talents along with her. The Monks wished to parent her into submission, the public wished to have her wed and bred into it.

Even Siena was guilty of the need to label her and tuck her neatly onto a categorized shelf. It was merely that the Queen's shelf was larger than most, perhaps able to accommodate the unexpected. To everyone else in Lycanthrope society, Syreena was admired as, say, a wild horse would be admired by the humans who captured it. Intelligent, yes. Even a bit dangerous. Something of power and beauty, meant to be broken to ride and bred for her bloodlines and genetic superiority. Serving dutifully the causes of others, never allowed to simply travel her own way.

If she had a self-created way.

In all fairness, Syreena didn't even know if she had a direction of her own. She didn't know if she was a single being, or always two halves, rather than a whole.

"Syreena?"

"Hmm?" She looked up, aware that she had lost track of her sister in her pursuit of her own thoughts. "I am sorry, what did you say?"

"I asked you if something was bothering you," Siena said, changing the question on the fly. She had seen the frown and confusion warring in the depths of her sister's harlequin features.

"Nothing out of the ordinary," Syreena brushed her off, seeming to shake off her thoughts as she shook back her hair.

Siena was not fooled. Lycanthrope hair was a living appendage, with blood flow, tensile ability, and even nerve endings. The toss of Syreena's head was their cultural equivalent to rubbing or shaking out one's hands, as if warding off a chill.

"Then tell me the ordinary," Siena invited softly, reaching to take her sister's arm and lead her into the depths of the cavern castle that made up their royal household.

"I was just wondering if I was up to the task you are setting before me," Syreena half lied. "You will be purposely standing me in potentially troubled waters. I am more used to avoiding such obvious situations of conflict. I am better suited to advising you what to do, putting you or others on your behalf into conflict." Siena laughed when Syreena gave a rueful chuckle. "Perhaps it will do me good," Syreena said a bit more brightly. "It may temper my readiness to throw others to the wolves in the future."

"That is the voice of a true philosopher, always hungry for a learning experience." Siena paused for several moments as they turned in the direction of Syreena's quarters. "Are you happy here, my sister?"

Syreena stopped, turning to look at the Queen with surprise. "Of course I am. Do you doubt my adjustment?"

"No. It took you some time, but you have adapted to royal life and responsibility quite well. But that isn't what I asked you. I want to know if you are happy . . . personally. In your heart."

Syreena smiled at Siena, linking their arms and guiding her forward once again.

"I am not as happy as you are," she teased her. "I do not have a handsome new husband making me happy every night"—she paused a purposeful beat for her own mischief—"and every morning, too, I am told."

Siena threw back her head, laughing with delight even as she allowed herself a bit of a blush.

"Damn, I hate being Queen sometimes. I cannot even use the bathroom without someone taking note of it." She self-consciously reached to fluff the thick, golden filament coils of her hair. "I think my attendants are already accounting for my breeding cycles in anticipation of an heir."

"Should I be watching as well?" Syreena asked archly.

"No." Siena chuckled. "Please. I will be staying quite far away from Elijah when I enter my heat cycle. At least for a few years."

"Ha! Now there is a trick I would like to see. Elijah has never struck me as the sort who would relinquish a hard-earned prize for two weeks, even if it is only twice a year. And you have never been through a mated heat cycle before. As hard as it is to keep from the bed of the opposite sex when you are without a mate, I hear it is nearly impossible to tolerate with one."

"And yet I am determined to forebear. Elijah and I must learn to live with one another before we think to bring children into the fray."

"How like my wife to view everything as a battle."

Siena and Syreena both came to a halt as the mocking comment rushed past them on a sudden cavern breeze. In a blink, the Demon warrior coalesced out of his element, metamorphosing from wind to flesh in a heartbeat, standing before them with all the assuredness of the cocky, powerful being that he was. He was a giant man, as golden blond as Syreena's sister, and roped head to toe with the musculature of a well-seasoned warrior. He wore faded denim jeans and a long-sleeved silk shirt the color of deep turquoise. The dye set off the bright green of his eyes as they roamed the figure of his wife boldly and appreciatively.

Syreena was the one who stood in the nude, but she realized that to Elijah, her sister was the only one standing undressed before him.

"Hello." He greeted Siena softly, his gentle tone taking about ten pounds of armor from his imposing appearance.

Siena's return greeting was nonverbal. She released her sister and glided eagerly into Elijah's opening arms. He hugged the Queen to his body, making her seem somehow much smaller and far more delicate by the reverence with which he did so. It was an impressive trick of perception. Syreena realized then that, as outrageous as it seemed from what she knew of them both, they had somehow become tamed to each other.

Which was not to say that they were either of them tame in any way. Suggesting such a thing to Queen or Consort would very likely earn a demonstration otherwise. It meant only that they were quickly finding a rhythm with each other that allowed one to flow in while the other flowed out. A tide that was powerful, volatile, and potentially dangerous, but a concerto of movement within itself. They were the very definition of what the Demons called an Imprinting; what humans called a soul mate. A perfect match. A meeting of life forces that transcended the limitations of the body.

Syreena could not help but envy them. She was happy for them, but she was also jealous, and she could not help herself. Siena had never tended toward domestication. Quite the opposite, in fact, swearing up until the day of her wedding that she would never marry, refusing to expose her heart and the responsibilities of her throne to the influences of a male. Syreena had always known that her sister's attitude had come from being raised by an irrational and bloodletting warlord of a father. The Queen had not wanted to repeat their mother's mistakes by risking marriage.

In truth, it had always been Syreena who had expressed wishes for a warm home, a loving mate, and a household of children in the letters the sisters had shared over the decades. Lycanthrope royals were allowed only one true mate, could have no other than that soul that existed out in the world somewhere only for them. Once they chose a lover, it was the equivalent of exchanging lifelong vows. It was supposed to be a bond without equal that would last through eternity, from one lifetime into the next.

And Syreena longed for it with all of her heart at times.

"Well, in spite of the fact that you two share a telepathic connection, I am certain that Elijah's stay at Noah's court these past two days has left you with a bit of catching up to do. So I will leave you both."

Syreena bowed out and away from their presence with haste, grateful that they were so close to her chambers. She made a quick escape into her suite of rooms before either of them could protest.

"Damn," Siena muttered.

"What is it?" Elijah asked, taking her face between his hands and tilting her head back so he could look into her eyes and divine her thoughts.

"Oh, nothing," she assured him. "I just realized that she never answered a question I had asked her. I will make her do so . . . at a later date."

Elijah grinned broadly as her ideas for what to do in the interim filled his mind.

"Someone missed me," he teased.

"Someone missed *me*," she countered even as his hands moved possessively over her back, drawing her ever closer to his warmth and his heart.

Chapter 2

Damien entered his home after his hunt, levitating down over the compound walls and landing on a third-floor balcony. The balcony led to a brightly lit library, and he entered, curious to see who had beaten him in the time it took to hunt and travel back to the Santa Barbara mansion.

He came around the shelves to the cozy sitting area several steps down into the center of the room. Sitting with her feet tucked up under her in a comfortable chaise, a book lying open in her lap, was Jasmine. She had not aged a day in nearly five hundred years, her skin still perfection, her black sweep of hair and dark eyes still as full of hidden, mysterious thoughts as ever. She was the one true presence he could not, try as he might, make himself grow tired of.

That is, she was the only surviving such presence.

Jasmine was one of the best hunters of his entourage, so it would not surprise him at all if she did hunt and return faster than he could, in spite of the fact that her hunting grounds were in Southern California.

But he knew just by looking at her that she had not hunted. Her body was chilled, not flushed with fresh heat. Yet she looked as if she were quite comfortable with her book and not intending to go out anytime soon.

"Jasmine?"

She looked up, clearly knowing he had arrived long before he had even cleared the compound walls. His presence was not one that went unnoticed to any Vampire of moderate skill. Since her skill was superb, she would have been aware of him the moment he entered the county, if not quite sure exactly who he was.

"Why have you not gone out?"

She closed the book, not even taking the care to mark her page. "I will. Are you suddenly my keeper, Damien?"

"Not suddenly. You have been a part of my household long enough to know I am everyone's keeper." He stepped lightly down, pushing aside a stack of books on the table across from her so he could seat himself directly at her eye level. "You are melancholy again," he noted directly.

"Don't they call it depression nowadays?"

Her glib tone did not sway him. He frowned slightly. "We are not human, Jasmine. Never were, never will be. Human terms will never quite suit us."

"I suppose not," she agreed. "And I am not melancholy. Nor am I bored," she added quickly when one of his dark brows picked up questioningly. "Don't worry. You won't find me causing mischief in order to entertain myself."

"Then explain to me why you are behaving so moodily."

"I believe I was born that way," she rejoined, leaning a little closer to him, the ends of her black hair skimming the tops of her shoulders as she did so. "When have you known me to be anything other than moody?"

"There is moody . . . and then there is this. I know you, as you say. You will start to neglect yourself, fall into torpor, and I will not see you for an entire century."

Jasmine actually smiled at that. He really did know her too well. The Prince was her oldest friend; her mentor, in fact. They had coasted over many centuries together, survived where their companions had not. She should be surprised if he did *not* know her.

"I would not be the first to do so. And you do not pester any of the others of us who become disenchanted with the present world and decide to go to ground for a while. Why am I earning your special form of concern? Why do you always pester me about this?"

"Because I miss you when you leave me, Jasmine. Do I need to say that?"

"Perhaps. It is nice to hear it." The slim beauty reached out with her long nails to run them down his face fondly. "I am well," she reassured him with a sigh. "Perhaps I am in need of something to occupy me after all. I do not know."

Damien smiled suddenly, transforming his serious features in a way that took years off his already permanently ageless good looks.

"It just so happens that I may have just the thing," he told her.

The sound of footsteps echoed in the caverns leading to the newfound Library hidden within them as Syreena approached the entrance. The traps had been removed, the trick of the locks disengaged for the time being. The stone that had protected the mysterious Library had been moved aside as scholars from differing Nightwalker species warmed the lonely shelves with the beginnings of a continued presence.

She stood at the opening for a moment, taking in only her second view of the remarkable room. The smell of must and mildew was a little less, she noted immediately. Leaving the cavern open had allowed fresh air to circulate in. It was a relief to her senses and probably those of all the other Nightwalkers.

The first step into the cavern took her from stone to a thin but intricately woven carpet. Though it was stained with the centuries and the dampness caused by neglectful trickles of water that had broken through the original seals put up to protect the Library, the craftsmanship of the red and gold rug was still apparent.

Immediately to the left and right along the walls were the first shelves of books. There was not an inch of wall space wasted. Whether they were carved directly out of stone or made of wood and secured into stone, there were shelves covering every inch of the walls, from floor to ceiling. On those shelves, packed in densely, were books ranging in both height and thickness, some of them quite tiny, others quite enormous. At first glance, Syreena could only read about one out of every ten titles. That was remarkable to her because she could read and write quite a few languages, both human and Nightwalker.

The main aisle was large enough to fit a row of tables comfortably down the center of the red runner, the books running the walls on either side for easy access. Someone had already lit several kerosene and oil lamps, setting them at acceptable intervals. The torches that thrust out from intermittent spots in the walls themselves were also lit and burning brightly. Almost too brightly. Syreena could feel the burn on her eyes.

This was as far as she had ever seen into the Library. The day they had first discovered it, they had been pressed into other matters and had not had the luxury of exploring it. Anya, the General of the royal Elite Guard, had been the only one to come back and run through it in its entirety, strictly as a safety measure, just in case the traps and such did not end at the door.

There were already two Monks and a Demon in the room. Syreena was positive there were more in the parts of the chamber that were out of her sight. She supposed they were just starting anywhere, grabbing the first book they came across. No one, as far as she knew, could understand the markings carved into the walls above the bookcases that were no doubt some sort of filing symbols.

They should probably appoint some sort of a librarian, she mused. Someone to coordinate the effort, keeping them from doubling back on their own work. Someone to track the volumes and be responsible for keeping everything complete. Someone to arrange for the repairs to the cavern that would be necessary to keep the water from flowing in and ruining any more of the volumes than it already had.

But while Nightwalkers could agree to share these findings, she would bet money that it would be nearly impossible for them to agree on something as individualized as assigning a librarian. Still, she would have to make the suggestion to Siena. The Library was in their territory, after all. Perhaps if they assigned someone without even asking if they should, it would become accepted as the norm and go unquestioned.

Syreena's speculations halted as a Nightwalker she could not immediately identify entered her perception. She was tiny, barely over five feet, and though she was quite pretty, she seemed terribly unsure of herself. She was creeping along the cases as if she were trying to tune out the fact that anyone else was even there.

She was not Demon. Demons were tall and tanned and dreadfully gorgeous in a very stalwart way, as a rule, and while she was very beautiful, the little thing was delicate and almost frail looking. Neither was she Lycanthrope or Vampire. Lycanthropes could always sense their brethren, and Vampires had no circulation to speak of. Not after a certain age, at least. It was clear to Syreena's senses that she had a rapid little heartbeat and a very efficient bloodstream.

Who else besides these three would be studying in a Nightwalker Library?

Syreena entered the room fully at last, making a straight line for the stranger. Her target noted her approach instantly and a look Syreena could only describe as panic seemed to cross her fine-boned features. She drew back, huddling against the bookshelf as the Princess stepped up to her.

That was when Syreena realized what she was.

"Hello. I am Syreena." She greeted the frightened girl gently, extending a hand of greeting. "You are Mistral, are you not?"

Syreena had only seen one other Mistral in her life. She was astounded that she was seeing a second. Mistrals were utterly reclusive. They did not associate with anyone other than themselves, and even then, outside of living in tiny villages together, they rarely gathered. They were xenophobic, they terribly feared crowds, and they very certainly feared those of any power.

The young Mistral female nodded in confirmation of Syreena's guess. She would not speak, the Princess knew. Female Mistrals were referred to as Sirens for a very good reason. The music of their voices alone was enchanting, dazing any who listened. It was an adequate defense mechanism. More than adequate. Like the ominous rattle of a poisonous snake, its effect was universally paralyzing. But also like the wise snake, she would rather slink away than face a challenge. However, Syreena was willing to bet that if put to the screws, one of the Mistral breed could do more than enough damage to an enemy. This would be easy to do to a mark that was entranced by their speaking voice alone, not to mention the utterly enamoring effect should they decide to sing.

It was fortunate that they were a dedicated nonviolent species.

The small-boned girl reached out and took Syreena's offered hand, shaking head to toe the entire while. As they shook in greeting, Syreena marveled that the girl had come there at all. She had not realized Siena had extended the invitation to the Mistrals, never mind that they would accept. This girl, despite her cowed shivering, had to be uniquely brave to have volunteered for this duty.

Syreena released her hand and glanced at the tables not too far away from them. She gave the girl a half smile and reached for one of the sheets of paper she saw sitting in a stack. She nodded to the pen clutched in the other female's fingers.

"What's your name?"

The Mistral actually smiled. She took the paper and, using the book in her hands as a lean, scribbled a quick response.

"Aria," it read.

Syreena liked her instantaneously. She knew it was a bias but did not care. Mistrals were shapechangers, too, but they only became birds. Lycanthropes ran the entire panoply of the animal kingdom. However, since they shared a like animal species in their transformed states, Syreena suspected they might enjoy some common experiences and insights. A bird's-eye view, as it were. It would just be a matter of gaining the little woman's trust enough that she would weed much of the enchantment out of her voice, like a snake keeping its unnerving rattle still, and allow a conversation. Siena's relationship with another Mistral named Windsong had taught Syreena that such a thing was possible.

Possible, but rare.

Clearly Aria was a rare bird to begin with, so it paid to hope for the best.

Before Syreena could speak another word, Aria suddenly stepped back from her and shrank into herself again. It was enough to put the Princess on guard. She turned to see what Aria was seeing.

Her breath caught.

Damien.

Syreena had met the Vampire Prince before, and she knew him on sight. It would have been impossible to forget him. Even though he was not presently using his ability to cast a net of altered perception and fear in front of himself, she still knew to regard his imposing presence with cautious respect. He was tall, like a Demon, defying the slender, willowy build of his species, bordering just above athletic with the anomalous width of his shoulders and his blatantly muscular build. Still, he carried himself with that casual and lean grace that all Vampires seemed to inherently have. He gave the impression of lazing carelessness, of ease and relaxation, but she knew from experience that it was a lie. A camouflage. The Prince could be at the ready with deadly quick ease.

Siena had seen him in battle. She had told Syreena of his performance with unleashed fascination. The Queen had said she had never seen anyone move so fast or seem to enjoy the kill so very naturally. For that to come from the Queen of a species who lived half their existence as animals of varying predatory instincts, it was quite the outstanding compliment.

Syreena's impressions of him had been different.

He had unnerved her, not to put too fine a point on it. Not quite as much as he was unnerving young Aria at the moment, but certainly enough to encourage her to keep her time in the same room with him down to a minimum.

The urge to tuck tail irritated her. It was not in her nature to be frightened or stirred up so easily, especially without any true explanation for it. This would be a very poor beginning to her duty here if she let him intimidate her. The only thing she had going for her was the fact that he had no idea she felt that way. Or at least she would so long as she purged herself of the thoughts quickly enough to avoid telepathic detection, just in case the autocratic Prince decided to nose around her thoughts. She imagined a man like Damien would not hesitate to breach the privacy of others' minds. He struck her as just the sort of empowered male who would see no wrong in such an invasion.

The Princess turned back to see Aria had utterly disappeared. Smart girl. Vampires were unpredictable and occasionally churlish. Syreena enviously wished for a moment that she had the freedom to beat a hasty retreat, but since she didn't, she turned instead to inspect the Vampire Prince and the svelte woman who stood by his side. She was quite obviously Vampire, tall and dark-haired, all fairly normal for the breed. There were very few blond Vampires in the world. Syreena could allow that the female was remarkably beautiful, save for the fact that there was something a little too old and a bit too disenchanted in her dark brown eyes. Her taut posture and resistant body language made it clear she was not exactly thrilled to be there.

Since Syreena had not been expecting Vampire representatives, she moved over to them to discover their purpose. They were welcome, of course, under the same sketchy guidelines as everyone else, but last night at a joint meeting to finalize the opening of the Library to the scholars, Noah had said that Damien had declined his invitation.

As she approached them, she saw a change come over the Vampire female. She was stepping into the Library entrance with an expression swiftly coursing across her face that no doubt they all had had the first time they had seen it. The hollowness in her eyes seemed to disappear and they filled with an avarice Syreena was actually quite familiar with.

The greedy hunger to learn.

A Vampire *scholar*? Now there was an amusing paradox. Not that they weren't one of the more brilliant and cunning species of Nightwalkers, because they were. However, they usually directed that intellect and energy to more . . . carnal and instantly gratifying pursuits. They were voracious sensualists. Nothing kept their interest for very long unless it engaged all of their senses at once. Certainly a roomful of books wouldn't often fit that bill.

Unless, Syreena speculated, one's lust and sensual pleasure was derived from reading and attaining knowledge. That would make this the site of a veritable orgy.

Damien noticed her immediately. Harlequin coloring aside, she was incredibly hard to miss. She was not tall or an outstandingly sexual-looking creature like her lioness of a sister was, but she was an unshakable presence just the same. As she walked toward him, her steps were straight and assured, only the slightest sway in her hips. He liked that, he mused absently. She wasted no movement, expended no excess energy. Why that was a keen little delight to him he had no idea. It wasn't as though he'd ever really been put off by a woman with a sensual wriggle in her spine, to be sure. There was simply something about the efficiency on this particular woman that made it appealing. Although, by the chill expression in her eyes, he probably should keep from smiling appreciatively about it.

But he didn't.

"Syreena," he said, his tone nowhere near as cold as her expression. He let warmth and speculation color his voice, purposely allowing her to hear it just to watch her spine tighten in irritation. "Jasmine, this is Princess Syreena. Syreena, this is Jasmine. She is . . ." He trailed off when he realized Jasmine had given Syreena a halfhearted wave before moving quickly toward the first stack of books she could reach. "She is apparently eager to get started," he mused in excuse for his companion's rudeness, chuckling under his breath while he watched her begin to rummage through the shelves. Jasmine had never been known for her winning ways with others, but her appetite for knowledge was rivaled only by her appetite for blood.

It appeared to Syreena that the Vampire Prince was undoubtedly quite fond of the lissome brunette. "I had not expected anyone other than Kelsey or you to be coming." Syreena broached him directly. "Why the sudden change?"

"Jasmine is an excellent student and quite loyal to me," he said by way of explanation, "a bill that Kelsey, while certainly loyal, does not reasonably fit. If you are worried, I give you my word she will not cause any trouble."

"Isn't that an oxymoron? A Vampire not causing trouble?"

Syreena had not really meant to say that. At least, not aloud. So she was startled when he laughed. He was rather handsome when he laughed, she found herself thinking unexpectedly. Oh, he was a handsome creature overall, his Nightwalker genetics seeing to that quite thoroughly. He had bright white teeth, no sign of fangs at all as they were retracted at the moment much in the way a cat hid its claws. He wore a closely barbered beard and mustache, the line of it trimmed along his jaw and accenting that masculine, squared contour. Another anomaly, she noted. Vampire males tended to be almost baby-faced, giving the illusion of an early adolescent hairlessness. Rarely did one cultivate facial hair like the Prince did. When taken in addition to the other slightly out-of-step traits he bore, it made her wonder if he purposely defied cultural norms, and if so, why?

His extraordinarily dark blue eyes gleamed with a merriment that made his features come alive. A thick braid of hair snaked over his shoulder, the end tip brushing just below his well-defined pectoral muscle. In that moment, the sheer beauty of him almost made him look like he was the most harmless man on the planet.

And that was probably what gave Syreena the chills.

She did not trust him.

She *shouldn't* trust him, she assured herself. Even though there was a relative peace between Vampires and Lycanthropes, who in their right mind could possibly trust anyone from a species that took great delight in using trust to suck in a mark they were playing with simply for their amusement? Syreena had heard stories, stories often concerning Damien himself, of exploits and exploitations that had the potential to curl her hair.

"There is no protection here," Damien mused suddenly.

Considering that the only people there were scholars and that there had been some very determined enemies excavating enthusiastically for this very place, he had a reasonable point. Yet she felt insulted despite agreeing with him.

"*I* am here," she noted coldly.

"Yes," he observed, his voice as slow and as speculative as his eyes while they roamed over her from head to toe in obvious measure. "So you are." He paused long enough to turn half his mouth into an infuriating smile. "Not to impugn your abilities, my dear, but I do not see how you would be sufficient to hold back a tide of magic-users and human hunters led by a turncoat Demon, should they decide to come back."

"Well, *my dear*," she countered caustically, "I suppose I will have to rely on the fact that they failed in their initial search and do not know of this place . . ."

"Yet," he injected.

". . . and the perfectly capable Nightwalkers who will be in the Library at the time," she finished, her tone mocking and hostile.

"And how many will that be at that time? Ten? Five? Jasmine included, I only see four at the moment. Hardly enough to even hope they will survive any attack in force. We will be forced to sleep within the daytime; our human enemies have no such limitations. Perhaps not even the Demon traitor, as powerful as she has grown."

Again, he had a point, Syreena felt. Actually, he had only thought of it quicker than she had. She truly was not in disagreement with his observations. So why, then, did she feel so offended?

Damien had to admit, he had baited her deliberately. He had wanted to ruffle that placid calm and marked self-assuredness she kept around her like a cloak. He remembered a night not long ago when he had seen determined and fierce protectiveness in her, as well as cold outrage, when he had watched her defend her sister from harm. It titillated him, the idea of getting under her skin and shaking that resolved composure. He could sense when her thoughts and emotions stirred, when she allowed herself to think hotly about how much she did not like him and that she absolutely would as soon take his head off his shoulders as trust him.

His impulse satisfied, Damien put aside his interest in her

with a wave of one hand and a dismissing turn of his body before she could respond.

The Prince walked into the Library and up behind the female who had come with him. He slid a hand around her rib cage, his fingers settling just beneath her breast as he leaned in and whispered something to her, an infuriating lilt of his lips and the brief cast of his eyes in Syreena's direction giving her the impression he was mocking her.

Syreena took a deep breath, trying to cool the rush of her temper. She had been giving in to this volatile aspect of her personality far too much of late. It was almost as though she was seeking a good fight. She had to admit, however, that she would have gained a great deal of satisfaction in slapping the smirk off the Vampire Prince's face. Political ramifications aside, even Siena would have appreciated the fact that he really deserved it.

Syreena was now in no mood to study. The Library was continuing to fill, the variety of Nightwalkers at a balance that assured maintenance of the peace they all studied in. Or so she told herself as she justified the action of leaving to get a breath of air. She walked out of the Library entrance, pausing to survey the three other caves branching off from just outside of it.

The network of caverns went on for miles, some of them too tight in access for something larger than an average-sized animal. This was why Lycanthropes enjoyed the caverns so much. Access to them was difficult, fresh water and hot springs abounded, and there were never any crowds or interruptions outside of the occasionally unfortunate spelunker. The temperature was constant; no matter what the season, it was always cool and comfortable. And perhaps most of all, it was always night. After a fashion at least. One could travel for miles through these networks during broad daylight and never once touch the sun.

Since exposure to the sun was rapidly poisonous to a Lycanthrope—sickening, polluting, and blistering them in a deadly sun sickness that could kill them far too easily—the advantage of the caverns was clear. A Lycanthrope who had been deeply envenomed by the sun would spend days in utter agony and sickened distress before finally expiring. Perhaps "easily" was a poor representation of such a death, a death Syreena's sister had almost succumbed to only a month earlier.

In the above world, it was now winter. A Russian winter, for that was where Lycanthrope territory was. The caverns had dozens of exits, both known and unknown, that led up into the wintry place. Syreena had entered by one that had formerly led to the hibernation spot of a Lycanthrope named Jinaeri, who had since vacated and found a new hostel for herself in anticipation of the Library traffic that would potentially threaten her winter rest.

Syreena wished she was of a hibernating bent. She could have used the solitude and the rest. But the falcon and her other aspect, the dolphin, were both migrating species. Her urges tended more toward a change in location, following the warmer seasons, than they did curling up for a long sleep. Perhaps this was why she could not quite sit still recently. Maybe this was why she felt so restless and found herself so easily stirred up.

That restless stirring led her to take one of the cavern paths.

When Damien looked up, the Lycanthrope Princess was gone.

He turned from Jasmine to look around the enormous room, his brow furrowed in momentary confusion. The Princess had not struck him as the type to run off and sulk, but he considered for a moment that his taunting may have caused her to do so. He tilted his head slightly as he used all of his supernatural senses to seek her out, just to see where she was. It was little help; the caverns created strange echoes in his sensory network, reflecting ghosts and shadows of presences that were difficult for him to sort through. The only thing he could be sure of was that she was not in the immediate Library any longer.

Why he cared, he did not know. He moved to the Library entrance, still searching.

Syreena broke out of the unexpected exit she had found, stepping into the crunch of untouched snow and the biting chill of winter air.

But it was fresh and clean and bracing as she breathed deeply of it with pleasure. At the same time, she folded her arms tight and close around her middle to conserve the warmth of her body. She was wearing a sheath dress knit of cashmere that was held up only by her bare shoulders and barely reached her knees. She wore a simple slip-on shoe, inappropriate for trudging through snow.

She was part animal, however, and designed to withstand those sorts of hardships. It would not bother her as easily as it would a human or even some of the other Nightwalkers.

She was in forestland, half of the trees standing stark and bare on the dark landscape, the other half hulking shadows of pine and other trees that kept their hearty foliage year-round. She began to walk, the crunching of her steps the only sound around her. Beneath that, of course, were the natural life sounds of the forest. However, even that would become quiet soon. In spite of her affinity to animals, she was still an apex predator, something to be feared more than harmonized with. In shapechange, she was only an apparent threat to smaller animals.

She was tempted to discard her clothes and become the falcon. She so enjoyed free-flying in the clear night sky. But she was supposed to carry out certain responsibilities on this first evening of the opening of the Library. It was bad enough that she had wandered off. She would allow herself a short, refreshing walk in the snow and then she would return. The purpose was to gain a clear head, to readjust her perspective. Nature in and of itself was a meditative process, so she was hoping she would find a calmer center for herself. She could not afford the mood with which she had greeted the Vampire Prince. It was her duty, in fact, to be just the opposite, to be cordial and diplomatic to all other Nightwalkers who did not threaten her.

Because there was no way, in practice, to put politics aside in these matters. An insult to any person, whether of the type of power Damien weighted or just the simplest citizen in the Nightwalker world, could have far-reaching implications that had the potential to begin wars.

Syreena moved forward slowly through the dark night. There was no moon in the sky, at least not one that could be seen through the heavy veil of dark clouds that hung low near the treetops.

She honestly needed to figure out what was wrong with her. It was as if she had reverted to the confused, volatile child she had been just before she had been sent to The Pride. But she was not a child. She was one hundred eight years old, well trained, highly intellectual, and emotionally centered.

Usually.

She knew that the effects of peace outweighed the effects of war. She knew that contention and surliness bred itself, just as softness of the voice and approach bred respect in return.

Syreena stopped suddenly when she thought she heard a sound behind her. She abruptly turned, her keen eyes divining and identifying all the objects in the dark. There was nothing there to be seen. Not even an animal. They were all sitting still and hidden until her intrusion passed.

She dismissed it as a random echo or a trick of her mind. If it were anything else, she would have sensed it.

She shivered with serious chill, but ignored the discomfort. Truly, her human form was the one she felt most exposed in. She spent a great deal of her time as the falcon. She would choose the dolphin more often if there were a ready source of deep enough water outside of the occasional cavern lake. At least in those forms she could guard or self-regulate against this type of temperature extreme.

Again she heard a telling sound to her rear. This time she whirled around and into an instinctive crouch. She balanced herself with a bracing hand in the snow as she peered into the darkness. Still, she saw nothing. However, this time, she could not dismiss it. She suddenly realized that she was not the only thing making the night forest feel unnaturally still and silent.

Syreena felt a sudden eddy of displaced air, the gentle puff of it stirring her hair from behind. As she turned back with violent speed, she realized she had been tricked. Tricked into turning her back to the actual approach.

And that it was very much a trick of the mind.

She narrowed harlequin eyes on the woman who had suddenly appeared in the darkness. She had only a heartbeat of time to note the familiar blond hair and the bright blue eyes that shivered with rage and madness.

"Let us play, Princess," the wicked female invited her with a soft hiss of breath.

Ruth.

Identifying the name of the Demon traitor who had turned to evil, joining with the black humans who toyed with corrupt magics they knew very little about, was the only thing Syreena had time for before the creature grabbed for her.

The Princess dodged, thinking on the run. She could not let Ruth touch her. If she did, the female Demon of the Mind would be able to teleport Syreena away from the familiarity and potential support of her homeland in the blink of an eye.

At least, she hoped that was the case. Ruth was an aberration now, a Demon who had used black magic. No one had ever done such a thing before, and Ruth had already proven to be capable of extraordinary power and ruthlessness.

"Let us see how much your sister loves that murderer she calls her husband when she realizes he is responsible for her beloved sister's death," Ruth threatened coldly.

Syreena felt a sudden and overwhelming panic, too sudden and too alien to be natural. The Demon was seeping into her mind, toying with it and altering her perception and her center of balance. Syreena stumbled as nausea overwhelmed her. Instinctively, she tossed her head to one side, exposing all of the brown of her hair.

But Ruth was a Mind Demon, and she anticipated the instinct even before Syreena could recognize she had put it into thought. Like a flash of lightning, she teleported herself onto the Princess's back, her sudden weight driving Syreena down face first into the snow. Syreena felt Ruth's gripping fingers sinking into her hair. Ruth's hands fisted, binding the living appendage that was her tresses so tightly that Syreena was forced to scream from the suffocating pain.

Once a Lycanthrope's hair was caught or bound, they could not change. The entrapment was a Lycanthrope's worst nightmare. On top of it, Ruth now had the contact she clearly needed to steal Syreena from the Russian forest. Battling her fear, the Princess knew her only recourse would be to disrupt the Demon's ability to concentrate. In spite of her skill, Ruth still needed to focus to perform the escape. The Princess reached back past her shoulder and raked out with outstretched nails, scoring the other woman nastily across her cheek and throat.

The physics of the fight called for a reaction to follow the action. Syreena was rewarded for her strike with a scream, but punished for it by the sudden wrenching of her head as the Demon woman clutching her hair reared back.

The pain was phenomenal as roots of her hair gave way to the stress of Ruth's amazing strength. She tore out so much of it that one of her hands pulled free in the process. Syreena fell back with Ruth's momentum as she was yanked over from front to back. They landed in the snow, and the Queen's sister felt the warm rush of her own blood pouring back into her hair. The saturation was so fast and so thorough that even the snow was pooling it in a swiftly melting hollow by the time Ruth regrouped enough to grab her around the throat with her now free hand. The hold was enough to remind Syreena that the woman had once been a warrior. A very good one, at that. One who had served in the three hundred year war between the Demons and the Lycanthropes. She knew all their weaknesses and, obviously, how to exploit them.

And Syreena had thought herself up to this challenge?

Ruth was cutting off her air supply, all the while forcing fear into her mind until her thoughts were so hazed over that she was paralyzed and could not think of a way to counterattack. The Princess suddenly realized that what made a remarkable fighter by her own people's standards was significant only when brought up in a cloistered setting. She had never fought a Demon hand to hand before.

It was clear why the Demons had so often been victorious in battle against them. Her father had truly been a madman to perpetuate such a war, madder still to think he could ever have won it. It was only now, seeing Demon power at its harshest intensity that she began to appreciate the restraint Noah's people had used all of those years.

That was her last thought before the world went black.

Chapter 3

Damien stepped out of the cavern exit he had traced the Princess to, his foot obliterating her smaller print in the snow. The cold hit him harshly, but he ignored it and closed his eyes. His head tilted as he reached out for her with better senses. She was a creature of both nature and power. It would make her easy to sense if she was not too far away. She might have taken flight for all he knew, in which case tracking her would become a much more complex project.

He opened his eyes and moved forward into the darkness, taking note of the deadly quiet around him. Special membranes flicked over his eyes without even a thought and, some distance away, a smear of pink residual heat stood out like a neon beacon. Damien could tell that there was no living being there, but one had been, so he continued his tracking.

Why he felt so compelled to tender an apology for what was probably a mostly imagined slight, Damien did not know. He had learned to obey his instincts, however, through a long lifetime that had taught him it was more often better to do so than not. As Damien neared the fading pink blur, he became aware of faint shapes to it. The least pronounced was a handprint in the snow. Then there was a sweeping flare of patterns he could not determine an origin from.

He flicked to normal vision and dropped to a single knee near the wide circle of disturbed snow. The only thing he could immediately determine in the darkness was that there were no footprints leading from the place, only Syreena's and his own leading to it.

He was about to give up, thinking she had obviously flown out of the spot, when he realized that the moisture soaking through the knee of his pants was not normal.

It was not cold.

It was warm.

The pungent tang of blood reached him a heartbeat after that thought.

The Vampire swore softly, cursing himself for his inattentiveness and carelessness as he scooped up a handful of the red-tinged snow.

Suddenly everything added up. All the pieces came together with dreadful clarity. Damien cursed again, realizing that his perceptions had been toyed with. There was no way he would ever miss a blood scent. Not even from a hundred yards away. His skills were beyond bountiful when it came to such things. He was the oldest and most powerful of his kind.

And he had been fooled by a simple little glamour.

He stood up, clenching his fist around the snow he held, letting it drip unheeded to the ground through tightened fingers as he extended every sense he had once more, this time circumventing the trick, pushing away the outside influence that had deceived his mind.

The scent and vibration of battle overwhelmed him instantly. There was fear and rage and desperation so intense that he could taste it right along with the flavor of blood that now rose up from all around him. Snow that had appeared white moments ago now showed the truth of the blood splattered into it. Residual energy and heat blanketed the area of the struggle.

He raised his hand to his mouth, breathing deeply of the scent of the blood he held gripped in his palm, familiarizing himself with the hormone and pheromone levels of it. It was Lycanthrope, clearly Syreena's. His fangs exploded behind his lips and he snarled softly.

That was when he realized he was clutching strands of gray hair between his fingers and palm along with the snow.

He threw down the compressed slush.

He had her blood scent, and now he could quickly and far more easily track her.

That was all that mattered.

Ruth took great pleasure in throwing the Lycanthrope Princess into a corner of the small stone room they had arrived in. All Syreena could do was protect her profusely bleeding head from striking the wall.

At least for the first moment.

The next moment she had her feet under her and was lunging with unexpected calculation at the Demon female. Ruth had forgotten that this Lycanthrope was not just some weakling little figurehead to a monarchy. Syreena was a Monk, and she had spent nearly her entire life with The Pride finding out what that made her capable of.

Her rigid bicep contacted Ruth's unprotected throat, knocking her right off her feet. The Demon hit the floor on her back. She got kudos for a quick comeback, however, as she swiftly used her position on the floor to kick Syreena's legs out from under her. The Princess lost her breath and saw stars as her back and head hit the stone floor. On top of the blood loss she was beginning to feel the effects of, it thoroughly disoriented her.

Disorientation was more than enough to give Ruth the advantage. The Demon shouted out a phrase Syreena did not comprehend, but a heartbeat later she understood it was a spell.

A *spell*.

A Demon casting magic.

The Lycanthrope knew this was so because out of thin air she felt hands closing around her throat. All she could do was gasp for breath and claw at her own neck for something that was not even there. There was nothing to latch on to, nothing to struggle with, except for the slim gold and moonstone collar she wore that was the badge of her inheritance to the Lycanthrope throne.

Ruth took the opportunity to regroup, straightened her clothing, and kneeled down over her victim. Syreena watched with wide eyes as the Demon smiled with clear contentment.

"There now, that is much better," she said, her tone almost motherly and soothing as she reached to pat the Princess on her forehead.

Syreena's face was turning red, her feet kicking out violently for some kind of purchase.

"If you sit still, I will let go," Ruth told her gently.

Syreena did not believe her, and it was apparent in her defiant eyes. She might die at the madwoman's hands, but she would not do so submissively.

"Oh, have it your way, then," Ruth snapped at her, clapping her hands and releasing the spell.

Syreena gagged violently. She rolled over, turning away from the Demon as she struggled to recapture her breath. Tears ran down her face and she fought the nausea and the headache lancing behind her swollen eyes.

"Now . . . let us keep in mind that I am a Mind Demon, and I can read your thoughts," Ruth said amiably as she settled herself into a comfortable cross-legged position on the floor just behind the Princess.

She was lying. Female Mind Demons were empaths. Only the males were telepaths.

"I am not lying," she leaned in to whisper to the misguided

Princess. "Though I can see why you would think so. It is true, I was once relegated to the shortcomings of my sex. Terribly unfair, really, how the men got all the goodies in our species. However, since I broke away from that hypocritical culture, I have found the way to unlock those abilities within myself. So let us save a good deal of time here and take my word for granted, hmm?"

"Bitch," Syreena croaked.

"I can see how you would think that, too," Ruth said, still using that affable tone as she reached to turn her captive onto her back so they could see one another. "But actually, you only have your sister to blame for this. She should have never taken that heartless murderer to her bed. Royal Consort, indeed! At least she had the sense not to make him King. Can you imagine?" Ruth's disgust was obvious, as was her hatred for Elijah. "But soon they will have an heir, making you rather obsolete, Princess, so truly it is best I use you to my benefit now while you still have some value left."

Ruth paused to reach out and sift her fingers through Syreena's dual-colored hair. The strands cringed, pulling back and slithering away from between her fingers. But it was easy enough for her to grab another handful of it, twisting it once around her hand to keep it from escaping again.

"Are you and your sister psychically connected? We never could figure out if that was the case between your people. You always had an uncanny way of moving in perfect concert in battle. No? That is too bad. I had hoped she would be able to experience some of this."

Ruth fisted her hand and pulled back hard.

Syreena's hair tore out of her scalp, flinging blood in a wide spray as it traveled through the arc of Ruth's powerful ripping motion. It was as if Ruth had just amputated a hand or foot from Syreena. Certainly, the blood loss and the pain were comparable. The Princess screamed, her feet kicking against the floor as her entire body convulsed. She catapulted into motion, using all her remaining strength to scrabble across the uneven floor and into her original corner. Once there, she huddled into herself, shaking with pain and sudden terror like an abused animal. She couldn't even see Ruth because of the wash of blood pouring over her eyes and face.

Ruth contemplated the hank of gray hair in her hand with a smile.

"This is going to be fun."

Tracking someone who had seemingly winked out of existence would be impossible for the inexperienced hunter. For the experienced hunter it would be intensely difficult. For Damien, it was a matter of having lived a very long life as a hunter who chased prey every single night. It had taught him how to track just about every sort of quarry there was, provided he had encountered it at some point and was familiar with its instincts and tactics.

For the moment, he was relieved that there was a trail at all. Whether or not the Princess would be alive at the other end would be something he would worry about when the time came. Hope came with the fact that there was a certain tension to this trail, indicating that someone had dragged Syreena against her will likely the entire distance.

He did not delude himself about how Syreena had been taken captive. The scent of a Demon lay parallel to every part of her path, and there was only one who would be so crazed as to attempt such a transgression on the royal's own territory.

Ruth.

Psychotic Demon bitch, he thought venomously.

She and her daughter Mary had single-handedly caused more pain and death for the Demon community in the past year than he would have thought possible. Now that Mary was dead, accidentally killed by her mother's own hand as Ruth had attempted to slay Elijah, there was no telling what she had in store for Syreena. And Damien had known the notoriously peaceful Queen Siena long enough to know that even for one as strong and practical in the ways of the world as she was, she would be hard-pressed to overcome such a personal, monstrous act and be able to maintain her peaceful ethics. How that would translate to the Demons would be hard to say. Damien could only take comfort in the fact that Siena was married to one and that would go a long way toward tempering her response. However, to lose her only sister . . . that could unavoidably affect a powerful monarch in ways that would have long-reaching repercussions.

The trail laid out before him was one of dragging energy. Though a teleport had all the appearance of starting cleanly in one place and popping up in another, it was more like a folding of space. A touching of the starting point to the ending point left behind something of a dotted line, as the crow flies, which could be followed if one knew what to look for and how to keep the track in sight.

The only thing was, it would take Damien a hundred times the amount of time to track it, and anything could happen in that time. So he flew through the air with all the speed he could muster, the wind burning over his skin and whipping through his clothing at hurricane force.

He barely noticed it, his entire concentration on his path.

As strong as she was, Ruth had her limitations. He did not figure her to be beyond the European continent. He had never heard of a female Mind Demon who could teleport more than a thousand miles' distance. Ruth, however, was the first and eldest of her kind. There was truly no telling what she was capable of doing.

Especially with the black arts to aid her.

It took Jasmine a full hour before she truly took note of Damien's extended absence.

Vampires were not in the practice of monitoring one another, but this was certainly an unusual circumstance. She was in another species' territory, surrounded by Nightwalker strangers, set to a task that Damien had said he would accompany her on for at least this initial visit, just to make certain everything was reasonably safe and calm before leaving her to her own devices.

Not that she needed protecting. It was simply that Damien had mentored her for most of her life, elevating her to the level of a personal favorite that no one else could lay a close claim to, and since then had always taken it upon himself to act as her guardian and protector. Much in the way an elder brother would protect a younger sister.

So for him to break promised plans without even so much as a word to her, was enough to stimulate a measure of curiosity, if not concern. Far be it for Jasmine to play guardian to a Vampire twice her age and power.

Still . . .

Jasmine walked out of the Library, looking into the cavernous tunnels all around her, even though she knew by sense that Damien was nowhere close enough for visual acquisition. It was habit, she supposed, to look just the same. He was strong enough to block his presence from anyone should he choose to. She just did not understand why he would want to do so.

As she paid closer attention to her surroundings, however, she began to pick up his trail.

So he was not hiding for any purposeful reason.

The track was mostly cold, telling her his passage had taken place long before.

She debated the wisdom of tailing him.

It could very well be the Vampire Prince had found something . . . or someone . . . to amuse himself with, and an interruption would not be welcome. A Vampire's attention could always be easily swayed in these ways. A race of pure sensualists, they rarely passed up a delight if it piqued their interest.

Although it had been some time since anything of that

sort had been unique enough to win the attention of the Vampire who had lived long enough to see it all.

Jasmine had spent the better part of five hundred years at Damien's side; she had seen the multitude of females he had gone through in that time alone, never mind the four hundred fifty years he had lived before she had even been born. While he still had appetites, he was no longer easily intrigued. It would not be like him, for all his Vampire nature, to suddenly see something that would distract him from a duty he held important. Especially when the duty involved a certain measure of political sensitivity and Jasmine's exposure to it.

Jasmine made up her mind, proceeding cautiously in his footsteps.

Damien landed at last, estimating himself to be somewhere just outside of Paris.

That struck a chord within him immediately.

From Lycanthrope territory to Mistral lands? Ruth had been evicted from Russia a little over a month ago, chased away from excavating the land just above where the rest of the allied Nightwalkers had made the monumental discovery of the Library. Now she was here, again in alien Nightwalker territory.

What was she doing there? Why had she dragged Syreena all this way? Damien realized that she must have taxed herself enormously, first with the initial travel to Russia, and now by returning herself and a passenger who was fighting her tooth and nail the entire way. Nevertheless, Damien realized that he should not give too much credit to that advantage. Ruth was no doubt well surrounded by hunters who would just as soon stake him out in the next dawn for a slow and painful conflagration, and magic-users who would want to do worse.

She was crazy, not stupid.

Damien moved into the shadows, blending into them with

a fluid motion he had always taken to so naturally. He was on a cobblestone path, village buildings on either side of him. It was a vintage city, exactly the type of setting where one would find Mistrals. However, it was too densely populated. Mistrals lived in close-knit groups, but usually in a country setting and with few more than twenty to a location.

This was a town of well over four or five hundred.

That only meant that Ruth had taken holdings less conspicuous than, say, trying to stay amongst Mistral villagers with the entourage that likely traveled with her. Ruth would stick out like a sore thumb in true Mistral settings.

Syreena's trail was growing more apparent the closer he got to her. The gentle night breeze blew her unique scent to him in faint traces that only a select echelon of stalkers would have been able to identify as hers. He, Siena, and Jacob, the Demon Enforcer, were part of that minimally select example.

Syreena was close.

He was approaching the situation almost blind. Only his knowledge of his enemy was girding him for this potential battle. The ideal choice would be to find a way to recover Syreena, moving in and out of the danger as undetected as was vampirically possible. The first thing he had to do was determine if she was even alive. If she was, then he must act on the moment. If she was not, he could take the time to regroup and bring in others who would help even the odds at retrieving her body and punishing those who had harmed her.

The thought was logical and practical, but Damien found it did not sit well with him. A sliver of chill bitterness walked his backbone at the idea of harm coming to one so special. The Princess was a one-of-a-kind creature. Her death would be a heart-wrenching tragedy, even to one such as himself who had grown used to seeing death and its many faces.

It was an intolerable idea, he thought to himself as he edged closer to a large stone storehouse that his trail was leading him directly to. He might be guilty of his passing frivolities, but he abhorred waste of any kind.

Therefore, even though there was a great potential that he was walking into a trap set for whomever Ruth would expect to hunt after Syreena—Siena and Elijah, for example—he would do everything in his power to see if the Princess could be saved.

As Damien came close enough to the building to touch the wall, warning bells screamed across his senses and instincts. The place reeked of magic, probably warning, repelling wards that would shoot first and ask questions an hour or so later.

Magic could be circumvented, given time and knowledge, but Damien was feeling an instinctive pressure that told him he was already riding low on time. He could shield his approach from Ruth for only so long. She was a master at the manipulations of the mind, and just as he had done, she would soon discover she was being misled and toyed with by an outside mental influence. Frankly, even with his mental power, he could never go toe to toe with a Mind Demon. His ability to sway the thoughts of others was strictly a hunting tool. It chased away ambitious predators so he would not waste time in power struggles, it baited and lured potential prey into well-crafted traps, and it even altered memory and perception so he could feed or come and go without arousing questions and suspicions.

Damien walked slowly around the perimeter of the wards, testing their power as unobtrusively and delicately as a member of a bomb squad would study an explosive.

He could only hope this all would not suddenly click to zero and blow up in his face.

Ruth was growing wiser over time, it seemed. This time her wards were layered to accommodate all Nightwalkers, rather than just Demons or whomever she would expect to encounter. She had learned her lessons well after the Nightwalkers had joined in collaborations against her.

She was not simply a loose renegade from her own people. She was a threat and a terrible danger to them all. Every encounter with her only supported that understanding more and more.

Damien flicked sensitive membranes in his eyes and immediately was blinded by the glare of heat from all the bodies tucked tightly into the central room of the building. There were back rooms, upper stories as well, and they had a scattering of bodies exuding heat within them as well.

However, it was the incredibly hot flare of a Lycanthrope he was looking for, and it was that burn that he quickly found. Rolled into a ball in the corner of an upstairs room she lay, the cool-toned body of her captor standing over her.

Oh, what I wouldn't give to have her heart beating in my hand, Damien thought angrily of Ruth. If for no other reason than to put an end to the havoc and the pain she wreaked so willingly. So ably. It seemed ridiculous that so hunted a creature could so easily elude the best hunting species on the planet.

The trouble was, she knew them and their abilities too well, from an insider's perspective. She used that knowledge in combination with her mental trickery until they were literally chasing themselves into circles. When they did run her to ground, as they had done once already, the fact that she was willing to sacrifice any number of humans to save herself had thwarted their capture of her. She was constantly throwing the misguided mortals into battle so they could distract her pursuers while she beat a hasty retreat.

Since she had a roomful of those same types of hapless people just beneath her feet, Damien had to formulate his plans in a way that would deprive her of the opportunity to sic them on him.

He levitated from the ground, staying in the shadows as he came very near the small window that led into the room where Ruth was storing her prize. The window was inconveniently tiny, little more than the height and width of his hand.

Clever, clever, he mused.

Small enough to keep out everything except, say, a Wind Demon in his molecularized form. No doubt fully equipped with a bar that would snap down on his head as he tried to reach for the tidbit of cheese Syreena had become.

Damien waited patiently for Ruth to exit the room. He was completely focused on his coming actions and on hiding his presence from her astute senses, except for the moment he took to calculate the time left until dawn. In a couple of hours, neither he nor Syreena would want to be running around unprotected. Ruth was quite capable of putting off the Demon lethargy that would try to drag her into sleep for the day. The eldest and most powerful of her kind could often circumvent that debilitation, at least for a few hours.

He and Syreena were less lucky. She would become the equivalent of tenth-degree sunburn, and he would start to smolder like barbeque coals. After only so much of that, Syreena would die from the poisons in her blood, and he would eventually become little more than a pile of ash.

They needed to escape, dodge the pursuit of not only the Demon, but the humans who had no shyness toward the sun whatsoever, and find shelter.

All within a couple of very short hours.

It took the better part of forty minutes before Damien's heat-sensing vision told him that Ruth had grown tired of her new captive and had left her alone. Whether that would last, he did not know. All he did know was that once he got hold of the Princess, he was going to have to figure out a way to keep Ruth from tracking them right back down again, just as he had done to the female Demon. He could shield himself, but he could not affect Syreena's trail.

He took the opportunity of Ruth's absence to peer into the window.

Damien could not see Syreena because she was tucked into the corner closest to him, out of his line of sight as he looked through the tiny window. What he could see was walls of stone that literally glowed with spells and wards.

Damn.

There was nothing for it. She was too tightly guarded. There was no way he would ever be able to slip beneath such powerful mystical fences unnoticed.

Therefore, he would have to resort to the direct approach, and break right through them.

Syreena was fading in and out of consciousness up until the moment stone seemed to explode and rain down all around her. The force was monstrous, shaking the entire room like an earthquake. The next moment was nothing but a storm of what she could only describe as hellish feedback. Power lashed all around her, some of it lancing through her. Luckily, she was too deep in shock to really even feel it.

She felt as though a firestorm was blowing toward her, and she had nothing but the curl of her own body to protect herself with. Even in her numbed state, she tucked her head down and tried to breathe as she waited for it to burn her to cinders . . . or pass over her.

Suddenly there were strong hands encircling her arms, trying to force her to her feet. She could not comply, however. Her legs simply would not work.

She felt a change in tactic, and she was scooped from the floor. She was so heavy, as if she weighed a million tons, that she could not imagine how it was possible for anyone to lift her.

There was a shift in position, the sound of a muttered expletive, and suddenly she was being thrown into the night air.

Chapter 4

Damien leapt out of the demolished room the same way he had entered, through the enormous hole he had made when he had rammed his body into it a moment ago.

Syreena was more than just dead weight in his arms. The insanely clever Ruth had bespelled the petite, light-figured woman he held with a weighting hex, making it seemingly impossible for anyone to lift her or take her away. It was like trying to fly with a full-grown bull elephant on his chest.

Still, he propelled them out of the prison and up toward the stars crowding the black sky. It was taxing, especially after the magical abuse he had just withstood not a minute beforehand.

On the plus side, Ruth could not fly, so her teleportation powers were useless. She could teleport into the night sky right in front of him if she wanted to, but she would promptly plummet to the ground and very likely die a moment afterward.

Ruth had to resort to other means. Damien could already feel her trying to pull his destination from his mind. If she won the image, she could use it to beat him there and would be lying in wait for him.

This was why he had purposely acted on the moment and had made no plans as to what actions he would have to take to thwart her. What he did not know for himself, she could not successfully take from him.

Magic-users could levitate, so he was not entirely safe in the air, either. He could sense and smell them leaping up after him. They were fresh, uninjured, and unburdened, so they would catch up to him very quickly.

This, however, was where he could shoot two birds with a single bullet. He hesitated in his fast upward flight, glancing down at his targets. He cast out a blanket of insurmountable dread and fear. He threw terror down at them as if it were a nuclear pulse.

The mayhem that followed their shattered concentration was instantaneous. In addition, even as bodies began to plummet back to the earth, he felt Ruth's drag on his mind faltering. She was trying to hold on to him *and* negate the effects his powerful hypnotic suggestion on her minions at the same time.

As formidable as she was, she would still fail.

The full power of Damien's mental ability flared into dominance, shutting the floundering intruder out with a painful backlash much like getting one's fingers trapped in the heavy closing of a car door.

He did not stick around to hear the echo of Ruth's scream of pain and outrage.

The effect of the weighting hex decreased the farther they got from the casting source. It took only ten minutes of fiercely fast flight before Syreena seemed to weigh little more than a feather in his arms, in spite of the fact that she was cold and dead limp.

She seemed so fragile, he thought as he took a moment to glance at her pallid, bloodstained features. It was not a term he would have ever thought to use when describing her until just that very moment. The sparkle of her vitality, he realized, had added an astounding potency to her presence. Now, as she lay limp and lifeless, he was overcome with the irrational fear that he might somehow break her to pieces just with the force of his necessary hold.

From the powerful aroma of blood lifting off her, he could tell she had been brutalized in ways in addition to the obvious, ways he could not immediately spy. It enraged him, the feeling intensifying as the call of the scent of it still managed to ferret out a hunger from within him. Nightwalker blood was full of the mysticism and power they all manipulated. To the Vampire, the bouquet of it was like the smell of an imminent gourmet meal cooking on the stove of a starving man.

Damien had never before had cause to be ashamed of that instinct, not in all of his long life, but he felt that burning and censuring emotion now. The last thing that he should be thinking of was what a delicacy she could be to his palate. A deadly delicacy, but a unique confection just the same. Unfortunately, he was overwhelmed by the pervading scent of her, made a little dizzy by it, and began shivering like a junkie being taunted with heroin while he was in withdrawal.

He had not hunted before escorting Jasmine to the Library that evening. They had arrived in the Russian province the night before, and out of respect for Siena's territory, had put off the need to seek prey until they had the opportunity to ask her official permission to hunt in her province. She would not deny them, of course, because they never harmed those they borrowed life from, but it was a political courtesy. Had it been a Lycanthrope staying in his territories, he would have expected as much and been insulted by less. Not that it was a matter that would lead to war or even an altercation; it was simply a demanded courtesy of their cultures.

So now, his hunger and draining energy was the price to

be paid for his civilized behavior. This was what made him vulnerable to the lure of the blood spoor that was spread over them both, more so than he normally would have been. The exotic nature of that spoor made the blade cut all the sharper and deeper.

It also told him that she was bleeding profusely. As strong as they were, even Nightwalkers could not heal fast enough to replenish blood supply at the rate the Lycanthrope was clearly losing it. He needed to find a way to provide aid for her. He had to find a safe haven, and he had to do it fast.

"Lyric, please bring me my sewing basket."

The small, slight-figured young woman looked up from her book of poetry to meet the large blue eyes that were the dominating feature in her companion's delicately shaped face.

"But it is Wednesday," Lyric said with confusion.

"Yes, Lyric, I realize that," Windsong said with a patient smile.

"You only sew on Thursdays," Lyric added.

"It is not a law that I do so," the older woman teased the adolescent Mistral. "We will be having guests soon, and I will need to repair that tear in my blue dress."

"Guests?" The young Siren actually choked on the word.

They never had guests.

They lived in a small French village—a tiny cluster of cottages, really—called *Brise Lumineuse*, with a total population of fifteen, not including the small children.

In all her nineteen years of life, no outsider had ever visited the little hamlet. In her ten years as Windsong's apprentice, they had only had two recurring visitors from the fifteen others who lived at the end of the long lane that distanced Windsong's chalet from the others. One was Thrush, Lyric's childhood friend. The other was Harrier, a handsome and sweet Bard who was to the elder Siren what Thrush was to her.

However, Thrush was in bed with a terrible flu and Harrier was currently traveling. So neither of *them* would be visiting anytime soon.

"Who will be visiting?" she asked her mentor as she tried to keep her hands from shaking by pulling them beneath the table and clasping them in her lap.

She had been there long enough to know it was a waste of time to wonder how it was that Windsong came by her knowledge.

"Lyric, do not ask me questions. Just fetch the basket."

Damien landed hard and with little grace.

He skidded to a stop on both knees, laying Syreena down on the damp ground. She was growing too cold too fast, and her breath was beginning to falter. He could not travel with her another moment without potentially killing her, and yet he was fully aware of the fact that their enemies had regrouped and were hot on his trail.

A lot of enemies.

"Syreena?"

He reached to touch her face, which was colder than even his wind-chilled hands. He did not have to touch her pulse to count it; he could do that by sheer ethereal senses alone. She was dying.

Rapidly.

He touched her scalp near her hairline, the most immediate site of free-flowing blood. Her hair had been torn away there, as if in methodical snatches. No doubt it had been a part of Ruth's delighted torture. Knowing her victim's weaknesses as well as she did, the former warrior had exploited them. It was clear Ruth had wanted to kill the Princess; Damien could tell that just by looking at Syreena. She had just preferred to do it slowly, with as much visible horror as possible. No doubt so she could find a perverse satisfaction or revenge, then return the corpse to the Russian territory as mutilated as possible, sending her message of vengeance loud and clear once the body was discovered.

Luckily, Ruth had not counted on someone of his strength being on her trail so quickly. That did not mean part of her plan would not succeed, he thought worriedly as he further assessed the Princess. Damien looked to his left and right, almost as if seeking help from the empty woods around him.

He truly did feel helpless. There were protocols to consider, superstitions between cultures that were hard to overcome. If he did what his instincts cried out for him to do . . .

Were she a Vampire, there would not be a moment's hesitation. But she was an alien Nightwalker. A Lycanthrope. And that made all the difference in the world.

Out of all the Nightwalker species, however, Vampires and Lycanthropes were probably the closest in ability, thinking, culture, and instinct than any of the others. If there could be any acceptable meshing of what he was contemplating, it could well be one of her breed that would make it even remotely possible.

It was written in their histories exactly what was and what was not acceptable for a Vampire palate. For instance, the blood of a being who partook of black arts and magics was utter poison. It was a powerful enough venom to kill a Vampire who partook of it within hours. Within minutes if the Vampire was young or weak.

Human blood was the mainstay in dietary needs.

Despite popular mythos, a Vampire did not kill with its bite. It was physically impossible to take in more than half a human's blood volume, and even that much was considered gluttony, so long as the Vampire was not wounded and losing blood as quickly as he was replacing it. So while weakness was inevitable, a human would recover from a state of prey quite easily. At the most, they would suffer from a mild to serious anemia.

Vampires were not stupid, however. Why harm their own supply of sustenance, when they could take from more than one vessel and have the humans barely miss a beat in their lives? That way their prey could live and provide sustenance another day.

As with all things in nature, it was instinct for Vampires to provide and take in balance. He had always believed that this was why they were equipped with coagulant systems to keep prey from bleeding to death, not to mention the notable side benefit of an antibody transference that could cure ill humans of a majority of illnesses.

However, very little in nature was perfectly universal. There were diseases that changed and mutated so fast that many antibodies would be obsolete almost instantly. Which meant there were things that even Vampires could not cure. Then there was the matter of what was nourishment, what was benign, what was deadly, and what was a great unknown when it came to the blood supply itself.

It was widely known in the Vampire world that Lycan-thropes could not benefit from the cure of Vampire antibodies. What was not as clearly known was what taking Lycan-thrope blood would do to a Vampire. Nightwalkers were taboo to Vampires, like sugar to diabetics—they could eat it, perhaps even survive it, but there was no telling what they would suffer for it.

This was Damien's dilemma of the moment.

As exhausted as he was from all he had done that night, he was not afraid to pit his power against whatever negative effects the introduction of Nightwalker blood would have on him. He had far more of a chance of surviving that than Syreena had at this moment of surviving without his aid.

The aid she needed was within his body, in the form of the injectable clotting factors that came into play after he had fed from a victim. In their mystical way, they would rush to all sites of open wounds and work their magic. He would have to take Syreena's blood, however, in order to trigger the coagulants she so desperately needed. One could not be stimulated without the other, just as a meal stimulus or something of the like was needed to trigger the injection of insulin into the human digestive system. A human could not simply think it into happening. Neither could any Vampire trigger his own injection response.

There was then the fact that she had lost so much blood already. To take more could kill her before it cured her. And after all those considerations, there was no guarantee the clotting agents would be compatible with her chemistry. It was very likely, but not a definite.

Damien suddenly grew tired of the frustration of his indecision. He no longer had time for the luxury of it.

He slid one arm beneath her shoulders, lifting her limp torso up from the ground. He slid her forward onto his thighs, the chill of her body penetrating him quickly as he drew her tightly to his chest. Gently, with a sense of reverence he did not understand the origin of, he brushed back what remained of the gray hair on the slope of her right shoulder. His dark gaze fell onto the artery that pulsed so weakly in her throat and he closed his eyes for a moment, exhaling as he said a quick mental prayer for her benefit and safety. When he looked at her again, he allowed himself to feel his incredible hunger for the first time in hours.

And he prayed for himself.

He was not prepared for how awesome it would be. The hunger was blinding, a sensation like no other, and he swayed under the power of it. It was dark and deep, insidious as it made itself known, telling him how long the actual craving had been creeping around in his subconscious and his veins. Only then did he realize how much self-censure and control he had been using all of this time.

Fangs erupted violently in his mouth, demanding their target ferociously. Need slammed through him in waves, erotic like the night, a mystery ready to be exposed. Without any hesitation, he struck at her with the speed of a biting cobra.

A second before he made contact, Syreena's eyes flew open. Something inside the female Nightwalker had known she was about to be attacked and had forced her into consciousness in the hopes that she could fight off any further harm. Like going into shock, it was her body's last-ditch effort to try and save itself.

So she was conscious when the fast and pointed piercing of Damien's canines struck her throat. However, she was too weak to do anything but gasp in surprise. Not because it hurt—the break through her skin was too quick and sharp to cause any prolonged pain. His mouth, however, was hot, like fierce fire compared to the deathly chill of her skin and body, and this was what shocked the sound out of her laboring lungs.

Syreena was aware that his strike was exactly that, a rapid piercing in and out directly over her carotid artery. She had always thought that a Vampire used the bite of his fangs like a straw or a needle, using them to suck blood directly from the main access point.

In fact, he simply used them to create the two wide initial holes he required. That had to be the case, because she felt nothing of his teeth a moment later as his lips, so warm and so damp, closed to make a perfect seal around the wound he had created. His tongue first slid over her skin, the burning velvet caress making her shudder hard in his hold. Then there was suction, increasing moment by moment with a surreal and erotic intensity.

Damien felt the violent tremor of her body. He was hugging her tightly to his chest, breast to breast, so the vibration of it made him quake in time with the aggressive shudder. He was dimly aware of her consciousness as her blood burst into his mouth. The heat of it intensely defied the chill of her body. That was his final coherent thought as the first taste of her flowed over his tongue. When the hot liquid slid down his throat, she burned him like a potent whiskey.

It could only be described as ambrosia. He had tasted the blood of human women thousands upon thousands of times, and always the pheromone content of it went straight to his head, filling him with a sense of sensuality and pleasure that was very akin to sexual desire. Syreena's blood was like nothing he could have ever hoped to encounter, even in his enormous lifetime. She was full of power, the layers in the bouquet of it like strong barbiturates that numbed in ever-increasing intensity. Unlike those drugs, however, he soared into an astounding high, rather than a relaxing, coma-like state.

He fell off his knees, sitting down hard in the wet grass and leaves, dragging her with him every inch of the way. He tried to think, tried to remember everything that was so crucial for him to keep aware of, but all he knew was her blood, the feel of her body, and the long, low groan she was releasing against his neck. Her hands slid up his back, her long fingers finding the path of his spine, following it up to his shoulders where they spread like wings to hold him.

"Damien . . ."

The rasp of his name on her lips sang through him like a high note. His body reacted with ultimate need and lightning-sharp arousal.

This was no pheromone-induced shadow of excitement, either. There was no mistaking the difference. His body burned, hardened with a violence of need that made him groan low in his throat. It was an oppressive weight, strangled by his clothing and his conscience. He should not be feeling this. Not when so much was at stake.

He could not have helped it, even if he had truly wanted to. And he could not make himself honestly want to. She was a sensualist's perfect fantasy. As she sustained him, bled into his body, he felt his senses expanding to accommodate the over-riding sensations and pleasures she was providing. Her scent, her luscious flavor, and the slow, slinky writhing of her body against his. His hands clenched into tight fists, balling up the fabric of her simple cashmere dress.

Leave her! Leave her now! his conscience screamed, completely in contrast to everything he actually wanted. What he wanted. Wanted. Craved. Syreena.

That was the moment her grasping hands went limp and fell away from his body. The hastening feeling of loss sent a note of warning and clarity into the haze of satiation and pleasure he was drowning in. Damien's eyes flew open as reality set in with its cold, demanding way. He suddenly recalled his purpose and that the life he held in his arms was in terrible threat.

The last thing Syreena felt before she drifted away into welcoming blackness was the second piercing of his teeth, followed quickly by a vicious burning sensation that began to spread across her neck and into her body.

Damien fell onto his back, gasping for air he did not even need, her slight weight falling over the top of his body. Freezing cold and moisture soaked into his clothing, but he was completely unaware of it. He could not move, could not think. He was nothing but a rush of feelings and sensations that the exterior conditions of the world simply could not touch.

He had succumbed to the immeasurable high of her inside him. Muscles and circulatory pathways contracted, shuddering and quivering in pleasure and the feelings of being beyond alive, beyond his own spiritual ties to that planet and that point in time. All he could do was stare up at the trees thrusting up all around him in an intensely distorted three-dimensional perspective. The stars in the dark night sky were spinning around the heavens, a blur of bright white light on a velvet black background. They streaked tails of light, as if his eyes were the lens of a camera left with an open aperture as the world turned on its axis.

He closed his eyes, feeling a little nauseated by it, trying to tell himself that it was just a mild hallucination.

What he could not so easily think away was the heavy ache of his aroused body. He felt as if molten steel had been poured into him, hardening him into an inviolable state. It was somehow sacrosanct, and his power was pure nothingness in the face of it.

He was dimly aware of her breath in the cradle of his neck. It meant she had survived him, and he was grateful for that. As they lay together in the night, she began to warm up against him.

"'Hours to go before I sleep,'" he murmured to the forest, the quote coming to his mind as reminder that he could not afford to waste any more time in this way that exposed them both to incredible danger.

But he could not make himself move. It was as if he had been given a paralytic drug. It kept him from moving, yet still allowed him to feel.

And that was when the pain came.

Damien cried out when it burst through him with sudden brutality. He could not help it. The wrenching sound echoed into the night, bouncing off the trees, a long, deep-timbreed roar of agony. He suddenly felt as if his veins and arteries were being stripped from his body, tearing clean through muscle, sinew, and skin. He convulsed beneath the charge, so hard that he heard a bone somewhere in his body snap in his sub-vocal hearing. He was aware, somehow, that he was being brutalized on an atomic level. With the altering of his body came the altering of his mind. He imagined, for a single, horrifying moment, that his chest was exploding, making way for the leaping escape of the dolphin that had somehow become trapped within. As the beast writhed into the air, it changed form into a falcon. From a falcon, it burst into the shape of a dove.

The soft little mourning dove floated on delicate wings to land beside his head. He blinked his eyes, and the next moment he was looking at small, bare feet.

Numbly, he followed the line of ankle and calf until he was looking up at the entire figure of a beautiful young woman he could swear he had seen once before.

* * *

Windsong knelt beside the Vampire Prince quickly, touching his skin to test the warmth of his body. It was the only way to tell if a Vampire was alive or not, provided they were not beheaded or burnt to ash. Those deaths were pretty much self-identifying.

Even in the darkness she could make out the blood still on his lips. Considering the matching wounds on the Lycanthrope's throat, Windsong was easily able to add up the evidence before her, immediately understanding what Damien had done and why he had been forced into such a terrible decision. The sacrifice he had made to save the vulnerable Lycanthrope Princess touched the sensitive Mistral far too deeply, and she had to blink back the sudden moisture in her eyes.

The flutter of bird's wings drew her attention up to the small lark lighting on the ground beside her. With a ruffle of feathers, the bird began to transform. In a minute's time, it became the petite form of Windsong's apprentice.

"Lyric, we must fashion litters and take them home as soon as possible. They need healing and protection."

"How can we protect ones such as these?" Lyric questioned nervously, even as she knelt to help Windsong turn the Lycanthrope Princess off the Vampire Prince, laying her out next to him.

"Just as we protect ourselves, dearest. With our voices and our wisdom and our hearts. Hurry now, there is no time to waste."

"Are they close to death?"

"I am not sure. However, I am positive they are being pursued. Move quickly, child."

Lyric did not ask another question. She hurried off to gather some strong branches together. She would not go far, Windsong knew, because she would be too afraid to. That was for the best, the Mistral thought, because for the next few moments she would not be able to keep any of her attention on her young charge.

Instead, she sat down on the chill forest debris, folding her legs beneath herself gracefully, her knees close to the side-by-side heads of the unconscious outsiders.

Windsong closed her eyes and took two long, deep breaths. Then, softly, she began to sing. The song was one of protection, and it was a powerful one. It would buffer the three of them from detection and harm once it had spread about them in a circle of comfort. That widening circle was only a matter of Windsong's exquisite voice warming up and expanding in exponential force. It only took a moment for the forest to begin to ring with the echoes of the notes, sung over scales that were sometimes perceptible only to animal ears. The eddy of the painfully sweet music drifted out, bewitching and confusing the senses of anything within its circumference, or anything trying to enter it.

"Syreena," Siena hissed softly.

She let the bloodied snow fall through her fingers, turning sharply to face the female Vampire.

"You believe Damien has tracked after her?"

"Since it is unlikely he would attack her, that is the only logical alternative," Jasmine responded matter-of-factly. "His scent leads to this place, then disappears just as your sister's does. Unless you think they are holding a caucus or trysting while your sister is wounded . . ."

"Syreena does not *tryst*," the Lycanthrope Queen snapped at the smaller female. "Why do I think you are seeing this as some sort of amusement?"

"Siena . . ." Elijah warned gently.

"Very likely because my species is easily taken in by a good intrigue. Lucky you, for that is no doubt why Damien followed the Princess."

Elijah reached out to grab his wife's arm when she lurched toward the Vampire female with a snarl rumbling out of her chest. "Siena! I am sure Jasmine means no insult and is only relating fact," he interjected quickly and soothingly.

"Of course," Jasmine said.

"Can you track them?" Siena asked her husband, ignoring the Vampire and grasping at the sleeve of his shirt.

"I can." Siena was forced to look at the outsider because of her husband's negating thoughts in her head. He could not follow Damien. His skills were not equal to the superb abilities of the Prince. "I can follow Damien anywhere he wants me to," Jasmine continued easily. "I assure you, he has not covered his tracks behind him. He wants anyone who notices this scene to follow him and perhaps lend him aid. Your Consort and I can fly after him. You, however, cannot. You will have to remain behind."

Elijah felt his mate's frustration soaring through her with white-hot intensity. She did not like this stranger telling her what she could and could not do. Even if she was right, the Queen resented her for reminding her of it. Siena's animal form was a cougar, a land-bound creature that could not cross bodies of water without the aid of other means, mystical or technological. For instance, Elijah could take her with him.

"No," he murmured softly into her hair near her ear, reaching to cradle her shoulders in his palms. "Stay here. In case Damien returns with Syreena. At least then you can inform us of it and we can return to you more quickly." He touched her chin gently, turning her eyes up into his own. "We will bring her back to you, kitten, if it can be done."

"I know," she said, the catch in her voice tight and painful. She blinked the emotion in her eyes away, turning from them both in order to hide it. Jasmine knew it was purely for her benefit. The Demon warrior was well aware of everything his mate felt, sometimes even before she was. It was the nature of the way they were joined. Even a Vampire knew this.

Jasmine spread her slim arms to her sides, fingers and

palms turned up to the sky as she lifted from the ground and into the night. The cold wind rippled through her loose shirt and hair as she hovered just above the couple's golden heads. She turned her eyes upward, her face away, so Elijah and his bride could say a brief good-bye without her obvious witness.

A moment later, the Demon was soaring up to her level, his stark green eyes penetrating the darkness as he looked at her.

"Lead," he commanded her.

"Be patient. This will be slow going, warrior," she warned him. "The trail is already several hours cold."

"I understand that," he said, glancing down at his wife in spite of himself. His worry for her was clear.

It was enough to touch even the jaded Vampire.

Damien's eyes flew open, the pupils contracting sharply in the bright light surrounding him. He shied for one breathless moment, alarmed that he had woken up in sunlight.

After a moment of adjustment, he realized there were soft hands on his back urging him to lie back into the warmth and comfort of the bed he had been resting in. He jerked around to see who was touching him, an instinctive show of fangs and a snarl behind his lips.

The young girl he sprang at yelped in terror, jumping out of her chair and knocking it over as she stumbled back out of his reach.

"Easy, Lyric," a soft, sweet voice soothed the girl as hands reached to steady her. "He will not hurt you. Will you, Damien?"

Damien hesitated when he heard his name, turning to focus on the new target. He realized immediately that he recognized her. "Windsong?"

"Yes, Damien."

He remained frozen in place for two beats as his mind

tried to reconcile all the information it was receiving at once. It was difficult to do, not only because of his shocky state, but because Windsong's voice was a natural hypnotic. The dazing lure of a Siren's voice was half pure beauty and talent; the other half was a trick of the mind. A Vampire of his skill and age was immune to the mind manipulation, but there would always be an effect of a Mistral's voice that he could not overcome. Not so long as the Mistral's intentions were well meant.

"Sorry," he murmured to the girl he had frightened before lying back with a sigh of immeasurable relief.

Safety. At last.

He remembered it had been intentional, setting down in the woodlands near *Brise Lumineuse*. He had intended to seek shelter there if and only if he had to. Apparently, Windsong had known he had become unable to reach her himself.

Windsong somehow always knew those sorts of things.

"My apologies, Lyric," he said again, this time far more sincerely. He glanced at Windsong and then turned studying eyes on the compact little dark-haired girl. "Your apprentice this century, I take it?"

"Yes," Windsong said. "How are you feeling?"

"Tired," he responded automatically. Then he realized that was very much the truth of it. He could not remember the last time he had actually felt weariness like this. This was not the weakness that came from too long a time between feedings, something he experienced with much more frequency, if frequency was the appropriate term. This was a tiring like . . . well, like it had been when he had once depended on circulation, oxygen, and a beating heart to power himself.

Like all Vampires, however, he had ceased to need those support systems around his one hundredth year. Now any use they got was purely habitual, like blinking or breathing. It was this lack of expected function that had started the myth that Vampires were the walking dead. In truth, it was merely that, as they matured, their bodies learned a new way to conserve nutrition while at the same time magnifying the energy it produced. It was an evolutionary efficiency and it was why they had become so prevalent as a species. Their brains functioned at higher levels, allowing for higher sensory abilities, the power to influence the minds of others, and the capacity to levitate and fly by the sheer command of thought. Not to mention the quick healing that all Nightwalkers enjoyed the benefit of in one form or another.

Apparently he had survived his deadly experiment with the ingestion of Lycanthrope blood, his remarkable ability to heal himself of almost any damage being his true saving grace.

However, he would not be repeating the act anytime soon.

He could still remember the pain and knew it would haunt him for quite some time. Like a child, he did not need to touch the flame twice to learn his lesson.

He felt leaden and heavy, but there was no hunger that needed attending, so he knew that was not the reason why. His body was nowhere near finished coping with whatever damage had been done. It made him feel helpless and he hated that. What he would not give for a good Body Demon medic in that moment.

"Syreena?"

"She is resting," Windsong assured him, resting a hand on his arm to keep him lying in the bed when his instinct was to get up and see for himself. He would be responsible if anything happened to the Lycanthrope Princess, and he would rather lose his head to a dull blade than see that happen.

The passion of the thought surprised him for a moment, so much so that he actually laughed aloud. It was out of place to the two women near his bed as well. He could tell because they exchanged curious glances. "Will she live?"

"Thanks to you," Windsong said, letting him know she was aware of what he had done to attempt to save her.

"Thanks to luck," he corrected her with a long, heartfelt sigh. "A lot of luck."

"Then we shall have to give thanks for your luck in our prayers before we sleep this morning," Windsong said.

"How long until dawn?" he asked. Normally, his body clock warned him when it was close to dawn, but he was not surprised to realize he was a bit dulled to some of his usual internal sensitivities.

"It is past dawn," the little apprentice said, her surprise that he did not know that all too evident in her sweet little voice.

"Thank you, sweetling," he said, his eyes drifting closed for a long minute. He did not see her blush at the intimacy of the endearment. "Right now, I think I would be mid-suntan before I realized that."

Lyric burst out in a surprised laugh, covering her mouth in shock at herself as she drew his attention back to her. He gave her a charismatic grin as he casually tucked one hand beneath his dark head.

"So you are studying to be a healer?" he asked. "You will be learning from the best. The woman you saved today would not have lived into adulthood if not for Windsong."

Lyric's eyes widened at that piece of information. "We mostly do herbal medicines together. Windsong will not take me to more serious cases."

"Because you are a long way off from learning those skills. One day at a time," the elder Siren lectured firmly, her large blue eyes sparing a knowing twinkle for Damien alone. "Is it not amazing how eager the young are to get themselves into hot water?"

Damien laughed and nodded. He had known far more than enough precocious Vampires with that very same trait. Jasmine had been one of them.

"Now, Lyric, resume your seat and your mending song," Windsong instructed her pupil, using her hands to guide the awestruck girl into her chair. "Lyric has an exceptional voice, Damien. I expect she will help you to sleep in no time."

"I do not doubt it in the least," Damien said.

He relaxed as much as he could in the bed, closing his eyes and trying to ignore the residual echoes of extraordinary pain that still lived in his memory and the nerves of his body.

As promised, Lyric began to sing to him. After a few unsure quavers, she fell into the familiarity of the mending song she had practiced over and over and over again; always waiting and hoping for the time she would first use it. She was amazed and honored that her first serious patient was the very powerful Prince of the Vampires. She could hardly wait to tell Thrush about the wild experience of the entire night. He would never believe her! She hardly believed it herself.

Lyric's voice flowed over Damien like a breeze that first rushed, and then lingered. The song itself was filled with soothing imagery, of fields and fresh air and moonlight that shone down on the wings of the moths flitting by. He allowed himself the luxury of being cocooned by this special form of magic. So long as Windsong was there, they would remain safe.

Damien drifted into a contented sleep with that thought.

Chapter 5

When next he woke, it was to the bright sound of song coming from a distant room.

He recognized the raw talent of Lyric's as yet untempered voice. Give her a few decades of intense study at her mentor's hand, he thought, and she would sound as easy in skill and as devastatingly beautiful as the voice that chimed in suddenly in chorus.

He lay quietly listening for long minutes. In spite of himself, they easily drew him into that half-hypnotic state that soothed even the harshest of souls. There was even a music in the way they carried out their tasks, which he came to understand was cooking their first evening meal. The heat of the kitchen and all its rich scents drifted on the notes their voices stroked and toyed with. Windsong's coloratura was a masterpiece in sound, Lyric's gentle soprano like the sweet crystalline tinkling of bells.

Damien sat up, running his fingers through his hair, trying to absently smooth it into a semblance of order as his eyes drifted over to the second bed in the room, situated perpendicular and to the right of his own. He assumed the beds were Lyric's and Windsong's own, surrendered for the well-being of their patients.

Patient.

The word did not sit well on a man like Damien, and he moved to get out of bed. He hesitated when he realized his bloody clothing had been stripped from his body, leaving him nude beneath the covers. Mistrals were not at all like his race, being far more conservative and reserved in all things except goodness and song. While Windsong was several centuries old, he was certain that Lyric was not used to such things.

He smiled to himself, even laughing under his breath. It had been a while since he had needed to think like a gentleman. He found it refreshing all over again.

He pulled a sheet with him as he rose to his feet. He was a little hungry, which was a good sign, and feeling incredibly light of heart. He realized, as he wrapped the linen fabric around his hips, that it was probably an effect of the song being tossed about with merriment in the distant room.

The Vampire Prince moved to Syreena's bed, leaning over her and touching gentle fingers to the bandages swathing her hairline. He sensed the strong and steady rhythm of her pulse, smelled the herbs that had been used to treat and bathe her. She smelled strongly of lavender, strangely enough a favorite of his. It compelled him to sit beside her on the bed, taking the time for a closer inspection.

She was bruised darkly across her face, but mostly on her throat. Her blood loss was retarding her normally quick healing or they would have been mostly gone by now, just as most of his damage had seemed to have healed over the daytime.

He noticed her hands were heavily bandaged and it surprised him. He lifted one from the handmade quilt she was bundled under, and unwrapped the gauze and strips of cloth in order to find out why. What wound had he missed there?

He made a soft, angry sound deep against his vocal cords

as he realized she had several wounds penetrating through and through her hands.

Bad enough the sick bitch had plucked the unfortunate Princess's feathers, but she had effectively clipped her wings as well, although the wounds would probably not last a tenth as long as the memory of their acquisition would.

Damien laid her palm gingerly onto his own upturned one, his fingertips of his opposite hand moving softly and gently over the wounds on the back of her hand. He heard her heartbeat alter and he looked up to her face quickly.

Her calico eyes were open, regarding him through half-raised lids and puffy, swollen flesh.

"Welcome back," he greeted her quietly.

She did not respond. Instead, she flicked her mismatched eyes over her surroundings in a quick, succinct inventory. "You came after me?"

Her voice was hoarse, her throat bruised by burst vessels from within, a result of the strangulations she had suffered.

"Once I realized what had happened," he told her.

He was instantly curious. Windsong and Lyric were still singing robustly in the background, yet she did not seem affected by it like she should be. It was a possible mark to her own mental discipline, but he found that hard to believe in her weakened and battered state.

"I thank you," she said on a sigh, closing her eyes and trying to shift herself slightly. She winced, a wholly slight response considering the magnitude of the pain she must be feeling.

"There is no need for you to move," he said soothingly. "You are being well cared for. Wait until you have healed some more before attempting to do so."

Her eyes opened again, this time a little wider, her awareness of him and her other surroundings clearly increasing.

"Where are we?"

"*Brise Lumineuse*," he told her, knowing she was familiar with both the place and who lived there.

It had been Windsong who had saved Siena from severe sun poisoning a little over a month ago. He could tell by the expression in Syreena's eyes that the Princess understood she was now doubly beholden to the generous Mistral.

Her eyes flicked down to the hand he held, and he followed her gaze. Damien realized with surprise that he had continued to stroke her softly as they spoke. He felt an incredible sadness as he looked at the wounds once more. He met her unusual eyes, not caring that she could probably read his emotions within his own.

"I am sorry," he murmured softly, his fingers replaced by the warm press of his palm.

"For what?" she asked.

"For taking so long to find you," he said.

He had nothing to apologize for, Syreena thought as emotion ravaged her features. Such tender sensitivity and concern from so unlikely a source stirred up the turmoil she had kept under tight control since this ordeal had begun. She could not stop the tears that leaked out of the corners of her eyes, but she turned her face away from him as she tried to regain control over her feelings of fear, anger and . . . and so many others she could not even face.

"Do not do that," he said suddenly, his fingers reaching to turn her face back to him. "Do not be ashamed of what you are feeling."

"This from one whose species feels very little and expresses even less?" she retorted, a bit of the fire he was used to snapping into the remark. It made Damien smile.

"This from a woman who has met a total of two Vampires in her entire lifetime?" he countered. "What you know of us from your Monks and your books varies greatly from what we truly are," he informed her.

Syreena was already beginning to realize that. But she did not like feeling so vulnerable and exposed to so utter a stranger. It had been a knee-jerk reaction to try to irritate him. She could deal with the barbs they tossed between them better than she could this wellspring of concern she had never thought him capable of.

Then she finally took note of his state of dress, or rather undress, and it occurred to her that he might be hurt as well. She recalled that there had been an explosion and the back-lash of a great deal of magic when he had arrived for her. It must have been an extraordinarily painful ordeal, one that only someone as powerful as he was could possibly survive.

Her searching eyes roamed the handsome planes of his face, the long, loose length of his blue-black hair, and his bare flesh over the span of his shoulders and chest.

"Are you well?" she asked at last when she saw no visible signs of harm on him. In fact, he looked far too healthy for a man who had been through so much in one night. She envied him his quickly healed body and the clearly robust health accented by his precisely defined musculature.

"So far, so good," he responded rather cryptically.

But the mystery of the comment disappeared in the next instant as she was flooded with sudden memory.

Syreena sat up so suddenly that she took him by surprise. She pulled her hand free of his and reached to take hold of his shoulders. The Princess repeated her scan of him, trying once more to find some sort of damage.

"Damien," she uttered in a voice full of shock and comprehension. "*Are you well?*"

He immediately understood the difference between her first question and then the repeat of it. He reached to take her hands from his shoulders, a soothing sound clicking off his tongue.

"Yes, I am well," he assured her, urging her back into a resting position.

She shrugged off the attempt, her pupils radiating her disbelief in his statement. "Why would you do such a thing? You could have been killed!"

"But I was not," he reminded her.

"You risked your life for mine as if you had no responsibility to an entire race of people! It was a foolish and ridiculous thing to do!"

"It would have been my mistake to make," he countered sharply. "I am not used to people criticizing my actions, Syreena."

"Well, perhaps they should! I would never have allowed Siena to do such a foolish thing!"

"Oh, really? Just as you prevented her from almost dying for the sake of her husband?"

It was a twisting knife in a very tender spot for her, and he knew it instantly by the expression in her eyes. It was only then that he realized she did indeed blame herself for her sister's near encounter with death that recent October.

"Was I supposed to let you bleed to death, Syreena?" he asked quietly, trying to take back the pain he had caused her with the balm of his words. "Why are you so eager to value my life above your own?"

"Because I am not so special that an entire people should be deprived of their monarch for my sake!"

"Lucky for you, I disagree with that assessment."

Damien understood, however, that there was baggage beyond her statement other than the immediate disagreement. Still, it did not measure up for him. She had never struck him as the type who devalued herself.

She looked at him as if he were completely insane for a long moment, her confused eyes searching over him for an answer and a logic that just was not within grasp. Then, without knowing why, she leaned in and kissed him.

Damien was shocked for a moment at the forward and illogical act, his hands reflexively circling her arms as her warm mouth pressed gently to his. Her unbandaged hand came up to lie against the side of his face, her contrary eyes sliding closed for a long, painful moment.

He felt, and then tasted, the salt of her tears.

She pulled away, only a couple of inches, her body trembling beneath his hands as he looked into her eyes with a confusion of emotions and sensations struggling through him.

"Why did you . . . ?"

"Because," she interrupted with a sob catching at her words. "Because it is a fairy tale, Damien. And in a fairy tale, the Princess always kisses the Prince who rescues her."

It was an enchanting and ingenuous thing for her to say. She was a woman of great learning, amazing strength, and a sense of logic that negated any illusion of naïveté, yet she was willing to expose herself as a hopeful idealist in order to express her gratitude. He realized that it was a preciously protected streak in her makeup that very few people were allowed access to. It subsequently meant more to Damien than the most profuse and eloquent words of any language.

"Syreena . . ." He paused to clear the coarseness in his throat. "I am no hero," he told her with rough quietness. "You should not make me into one."

She defied the statement by forcing it into silence with the cover of her mouth.

This time Damien saw it coming, but it made him no better prepared. This time it was not a quick and simple expression of impulsive gratitude she was reaching to express. This was a little different, and on an instinctive level he knew it.

Completely in spite of the soundness of reason that rang stridently in his head, Damien allowed himself the luxury of the feel of her lips. Caught less off his mark and having had a moment to think about it, he returned the intimacy with equal warmth and measure. From one heartbeat to the next, his hands found their way into the hair at the back of her head, his fingertips sliding with careful languor, mindful of all she had suffered and been through and in no way wanting to cause her even a moment of additional pain.

Syreena was also sliding her fingers into a position that held his head to her, just in case he thought to argue with her any further about her desires in this matter. His darkening eyes were looking directly into hers, seeking for things beyond both their comprehension. She met his searching gaze with eyes full of surety and strength. She knew what she wanted, amazingly enough without a single doubt or second thought. This moment, those fascinating eyes messaged to him, was to be precious for them both. The next moment would come soon enough. But this moment . . .

This moment was for thanking, for gentleness, and, most of all, for feeling something that had no pain, struggle, or immediate ramifications to it.

It simply would be what it was.

A kiss.

A kiss between a man and a woman.

Not Nightwalkers. Not a Prince and Princess. Not a Vampire and a Lycanthrope.

Simply a man and a woman.

Damien's eyes closed as the keen purity of that ebbed into him. He seemed to suddenly realize that her mouth was a soft, heated fullness that had nothing to do with bruised tenderness. That she had flavor, in both bouquet and taste, and it was like tasting heated syrup. She was liquid and soft solid and every other essential that was natural to life.

At the same time, he understood that she had never kissed a man before.

Never in all of a century of life.

I have lived in a cloistered setting, forbidden any opportunity to form attachments or affections outside of a student-teacher relationship. What I was starved of at first, I was soon too complacent and numbed against after so many years of deprivation. So I never sought it.

These were her thoughts, easily read even if he had not been able to study them.

So the kiss was also an act of total bravery. A baring of her soul and her vulnerability because of her inexperience. It ought to have been awkward, but it was not. She moved against his mouth in delicate increments so that there would be no clumsiness on her part. As with all things she had taken on in a lifetime of being a student, she gave an exemplary performance of her quick ability to learn and adapt.

Damien's lips stroked against hers, opening slowly until she was mimicking him perfectly. She anticipated him, though, her little tongue touching his lips before he could seek it out himself. His breath fell quick and hot against her, the reflex automatic in spite of its lack of requirement. She exhaled into his mouth as he reached deeply for her, perfecting the hungry seal of their mouths.

He lost sense of everything but the exquisiteness of her kiss and the piquing interest of his own body. She smelled of lavender and those indefinable perfumes that had led him over miles of land and sea to find her. The exposed nails of her other hand skimmed down the thick column of his neck, making his throat convulse with an uncensored sound of pleasure. She slid her tongue over his, letting them touch and twist together in an erotic dance of sensation and curiosity turning into a purer appetite.

Damien loosed a hand from the cling of her hair, drawing it down the back of her neck and the bare track of her delicate spine. She shivered under the caress, the shudder pulling her in closer to his chest.

The Vampire Prince broke from her mouth when her bare torso connected to his, the heat of her naked skin unbelievably intense and almost bracing. He struggled for equilibrium, touching his forehead to hers as his gaze fell down onto their touching skin.

He had never known how much depth there could be to so seemingly simple a bodily contact, the most remarkable thing being the intense heat that emanated from her and into him. It brought back memories of the taste of her blood, the way it had bled hotly into him, the way she had writhed beneath the intrusion of his bite and the subsequent feeding.

Damien groaned, the sound mutating into a soft growl full of desire, sensuality, and frustration. He pulled her forward so her cheek was pressed to his, taking a moment to appreciate the heat of her flushed face before he had to move away from her.

"Don't," she begged him on a whisper, her hands tightening to hold him to her.

"I have to," he argued roughly, his fingers betraying his actual wishes as they stroked up the supple skin of her bare back.

"Why? Why do you have to?"

"So many reasons," he sighed into the soft, feathery tresses falling over her cheek and ear.

"Are there any reasons to stay?" she asked.

"So many more," he confessed, but he pulled back from her all the same. "You have thanked me, Syreena, expressing your heartfelt gratitude in wonderful measure," he said kindly, his tender thumb brushing at the traces of moisture from the kiss that had been left on her enflamed lips. "But this is where gratitude must end. Anything beyond this . . . must come perhaps another day . . . for other reasons entirely."

After delivering that truth, Damien extracted himself from her hold with patient but persistent gentleness. After a moment, she let her hands fall away from him and allowed him to lay her back against her pillows while he pulled the quilt up snugly around her.

He hovered over her a moment, nose to nose with her as he mined her thoughts through her eyes. Syreena wondered if he was even aware of the way he was absently stroking her sensitive hair.

"There is one thing a Vampire of great age enjoys more than anything else in the world," he told her, "and that is to be deeply and delightfully surprised. You, sweetling, are a veritable bundle of surprises."

She smiled at that, feeling his sincere bafflement at his realization. Then the Prince drifted a brief kiss of his lips across her forehead and left her bedside.

* * *

Elijah walked around the little cell of stone slowly, his keen eyes in search of any clue that would explain what he was seeing. He glanced at his temporary partner, who was crouched near a corner full of dark stains of blood.

"This is where they were keeping the Princess, of that there is no doubt," Jasmine murmured, her voice distant as she sorted through her sensory information. Elijah had already divined that from the evidence himself. He was waiting for her to tell him something he did not already know. "Magic-users, hunters . . . a Demon." Her dark gaze flicked up to him questioningly.

"Ruth. A traitor."

"Ah yes. Her." Damien had shared the story with Jasmine, as well as his insights and speculations on the matter. "Well, they have all abandoned this place rather quickly. They have several hours' head start, since we had to stop for the daylight."

"I will worry about them later," Elijah told her, reminding her his interests lay elsewhere.

"The damage is from Damien, of that I have no doubt. From this point I have no sense of his trail whatsoever. But I expect that is because he is now purposely hiding it in order to throw off pursuers. What is not hidden as easily is the spoor of the Princess's blood. She was clearly bleeding with profusion."

Jasmine did not point out the obvious. The warrior had eyes in his head. They both could see the remains of the massive loss of the precious fluid that had pooled and sprayed all about them. Neither of them could see how she would ever survive such a depletion, no matter how quickly Damien might find aid for her.

"Wherever she is," Jasmine said, "whatever her state, she is with Damien. We can be assured of that much."

"We're in Mistral lands," Elijah noted as he walked out of the room and into the loft leading around the storage room below. "They have been here for a while," he observed when he saw the cots, supplies, and all the evidence of their inhabitance.

"It does not look as though these others were prepared for leaving," Jasmine said as she followed in his footsteps. "They were mid-mealtime when Damien arrived," she added, looking down at the long tables full of half-empty plates and upended mugs. "I do not understand. Why would an enemy take a leisurely meal when so dangerous a prisoner was being kept just above their heads?"

"Perhaps they did not know there even was a prisoner," Elijah said. "I have a feeling Ruth was acting on her own agenda, and as usual left these fools in the dark."

"I would have to agree. You are right. She is quite deranged. Only manic persons make these kinds of impulsive choices."

"It certainly is not the way I taught her to think," Elijah said grimly. "Not what I know her to be capable of." He turned to the Vampire. "We better continue on after Damien and Syreena. As much as I would like to, I can't afford to chase these necromancers down until I am certain they are safe."

"Agreed," Jasmine said, admiring his logic and his ability to circumvent the very powerful emotional instinct to seek out his enemy. It was what made the difference between a warrior, and a leader of warriors. It was why Jasmine was certain Elijah would catch up to Ruth in the end. Ruth was a poor leader, wasting her energy and her resources to satisfy her emotional needs, rather than satisfying a proper strategy.

Assuring herself in this way, this time she followed the warrior as he took off to track Syreena's trail.

Damien stood out in the cold darkness, letting the night wind blow over his body. It rippled through his freshly laundered clothing, snapping back his retwisted braid.

He was in need of a feed.

He pushed the need aside easily, however. He could not in good conscience leave the cottage and those within it for any amount of time. Windsong and Lyric had put themselves at great risk for his benefit, and he would not leave them to their own devices when he had potentially led enemies straight to their doorstep. Windsong's protection songs were quite impressive, but they would not work forever, nor would they keep out someone like Ruth who had no doubt become largely immune to such manipulations.

Frankly, he was surprised she had not already come.

It was a logical move to let her prisoner slip away at this point, because if one Nightwalker had been able to track her, there were likely others in his wake. If it were Damien, he would have concentrated on misdirection and other tools to mislead anyone trying to find them as they escaped their discovered stronghold.

But logic was rarely a part of the thought processes of a woman driven in the way Ruth was. It would be very like her to ignore wise tactics for the sake of personal gratification.

At least, it was at this point.

It was clear that Ruth had discarded all sense of self-preservation for the present. If only her lackeys would come to realize that, maybe they would stop following her commands so easily. If they were eliminated from the equation, it would make her capture much more likely. Magic was such a nonquantifiable resource. There were no set guidelines. The outline of possibility changed with the variables. Until now, for instance, no one had known it was possible for a Nightwalker to even use magic.

What a frightening prospect that was. Black magic had one true universal: it corrupted unanimously. It was why magic-users smelled so vile to Nightwalkers, this corruption that went soul-deep. It was . . .

It was the antithesis to the love of soul mates.

Elijah and Siena were soul mates. Theirs was a love that had transcended cultural taboo, their personal independence of spirit, and had managed to defy every written rule of the Nightwalker world. While magic could accomplish these things as well, the effects were the telling point.

Siena and her mate were now a synchronous being. They had come into harmony to create a unified force that was impressive and powerful. It was rapidly destroying walls of prejudice and suspicion; it was eliminating the possibility of any future wars between their two disparate societies. It was building a prospect for those in the present, and their children of the future.

Magic only created discord. It hurt, it harmed, it tore carefully sewn seams to shreds. Nature became unbalanced and suffered under its poison. An example in the starkest sense would be the magical act of a Demon Summoning. It stole the named Demon out of his or her life, entrapped them in a poisonous pentagram, forcing them under magic's sway. It mutated them into monsters without souls, without conscience, the ultimate insult to a member of a species who were normally so moral and conscious of their behaviors.

Magic had its ways of hurting Vampires as well. He had seen them murdered with it, eviscerated, decapitated, and paralyzed, left on the ground until the dawn came.

It would never be truly eradicated, the Prince realized, until every spell book, every scroll full of those cursed words, was burned into nothingness, and then those who had such things in their memories were also destroyed.

It was an impossible prospect. The discovery of spell compendiums in the hidden Library had shown him that. For 100 years magic had been quelled, but its recent resurgence made it all too clear it could not be eradicated.

"Damien."

Damien turned sharply, surprised to realize he had been so deep in thought that he had not heard the approach from behind.

Then again, she was hardly a threat.

After a fashion.

"Syreena, you should be resting."

"I can't sleep," she said with a shrug.

She had wrapped herself in her quilt to keep herself warm. He saw the flash of a powder blue skirt around her knees. Apparently Windsong had lent her a dress to replace her torn and soiled one. Her feet were bare, and just the sight of them on the cold ground was enough to give him a chill down his neck.

"Come here," he commanded gently, beckoning her forward.

She obeyed without argument, a testament to how vulnerable she still was and still felt. He reached around her slight figure, scooping her feet off the ground and raising her up into the seat of a boulder that was just beside him. With the quilt beneath her to protect her from the cold of the stone, it was an improvement, if not much of one.

The rock situated her just above the level of his waist. He did not join her because there was not enough room on the slightly slanted surface. Instead, he leaned his hip against it near her knees, facing her as he gave her a good study from head to toe.

"I have only been sick once before in all of my life," she mentioned quietly as she turned her face up to the pronounced stars above her.

"This is not a sickness," he reminded her gently.

"It feels the same. If not worse."

"I can imagine."

"It was when this happened," she noted, her fingers sweeping through the brown strands of her hair first, and then what remained of the thinned gray.

"What color was it originally?" he asked out of honest curiosity.

"Hmm. I actually don't remember. It was so long ago. I think I asked Siena that question in a letter once and she conveniently ignored it."

"Perhaps so she would not allow you to bias yourself against half of yourself."

"I agree," she said with a nod. "It was very hard to accept being so different in the beginning. I imagine I was a bit of a nasty thing to be around at the time. It is strange how things that are so important to us when we are younger become so impossible to remember later on."

"I don't remember much of my first one hundred years," he said. "It was all something of a blur." His half-smile of mischief reached his eyes, making a liar of him.

"I see. Caused a bit of trouble, did you?"

"A bit," he chuckled. "Too much. Too much fun. When we are young, we do not understand that such a thing is possible. Not until we hit the downside of the mountain." His smile faded as he looked up at her. "I fell into torpor shortly after that. My disenchantment was by far the worst thing I had ever felt before or since. I literally found myself a hole and curled up for one hundred twenty-one years. When I woke, I made a pact with myself to be more gentle and appreciative of my time and my amusements. I have not needed to sulk in that way since then."

"Which is why you have accumulated the power and wisdom to become Prince of your peoples."

"I suppose so." He studied her features for a long moment. "Do you never resent the fact that all the course your life has taken has been decided by someone else?"

"I do. Resent may be too strong a word, though. Resentment is for childhood. Adults are merely frustrated."

Damien understood her distinction all too clearly. Her position did not allow her the luxury of a good old-fashioned temper tantrum.

"Perhaps one day you will have the opportunity to go your own way."

"Perhaps. Perhaps after Siena begins her family, securing the line of the throne. Even then, I am her most trusted and essential advisor. I am logic when her emotion is harmful. She needs me."

"And what do you need, Syreena?" he asked her softly.

"I need to be needed," she said at first, assuring herself that it might be enough to satisfy her. However, they both knew that was not the entire truth. "Why do you ask me this?"

"The question should be 'why don't you ask yourself this?' " he remarked.

"I see. You suddenly know me so well?" Her tone was mean and clipped, defense mechanisms so obvious they were like a neon sign saying KEEP OUT!

"I know what it means to have responsibilities and to be the focus of everyone else's expectations of me. I know what it means to be royalty, Syreena. I am the closest thing you will ever know to yourself besides your sister."

He had too valid a point, Syreena realized angrily. He read her too well, for all he was a stranger. It made her feel even more vulnerable, a feeling that she would always despise in herself. She hated being weak in the face of anything.

But why not? she thought bitterly. She had proven herself to be nothing short of weak in the past twenty-four hours.

Damien knew her confidence had been shaken. He had known it from the moment he had found her huddled in the corner like a sick and frightened puppy, beaten and bleeding and terribly defeated. She had nothing to be ashamed of, she just did not understand that. She did not realize that Ruth could have done just as much damage to any one of them— Noah, Siena, and himself included.

"Syreena, do not blame yourself for being victimized," he said quietly.

"What do you know of what my blame and my feelings are?" she snapped with sudden acrimony. She leapt from the rock in her anger, stumbling as her feet hit the ground. He instinctively reached to balance her with a helping hand, but she struck him away. "Stop trying to help me! The rescue is over. Your duty to my sister is fulfilled. You do not have to be so *nice* to me any longer!"

She stalked off, but he quickly followed at her heels.

"I do not recall your sister ever entering my mind when I decided to come after you," he shot at her back.

The remark made her come to a halt. She whirled around to face him, her bicolored eyes narrowing with suspicion and rage.

"Don't you dare patronize me!"

"I was not aware that I was."

"Why are you doing this? Why are you still here? *Why are you following me yet?*"

"Because you apparently need to be followed. You need to be protected. And, as you said yourself, you need to be needed."

Damien could understand her sudden expression of surprise. He did not know where that last item had come from.

"In what way could you possible have a need for me?"

The multitude of answers that flooded Damien had the power to make even a Vampire blush. Where it came from, again he had no idea, but it was there all the same, bright and bold and piercingly sharp. It was an instinct, and he had lived by them too long to start ignoring them now.

"How is one to find out the answer to that if you keep walking away from them?" he said instead.

"Do not take pity on me just because I wept all over you before. I am not some weakling girl who needs a pat on the head and praises."

"Everyone needs praises. And if you were a weakling, Syreena, you would earn my disgust, not my pity. I have a very low threshold for people who sit around crying, waiting for everyone else to save them."

She didn't have a way to be immediately angry with that, and Damien knew that was because she agreed with him. She floundered, searching for a way to keep her temper up. She was having difficulty because it was not him she was truly angry with and he was not providing the necessary target for her temper.

He was struck by how like her father she was in that respect.

"I am not!" she bit out, newly furious, marching back up to him with as much dignity as she could muster considering her weakness and soreness. "Don't you ever say that again!"

"I did not say it," he responded. "I thought it. If I had wanted to share, I would have given you permission to access my thoughts."

What he was not telling her was that he was shocked that she had even been able to do so. Very few beings could read his well-protected thoughts even when they *did* have his permission. How had she done so? Lycanthropes were not telepaths. They only divined things through a collection of vibratory data and a fairly acute sixth sense. Syreena had caught on to him fairly word for word, by the potency of her reaction.

She took a moment to be equally confused, her expression telling him she was also trying to figure out how she had done such a thing.

"In any event, I meant your temper, not in the essence of who you are," he explained calmly, his dark, midnight blue eyes never wavering from hers. "It is nothing you do not already know."

"I don't need a total stranger telling me so," she retorted. But her words were losing their punch. She was tired, upset, and trying too hard to blame him for how she was feeling.

"What you need is rest and peace, Syreena. You are too hard on yourself and you are thinking too hard for someone who should just be letting herself heal."

"Will you please stop telling me what to do," she sighed.

She collapsed where she stood, too tired to even hold her own weight anymore. Damien moved like a blink, his speed bringing him to her before she had sunk even two inches below her height. The Vampire Prince swept her up into his arms, high against his chest until her heavy head settled in the nook between his right ear and shoulder.

In spite of himself, he pressed his cheek against hers, letting her feel his warmth and the security of his presence.

"Stop this," he whispered into her tiny ear. "Stop trying to prove to me how full of quills you are."

"I don't . . . I don't understand you," she cried softly. "I don't understand what you want!"

"I know," he murmured. "And I am not surprised."

He shifted her closer and began to walk back toward the cozy cottage sitting some distance back in the darkness.

"Tell me what you want," she pleaded.

"I want . . ." He paused long enough to laugh at himself on a soft breath. "I want to know what you want. And since you do not know what that is, I will have to wait to find out."

Chapter 6

Syreena lay bundled beneath clean, warm covers an hour later, trying to figure out what he had meant by that.

She heard him speaking with Windsong in the next room. Every time he laughed, she had to fight the urge to be curious as to why he was doing so. It was an infectious thing, in no way as dark and mysterious as he was. It made her want to hurry into the room and ask what the joke was.

She wanted to hate him, but she realized it was impossible. She had even found his confession of degeneracy to be fascinating and character defining, not a scandalous waste like she had been trained to think. In truth, he was nothing like she had tried to make him out to be. He was painfully courteous, even when she railed at him, charming without malicious intent, and terribly wise despite his claims to be less than judicious in his behaviors both past and present.

The Princess realized she had been taking out her foul mood on him, that she was angry with herself for ending up in this entire predicament. He had borne it patiently, even with an ounce of wisdom and a dash of seemingly infinite serenity.

She sat up in her borrowed bed, pushing back the brown side of her hair, which clung wildly to her bandages. She began to unwrap her hands, suddenly tired of their restriction and the way it made her feel like an invalid. She couldn't be as liberal with the coverings on her severely damaged head, so she satisfied herself with the freedom of flexing her fingers and her hands. All that remained of the penetrating wounds was the angry red indications of where they had been. They were also very sore, even a bit painful, but it was nothing she couldn't bear if she put her mind to it. In another few hours it would pass. The more she healed, the stronger she would get.

But it would take a very long time to grow back her hair.

She felt like Samson, shorn to the quick and left betrayed by the resulting weakness. Had love also betrayed her? Like that biblical character had allowed love to become his weakness, had she allowed her love for Siena to weaken her? Or had the Queen's love for her left Siena vulnerable?

Syreena despised the idea that she was considered a weakness to Siena. Worse yet, one that could be exploited in order to attain revenge.

"Stop it!"

Syreena jolted in surprise as the deep bellow preceded the sudden slam of the bedroom door.

She saw the livid fury in Damien's eyes and looked down at her bare hands and the bandages in her lap. "I don't need them—"

"I am not talking about the bandages, Syreena!"

He strode across to her, his irritation evident in every step as she tried to figure out what he was so mad about. Her heart was beating rapidly as he faced her, paused for a moment, and then kneeled down on a single knee before her.

He reached for her wrist, closing long, strong fingers around it and tugging so she would be sure to meet his eyes.

"Are you so bent on punishing yourself?" he demanded of her, his deep blue eyes radiating with the break in his patience. "Will you take on a definition given to you by a mad-woman to satisfy that desire? Just because Ruth's convoluted logic made you her means to get to your sister does not make it the truth!"

"How did—?"

"I swear, you are enough to try the patience of a saint. Or is this what you are trying to attain? Sainthood? No wishes of your own, no ambitions of your own, no love and no lovers? Everything for everyone else? What is it you hope to achieve with this thinking, because I know the purpose escapes me!"

"It escapes me, too!" she bit back defensively. "Unlike you, the world has not been my playground, Damien. One day I was a child like any other, with all the freedoms a child should have. The next I was waking from a fever, and from that very instant my entire life has been mapped out for me. I have been shaped to obey everyone else's ideas of who and what I should be. It is all I know!"

"It is all you will allow yourself to know. I have seen you stand up against this conditioning before. You did it the day you defied your teachers for Siena's sake. Why can you not do it for your own sake?"

"Who the hell do you think you are? You are not my keeper! You are not my teacher! I have enough people telling me what to do!"

"I am the one you chose to show that child to just a few hours ago, Syreena. The child inside of this woman who still hopes in spite of herself and in spite of a century of people trying to wash it out of her."

The kiss.

She knew that was what he meant. A part of her even knew there was truth behind his words. She had indeed shown him that part of herself. She had kissed him simply because she had wanted to. No one had told her to, no one had expected it of her. It had been an impulse of her own desires and her own wishes, born of a longing for things she had relegated to a low position on her list of things she might get around to one day, once she was finished doing everything that was expected of her.

"Stop talking to me as if you know who I am," she said, her entire body shaking with emotion as she tried to free her hand from his grasp.

"Only when you admit that even you do not know who you are," he countered sharply.

"Shut up!"

"Very snappy comeback, sweetling. All that education and that is all you can think of?"

She threw out a word of even less sophistication.

It made him laugh. "You know, I think your temper is the only thing left for you to truly lay claim to," he mused tauntingly.

Syreena smacked him.

A little too hard.

She yelped in pain, nursing her stinging hand to her lips as she groaned and cursed against it. Her only satisfaction was the impression of her fingers just above the line of his beard.

She had also cut his lip against his own teeth, and he touched the bleeding spot with a finger. He looked at it with amusement. "So, I guess Siena is not the only catty one in the family," he observed.

"Why you—!"

She leapt at him, ignoring all the reasons why she shouldn't, her hands going right for his smug face. It didn't even enter her thoughts that he was far faster than she was and could have stopped her quicker than a wink.

He fell onto his back on the floor, his head striking the wooden floorboards with a satisfying whack. She scrambled over him, straddling his waist as she tried to get her hands around his fool neck.

He had her by both wrists, however, and there was no way she could ever overpower him arm to arm. She realized she was in a bit of trouble only when he suddenly rolled her over onto her back, laying his heavy, powerful body over her and trapping her beneath him.

"Get off me!"

He ignored the furious command. Instead, he pressed her hands gently into the floor and looked down into her livid eyes. He felt her trying to dig her heels into the floor for purchase, her entire body wriggling in resistance and in search of escape.

"Keep it up," he encouraged her with a sly smile. "It is about time you had a little foreplay."

Syreena gasped, outraged, shocked, and flustered all at once. She froze in place, finally aware of the position he had caught her in. He lay flush against her, and she had managed to put him directly between her thighs.

"Oh . . ." she said, the strangled sound all she could produce in her shock.

"I should think so," he agreed, his infuriating grin widening as he looked down at their meshed bodies with clear speculation. "Let us see, now . . ."

Syreena shivered as he took a second inventory, except all he used was his sense of smell. He started at her neck, the feel of his breath a curious stimulant as he moved his face down over her shoulder, across her throat, and down the arch of her breastbone right between her breasts.

It was a terribly erotic thing to do. She just could not figure out why he was doing it.

Damien wanted to keep her off balance. She did not think in an orderly fashion when she was working on instinct.

In his opinion, she could use quite a bit of that.

He had, however, forgotten to take his own instincts into account. She still smelled of lavender, but now she carried the scent of the night on her as well. Her time out of doors clung to her like a perfume. The only difference was that she had warmed it, robbing it of its biting chill.

Of all Nightwalkers, Lycanthropes had the highest normal body temperature. He had always seen that in his heat vision.

It had never prepared him for being this close to that heat, however.

"Damien, don't . . ."

"Damien, don't what?" he demanded against the fabric of the dress she wore. He lifted his head so he could see her eyes. "What don't you want? What do you want, for that matter?"

"I . . ." she stammered, everything so confusing and unexpected. If she could only think! "I don't want this!"

"This? What is this?" he asked, clearly being obtuse on purpose. He drew the tip of his nose up the long plane of her neck, inhaling her fragrance the entire way. "Don't do this?"

"No," she breathed, closing her eyes as she tried not to feel the rush in her pulse that responded to his curious caress.

"So I should do it?" he asked, immediately repeating the action.

Syreena exhaled with a shudder, the tremble vibrating against him everywhere. He closed his eyes for a moment as he absorbed the reaction.

"Damien . . ." she tried to complain breathlessly.

"Not good enough?" he questioned.

He improved the touch by using his lips instead.

She turned her head in spite of herself, giving him just a little more access, probably not even realizing she was doing so.

Damien was suddenly caught in a web of his own making. The slight gesture exposed the beat of her pulse, the conduit carrying her blood pounding against his mouth in provocative rhythm.

It took a very long series of moments, but he jerked back from the temptation.

Syreena opened her eyes when she felt the abrupt movement. He turned his head aside, cursing under his breath. It was at that moment that she realized she was not the only one reacting to his manipulation. She pieced together the memory of what she had done to disturb him, immediately realizing what she had inadvertently accomplished.

Normally, she might have apologized for her unthinking actions, for baiting him against his own nature, but she realized that she was not at all sorry for it. A tumult of choices opened up to her, and she knew that if she contemplated it too long she would end up doing whichever one she thought she was *supposed* to do. She would do what was proper; what was expected.

And she did not want to.

Then she understood that this was exactly what he had been trying to make her comprehend. That there was a choice beyond what others chose for her to do, if only she would listen for it.

Damien released her wrists and went to back off her. It had not been his intention to endanger her. He had not meant to stimulate himself in this or any other fashion. He should have realized from the start that it was not a safe game to play with her. She tickled his senses far too easily. She was so different, so unique, and just the sort of thing that he would crave.

Especially since he had tasted her already.

No, wait. The opposite was usually true. He almost never yearned for the same thing twice. Not when it came to a feed. To him it would be like dining on leftovers. Dull, cold, boring.

Confused, he pushed his hands against the floor and rose away from her warm body.

He was not expecting her hands to snake into his hair and pull him back, so he fell easily to her wishes. His nose bumped into her neck and he realized he was precisely where he had started with her.

With his mouth pressed firmly to her pulse.

She chose that moment to lock her strong legs around his hips, seriously trapping him to herself.

Great. Now *she grows a will of her own,* he thought heatedly.

"Syreena, don't," he murmured against her skin, realizing he was pleading with her.

"Syreena, don't what?" she countered softly, turning the tables with an artful twist.

If he were looking at the saucy little thing from a distance, he would have laughed.

But the truth was he was too close for comfort.

"Syreena, I have not fed tonight," he reminded her gently.

She did not respond. He felt her turning her head, felt her nose drifting up the column of his neck, over his ear, and into his hair. When he realized she was taking in his scent with slow purpose, he had to bite back the groan welling up in his throat.

Syreena thrilled to his reaction to her play. She did not know why it delighted her so much, but it did. And she knew he was reacting. She could feel it with every inch of her body, wherever she contacted him. He had tried to frighten her away, but she realized she was in no way afraid of him. She probably should have been, especially considering his warning, but she was not.

She understood it was because she trusted him. Because he had never given her reason not to, and had given her dozens of reasons why she should. Mostly, he had proved it by telling her the absolute truth.

A truth that even her sister was unaware of.

"I think I need to return a favor," she whispered softly into his ear.

Damien had no idea what she was talking about, but it had an almost ominous ring to it. He tried to push away from her once again, but she chose that moment to open her mouth and place it against his throat where his pulse would be.

Amazingly enough, his autonomic systems reacted to th
erotic nip and provided her with exactly that.

A pulse.

A Vampire's neck was a key erogenous zone. And it wa
very clear as she scraped her teeth across it that she actuall
knew that. Damien cursed, dragged in a reflexive breath, an
instantly tried to roll away from her.

The nimble little minx clung to him like superglue, rollin
with him until she was straddling him once more. He reache
for her waist and tried to push her away.

"You are the one who wanted to know what I wanted," sh
reminded him as she resisted him with an easy twist of he
body. Eluding the grasp of his fingers entirely, she swep
her neck and throat across his lips, covering his eyes with th
silky rainbow of her hair.

This time there was no stopping the sound of hunger tha
erupted from his throat. She laughed with pure delight whe
he released the heavy groan of tempted pleasure and reflex
ively sank a hand into the hair at the back of her head. Th
noise he made stirred something inside her, an answerin
beat that sought a certain rhythm with which to match.

"Syreena," he said breathlessly, "you are playing with fire."

"I've been burned by your fire before," she countere
carelessly.

Damien's fingers curled into a fist in her hair, letting he
know she had flustered him enough to forget to be carefu
with the bruised tendrils. That felt somehow powerful an
exciting. He was always so composed, so holier-than-tho
patient, that it just begged her to rattle his cage.

She felt his mouth open against her skin, his tongue
drawing a ravenous line up her pulse. A moment later he
seemed to realize what he had done in spite of himself, an
once again tried to seize her and push her off him.

"Syreena! Stop!"

"Why should I?" she demanded, her determined eyes

lashing wicked fire down at him. "You don't like aggressive women?"

"I like them too damned much!" he bit back.

"Good!"

Her hands became very aggressive very suddenly. Using the way he was pushing against her as a support, she slid them down his chest, onto his stomach, and over his hips. Her path back up was far more blatant, pressing up over his fly, his navel, and on until her nails scraped over his nipples.

Damien's head jerked back, his entire body twisting to match the ripple of her bold touch. He swore savagely as her fingers ended their journey in his hair, jerking his head forward once more, thrusting his mouth against her pulse yet again.

This time there was no stopping his reaction. Fangs burst out in his mouth, the violence of the eruption making him suddenly dizzy. Instinct took over from that moment, and there was nothing civilized left as he reared back and forward again with blinding speed.

The strike was so quick that she hardly even felt it. But she felt the subsequent closure of his mouth over the opening he had made. Syreena released a strangled sound of utter pleasure. Her body released endorphins and adrenaline in response and she immediately became dizzy with the rush of them. It took a full minute before she realized she had somehow ended up on her back beneath him again.

She gasped a distorted encouragement to him, trapping his head against her, afraid he would stop the overwhelming pleasure of it before she could come to understand it. As he drank of her, he was pressed tightly to her, his body broadcasting his incredible arousal to her with its sudden heat and hardness. His hand was gripping her waist just a little above her hip, the coolness of his fingers fading as they were flooded with the warmth of what she presumed was her blood.

This time she was fully aware of the desire that screamed

through him with the madness of a banshee. She was cognizant of the narcotic she was within him. For a moment, she even saw herself and felt herself through his eyes and his body. For that space of time she knew what it meant to be male, holding the body of a female who aroused and impassioned him beyond reason of thought. She knew the taste of her own blood and the way it flushed and nourished him.

She also knew with perfect clarity how he saw her as a person.

As a whole person.

As she faded back into herself, it was with a sense of unimaginable completion. In a single moment she had experienced the fusion she had sought between her two halves and of her life. She experienced it through the eyes of an outsider who had never seen her as a before or after picture, as a student or an advisor, a falcon or a dolphin. He saw it all. Liked it all. Wanted it all.

If it were possible, she was sweeter and more intoxicating than the first time. The chemicals flooding her bloodstream were like spices and wine, making him drunk with the three dimensional flavor and effect of them. The most startling was the spiking of her hormonal levels as she was roused to passion. He felt the weight of her breasts pressed against him, the heat between the legs which still clasped him so tightly. For the first time in his life, he became aware of the possibility of mortality.

If he were inside her, deeply embedded in her heat and clutched by the pleasure that was even now quaking through her, he could give way to the idea of death without batting a single eyelash. That would be the pinnacle of life itself, he realized. And since it was not likely he would ever be claimed in such a way, at least not anytime soon, it opened up the idea that he could repeat the pleasurable visitation again and again and yet again.

As if in response to his thoughts, Syreena arched up roughly beneath him, convulsing and crying out with a rap

...rous exultation. He absorbed the buck of her body, felt the ...wirls of heat racing through her, and could define the scent ...f feminine musk coating her trembling being.

It was when she went quiet and limp that Damien started ...o come to his senses again.

And in that single horrific second, he realized what he ...vas doing.

The Vampire Prince launched himself away, falling over ...n his haste and hitting the floor hard. A bitter taste filled his ...nouth and he realized he had forgotten the finishing bite.

He tried to move, to get back to her, to stop what could ...nly be inevitable if he did not complete his feeding the ...roper way.

But he was paralyzed and could not move a single inch ...urther.

All he could do was turn his head and watch as her blood ...ooled beneath her neck and head.

"Merde!"

Windsong could not help the exclamation that burst out ...f her when she opened the door to her bedroom and saw the ...rince and Princess lying on the floor.

Syreena was laying in an ever-widening ring of her own ...lood, and Damien was seizing fitfully.

"Lyric! *Lyric!*"

She screamed the name even as she stumbled to kneel be-...ide the Lycanthrope Princess, quickly putting her hand on ...he wound on her neck in order to stem the flow of blood.

"What is it? There's no need to yell at me, Wind—"

Lyric broke off with a horrified gasp, slapping her hand ...ver her wide-open mouth in her shock.

"Get me my bitters! Hurry, girl!" Windsong commanded ...arshly, her tone galvanizing the young woman into obey-...ng.

Lyric scrambled for the bag of herbs that always sat at the

ready in the kitchen. Meanwhile, Windsong reached to pre
her hand to Damien's chest.

"What in the world possessed you, Damien," she mu
tered under her breath.

Softly, slowly, she began her most potent healing sor
shy of the Spirit-singing. The Spirit-singing could not l
done without a healthy spirit, and hers and Lyric's were n
compatible with the victims lying on the floor.

She did not break a single note when Lyric skidded ba
into the room, falling bravely to her knees beside her ment
Windsong knew that the sight of blood was something Lyr
had not faced as yet, so she was proud of the girl when sl
slid through the liquid to reach Damien's thrashing head a
prevent him from harming himself. She immediately chime
in with her less experienced song, a totally different temp
and composition, meant to soothe a body in shock. Lyric ha
only learned the song the night before, when they had four
the two in the forest. She had learned it on the fly, and no
prayed her memory did her good service.

Windsong was in and out of her herbal bag without eve
looking at it, knowing by touch exactly what was what a
where it was located. She quickly removed her hand a
smeared a coagulation salve on Syreena's throat.

The herbs worked swiftly, but the Mistral did not miss
beat in her song to sigh with relief. Instead, she reached ba
into her bag and then forced a blood-building liquid dow
the Lycanthrope's throat. She felt for Syreena's pulse on tl
opposite side of her neck, the side that was still healing fro
the previous night's encounter with Damien's bite. It w
weak but growing in tempo, and that was all that mattered

She then turned to her second patient.

Damien's skin was gray, and then flushed, and then
strange color that looked similar to the tan coloration of
Demon's skin. For this, Windsong was at a loss. Vampir
were totally alien to her. They had no circulation to speak o
no pulse and no breath, and the mysteries of their nutritio

both good and bad, were utterly beyond her skills. All she could do was support him with her song and use the intent of her eyes to encourage Lyric to do exactly what she was doing.

Syreena woke with a sharp intake of breath, her eyes flying open. The first thing she noticed was the bereft feeling of weightlessness.

That is, the lack of Damien's weight lying across her body.

She had apparently passed out again.

"Damn," she muttered, sighing in frustration at herself.

She turned her head and immediately winced at the incredible soreness on her neck. Not that she was very much aware of the last time Damien had fed from her, but she didn't remember it hurting so badly.

She sat up, immediately reaching for a brace as the world spun around her. Her fingers touched hair, and she was aware suddenly that someone was sitting on a chair at her bedside, sleeping soundly with their body bridging the distance between chair and bed and their head on the mattress. She noticed Lyric's hair color immediately.

"Lyric?"

"I have tried to wake her. She is exhausted, poor thing."

Syreena looked up at Windsong, who was seated in a similar fashion next to Damien.

Damien.

The Princess darted her gaze to his face immediately, instantly becoming aware that something was terribly wrong.

"Do not move from that bed." Windsong anticipated her, her stern voice immediately rooting the Lycanthrope in place.

"What happened?" Syreena demanded of the Mistral.

"Perhaps you should tell me. Why on Earth would Damien repeat an act that very nearly killed him the first time?"

"Killed him?"

"He did not tell you that?"

"No," she said, her stomach suddenly queasy, the room spinning a little faster. "He said he was fine. He made i seem . . ." She swallowed convulsively. "He made it seem like it was nothing to him."

"Well, I assure you, it was something. He keeps going cold and hot by turns. I am no expert on Vampires, but I know they have a body heat that ebbs in one direction over the course of the day. From hot to cold and not back again. Not until they feed." She cleared her throat a little. "Feed normally, that is."

Syreena's heart skipped a beat. "Do you know what this will do to him? Will he live?"

"I think so. He did last time. He is a powerful being, not to be underestimated. Besides, Lyric and I have brought you both quite far in a short while."

Syreena looked down at her hand, which was absently stroking the sleeping adolescent's head. So much for her first bid at independent choice, she thought painfully, blinking her eyes in an attempt to escape the burn in them. She refused to sit around and weep like a child. It would do no good.

Stop that . . .

Syreena laughed a bit hysterically as Damien's earlier words filtered into her thoughts. If only he'd known what he had been setting himself up for.

I do know. And I would not trade away a minute of it.

Syreena gasped when she realized it truly was his voice she was hearing in her thoughts. She fought off Windsong's enchanting command and struggled to get out of bed. She pushed past the bewildered Mistral and fell onto Damien's bed.

"Damien? Can you hear me?"

She could tell what Windsong had meant immediately. Damien was hot to the touch, feeling almost feverish, if such a thing were possible in his kind. She pressed her hands to his chest, feeling his heated skin and taking it in as an affirmation that he was indeed alive.

"Syreena . . ."

"Shh!" The Princess hushed the Mistral sharply.

Syreena . . .

"Damien! Damien, why did you do it if it was going to hurt you? Why didn't you tell me?"

Stop worrying. I will be okay in time. I am grateful that you are not harmed. I was worried I had hurt you badly.

"No. No, I am okay. Just tired."

Windsong was baffled. For a minute she thought the Princess had gone straight around the bend, but after a moment of listening to the one-way conversation, she began to get a sense of what Syreena was hearing in her own head.

Of course. Vampires were capable of speaking to the minds of others. Usually it was images and illusions, she mused, but she supposed a conversation would not be such a stretch. She watched with fascination as Syreena leaned close to the Prince, who looked like he was in a sound and peaceful sleep. Apparently he was, but only in body. His thoughts were quite alert, it seemed, and eager to check on the Princess.

Bemused, Windsong stood up and moved to leave the room for a moment. She would give them only a minute, and then she would command them both into sleep. Whether they liked it or not.

The elder Mistral went into the kitchen to check the blue dress that was soaking in the sink. She had been forced to replace the bloodstained garment with a night rail on the Princess, since the dress Syreena had arrived in had been beyond reclamation. She was not worried because she knew the right combination of herbs and agents needed to remove the red staining.

Satisfied with its progress, she immediately returned to the bedroom.

She stopped short on the threshold of the door and pressed her fingers to her lips to keep herself from smiling.

The Princess had crawled into bed next to the Vampire, her head pillowed on his chest and her hands wrapped tightly around one of his as if she were afraid he would escape while she wasn't paying attention. She was so exhausted that she had immediately fallen asleep the moment she was certain he was safe.

Windsong decided to let her sleep.

She crossed the room and nudged Lyric into the vacant bed, rolling the young girl over until she was faced away from the sleeping duo. Then, glancing at the clock that indicated it was far past noon, she left the room and retired to the couch in the little living room of the cottage.

Chapter 7

It was an hour into the dark by the time Elijah and Jasmine finally set their feet onto Windsong's property.

There had been no trail; everything was a jumble of confusing paths and directions. In fact, it was too much of a jumble. Elijah and Jasmine had agreed that someone was trying to hide something, and it had not taken Elijah long to add up the pieces of the puzzle that was relatively rudimentary, provided you knew all the players involved. There was history between Syreena and Windsong. Damien had known Windsong for centuries. It only made sense that she would be the one he would turn to if Syreena was wounded.

Elijah turned to look at Jasmine. Her eyes were closed and she was concentrating. Her smooth brow furrowed as she tried to piece together what she was sensing.

"I think . . . I think they are here. Can you detect them? Usually if I am this close to Damien . . ."

She shook her head, very obviously vexed by her confusion.

"I have a better idea," Elijah said, lifting a brow as he strode quickly up to the door.

He knocked.

"How . . . succinct of you," Jasmine said dryly.

"Whatever works," he said with a shrug.

Windsong answered her door immediately and without any caution. It was as if she was expecting them.

The Mistral did not speak, a courtesy to the Demon who would not be able to circumvent the thrall of her voice. Instead she used a gesture of her hand to usher them inside and across the main rooms. Knowing exactly why they were there, she cracked open the bedroom door and let them both have a momentary peek at Damien and Syreena.

Jasmine gasped when she saw the Prince was not awake and moving about by that hour. She knew Damien chafed to be up and about come the night. Instead, he was sleeping peacefully well beyond darkness, and he was using a diminutive Lycanthrope female for a blanket, his arm settled securely around her shoulders as he held her to his chest.

When Jasmine went to move into the room, Windsong immediately stepped into her path. The sharp look she gave the Vampire female was coldly pointed and clearly nonnegotiable.

For Elijah's part, he was satisfied that Syreena appeared to be alive, somewhat well, and in relatively one piece. Through the bonding he shared with Siena, the moment he knew these things, she knew them. For the first time in days, they both were able to sigh in relief.

"Siena thanks you," he said in earnest to his hostess a heartbeat later. "She says that if you ever need anything—"

Windsong raised a hand to silence him. She knew how far and in what ways Siena's gratitude could serve her, just as Elijah knew there would probably come a day when the favor would be called in. The warrior was content. He immediately took a comfortable seat in the little living room that made him seem even more of a giant than he normally appeared to be to those around him.

Jasmine was not so easily satisfied, but she did not see that she had much of a choice.

Personally, she would not be happy until she saw Damien walking and talking like normal. She did not like the idea of him behaving out of the norm. Not that he could be called predictable, but she just knew him so well.

She supposed his protective behaviors had rubbed off on her after all.

Jasmine folded her arms tightly to her midriff and stepped away so the Mistral named Windsong could close the door. She was flooded with questions and the need to know what had been happening all of this time. For a moment, she resented the warrior's presence. Were he not there, she would be able to speak to the Mistral and get the answers she craved.

And what she wanted to know, more than anything else, was how she could be standing a room away from Damien and yet still feel like he was not even there.

Syreena felt a tickle along the ends of her hair, and it stirred her out of her deep sleep.

She opened her eyes, a long exhale shuddering out of her as the tickle caused a chill to steal down the back of her neck. She tilted her face upward and looked into midnight blue eyes and a half-cocked smile. Damien had her hair wrapped softly around one finger, the tickle she had felt, and was absently running his thumb over it. When he noticed her looking at him, his smile grew exponentially.

"Hello," he greeted her amiably.

"Hello?" She lifted her head and her eyes widened incredulously. "Is that all you have to say to me? Hello?"

"It is a traditional start," he pointed out.

She growled at him in a pique of temper, shoving herself off him and the bed so she could stand and glare at him with her hands curled into fists.

"Damien! What in the world is wrong with you?" she demanded to know. "Do you have a death wish or something? Why didn't you tell me . . . Why did you let me . . ."

The serene lift of his brow only infuriated her further.

"You are a total psycho, do you know that? You're just like those crazy humans who play with snakes they know could strike them dead in a heartbeat!"

"Syreena . . ."

"Don't you Syreena me! Don't lie there with that obnoxious patience of yours and act like I am getting hysterical as if I was some . . . some frail, missish thing who saw a mouse scurry across the floor! Damn you, Damien, you need a keeper!"

Damien stopped trying to speak. She was not going to let him do so, and he could actually understand her fear-driven outrage. The Prince could not defend his misactions any more than she could, and she was probably right in any event. It had been a very stupid thing to do. But it had been his fault and his responsibility from beginning to end, and he would not let her take any part of the blame.

Syreena suddenly stopped scolding him, her head cocking with that certain sharp attentiveness that he was so familiar with.

He turned his attention to what she was sensing.

"Oh, this is just great!" Syreena threw up her hands and they landed back at her sides with a slap on each thigh.

"Did you expect your sister to just sit and wait for you to reappear?" he asked.

She told him quite succinctly what he could do with his logical remark.

She crossed over to the empty bed, ignoring him completely from that moment on. She stripped off the nightgown she was wearing, giving Damien's appreciative eyes an excellent rear view of her athletic little body. The next moment, she hid it again, this time under the borrowed blue dress.

She turned back to face him as she gingerly freed her hair from the neckline of the dress.

"I don't want Siena to know about this. Do you understand?" She put her hand to her throat, fidgeting with the slim gold and moonstone choker that indicated her rank in the royal household. Between twisting out the kinks in that and carefully arranging her hair, she was able to conceal the marks on her neck caused by his most recent taste of her. The others had already faded to small pink dots of freshly healed skin. "There are rules in our society, taboos and laws and superstitions, and we have broken so many of them it makes me dizzy."

"Blood loss makes you dizzy, Syreena. Breaking the rules scares you to death."

"I'll tell you this much," she snapped back. "You could use a healthy dose of fear, Damien! You are a menace to yourself. I'm just glad I am going to be very far away while you trot off somewhere else and self-destruct."

With that, the Lycanthrope Princess marched out of the bedroom, slamming the door behind her.

"Kitten?"

"Hmm?"

"Kitten, you are wearing a hole in the carpet."

Siena stopped pacing back and forth and looked at her husband, who was lounging in their bed looking like he did not have a care in the world. It made her want to smack him in the head.

"I heard that," he warned her, chuckling.

"Are you sure? I mean really sure?" she asked for the tenth time that night.

"Siena . . ."

"Oh, I know," she said with a frustrated sigh and a wave of her hands. "What I want to know is how she does it. How does that conniving little bitch just slip away into nothingness? Our best hunters have tried tracking Ruth, mine, yours and Damien's, and none of them can seem to hold her trail. Not even Jacob! He is your Enforcer, designed to hunt down renegades from your species, and even he is baffled! I want to know how she does it!"

"She does it with her considerable power," Elijah reminded her gently. "We could be standing on her head, but she can manipulate our minds into thinking she's a thousand miles away. I'll tell you exactly who will be able to catch her one day."

"Who?" the Queen asked, sounding terribly eager and avaricious in spite of herself. Siena had reached the end of her infinite tolerance. Ruth had attacked her family once too often, and like the fierce lioness that she was, Sienna would protect her family with her own life if need be.

"My money lies on Damien or Magdelegna. Legna is the only Mind Demon powerful enough to beat Ruth at her own tricks." He sighed in tandem with his wife as she finally climbed into bed with him. "But she cannot risk a hunt until after she gives birth."

"What of Damien?"

"Damien is . . . Damien is immune to her trickery when he is paying attention for it. He is also the best damned hunter I have ever seen, next to Jacob."

"And yet he has had no luck in the year since this all began. The closest he got to her was when he rescued Syreena. Damn, I wish I had sent more people with you. They could have at least tried to track her."

Elijah encircled his wife's shoulders, drawing her delightful body very close to his. He kissed the curling hair at the arch of her forehead with affection. "You know they would not have had any luck. Don't fret, Siena. I promise you, Ruth's days are numbered. She will turn up again."

"That is what I am afraid of. She is up to something. Something to do with the Library and now being in Mistral lands.

I don't like it. It gives me a chill thinking she is running around loose out there." Siena snuggled deeper against him, trying to ease the chill in her body that had nothing to do with the cold of the cavern castle bedroom they shared. "It is you she hates, Elijah. In her twisted mind, she believes you killed her child. I am afraid of her catching you unprepared and hurting you like she did—"

"Siena, that is not going to happen. Not again. I made a mistake, I know, and nearly got killed for it. But you can bet there won't ever be a repeat. Don't be afraid of her. That is what she wants. She wants you to be afraid for me, afraid for Syreena."

"I won't be afraid of her . . . not after I rip the little bitch's heart out."

Elijah laughed at that, the rich timbre of it echoing down several cavern corridors. "That's my girl," he said, just before capturing her mouth and starting her on a path full of completely different topics.

Syreena got up from kneeling in front of the prayer altar she had been meditating in front of for the better part of the past twenty-four hours. She was not allowed to fast as she continued to recover from her ordeal of a week ago, and she wished the Monks would relent on that issue. She was fine, really, her blood supply quite back to normal. Perhaps if she fasted, her attempts to meditate would prove more useful. It had always worked in the past.

There was no use speculating about it, Syreena thought with a defeated pout. Besides, the food that was or was not in her belly had nothing to do with why she was having such a hard time focusing.

She was wondering how Damien had fared after all he had gone through. Because she had not been forthcoming with her sister, Siena had seen no need for more than the usual inquiry about his well-being in the aftermath.

But Syreena knew better.

She also knew that she had shown him damn little appreciation both for what he had done for her, and for her part in the second incident. Why she was so testy and volatile around him, she could not say. There was simply something about him that put her on edge or stirred her up. One or the other.

That thought brought back far too many highly sensitized memories for Syreena's comfort, and she restlessly began to pace the halls of the monastery of The Pride.

Having grown up in the enormous underground monastery, she knew it better than she knew the royal castle. In a sense, these caverns and rooms carved through the massive Russian mountain The Pride was located in were more of a home to her than her birthplace. At the same time, there was no fond love and affection to be found in these halls. Lectures, professors, and discipline, yes, but nothing quite resembling kindliness.

Not that she had been abused or truly deprived. She had thrived in every other way imaginable. She had benefited from an education beyond measure, and the knowledge of how to settle her soul when it was most disturbed.

Well, usually.

Syreena had come to lick her wounds in this place because at least here she could be assured of no one taking overmuch interest in her emotional well-being. The Monks would think her quite capable of managing herself. Siena would not be so easy about it. Though the Queen would mean well, wanting to be a sister, Syreena did not think she could bear up under too much scrutiny at the moment.

Again her thoughts turned immediately to the Vampire Prince.

She felt herself flushing and absently raised a hand to cover the telltale blush of her cheeks.

She had never felt anything like the wildly precarious things he had managed to create within her. Perhaps it was because he was so terribly dangerous, both to her and to himself, that made it so. She had never been a thrill seeker before, however. Outside of her position in the court, she led a rather mundane lifestyle. While living in the monastery she had been required to be celibate; as a Princess she was required to remain so until she found her mate for life. Between the two, she had long ago become used to it not being a factor of interest.

Damien was the first to ever shake that particular tree within her.

Although it had been more of an earthquake than a shaking. Everything that had happened in the wake of it had been a testament to why breeding across Nightwalker species was so strictly frowned upon. Siena and Elijah were the exception, and it had not been an easy adjustment for everyone to make. In fact, the court and Siena's people were still adjusting to it. Some far better than others.

But at least they did not cause harm to one another. They were both clearly thriving and robustly happy. Such a thing was clearly not possible between Damien and Syreena. It had been foolish of her to even attempt to think otherwise. More foolish of him, considering he had already been aware of the painful ramifications of playing with that fire.

Syreena made a frustrated sound and stopped to lean back against a cool wall for support as she rubbed at the ache in her temples. No matter what she did, she could not stop herself from thinking circles around this issue. Why could she not convince herself that this was simply the end of a string of bad choices? Why, in spite of everything, did she still have this overwhelming craving to seek him out?

Footsteps approached her and she quickly resumed her walk. She passed a pair of Monks and they nodded to her in polite acknowledgment. She nodded back, using great mental effort to not cover the bare patches along her ragged hairline when their eyes fell onto it. She wished she could tolerate wearing a shawl or scarf over it to guard herself from such observation. But where all Lycanthropes balked at confining their hair in any manner, she found she was even more re-pelled by it than before.

It would take years before it became unnoticeable again. And it would never all match in length again. There was an ironic humor involved in it as well. Until her hair reached a certain length again, the dolphin would be forced to lie dormant within her. It was almost as if she were being cosmically punished for her resentment of her two halves. Now that it was out of reach, she suddenly wanted it back with all of her heart.

The Princess self-consciously reached to comb fingers through her soft brown hair, arranging it to cover the bare places. The effort was obvious, considering the even part that was normally there, but it was better to look like a zebra than a victim. At least there were those who naturally had striped hair color in their society. Those who did not know her would not look twice at it.

Unfortunately for the Princess, there were few people who did not know her.

Still, it was better than nothing.

The Vampire Prince was brooding again.

Jasmine sighed softly as she spied on him from the balcony of the mansion. The turn of the tables was unnerving. *She* was supposed to be the moody one. However, she did not have that luxury any longer. She was too overcome with concern for Damien.

He was walking the darkened gardens sprawled out just below her, heading toward the cliffside where he would no doubt spend another collection of endless hours staring out at the Pacific Ocean.

Jasmine assumed it was toward Russia which he looked.

She did not assume this because he had confided in her about anything that had occurred. She had been left to her own devices of deductive reasoning on that matter.

The Princess could possibly manage to hide the truth of things from her sister and their people with tricks of hair and jewelry, but a Vampire could not be fooled in such ways. The bite of a Vampire was something like an animal rubbing up against a tree, a marking that outlined territory and pronounced the power of the beast within its borders.

A Vampire could always sense when another had been before it. Since they were so territorial by nature, that was how they managed to keep from treading upon each other's toes.

So anyone who crossed close enough to the Lycanthrope Princess would know that Damien had been there before them.

Besides that divination, Jasmine had been quite shaken by the simple sight of them sleeping together in the Mistrals' home. Damien went to bed with his women, but he did not sleep with them. She imagined it was because he did not trust any of them as far as he could throw them. Or perhaps it was because the intimacy of it was too potentially misleading. Damien did not like for his enjoyments to form attachments to him. He preferred to keep that in accord with his own wishes. Infatuated females were too much work and headache if he did not want them to be infatuated with him.

It had taken four years for him to show any affection for Jasmine, though she had been aware of it long before the expression of it. Even now, it was a part of how they functioned that she would always protest any need of him. Neediness was unattractive to Damien. In truth, while they were deeply friendly and caring of each other, she did not need him in any overtaxing way. She certainly did not claim a dependency on him. They had never been lovers, though she had contemplated it once. She had decided long ago that she would rather have his unending interest in friendship rather than his passing fancy in bed. Jasmine believed this was what had kept them side by side through the centuries.

Damien was also not forthcoming about what effect his little marking of the Princess had had upon himself. Jasmine knew, however, that there had very much been an effect. This knowledge was what had prompted her to send all the others who shared their home, friends and servants alike, away to another of Damien's households for the time being. She had conjured up an excuse about diplomatic obligations and traveling, something they were used to. Whatever happened, the others must never be made aware of any changes in Damien. Change was often viewed as a sign of weakness in their society. Weakness, even among friends, had a way of causing huge amounts of trouble and danger.

They would quickly be able to sense what she had sensed about Damien, that there was indeed a difference. The Prince could not have been ignorant of it, either. It was impossible. If she could sense the differences in him, then he could feel them in himself. However, there was no way she could get a true sense of the nature of the change so long as Damien was actively blocking her. Only his invitation would allow her evaluation of what alterations there had been.

It was all too disturbing. Which was why, she supposed, the Prince kept sitting at the edge of a cliff looking toward impossible things night after night.

Jasmine was as silent as the grave she purportedly slept in. If a single whisper of these events got out, it would be like blood in the water. Ambitious Vampires would be sniffing at Damien's heels in search of his crown, seeing all of this as a weakness to be exploited.

Part of Jasmine wanted to go out and see to it that all who knew of it remained just as silent. Permanently. Anything to protect him, as he had always protected her. But considering who the parties were, she would end up setting everyone involved at war, more or less.

Besides, Damien would probably frown on the indiscriminate assassination of heads of various Nightwalker provinces.

Oh well.

Jasmine was not a very patient creature. It was probably why she so easily grew weary of the world around her. She stretched out her arms and rose up into the air, the breeze fluttering through her long, loose hair. She could smell the salt of the ocean on the wind, even though they were set back a distance from the water. She skimmed the treetops in a position perpendicular to the ground, following in Damien's wake, the tips of her booted feet smacking an errant leaf here and there as she went. Her ankles were crossed, a preferred position when she flew that made for less wind resistance and effort against her legs.

She set down on the gravel path with a gliding walk that made an obvious crunch. Damien had already taken his seat on the stone bench just steps from the edge of the cliff.

He turned at the sound of her feet.

Damien had been expecting the confrontation eventually. He knew Jasmine was not the sort to beat about the bush when she had issues to discuss. "Jasmine, why can you not just let it be?"

"Very well. If you will stop mooning about the manse, I will not ask a single question."

"I do not moon about," he said shortly, turning back to the dark sounds of the ocean tides.

"Moon, mope, melancholy, pout . . . call it what you will, but you are most certainly doing so. Do not think you will pull the wool about me, Damien. I know you too well."

"And not at all," he said sharply.

"Yes. Even after five centuries. Although I do know enough to know that this behavior of yours could lead you to risk everything important to you."

"Perhaps what I viewed as important before is not now."

Jasmine was certain that had she a heartbeat, it would have skipped in tempo just then. This was beyond mere moodiness, she realized. It was not like Damien to question his goals and his rather steady ideas of what he wanted from the world.

She moved to his side, sitting on the cold bench and leaning into the warmth of his body as she often did when they spoke of serious matters.

"Damien, I am your best friend. Why will you not tell me what is hurting you so?"

Damien turned his head to look at her as she rested her chin on his shoulder. Jasmine rarely pulled this particular ace on him. Professing her understanding that she meant so much to him was something spared for cataclysmic events. For the first time, he saw himself as she must be seeing him. Altered. Forever changed. A stranger she did not know and was afraid of meaning nothing to. This was how she expressed her love for him, and he immediately regretted pushing her to it.

He reached around her shoulders to hug her close to himself. "Do you remember 1562?" he asked her, whispering his words softly into her hair.

"The French uprising?"

"Before that."

"Ah. The freckled queen of England."

"Yes," he agreed. "It was just before I found out she had contracted smallpox." He smiled against the silky strands of midnight pressed to his lips. "It was the last time we were all together."

"Simone, Racine, Lind, Jessica . . ."

"Dawn," he added.

"Silly chit. Getting herself killed on a French battlefield, of all things. Turning a feast into a funeral."

"It was a mistake. We all make them. Unfortunately for Dawn, hers was a fatal one. If you recall, we had a rash of mortal mistakes within that group over the next century." He released a melancholy sigh, reaching to rub at the spot between his brows, as if he had a headache. "Anyway, I had turned her away that night in England. I always thought there would be time."

"Damien, she warmed your bed, not your heart."

"No. I know. But she is the example of all those I always thought I would get back to later, yet never again had an opportunity to."

"Why are you talking of this now?"

"Because there is something I need to get back to. Not tomorrow, not a week from now. This very instant."

"You mean the Lycanthrope Princess, I take it," she said softly, not believing what she was hearing. "Damien, she means nothing to you."

"Are you so certain of that?"

Jasmine lifted her head to look into his eyes with surprise.

"I am no longer certain of anything about you anymore, I am discovering. Who is she to you? Just tell me what happened. I want to understand. I cannot support you if I do not understand. And believe me, if you are thinking what I think you are, you are going to need my support."

Damien paused for several beats, the fingers of the hand around her back stroking against her shoulder absently as he reconciled his thoughts for her.

"Do you know why we do not wed for life, Jasmine?"

The question seemed out of left field, but she played along. "Because we need variety too much. Because we do not believe in silly old practices of that kind like Demons and Lycanthropes do."

"Or because we do not do what we need to in order to find that type of partner."

"I do not understand you," she confessed.

"I am the longest-lived member of our species, Jas. In all that time, I have never seen a Vampire fall in love, wed, or mate for life. I think I have figured out why."

"Damien . . ."

"Because we do not feed from Nightwalkers."

She laughed out loud. "I do not understand what that has to do with—"

"Perhaps," he interrupted her, "we will find something about it in the Library. The Library goes much further back in joint Nightwalker history than even we have conceived of. Perhaps it will know the truth about why we forbid ourselves to drink the blood of Nightwalkers. Think about it, Jas. Think of how we are, of all that is missing. Why don't you love me, for instance?"

"Damien, that is a ridiculous question."

"Is it? We have known each other all of your life. You became a part of my household five hundred years ago. We are very likely the two closest Vampires on this planet. I have never met anyone with our friendship, our companionability, in our culture. So, though we have lived side by side and, as you pointed out, been the best of friends, why did love not follow? I mean outside of my clear regard for you."

"Because love does not work in such ways," she reasoned.

"Then how does it work, Jasmine? Have you ever been in love? How can every other intangible feeling and state of being that exists for every other species, Nightwalker and human, exist for us, except love? And do not tell me love does not exist, because I have seen proof with my own eyes that it does." He reached for her chin and made sure she met his gaze as it bored into her. "Do you know any Vampire capable of being in love?"

"No, Damien. We are too selfish for—"

"How convenient we make that excuse," he argued irritably. "What a pat little rationale for walking away from those grapes we cannot reach. Even humans, who think they are in love and change their perception of it later on, *thought* they were in it. We never even mistake it. We simply say we are not cut out for it." He shook his head. "You said just a moment ago that I never loved Dawn. As if, were it someone else, you thought it was possible. Yet now you say it is not possible. Which is it?"

"You are confusing me, Damien, and talking yourself in circles. Are you trying to justify your desire to go back to the shapechanger?"

"If it were just desire, I could ignore it, you know that. It is obsession. I think of nothing else. I want for nothing else. My mind repeats certain incidents I shared with her over and over again."

"That sounds like infatuation."

"A convenient adjective those who are afraid to feel with this kind of passion use to justify themselves and their behaviors!" Damien could not sit a minute longer. He stood up and paced away from Jasmine before turning back. "But I have felt infatuation. I know what it is. It is not what this is."

"Then what is this?"

Damien halted, turning to look at her. His hands, which always moved in gesture with his speech, settled onto his waist.

"This is what happens when a Vampire takes the blood of a Lycanthrope into his body."

"And what is it? Love?" She laughed in spite of herself. "Do you know how ludicrous this sounds?"

"Can you be so quick to argue me otherwise? For Demons, all it takes is a touch to turn on that connection to their soul mate. For Lycanthropes, it is the act of lovemaking. Even Mistrals and Shadowdwellers have comparable triggers. What is it for us?"

"So you think it is taking the blood of a Nightwalker? But we do. We drink of each other. The strong who bring blood to the ill from within themselves, mothers who bring to their young, and, of course, during certain levels of sex."

"But never from *other* Nightwalkers. Never. None of us. Even the most reprobate, reckless, and feckless of us have always seen that as the ultimate taboo, the line even they will not cross. But not because we are afraid it will kill us like the black poison of magic user blood will. So where is the fear? How was it bred into us?"

"You are asking all these questions for a reason, Damien. What is your point?"

"I am not sure. I have no proof, no logic. Only supposition." He turned to face the cold wind blowing off the ocean, letting it sweep over him, as if to cleanse himself, for a very long minute. "I only know of two ways we can find out."

"I have a feeling one requires you to pursue a certain Nightwalker Princess."

"I do not deny that." He cocked his head back in her di rection. "She has become a part of me, you know. I have fe from others, and yet her blood remains deep inside of m systems. This I have proof of, at least."

He reached for her hand, pulling her to her feet and draw ing her close. He laid her head on his shoulder with the pres sure of a gentle hand. "Tell me what you notice," he whispere to her.

Jasmine closed her eyes and reached out into him wit her every natural and supernatural sense. She had bee wanting to do so for too long to refuse the invitation.

Her eyes flew open in shock a second later.

She could smell the scent of the Princess on him. No. No on him. *Inside* him. He was actually still there, that stron woodsy, male scent that was so uniquely Damien and a compelling as he was. However, she had spent three day tracking them both, so she knew the fingerprint of the Ly canthrope just as well.

"How is this possible? We never carry the mark of prey They carry the mark of us."

"Who preys on the predator, Jasmine? Who are we i danger from?" He laughed as he let her step away. "I think i is different for everyone. For me, I think it is a female with eyes of different colors half the world away from here."

"Did it never occur to you that it is just because she is a mutation? She's abnormal, Damien. She is poison to you! saw you when we arrived at the Mistral's home. I have never seen you so ill. I am stronger than you were then even when I have fallen into torpor."

"Necromancers are poison to us. Poison is something that kills. I am yet alive."

"Merely a different sort of snake," she insisted. "Some just kill you off a little at a time with necrosis."

"What of that which makes us stronger, Jasmine?"

"In what way are you stronger? I see only insecurity, fancy, and weakness, and so will everyone else! I warn you, Damien, there are those who will kill you if they hear you speaking in such ways."

"I think not."

The sentence was left hanging in the air between them as, right before Jasmine's eyes, Damien winked out of existence.

She gasped, horrified and frightened for a moment. Then she felt something fall against her cheek. She snatched it up and turned toward the moonlight.

Lying on the tips of her fingers was the feather of a raven.

That was when she heard the beating of wings.

She whipped around just as the raven soared over her head and came in for a clumsy landing on the bench behind her. Again, there was a shift in her sight, and Damien sat in place of the bird.

"My landings leave something to be desired," he said softly, "but I believe with time and practice it will change."

"That . . . that is not possible! That is a Mistral's trick!"

"Or the trick of Lycanthrope blood in the body of a Vampire," he told her pointedly.

Jasmine could not speak. Her voice would not work, even if she could formulate a single thought. The condition lasted for many harrowing seconds.

"What is the other way?" she asked hoarsely at last, swallowing hard as her head spun with what she had just seen. "You said there were two ways . . . ?"

"The Library, Jasmine. For which, I am afraid, I will need your cooperation."

"Damien," the female Vampire said, still half in shock after watching his thrilling and terrifying transformation, "you are asking me to look for a Holy Grail; a treasure you only hope and suppose is out there. What if it is just as impossible to find?"

"I expect it will be. But it will be more possible if one

who reads our ancient tongue is there. One who has a vested interest in researching our part of it. I know you were curious and compelled before, but now I want you to be driven. If not for the potential importance to me, then to the effect it could have on so many others of us." He raised an elegant hand and beckoned her forward. She obeyed automatically, moving closer to the bench until he could reach to take her hand. "It changes everything, knowing what my hopes and speculations are in this matter. Not for me, but for you. You will be tempted to shy from this. You will want to fear anything that threatens you with potential for commitment. I know, because a week ago I would have reacted the same way.

"Unfortunately, you will not have the song of the blood of another inside you luring you toward acceptance and spurring you into action. Your instincts will scream at you to lie to me, to burn evidence I need to support my theory and to do anything you possibly can to avoid the idea that there could be a way of tying yourself to a complementary being irrevocably, day after day after day, for the rest of your existence." Damien had to stop as he fought off the chill that walked his spine, the cold dread of it a remnant of similar feelings that faded as the time apart from Syreena grew longer and more strained.

"Why?" She struggled on the question, realizing he was terribly correct. "If I am not meant to feel this way, then why do I?"

"I do not know. I am hoping this is what you can tell me."

"I . . ." Jasmine broke off and sat beside him, her fingers feeling numb and cold in his grasp. "The anxiety building inside of me," she explained her knuckles pressing against her solar plexus as if she were experiencing pain. "I am afraid of so little, Damien, yet this thing terrifies me out of proportion. This is instinct. I am used to embracing instinct."

"So is this," he countered, indicating the feelings within his own body. "You have to trust me. One of these instincts is natural. The other is somehow not. You need to tell me which it is. I need to know before it drives me mad."

"You have felt as I do for nearly a millennium, Damien."

"The time spent on a pursuit does not matter if it turns out to be a false path in the end. All you can do is seek backward until you pick up the true path and can follow *it* instead. It is an old hunter's philosophy, sweetling. One I know you can grasp. There is only one true path here. Let us find it together."

Jasmine sat in silence for a minute, the fine tremor that shivered through her body betraying how rattled she was. Damien, however, was counting on his knowledge of her. Jasmine thrived on intriguing ideas and thoughts. For a Vampire, the more dangerous the stakes, the more diverting and delightful the prize of success was.

Life was not worth living if you were not willing to risk it.

This, he realized, was why they shorted out so easily. There was so little for them to fight for, to defend and crusade about. Without things like this to drive them, they became like Jasmine, constantly growing depressed and bored, so lost for lack of having a purpose that all they wanted to do was sleep.

"Very well," she said so softly that he would have missed it had he no supernatural senses. "You are right. Something is not right here. But I warn you, Damien, I do not agree with the idea that the way we have lived and related for so long is the wrong one. My goal is to seek proof, even if it is proof against your desires."

"I expect nothing else," he assured her.

"And I will act on my findings, Damien," she warned him a bit more ominously. "I will do everything in my power to separate you from the Lycanthrope forever if I find out she is the wrong choice here. If she is the poison, I will administer the antidote. I would rather kill her and risk ages of war than lose you to something that will eventually destroy you. We need you too much. *I* need you too much."

The statement did not rattle him as it was meant to. She

was baiting him with her threat to harm Syreena, but eve
more, she was trying to push his buttons about neediness
Jasmine apparently did know him very well. Such state
ments were a quick way to get dismissed from his compan
because they made him uncomfortable and the strings a
tached caused too much inconvenience.

At least, it had.

Before he had demanded to know what it was a femal
with bicolored eyes and the contrary heart to match ha
needed.

And now everything was different.

"What of you, Damien? Are you going to run off to Rus
sia and profess love to a total stranger?" Jasmine could no
bear the idea of him behaving so irrationally.

"No. I am not saying I am in love with her. But I am goin
to find out if I can be."

Chapter 8

Syreena rolled over restlessly in her bed. The room was pitched in darkness, the silence of inactivity deafening. She knew that dusk was still an hour away. Though daylight did not reach into this depth of the monastery, she refused to get up. She was exhausted from roaming the hallways endlessly, her thoughts and body behaving like an impatient whirligig that refused to wind down. If she left her bed, she would do just that.

But being in bed only stopped the walking, not the pacing of her mind.

It was time for her to return to Siena. At least there, she would have something to do besides self-reflection. Her life at Siena's side had proven to be a busy one. There was catharsis in being distracted from disturbing thoughts and feelings. She was not so ignorant as to think they would go away, but at least she might forget them for short spurts of time as other, more pressing troubles crowded them out. That in itself had to be a relief of some kind.

Besides, she had to face their people at some point. She could not stay away waiting for her hair to grow so they would not look at her in that way she had grown to despise so quickly. She was healed enough now to resume her work; she had been able to access the falcon for short periods of time twice already. The missing feathers were not flight feathers, which meant she could still assume the Lycanthropic form she used most often anyway. The length of time she could become the bird would grow as she recovered from her trauma.

At least, she hoped so.

She would not confess it to anyone, and almost didn't wish to acknowledge it herself, but something was different about the shapechange experience.

Different, to her at least, was rarely a good thing.

It was hard to pinpoint or describe how it was changed. It was the same shape and coloration, the same process of concentration combined with head shaking that brought it on and the body shaking and focus that reversed it. She could fly, glide, and cry out in the voice of that side of herself. In her second form, the one Siena jokingly referred to as "the harpy," she was still a woman, covered in falcon feathers and sprouting large wings. A form which no doubt had started the fanciful notion of angels or, as Siena said, harpies. Perhaps both, only it depended on the temperament and the actions of the individual Lycanthrope that had created human perception of them.

The fact that she could not access the dolphin was highly expected. The same went for the "mermaid" she became in the combined Lycanthropic form of humanoid and dolphin.

So what was so different?

She was almost afraid to return to her sister's household without being sure. It had something to do with Damien's bite, of this she was reasonably certain, but it must not be anything of great note if it was not immediately apparent.

Frustrated by the constant vacillation of her thoughts, Syreena flipped over onto her stomach and buried her head beneath her pillows. She put her hands over her ears and hummed to herself, filling her head with the sound and vibration of it for several minutes before she began to feel comfort. She did not care that she was feeling a little suffocated with her face pressed into her bedding. All she wanted to think about was the tune she was humming, hoping that if she let it overwhelm her enough, she could actually manage to doze until a little past dusk.

Even forty minutes would be a welcome respite.

She hummed louder and more urgently when she realized she was in danger of thinking again. She was softening, forgetting snatches of her melody as it began to work about fifteen minutes later.

Damien smiled as he listened to her sing half in and half out of her sleep.

An impending snowstorm had blocked out the sun early that evening, much to his pleasure, but she would not know that down in the belly of the monastery as she was. He had found her easily enough. After spending the day as Noah's guest at his residence in England, Damien had used the storm to take him to one of the more distant, lesser known entrances to the monastery caverns. Having been a fixture around the Lycanthrope courts on and off for most of his lifetime, he had come to know a few things about how to get around. Truthfully, however, it had been more about following the pulling instinct in his gut that had led him to her so quickly.

The advantage to the raven form he had suddenly become capable of was that Lycanthropes would not question the presence of a black bird fluttering its way through their halls. They were mostly asleep still, but those whom he had passed had not even looked twice at him as he had skimmed his way past.

He liked being a bird, he thought as he unfolded his arms from across his chest and moved closer to Syreena's bed. It was a light body capable of extraordinary speeds. Its aerodynamic form was a marvel, in spite of its apparent defense-lessness. He felt as though he suddenly had an insight into what it was like for Syreena.

Freedom and speed at the price of vulnerability.

Always a trade-off. He wondered, for a moment, what the vulnerabilities of her other third were. He was already getting an idea of the ones present in her current form.

The Vampire Prince stopped when he reached the edge of her mattress, taking a moment to allow himself a leisurely look at her slender and athletic figure. She was bottom side up, and it made him smile wider as the quilt she lay under followed the shape of her legs up into the swell of her back-side, then flowed abruptly down again to the exaggerated arch of the small of her back. The end seam of the handmade blanket stopped in the middle of her spine, allowing only for the flow of soft, peach-shaded skin.

He could feel her warmth even from the relative distance where he still stood. He had an impulsive thought, comparing the probable chill of his hands pre-hunt, as they were at the moment, in contrast to the superheated warmth of her Lycanthrope body. He imagined that if he touched her on the back that very second, she would jump out of bed high enough to hit the ceiling.

He had to suppress a chuckle along with the urge to do mischief. Play could wait until after she knew him better. At present, such tricks would very likely cost him his head.

Her sleepy song, a Lycanthrope lullaby sung in rounds, faded in and out of strength. It told him the story of her struggle to sleep, and he could easily sympathize. He also took comfort in it. It was the first sign that he was not the only one struggling.

Damien moved his eyes to the twisting combination of colors that made up her long hair. Most of it lay across her shoulder blades, the rest pooling down her ribs on the side nearest him. The fact that there was far more brown than gray settled an ill feeling on him. She had suffered much pain and had seen no justice for it. Hopefully they could somehow rectify that together.

As far as he was concerned, Ruth deserved vengeance from him just as much as she did from Syreena. The idea of the twisted bitch laying harmful hands on her made his blood boil with a possessive outrage. It was a bracing feeling, but he did not shy from it. In fact, he rather liked it. This was what he had been trying to explain to Jasmine.

Passion. There was nothing cool, dull, or blasé about it, and he really liked that. Would it fade in time? Was it just another brief delight that time would take the pleasure from?

He was not sure, but in the moment, feeling it as he did, he could not imagine it happening. That was quite a testimonial from the heart of the world's eldest Vampire.

Damien slowly dropped to a single knee beside the bed that cradled her so cozily. He leaned forward, just past her upper arm, and purposely exhaled across her shoulder and the sensitive hair lying over it.

She twitched in her dozing state, lifting her shoulder as if to escape the sensation.

Damien's lips drew up on one side, grinning.

He repeated the airy caress, long and slow, watching as her skin broke out into a chilled wash of goose bumps.

Syreena started suddenly, jerking her head up and out of the cocoon of pillows. A quick hand swiped away the hair hanging lazily across her face.

She turned her head and looked into fathomless eyes of midnight blue.

"Damien," she said, her breath leaving her in a sudden rush as inexplicable delight and excitement rushed her from head to toe. She did not know why, but she did not fight the feelings. They felt too good. It was the best thing she had felt since . . . well . . . since she had last touched him.

"Damien," she repeated breathlessly.

Damien was not expecting this reaction. He had somehow thought she would be angry with him. At the very least resistant to even seeing him again. When he had last seen her, she had shouted at him with fear and frustration.

Because she had been afraid for him.

That was when he realized she was happy to see him because it meant he was well. Unused to the regard of someone who wished to see him protected, at least someone besides Jasmine, Damien was a little overwhelmed. He found himself unable to speak even to greet her.

Syreena sat up suddenly, reaching to grasp his shoulders as she dragged him up for a closer inspection. He followed the powerful strength of her guiding hands until he was seated beside her on the bed. She drew herself onto her knees, shoved back her straggling hair once more, and began to inspect him with quick, intense eyes. Her hands flew where her eyes did, touching his shoulders, face, and chest in turn.

"Are you well?" she asked in an extreme whisper.

He responded by dodging past the torturous gentleness of her hands and catching her mouth with his. Syreena made a sound that was nowhere near surprise. He knew it well. It was relief. He was feeling it, too, he thought, as he kissed her taste from her soft lips. He caught her head into one large hand, holding her to him so she would not leave before he was over the initial scream of reprieve rushing his entire being. Despite what his mind struggled with, his chemistry knew what it wanted and what was compatible with it.

Compatible being too mild a term.

Her hands lifted to his face, her fingers flickering soft touches over his cheeks and the corners of his eyes. She invited him further with an exquisite parting of her lips and the hot firefly flick of her tongue against his.

The room around them filled and echoed with the sounds of breath, the rustle of his clothes, and the creaking of bedsprings as she shifted her body into his open embrace. Syreena slid into his hold and his lap as he kissed her with the intensity of a creature seeking sustenance for life. Her heart was pounding in her ears, as well as against his chest.

Damien felt it with ease since he had none of his own to confuse the signal. His head began to buzz with that strange high she gave him when he had fed off her before, but all he was feasting upon this time was her sweet mouth.

And that was when he realized it was not her blood that had done it at all in the first place. Not in the strictest sense. It was her, period. The chemistry, the movement, the passion.

He broke off their kiss suddenly in his shock, capturing her face so he could pull her under the scrutiny of his eyes. Searching her bewildered features, he realized what his mistake had been.

Having never known a true passion, he had been paralyzed by the feelings of it when she had unlocked it within him. Passion or love? Love or just unbelievable desire? He did not know. All he knew was that he had never felt anything like it, and that the pain of leaving it was blinding. That was what his body had been trying to interpret for him in the easiest emotions he could relate to. The change caused by her blood to his systems was unrelated. In the strictest sense, at least.

He laughed suddenly, the laugh of understanding dawning on a mind too long mired in confusion. "I knew it," he whispered to her, sounding momentarily cryptic. "I knew I should always trust my instincts."

Before she could question his meaning, he had her mouth caught to his once more. Her head immediately reeled with dizzy pleasure and the understanding that his words were meant to be complimentary to her. She definitely took them as such.

"What I meant," he said against her seeking lips, "is that you could never have hurt me. I only regret hurting you."

"You did not hurt me. Quite the opposite," she assured him. "I have never felt anything like that in my life."

"You almost bled to death," he scolded in a very gentle argument that lost its punch by being bracketed with the kiss of his mouth.

"It was because you were not prepared for what you were feeling, wasn't it?" she queried.

"How do you know that? Damn it, it has taken me until just now to figure it out." He lifted his head so he could see her sparkling eyes.

"I honestly do not know. I just figured it out, too."

"Oh. Well, I feel better, then." He chuckled.

Syreena laughed at him, wrapping slim arms around his neck and hugging herself to him tightly.

Until he touched her back.

The Princess yelped in shock at the bracing cold of his hands, jolting so hard out of his lap that she fell off the bed and onto the hard cavern floor, with nothing but a thin carpet to cushion the blow to her bottom.

Damien immediately realized what he had done and cursed in unison with her as he reached to help her.

"I am so sorry," he said in earnest regret. "I completely forgot. I am chilled because of the weather and the fact that I have not had the opportunity to hunt yet. Forgive me."

"That," she gasped, "will definitely wake a girl up in the evening." She reached for his offered hands, letting him pull her back onto her feet as he laughed at her remark.

"I should think so. I am sorry, I assure you."

"I know. There is no need to apologize." She exhaled and pressed a hand to her pounding heart. "I only need a moment to catch my breath."

Then she abruptly lifted her head and turned to view herself, him, and the entire room.

"Um, I am not sure if you are aware of this, but you are in the monastery of The Pride."

"I am aware of this," he countered, lifting a brow in obvious curiosity. "I have been welcome before."

"Yes, but . . . not in the bedroom of the royal heir who is a Monk and is supposed to remain celibate whenever she crosses the threshold."

"And so you have, courtesy of my cold hands," he said with amusement.

She laughed, realizing how easy it would be to enjoy his company if they actually managed to spend enough time on the same side of an interest.

"However," he continued graciously, "if it makes you uncomfortable, I will leave."

"No! I mean . . . well, yes. What I mean is—"

"Perhaps," he interrupted her, catching up her free hand so he could place a calming kiss in her palm, "perhaps I will go for my hunt and meet you elsewhere on the other side of this threshold at a later time."

She became thoughtful and silent for a moment, and Damien was tempted to peek into her thoughts. Instead, he resisted the urge and patiently waited while she gathered them.

"Damien, why have you come here?"

"You know why," he said without hesitation. "I have come for you, Syreena."

"But . . . Damien, I can't . . ." Syreena made that characteristic sound of frustration at her uncharacteristic stammering. "I don't have the freedom you do. I am of the royal line and that means—"

"I know what that means," he said firmly.

Syreena blinked, then stared at him in momentary shock.

"That means," he continued softly, pulling her a little bit closer so he could bask in the wash of her body heat, "that I will meet you later to discuss it. For the moment, I hear footsteps in the corridors. Your brethren are awakening. Since I do not wish to trespass on any rules, I will catch up to you later at your sister's holdings. Is this acceptable?"

"Yes," she said quietly, nodding as he brushed cool, affectionate fingers along her distorted hairline. The touch was tender and almost alluring. It was as if he saw the spot as an advantageous charm, not the mutilation all others saw it to be, herself included.

He stepped back from her, and then, to her shock, he shapechanged into a raven and flew once around her before winging off into the outer passages.

"He did what?" Siena was not sure she had heard her sister right.

"He took my blood. Twice."

"*Twice?*"

Siena exhaled in worried frustration as she paced across her sister's chambers for what had to be the hundredth time. "And I just saw him shapechange into a raven, Siena. I have never heard of a Vampire doing such a thing."

"I have."

The sisters simultaneously looked at Elijah.

"So have you, come to think of it," he amended himself. "In human folklore, there are stories of Vampires being able to change into the shapes of animals."

"Yes, but humans also think staking a Vampire in the heart will kill them," Syreena argued.

"They are not entirely wrong," Elijah said. "A trauma of that magnitude would eventually cause a Vampire to bleed to death if he did not replenish himself. Just like it would you and me."

"That is an interesting point," Siena murmured. "But shapechanging? I have always heard that throughout Nightwalker history that was limited to us and Mistrals."

"And Demons. And Shadowdwellers, too, actually."

"Wait." Syreena held up a hand when her sister went to question her husband. "You mean that you change with your elements, and that 'Dwellers can become the shadows themselves in order to hide the substance of their bodies."

"See, she didn't go to school for a century without making progress," Elijah teased them both.

"So Vampires are the exception," Siena argued. "They are Nightwalkers who do not change form."

"And yet, in ancient human texts, there are tales of Vampires turning into bats, birds, wolves, mist, and shadow. I think there are others," Elijah said, "but I am not the scholar here, so I do not recall what they are. But I will ask our scholar what she notices about this particular list."

"They are representative of several forms from every Nightwalker species," Syreena responded instantly. Then she truly saw what path he was leading her to, and her eyes widened enormously. "If Damien took in my blood and became a bird, what would happen if he drank of a 'Dweller?"

"He could have the power of shadow?" Siena stood up and joined Syreena's pacing progress. "And one who drinks of a Demon?"

"It would depend on the Demon," Elijah speculated.

"Water. Fire, Earth, and Air . . . the Mind and the Body. These are all your people's elements, Elijah."

"Mist, smoke, dust, wind . . . teleportation and healing," he reported in turn. "I have read human fiction dating back to the dawn of humanity where they first speak of Vampires, saying they can do these things. So why are the Vampires we know now incapable of them, except for Damien?"

"Because Damien drank from me to save my life . . ."

"And because they believe that Nightwalkers, next to magic-users, are the ultimate taboo." Siena bit her lip and folded her arms beneath her breasts. "Damien must have fed from you to give you the benefit of the coagulants you needed when you were bleeding from your damaged hair. We all know it can be as bad as slicing an artery if we lose enough of it."

"I lost enough of it," Syreena said grimly, her hand going self-consciously to her hairline. "He went against the grain of everything he knew, risking his own life, just to save mine."

"A profound act," Siena agreed, appreciating her sister's disturbance enough to put an arm of comfort around her shoulders.

"The ramifications of which are very enlightening," Elijah mused. "I wonder if it is just Syreena."

"What is that supposed to mean?" the Princess snapped at her brother-in-law.

"It means," Elijah responded calmly, "that I wonder if it is a cumulative thing or limited to one effect per customer. Can he feed, for example, on me and then be capable of raven and wind? Or does it switch to wind and purge the raven? Or is it raven and now no other?"

"Oh." Syreena backed down sheepishly. "My apologies, brother."

She did not notice the shock on their faces. She had never referred to Elijah with such intimacy before. Though she had respected him, she had never warmed to him personally. It made her apology full of impact.

"Understandable. It was a poor choice of language," he said with unusual grace for him. He was learning a great deal about diplomacy, even in his short time in their court. It was necessary to have when in a household of people who did not trust him, save the fact that he was in the heart of their Queen.

Then again, Elijah had won over many people just by being very obvious about how deeply entrenched the Queen was in *his* heart. If Elijah had ever been shy about showing affection in front of others, no one in the Lycanthrope court knew about it.

"Nevertheless, it is an excellent question. One, I am willing to bet, that is riding on Damien's heels as well."

Syreena did not like the sound of that. It bothered her, for some reason, to think of him running around biting random necks as a way of accumulating power.

In fact, it bothered her thinking of him biting necks, period.

Female necks especially.

She had seen enough even in her sheltered lifetime to know there was a difference for him between males and females. Their own intimacies aside, she had always had a sense that there was a pleasure involved when Vampires took the blood of the opposite sex, no matter what species. And Vampires were certainly not above dallying with humans. To be fair, neither were Lycanthropes. That was how half-breeds had come to be. Anya, Siena's General, was a half-breed. She was clearly of vulpine descent, a vixen had she been full bred. Instead of shapechanging, however, Anya was a permanent mixture of human and Lycanthrope. She had all the looks of a human, but the skills, claws, and features of a vixen.

Syreena wondered briefly if there was possibly a Vampiric equivalent to a half-breed. She had never heard of one, and to her knowledge neither had anyone else, but they were fast learning that even for an ancient species, new and different things were always possible.

"I would be interested to see if there is anything about this in the Library," Siena said.

Syreena, however, was not paying attention. Instead, she was overwhelmed with the desire to find Damien, to have him at her side. She tried to push the impulse away, realizing it was a ridiculous jealousy she had no right or claim to.

She was unsuccessful, however.

Without another word to her family, she transformed into the peregrine, her empty dress fluttering to the floor before their startled eyes as she soared free of the neckline.

"Syreena!"

Syreena reeled, dipping an apologetic wing, and soared into the cavern corridors.

Damien eased his sleepy prey to the chilled ground.

The canine sitting patiently just behind him, its tail wagging against the concrete, was looking up at him expectantly when Damien stepped back from his need of the animal's master.

"Good boy," the Prince praised the animal gently. "Now, I expect a few licks on your friend's face after I am gone will rouse him. I do not recommend letting him sit in the cold long. These humans do not have your fur to warm them."

Damien knew the dog understood him. An animal mind was very different from a human one, but with skill could be just as easily touched. Besides, the dog understood the circle of nature and the predator and prey who revolved within it. So long as Damien caused the man no harm, the beast was not inclined to harm him in return.

The Vampire stepped away from the guard and his dog, falling back into the shadows of the building they were protecting. With a hard, pushing thought, he produced an altered perception onto the man he had fed from. It was designed to blur reality, allowing the man and all others who looked at him to perceive nothing marking his neck during the time it would take him to heal. Damien did a last sensory check of the area to assure himself that both man and beast would remain in safety for some time after he had gone.

To his surprise, he was aware of Syreena approaching him.

The speed she used was a marvel to him. Perhaps, with practice, he would attain such grace and swiftness in the raven form. It was easy to become the bird, but less easy to *be* a bird. For instance, cold Russian nights and wings not agreeing well with one another was an important detail that would not have occurred to him normally.

Syreena changed form midair, but landed on the balls of her feet with amazing grace and balance just the same. She swung back the hair that had peeled from her body after changing back from its feathered state.

She was quite a sight to behold, the Vampire thought, feeling a little light-headed as he did indeed behold her. She was standing on the icy ground in her bare feet. In fact, her entire body was bare. Bare and obviously chilled, he thought, a slightly naughty smile toying at his mouth.

"A bit cold to be flying about," he noted, drawing her attention to the place of his concealment. Given time, she would learn how to divine him from the background of darkness he wore so well. For the moment, he joined her in the light of the nearby streetlamp.

"Funny that you should know that," she countered.

He would not bother to pretend that he was ignorant of her reference to the raven form she had so recently seen him take. It must have been quite a shock, yet she seemed level and matter-of-fact enough.

"Ah, yes. Noticed that, did you?"

"I'd have to be as dumb as a post you weren't roosting on to miss it. I can imagine the theory behind this development. I should like to hear about it."

"A discussion we can have in more comfortable surroundings than this." He took her elbow in hand, drawing her close to the very warm flush of his recently fed body. "You look like you will freeze to death in another ten seconds. Your lips are blue."

He reached up to rub a knuckle over her bottom lip. He dropped his hand back to his side, but on the way, she felt his very warm fingers stroke down over her neck, collarbone, breast, and tightly thrusting nipple. Even though she managed to repress any obvious sounds of the effect the intimacy had on her, there was no concealing the rush of her breath on the cold air. It clouded instantly, betraying her as it ebbed against him.

Damien was terribly intrigued, and suddenly found himself with an appetite that had nothing to do with predator and prey. Then again, he sometimes was overwhelmed with the feeling that she could provide a sweet sustenance for him in ways far beyond the nutrition of blood.

"Come, let us find shelter."

Damien went to sweep her up into his arms, but she stepped back out of reach. With a shake of her head and body, she was quickly covered in feathers. This time, however, she maintained her feminine form. Large wings expanded from the joints of her shoulders and she drew herself up into the air, turning a dark avian eye down to him briefly before she soared off into the cloud cover.

Damien maintained his usual form and followed her.

It did not take them long to reach the mountain range that housed the caverns of the royal holdings. Syreena led him through a back entrance that he suspected only she knew about. By the time they reached the true beginnings of the underground castle, they had been traveling underground a good twenty minutes.

Syreena settled into a semiprivate alcove with a pool of steaming water in its center. She shook form, and, without a word for him, she dove into the clear pool head first.

He moved to the edge of the rock rimming the small but deep lagoon. It was clearly a hot spring, and an ingenious way of warming up after standing in the cold.

Damien waited for her to surface, well aware that though she could not change into her second form of the dolphin at present, she could still hold her breath for as long as she needed or wanted to. She took to water like she took to the air. It meant that if she had to, Syreena could travel the earth, the air, and through water. It was an excellent ability to have. It meant she always had alternatives for speedy travel and that very little could stand in her way, save perhaps solid rock.

And, he realized, he could claim the same. Though he was not fond of the water, he could swim well, and his lack of need for air could benefit him with that. He walked the earth as she did, and even traveled the air. But with the change in size his body went through to become the raven, it allowed him a new sort of access he was quickly coming to appreciate.

He saw her streaming up through the clear water, heading toward him and the surface. She broke through with a long intake of air, slicking back her hair with her hands automatically. The Vampire squatted down low, so that he was much closer to her as she held on to the ledge and treaded water.

"Better?" he asked.

"Some."

The response was enigmatic, but she pushed back and swam away before he could question her about it. He straightened to his full height again and watched as she floated lazily across the surface, her lithe body turning and twisting, diving and surfacing, giving him teasing flashes of flank and skin, and of long, graceful arms and gently arched feet. He walked the edge of the steaming pond slowly and thoughtfully. He barely spared a glance for the carved stone archway leading into the circular chamber and the intricate art etched into the faces of the walls. There was a stone bench, a part of the wall itself, that circled the half-moon alcove from one side of the entrance around to the other. He did not make use of it, instead moving around her as she played in the water.

She turned to look at him after a few minutes and then swam to the edge nearest to him. With capable hands, she hauled herself onto the dry stone and up onto her feet. Water cascaded from her long hair, splashing over the ground, his shoes, and the lower part of his pants. He cocked a brow at her, realizing there was a little bit of malice to the supposedly innocent accident.

"Passive-aggressive behavior does not become you," he informed her mildly.

"Neither does jealousy," she said, her tone tight and strained. "And yet, I am still engaging in it. Perhaps you can tell me why that is?"

"Jealousy?" He mused over the term with blatant curiosity, one that was tinged with a little too much amusement for her liking.

"Don't be so smug," she warned him. "Not until you have seen a jealous Lycanthrope." She growled under her breath impatiently. "Tell me why I feel this way! I hardly know you. I have no claim on you, nor do you have one on me. You seem to have a wisdom about all of this that I do not. I want you to tell me what is going on!"

"Your premise is in error. We do have claims on each other."

"Because you drank my blood? What is that to you but a meal? Just another tasty tidbit before the next comes along."

"Hmm," he murmured.

He let his eyes roam over her slowly for a moment, memorizing her shape where it was sleek and also where it was soft and round. His obvious appreciation made her body shift in spite of what she preferred it to do. How could he turn her inside out so easily, with just a look? She walked the world in the nude without interest or care, yet one glance from him and she felt truly naked before him.

"There are certain foods that can never be topped, Syreena. Did it not occur to you that you are perhaps the tastiest tidbit of them all? That against you, all the others pale dramatically in comparison upon my palate?"

"Is that how you see me?" she asked, her bewilderment terribly obvious to them both. "I admit, I have no idea. Everything we have experienced together so far has come from necessity or impulse. You seem to know so much, where I am lost and baffled."

"Is that your impression?" Damien reached out, brushing droplets of water from her forehead above her left eyebrow. "I can see how it would appear so, but I assure you it is not always the truth. You see, Syreena, I am working with the experience of a long life of living by my instincts. It has always served me well. What you perceive as ease of understanding is merely familiarity of action."

"Perhaps that is exactly what I am afraid of," she noted quietly, turning away from his touch and walking around him.

He was left to follow her the short distance to her chambers. "Would you mind clarifying that remark?"

She ignored him for a minute, reaching into her wardrobe for a short sheath dress made of olive green silk. It shimmered over her head and down her body, with only a slight twitch of her hips to settle the loose fabric in place.

Damien took the opportunity to look around the room, taking careful note of the Spartan setting that resembled the conditions at the monastery. She had no waiting room or parlor, and no ladies catering to her needs as her sister did. Siena enjoyed her privileges and her luxuries, and though little things like the fabrics Syreena wore and the silky sheen of her bedding attested to the fact that Syreena enjoyed a certain level of luxury herself, it was clear to him that it did not extend too far beyond her person.

She was a private person, as he had become over the years. He expected her cloistered upbringing was behind her penchant for solitude. She was definitely a thinker, someone who meditated on her approaches, thoughts, and actions, keeping her settings as simple as possible in order to avoid disturbance or distraction.

If she had not been the type to deeply consider her actions, she might have come at him with the full force of this jealousy she was laying quiet claim to, instead of walking carefully around its edges, just as he had walked the edge of the hot spring.

"Am I merely your latest instinct, Damien?" she asked abruptly, the brush of her hands over the hips of her dress broadcasting an uncharacteristic nervousness that the Prince picked up on instantly.

"The latest? Yes. Merely? No, Syreena. By the nature of who you are, it could never be a mere thing."

She sighed, but not with relief. It was more a sign of growing agitation. "You have such a way with words. I never know if it is just because of years of practice, or because you have feeling behind it. What I do know is that Vampires are hard to impress and not known to show their emotions. Yet you do not hesitate here?"

"No. I do not."

"I need you to explain why," she insisted, stepping closer to him. She was warmer than usual, her body superheated from her swim. He could feel it even though she stood a good yard away yet. He suspected her rise in emotion had something to do with it as well.

"I already told you, I am not certain why. It just is."

"And what will 'just' be tomorrow? Will you take the blood of another and find yourself acting on instinct as well?"

Ah. The point, Damien thought with an inner smile. "Let us say that I did. It would not change how *you* feel, will it?"

"That depends on how far I let this go. I will not play the odds like my sister did. She gambled that making love with a man not of our species would suspend the mating rules. She lost her bet, although in actuality she won, because Elijah is her perfect complement. Only a male such as he is could temper my sister."

"And what kind of man would temper you, Princess?" he asked silkily, moving a step closer, the single advance closing the distance between them to mere inches.

Syreena looked up to meet his eyes and was aware that he was finding some sort of amusement in their conversation. For once, however, she sensed that it was not at her expense. She understood that it was just who she was that he took so much delight in.

"If you mean for it to be you, Damien, you have to know that, for me, there would be no going back. There would be no other choices. For the rest of my life, I would want only you, and never anyone else. It is written in genetic code on every cell in my body. No member of the royal household has ever been successful at defying it. They never even wanted to."

"And as I understand it, that applies to your mate as well."

"Usually. But this is uncharted territory. You are not Lycanthrope."

"It worked with Elijah," he pointed out.

"An extraordinary chance of luck. Demons have the Imprinting. We have it, too, only we call it something else. I have never heard of such a bond between Vampires."

"Vampires also never shapechanged before," he reminded her softly. Again, he reached to touch her, as he seemed always compelled to do when close to her. "Syreena, I cannot guarantee what I do not understand myself. I understand the risk involved on your behalf, and that you do not see it as being as much of a sacrifice on my part, but," he said, his fingertips brushing that spot on her hairline that was already sprouting downy-soft growth, "if it will make you feel better, I will tell you that I have thought of nothing but you since we parted. I cannot sleep; I take no joy in feeding. Jasmine says I am moping and melancholy."

The terms used against someone like him were comical, and she laughed in spite of the anxiety twisting beneath her breastbone.

"I have not experienced this state of disenchantment for nearly eight hundred years. I cannot afford the luxury of such things because I have a species to care for. And yet, I indulge in it in spite of myself. No one, no female of any species in all the years of my life, has affected me the way you have. I have had obsessions and infatuations, but none were like this. Is that what you want to know, sweetling? Or do you want to know that I will not one day actively seek a way out of your arms when I grow tired of you? Perhaps you wish for a promise that I am not thinking of taking you to bed simply for the experience of intimately knowing a one-of-a-kind creature, who has no genetic equal?

"I think that no matter what I swear to or promise to, you will find another reason to worry. Your insecurity shows, Syreena. Your need to believe in yourself and to have others believe in you is sharp, and it must be so very painful when we do not live up to your hopes." Damien ran those gently searching fingers back along her hairline until they were circling the back of her ear. It was a sensitive spot, and she shivered under the caress.

"All I can tell you," he continued quietly, "is that from the moment when first I saw you, I saw beauty. I saw strength and determination. I saw the sweetness of your love for your sister. All of this I saw while we were in the dark. Remember? I saw nothing of your eyes or your hair. I saw nothing of your crown. I took nothing from your bloodstream. Even then I felt myself intrigued by you. I felt desire for you. Perhaps it was because you were threatening my life. I do find that particularly sexy."

"Damien!" She laughed in shock, reaching to touch his chest because she couldn't bear not to any longer.

"Your heart is as harlequin as the rest of you, Syreena. Gray in some areas, natural in others. I would learn them all, if given a chance. And while I do not deny that I want very badly to take long amounts of time exploring everything about you . . ." He paused long enough to run his eyes down her body, his inference as clear as the increasing beat of her heart. She felt heat slipping through her everywhere at once, until she was light in her head over it. "In this instance, however, I see that I must leave you to decide when you wish to come to me and soothe my desires."

Damien's fingers slid from behind her ear to the back of her neck, his thumb stroking over her cheek as he pulled her closer. He touched his lips to the corner of her mouth. She closed her eyes, her slight body shivering in excited anticipation. She understood what he was saying. She realized that he would walk away and give her time to think, if he had to. It relaxed her, opening her closed and suspicious thoughts to possibilities just out of her reach.

"I suspect such a thing is not possible," he murmured against the skin of her cheek after a moment.

"What is not possible?" she asked on a whisper of breath.

"Soothing my desire for you," he said, the sudden rush of longing very apparent in his heated voice and the unrestrained fingers sliding around the curve of her ribs, gripping her side as if she were a prized possession he wanted to keep very close, lest another covet her. "I cannot imagine a hunger like this being satisfied with a small taste."

Syreena closed her eyes, inhaling deeply, letting the obvious changes in his scent wash over her as he let a few of his restraints slip away. It allowed her a startling insight into how she could arouse him even when he was simply holding her close to himself. She marked all the attractive, delicious changes in his chemistry, and how they seemed to cycle through her blood, awakening the response within her own systems.

He was breathing against her, telling her that he had switched into that place where he began to lose his control over how his body functioned. The reflex was a compelling clue, one that gave her a strangely prevailing sense of satisfaction.

"You enjoy your effect on me," he noted on a low, aggressive pitch. "I know because it radiates from you like a sun, searing through me." He turned his mouth an inch so he could kiss her in a short, forceful style, making quick work of relearning her textures, her warmth, and her incredible sweetness. "Be careful, Princess," he warned on a hot and rapid breath, "or you will start a fire that I will not be able to control."

It always amazed her how, when he began to touch her and kiss her in such ways, it never took long before she couldn't care less about consequences. His warning had little impact when pitted against the flavor of his mouth and the feel of his domineering hands.

"I don't know what to do with you anymore," she said with wired emotion, her hands gripping at the fabric of his shirt along his sides. "You say all the right things, you *do* all the right things. Even things I deem mistakes, you manage to explain away as if they had all the logic in the world behind them. Where do you get your unshakable surety, Damien?"

"For me, it is a survival instinct, Syreena. Without it, my throne would fall into someone else's hands . . . along with my head to the ground. I cannot afford the luxury of second-guessing myself."

"You cannot possibly know how much I wish I could say the same," she said longingly.

"You can, you know. You have no one you need answer to.

Not unless you wish to answer to them. But first," he said, taking her by the arms and easing her away from his over-eager body, "first you need to figure out what question you need to ask yourself. I know I could easily sit here and influence you," he said, stroking stimulating fingers down her throat to prove his point, watching the effect it had on her already erratic pulse. "Syreena, you have let the world manipulate your life enough. I will not tell you what to do. I will only tell you your options."

"Tell me my options, Damien. Make it clear. Do not couch it in pretty words and elusive observations. Be straight with me. Tell me what you want from me—from us, if there is to be an us."

Damien looked down into her serious bicolored eyes, knowing exactly what she wanted to hear. He was surprised to realize how much he wanted to say it.

"I want to learn how to love you, Syreena. And no, I do not mean make love to you. I believe I can figure that out well enough." The sparkle in his eyes and the pointed twitch to his brow made her laugh. "I want to learn why it is and how it is you have effected these changes inside me, both physically and spiritually. I wish to know how one such as myself, so nonchalant in emotion all of his life, can be so moved by a single little creature like you.

"This is not a phase for me, Syreena. This is not a fancy that will flit out of my system. I have lived long enough to know what is and is not unique to my make-up. If you want promises, I will find ways to make them and keep them. If you want forever, sweetling, then I will gladly live another long lifetime." He let go of her, his reluctance obvious. "Now it is up to you to decide if these things will make you happy, if they are something you will want with equal measure. Be warned," he said, holding up a hand to stay her interruption, "because there is another side to this. We both have responsibility besides to ourselves. If we cannot reconcile these things, then the choice becomes one of what we are willing to give up for the sake of ourselves. Even I have not had time to consider that. I have only had time to realize that it is not so important to me as it once was, and that, perhaps, is the first step. Do you understand my meaning, Syreena?"

"You speak of our thrones, Damien. So, there is something we must answer to after all."

"Again, only if we wish to."

"Wishes cannot come into it, Damien. I am Siena's heir. There is no changing that."

"Only if you do not wish it to change. But that is not the immediate question. It is merely an affected consequence of the answer. Discover one, before worrying about the other."

"Find out what my heart wants, without considering my responsibilities?"

"To you, that sounds irresponsible, I know. But it is the mark of true freedom, Syreena. To follow one's heart and instinct above all else. I may not have much of a heart, but I do know that much."

With that daunting remark, he reached to press a lingering kiss to her forehead and then turned to leave her.

Everything inside Syreena wanted to jump at him, leap at him and grab him, hold him in place so he could not leave. Her skin screamed with his absence, her pumping heart abusing her with a flood of sickening dread that rushed her every major artery. It was as if he held a tether to her spirit, and he was ripping it free of her as he went.

Chapter 9

"Damien! Damien, wait!"

She launched herself at his back before he could cross the threshold. Her hands hit his shoulders, her chest slamming into his back as she wrapped her arms around him. Her eyes stung with tears, tears of such sudden relief she could hardly breathe.

Damien closed his eyes, a pained expression flitting over his features as he reached to enfold one of the hands grasping him. He struggled within himself for a long minute as she clung to him with such desperate need. He wanted to stay. More than anything. But she had so many doubts. He could not bear it if he caused them both a great deal of pain simply because he could not bring himself to be patient and to do the right thing.

"Syreena . . ." he argued hoarsely.

"No! You are right. It is my choice! No one can make it for me. Not even parts of myself. All I know is that I cannot bear for you to leave me with a totality of being I have never experienced before in all of my life. Every grain of life inside of me protests it. Damien, please . . ."

Damien turned slowly, letting her push herself into the entire length of his body, although the intimacy of the contact was so taxing to his strength of will.

"And ten minutes from now, you will doubt me all over again," he whispered into her hair.

"No. No, I won't."

"You cannot be sure of that."

"Yes, I can! Yes, Damien, I can."

She reached for both of his hands quickly, bringing them up her body until his fingers were resting around her throat.

His touch fell on precious metal, gold and moonstones, the necklace that was her badge of royalty.

Damien understood her intent immediately.

There was mysticism attached to these remarkable pieces of Lycanthrope jewelry. They were capable of always fitting the wearer, no matter what shape or form they were in, transforming as they did. But more significantly, no one knew the secret to how to remove it. The legend of the jewelry said that there was only one way it could ever be removed.

By the hand of the royal's one true mate.

"If it is meant to be, your touch will tell me so."

"I see," he said softly. "So you cannot decide after all. You must once again depend on something outside of yourself."

Damien tried not to feel the painful disappointment that shuddered through him, but it was too strong and too encompassing. He pulled away from her, a bit forcefully under the might of his emotion, and pushed her hard from himself.

"Grow up, little girl," he snapped as his temper reeled out of rein. "Until you do, do not torment me with your teasing and empty pledges. Despite rumors to the contrary, even my heart is sensitive."

With that, he violently morphed into the form of the raven and left her.

Shocked into paralysis, her numb fingers still on her throat where she had led him to touch her, Syreena stood unmoving and unfeeling for a moment. Then she was overwhelmed with pain. Unable to control her own body a second longer, she collapsed onto the floor of her bedroom.

"Elijah, this is not like her at all," Siena said worriedly.

The giant blond man reached out to stop his wife's jittery pacing, drawing her curvaceous body into his, nuzzling her neck where her collar usually was when they were outside of their bedroom. In her unceasing worry over the well-being of her young sister, Siena had forgotten her badge of office that day.

It allowed him the advantage of exploiting the spot on her throat that he knew was terribly sensitive for her. He could always distract her with a kiss in that place. It worked, a pleased sigh leaving her as she cuddled voluntarily closer to him. He smiled against the sweet scent of her neck.

"Kitten, you need to stop worrying about a woman who is over one hundred years old."

"She could be a thousand years old, Elijah, and she will still be my sister."

Elijah knew that, and regretted making it sound otherwise, but he felt as though Siena was overprotective of the Princess, who was obviously able to care for herself. Unfortunately, since Ruth had harmed Syreena, Siena had been even more concerned with her sister's safety and soundness of mind.

"You know I didn't argue that," he admonished her gently. She could read his thoughts, so he knew this was true. "Syreena is entitled to her privacy and her pouts just as any of us are. The last time you tromped through the house in a fit, she was wise enough to give you space. You need to respect her in kind and trust her to come around to you when she needs you."

"I do," she argued.

"You don't. You expect her to advise you, but she never lets you advise her, and that puts you out. So you simply hand out commands and instructions and stick your pert little nose where it probably does not belong."

"Elijah!"

"Siena, if I was going to lie to you, I would make a terrible husband. Who can fearlessly tell a queen her faults, if not her mate?"

Siena released a signature growl of frustration, trying to push him away so she could be vexed without the warmth of his comfortable body to distract her from it. But moving him was like trying to move a mountain. He didn't budge unless he wanted to.

"Don't sulk, kitten," he murmured close to her ear.

"Stop trying to charm me when I am mad at you!"

"I have no charm, sweetheart. You know that."

"You are nothing but a bully. You always have been." Her accusation had no punch, however, because she laid her cheek against his shoulder and easily stopped trying to fight him for the sake of her temper. "I am lost without her, Elijah. She is always the steady and practical voice in my ear."

"There is another voice now, kitten," he reminded her. "And Syreena must be free to go her own way. The days of locking her up in safety are long past. I know you realize that."

"But—"

"Siena," he scolded.

"Elijah, she is so sad. I feel it with every fiber of my soul. And I know it is somehow Damien's doing. I want to find him and beat the sense out of him!"

Elijah understood her frustration all too well. He glanced over the edge of the balcony in which they stood, looking down at the Princess who was sitting in sad solitude in a lonely alcove, below and across from where they stood. Syreena had been inconsolable over the past couple of days. Though she showed no obvious emotion, there was no spark of interest or concern within her for anything but her own thoughts. He was aware that Siena had even tried to fabricate concerns, trying to draw her out in the role of advisor at the very least. Siena's sister had merely put her Queen off, claiming to be unwell, busy elsewhere, or any other convenient excuse she could think of to go sit in her own company.

The warrior tried not to be angry with the Princess for the distress she was causing his wife. The problem was more Siena's than it was Syreena's, as he had already pointed out to her. Still, when she hurt, it hurt him. It was the nature of the way they were mated. He could accept that one slight flaw, though, because of all the benefits that also came with such a depth of connection.

He had been tempted to approach Damien himself several times. Just for the sake of understanding. Or, perhaps, it was because Siena wished for it so vehemently. Sometimes her desires were so powerful, he could mistake them for his own. The reverse was also true. So he maintained his ideals about the situation, hoping the sensibility of it would eventually rub off on her.

"I would not bet the castle on it," she retorted tartly.

Elijah chuckled at her, pressing an affectionate kiss into her sprung-up hair.

"I am hopeful, Siena, *not* an idiot," he informed her with amusement.

Jasmine ran absent fingers over the spines of books, slowly reading what titles she could, looking for something, anything, to help her in her search.

Her home was in turmoil because its master was equally so. Though he was far more adamant about keeping the matter to himself this time around, Jasmine was almost positive he had faced some sort of rejection at the whim of the Lycanthrope Princess.

Damn her to hell anyway, Jasmine thought with easy venom.

Damien was not used to being gainsaid, nor was he accustomed to the rejection of a woman. Considering the hope and unusual idealism the Prince was investing in the ungrateful chit, Jasmine imagined it was all the more painful and scarring to the male Vampire's ego to be rejected.

Without knowing why this had come to pass in so unsatisfactory a manner, she was left to guess. In her concern for Damien's well-being, even though she was convinced the little snob did not deserve him, Jasmine had to find proof without prejudice to support her Prince's pursuit of the foreign baggage he had taken such a fancy to. It was the only way to rectify the situation. If Jasmine could prove that Damien's theories were couched in fact, then the shapechanger would have to at least listen and consider the possibilities.

She only wished that she could read faster.

Damien walked his dark gardens, his thoughts deeply fixated on a frustrating woman half the world away from him. She may as well have been sitting in his lap whispering her doubts and insecurities into his ear over and over again. He had not hunted once since he had last seen her, and the cold of his body matched the ice coating his soul. As distracted as he was by thoughts and emotion, it would not be wise to walk the world and expose himself to the innumerable dangers that could await him. He would end up getting himself killed if he was not careful.

As it was, he was aware of powerful presences flitting too close to his home and territory. They were Vampires, two of them, and they were lurking in wait for an opportunity to confront him. Normally he would have faced them down immediately, but he was uninterested and disinclined to do so at the moment. Let them come and take their chances, he thought wearily. What did he live for, but to amuse the occasional embodiment of avarice? Let them covet his position, his grounds, and his home if they liked.

They could have it all, for all he cared in that moment.

Jasmine would be fine on her own. She had told him more than enough times that she did not need him to protect her or advise her. She had been telling the truth of it. He had probably been using her as an excuse to remain aboveground for these many decades. He had needed her far more than she had ever needed him.

Which seemed to be a running theme in the women he was attracting of late.

Damn her.

It had been well over two nights since he had left her. In all this time, she still could not make a choice? Why should that surprise him, he asked himself. She had not made a free choice for herself in her entire life. It might well take another one hundred years before she would be able to figure out how.

And he would be damned if he was going to sit around waiting for her.

Not in a way that would continue to be as painful as this was proving to be.

On some level, Damien was aware of his affectations, their causes and the logic to them. However, the harder he tried to reason himself out of his despair, the worse it seemed to become. He was thwarted by the catch-22 of needing something beyond all reason, and needing that something to have a reason for being with him beyond *her* ability to reason.

It made no sense, and yet all the sense in the world. It was the only truth he wanted to hear. He was deaf to all others.

Unaccustomed to this depth of feeling, Damien was floundering. That, he supposed, was because he was doing the opposite of what he had done all of his life. He was acting against instinct. His inner compass pointed back to Russia, yearning to go to Syreena and make her understand what it would mean to her to choose him. Why could he not be satisfied with her logic? It would get him what he wanted, just not the way he wished to get it. What did it matter, if the end result was the same?

But it would not be the same, and it was instinct that told him that as well. If he manipulated her choice, coerced her decision, he would leave her too much room for doubt. If she could not believe in him now, she would not believe in him in the long run. He was positive that everything inside Syreena was screaming for him, just as he cried out for her. Yet she fought herself and resisted and stumbled around waiting for someone to tell her what the right choice was.

In her heart and soul, she should already know.

Like he knew.

If she wanted guarantees, she would find them only inside herself. He had already said all he could on the matter. But apparently that was not enough for her. And why should it be? She did not trust herself, never mind anyone else.

Damien made his way to the bench that had become like a second home for him. He straddled the cold stone and sat down, gripping the edge of the seat in tight, icy hands as he turned toward the wind blowing with wintry chill off the ocean.

He was tired and weakening. He was aware of this. Soon he would be forced to either snap himself out of his gloom, or he would have to go to ground, hiding himself from the above world. It was the only way he could survive. If he remained in this state, it was only a matter of time before someone challenged him. In his present condition, he had little hope of winning.

Let them take it all while he slept protected in the earth. Syreena's indecision might be killing him slowly, but he would be damned if he would let his greedy brethren pick over the bones.

Let them have it.

It meant very little anymore.

When Damien woke hours later, it was to find himself looking up into a sky pinking with the dawn.

He sat up quickly, realizing suddenly that he had fallen asleep on the stone garden bench. As he did so, he faced the full force of the rising sun. He flinched hard, throwing up a hand to protect his eyes even as they began to sting with painful tears from the exposure. A couple of days ago, while at peak strength, he could have born this early breach of sunlight. In his weakened state, it was another story entirely.

He cursed himself for his carelessness and struggled to his feet while protecting his exposed skin with the turn of his body. He turned to hurry back to the house, his need for protective shade quite sharp in his mind and on his skin.

Then, as if deciding the entire thing was a trick of mind over matter, he stopped all progress toward shelter.

He dropped his hands slowly and turned back toward the growing sunrise. He realized then what a beautiful thing the deadly sun could be. It, too, was a predator of sorts. Only it was at the top of every food chain. It fed on everything. The sun gobbled up the darkness with a quick and gluttonous appetite. Then it nibbled or chomped at Nightwalkers as if they were dessert. It sapped the energy from Demons, it made Lycanthropes blister and boil as essential nutrients were violently withdrawn from their bodies.

For him, it would nibble at his flesh in bit-by-bit burns, until he truly was nothing but ashes and dust, devoid of water, blood, and life of any kind.

"Damien, what are you doing?"

Jasmine grabbed at the Prince, panic flying over her with the wild, galvanizing need for action. She was more than powerful enough to force Damien to her will while he was in this state of lethargy. She seized him and dragged him with blinding speed into the manse, behind the safety of strongly tinted windows and tightly drawn drapes.

Out of immediate danger, she turned more gentle, helping Damien find a seat on a large sofa before a cold fireplace. Once he was seated, she dropped to her knees in front of him, wedging them between his ankles as she clasped his cold hands in hers with a grip of fearful anger and concern.

"Damien, she is not worth this! No woman is worth your life! You could have been killed. Please . . . I am begging you to stop hurting yourself like this."

The attention he turned to her was only half there, the distance in his eyes telling her how unreachable some of the most integral parts of himself truly were. It was as though this silly woman had stolen the heart out of him. He was grieving, and she felt it keenly from him. So much so that her perception of it nearly drove the usually serene Vampire to tears.

"Damien," she cried in a whispered, hitching voice.

Jasmine threw her arms around his neck, hugging him as hard as she could, consoling him as she assured herself that he was safe and alive. She realized she could not leave him again. It was too dangerous. That, however, was only a temporary stopgap. If he did not hunt, Damien would fall into torpor. It would only take another couple of days for that to happen. Since she had never experienced the other side of the equation, Jasmine was overwhelmed with understanding of what she had put Damien through each of the several times she had fallen into it herself.

He was so cold to the touch, and it added to the chill his mental state was leaving on her soul. If she could be in a room with that thoughtless, coldhearted bitch of a Lycanthrope for two minutes, then Damien would truly have something to grieve for. Jasmine wanted to kill her.

The passion of the thought was so strong that Jasmine's fangs appeared with aggression and hostility. She made an angry vocalization, rocking her beloved friend in consolation still, in spite of her naked outrage.

"Damien," she murmured into his ear, her fingers stroking down the back of his head and his braid. "You must feed. Come," she coaxed softly, drawing back her hair as she settled his mouth to her neck. She had fed herself only an hour before dawn, so the scent of the hunt and the heat of the prey's blood she had taken were still evocatively fresh. "Let me sustain you," she pleaded in his ear.

Damien was only dimly aware of any appeal her offering might have. Therefore, it was easy for him to turn away. He had no appetite, no desire to experience the feelings that accompanied a feed, especially that from a female.

Even if it was Jasmine.

He pried himself out of her grasp, discarding her invitation as he stood on his feet and stepped over her kneeling form.

Without a word, he left her. He retired to his chambers where he would sleep the rest of the day until darkness moved over the world again.

The first thing to penetrate Damien's sleeping senses was the gentle scent of lavender.

It shocked him out of the depths of sleep and he sat up with a sudden movement, twisting around so he could see the entire room.

In the night of the room, he could see the shape of a vase near his bed, and it was full of fresh flowers and branches, including heather and lavender.

His heart sank along with his unexpected, and now crushed, hope, and in a fit of rage he grabbed the offending vessel and threw it across the room. The glass burst, sending water and blossoms everywhere.

Was he so awful a creature that she could not possibly reconcile herself to spending a lifetime with him? That she could not even bear to try? Was this the ultimate trick of fate? He had committed a long list of sins in his many years, so maybe this was the ebb of a painful karma he must suffer.

Damien growled dangerously, warning the outer forces of the world to back off him. Hadn't he compensated for his flaws as best he could through the centuries? How many lives had

he saved, how many improved, because of his careful inter-
ference and selection? He had lost count long before he had
saved the life of the English queen who had lived to reign
with remarkable strength for nearly seventy years. He had
always thought that the gifts of the Elizabethan Renaissance
had been an extraordinary contribution to the development
of the human race. It was an era that might never have existed
had the Queen died of smallpox that year he had met her.

Was there no karma for those things? Was there no angel
of mercy and appreciation flying around him now, acknowl-
edging that he had committed dozens of such integral acts,
and now it was time that he experience the peace of a thriving renaissance full of freedom, unimagined beauty, and,
most of all, love?

He had never believed Vampires to be the demons they
were commonly thought to be, but if dwelling in the depths
of hell made him a fiend, then a monster he most definitely
was, because this existence could only be described as un-
adulterated hell.

His pique of temper had only made the spread of the
scent of lavender worse within his bedroom, he realized after
a moment. He got out of bed, throwing aside the sheets that
had become snarled around him as he had slept fitfully. He
strode across the room to his wardrobe, determined to dress
and force himself to hunt that night. Perhaps force was not
even necessary. As his emotions elevated, his desire for a
savage stalking rose in equal measure. It was dangerous to
hunt by emotion alone, but at that point, he did not care. It
was better to risk his life trying to regain his health than it
was to drift further into the self-serving pity he was dwelling
in as if he would make a permanent home of it.

But first, he thought as he pulled on a pair of slacks with
jerks of driven irritation, first he was going to burn those
cursed flowers and get that scent out of his house.

Damien did not even grab a shirt as he angrily turned to
do just that.

And nearly knocked over Syreena in the process.

He automatically reached to steady her, his hand closing on her arm around her bare bicep. He felt himself immediately drawn in by the soft texture of her skin and the amazing sculpture of the sure muscle beneath. She was so warm, especially compared to him. Through the shadows of the night and the room, he could see her strange eyes, especially the gray one, looking at him as if she could see right through to his back.

Damien was stunned that she was even there. However, his recent bout with false hope only minutes ago had jaded any chance of him feeling that optimism again. And in spite of his surprise, he was still quite livid. Since she was the source of it, he took no pleasure in seeing her.

Or so he told himself.

"What are you doing here?" he demanded coldly. "Come to torture your pitiful suitor with your vacillations and never-ending questioning of his intentions?"

"No," she said, her dulcet voice alien in the harsh emotion filling the room as it emanated from him.

"Go home, Syreena," he said roughly, failing as he tried to keep the emotion out of his voice. "I do not have the answers you are looking for."

"Damien . . ."

Damn her, he hated it when she spoke his name. She always said it in such a way, in such a tone, that she could turn his nerves inside out upon themselves. It was unfair that she could provoke a response in him when she was so clearly cold to him in return. In spite of her earlier responses to him physically, she had proven to be frigid toward him when it truly counted.

"Do not say another word," he warned her, holding up a hand in a sharp gesture that made her jump in her own skin a fraction of an inch. "You have had three days and nights to speak to me, Syreena, and your opportunity is gone."

Or it will be, he thought vehemently, *as soon as I can get away from her and get some fresh, revitalizing warmth into my system.*

Syreena understood why he was angry with her. He was right, after all. She had spent days balancing on the edge of a choice.

A choice, she had suddenly realized, that was never truly a matter of selection.

It was what Damien had seemed to know from the start. The only choice she could make was to ignore the demands of her heart and her spirit, both of which she had tried to ignore no matter how loudly they had screamed at her. In truth, there was no choice.

She was meant to be his, and he was meant to be hers.

She had searched day after day for outside proof of this, only to realize that there was none, and never would be. The proof was stamped in the desires of her soul. It was the instinct that had been born in her, flipped on like a switch, the moment it had flipped on as brilliantly in him.

Only he had seen the light, and she had been blinded by it.

"Damien," she protested gently, needing to tell him that she understood now. She comprehended all he had been trying to say, as well as understanding exactly how much he had accepted on faith and feeling while she had floundered around and caused him what must have been an unbearable agony of the heart. If she had been in pain these three days, then he had been in torment.

"I said you are not to speak to me!" he snarled in sudden temper, coming so close to her with his violent emotion that she took a reflexive step back.

Then she rethought the action, and shifted her weight back onto her forward foot. She bumped into his aggressive, imposing body as he towered in justifiable outrage.

Damien faltered when she did not give way, instead insinuating herself into his personal space. Her warmth, scent, and presence invaded him like a virus, all the familiar symptoms of reflexive need and desire unfurling along the planes of his form that were closest to her. She raised her hands, the flats of her palms toward him, reaching to touch him on his bare skin over his chest. Like a whip, his hand shot out and grabbed one of her wrists painfully, twisting it and her hand back in order to force her to change her mind about coming into contact with him.

She winced in pain, made a sound in reflection of it, and then turned her gaze up to his glare.

"You can break it if you like. It will not deter me," she told him softly.

She touched his cold skin with her other hand, immediately catching a shiver up her arm. Damien caught the reaction and gave her a bitter smile.

"I have not hunted since I left you. I do not suppose you are offering me a dinner date, are you? As you can see, I could use a little warming up. One woman or another will not make a difference to me."

"Are you so certain of that?" she countered quietly.

"I am positive of it. Your blood could warm me, Syreena, but my heart would stay just as cold to you as it does this moment."

"Very well."

She swung her head to one side, flinging back her hair until her collar glinted in the darkness. What shone even more luminescent, however, was the pale line of her throat, which she offered up to him with closed eyes and a stretch of her body.

Instead of the touch of his mouth, however, it was his forceful hand that closed around her neck. She released a strangled gasp as her eyes flew open.

"What are you, insane?" he hissed in accusation as he jerked on her wrist in his anger. "If you want to play with fire, Princess, I suggest you go find another flame. I'm not biting, if you will forgive the pun."

"Why not? It's just another feed, right? You have a demand; I have a supply. It is a simple logic."

"Logic?" Always, always logic with her. Always practical, everything with clear and tidy directions and explanations. "Logic dictates that when a Vampire is this livid, Princess, that you best hightail it out of the county lest he rip out your throat!"

"So much bark, so little bite," she observed tauntingly.

Damien had half a mind to show her just how much bite a Vampire could have when he was uncontrolled. It did not help that he was already suffering from all too clear memories of her taste, the richness of her extraordinary flavor and its effect on his systems. He had likened the experience to a drug in his mind several times, and he was beginning to realize he was fast becoming an addict.

Damien pivoted, slamming Syreena up against the wardrobe so hard that she lost her equilibrium. The room spun around her, making her quite dizzy. She tried to get purchase with her feet, but the bare floor was too smoothly polished to provide traction for her bare toes, and he was holding her up too high for her to touch the ground with her heels.

It did not matter a moment later, because the full weight of his large, powerful body was crushing her back against the solid piece of furniture a moment later. It was a punishment, not an embrace, but she could not help feeling as if she were being rewarded all the same. As chill as he was, the shape and feel of him, especially in this wild aggression, was a mighty stimulant to her senses, which had been so starved for him. It did not even bother her that his hand was restricting her breathing. She should have balked, considering her recent experiences at Ruth's hands, but the truth of the matter was that no matter how hard he railed and bullied at her, she was not afraid of him. She knew he would never be capable of hurting her.

That had been the whole point to all of her recent revelations.

He could never hurt her. Not physically, not psychically, not emotionally. Not even when she had so clearly hurt him in all three ways. In spite of his roughness, his coarse words, and his raging, nothing he had done had hurt her.

Now she had to make up for not being as gentle with him.

She fought him for the first time, twisting her wrist free with lightning speed while she wrapped her leg around his left knee. She straightened her leg hard, collapsing the structure of the brace of his legs. He fell to the desired side, and she made sure she followed him down.

Damien's backside hit the floor, and then, as her falling weight struck him, his shoulders went down onto the polished wood. As he moved to brace his feet, her bottom settled across his hips, and her hand went to his throat. She successfully pinned him in place with remarkable skill and strength. Even in his weakened state, it was quite an accomplishment to best him in such a way.

Before he could say a word, before he could move a muscle to attempt to throw her off him, she pushed his face aside and leaned forward across his chest. It exposed his neck to the strike of her mouth.

She had learned well, he realized as the warmth and dampness of her mouth closed over him in the most stimulating place available in that erogenous zone. It was a shock to his cold systems, all that warmth, but not as much of a surprise as the bite of her teeth that followed.

Damien fought the answering response of his body with the entirety of his will. He would not fall for this trick twice. He would not allow her to manipulate him whenever she wanted to, only to change her mind again later and leave him reeling and hurting. She already had too much power over him, and he would not allow her to have any more.

He reached up and grabbed her by almost the whole of her hair, squeezing his fist around the tendrils, which immediately began to squirm for escape. She gasped, breaking off her contact with his throat to lean her head back.

Only he had expected her to sit up away from him in the process. Instead, the arch brought her entire torso flush to his and caused her long throat to flash its pulse at him with tempting flirtation. It was different this time because it had not been by her design. The truth of the matter was he could not shut himself off from the effect she had on him.

Angry, with himself as well as her, he pried her clingy body off his, literally throwing her across the polished floor. She skidded nearly the entire length of the room, the friction burning her skin at several points. She sat up, trying to shake her head on straight as he scrambled to his feet.

"Stop making a fool of yourself, Syreena! You are a princess, for the love of—!"

"Oh, now all of a sudden that is important?" she barked back at him, gaining her feet and stalking right back over to him. Her approach was so volatile and aggressive that Damien was afraid she would find a way to touch him again. He did not know if he could bear much more of that, so he backed up in the path of her advance.

Until he hit the wall, at least.

The minute she had him cornered, she reached to thrust insistent fingers into the hair at the back of his head, and as she pulled him down, she thrust her body up against his.

She was able to capture his mouth.

Syreena did not kiss him for long, just with a hard seriousness that was sure to invade his senses and his memory in the quickest way possible. She broke away from him, placed her fingertips on his chest, and raked her nails down his bare skin with barely repressed violence.

He roared in outrage and pain, and then found himself glued to her mouth once more. She worked the kiss hard and hot and with unbelievable aggression. Damien's entire world began to reel as he was assaulted by all the stimuli she was using to bombard him. He quickly found himself struggling along the border of those sides of himself which were civilized, and those which were not.

For a minute, he could not remember that he had taught her how to kiss. She was working on an instinct that had nothing to do with what they had learned together. It was wild and intoxicating, raping him of his will and his resistance just as she knew it would. She pulled him by his hair to break him away from her mouth, and he made a strangled sound that crossed between regret for her suddenly absent lips and fury for her assertive abuse.

Then she slapped him so hard that his head almost turned completely backward on his neck.

This time, when he sprang back to look at her, it was with a roar, a violent flash of aggressive fangs and raging attitude. He grabbed her with an animalistic snarl, flipping their positions against the wall with a slam of their connected bodies. She made a sound as the air rushed from her lungs, but it was clearly one of satisfaction and not protest.

She had pushed him where she had wanted him.

Too far.

Beyond thought, beyond pain, beyond the ability to do anything but act on the instincts he so heavily depended on. It was the only way she figured to make any progress with him. She needed the naked emotions and reactions. It was the only way to cut through the stubborn anger he was shielding himself with.

She witnessed her overwhelming success when he nearly wrenched her head off her neck in his blind bid to expose her vulnerable pulse.

His teeth were in and out of her skin in a flash, her blood pulsing hotly over his lips and tongue. The minute the feeding began, she knew he would not stop until he made up for the starvation he had suffered the past three days. He was beyond coherent thought, she knew, and nothing could change that once her potent blood began to fill his needs.

She reached for his clenched hands and put them on her body, bearing the bracing chill of them as she dragged them over her warm skin. She led him to her breasts, gasping raggedly as the cold contacted her nipples, making them contract in immediate response.

The feel of her hot skin, and then the sudden fullness of her breasts pressing into his hands, penetrated the haze of his hunger with a sharp, spearing intensity. It combined with the erotic narcotic of her chemistry sweeping over his tongue, wrenching his body into a new awareness and a brutal form of arousal that started from the inside and exploded outward. As his hands flowed over the flesh she had boldly invited him to, she groaned on a hitching breath near his ear.

As he was swept up in the spinning awareness that swirled through him, his hands split direction over her wonderfully soft skin. One hand remained at her left breast, feeling the weight and warmth of her, understanding that he had wanted to cradle her in this way for so long it seemed like he had been born with the craving. The other hand skimmed her breastbone and defined abdomen, sweeping wide around her ribs until he was coasting down over her hip, her sweetly rounded backside, and down to a slender, powerful thigh. He traced the line back, but on a totally different path, the feel of her bleeding sensation into him like sound vibrations that tripped across every nerve.

As his hand roamed her body in bold sweeping motions, she felt it warming and then superheating in temperature. She slinked against him, clinging to both his hands and his body in every way she could manage. All the while, the persistent sucking of his mouth was making her wild with shivers of delight and liquid with heat that could not be bled from her no matter how deeply he drank. Syreena reached to stroke her hands up his chest, her nails safely retracted this time because she just wanted him to feel her touching him as thoroughly as possible. His skin was smooth and incredibly firm, the coolness of it fading in increments with every searching stroke she visited against it.

It was an amazing experience in contrasts to feel him go from empty chill, to blushing warmth, to flowering heat.

Better yet, her entire bare body was sharing in the swirling changes in temperature as it slid against him like poured water. Her fingers and palms heavily traced the etching of his musculature, starting on his chest and working out in wide, sweeping circles. His body was incredibly fit, firm and smooth, and the more she touched him, the more she craved him. The Lycanthrope Princess made it clear that she could not get enough of touching her Prince. When she had covered his bare skin twice, her hands slid down his spine and over the waistband of his slacks. Her fingertips traced the taut curve of his backside and the flex of his tightly braced thighs as far as she could without breaking the contact of his mouth drawing on her throat.

Damien felt as though she had lit him on fire. Between the work of his mouth and the work of her eager hands, he was consumed in flame. Her hands flowed forward, bracketing his hips, and then her fervent fingers slid deeply into the pockets of his pants, her palms turned toward his body. The moment she touched him through the thin fabric, he lurched into her light little body and sank his teeth into her a second time.

Syreena gasped as a familiar burn flowed through her neck, and an unfamiliar heat penetrated to her curious hands. He was massively aroused, a bold and thrusting hardness that begged for her touch. She slipped free of the confining pockets and, drawing back the waistband of his pants by a belt loop, she slipped an ambitious hand down the softly furred path of his lower belly.

Damien finally lifted his mouth from her, his head snapping back into an arch as he groaned with the magnitude of pleasure that her touch closing around him delivered. It was as if her touch were sweet venom, and this time she was the one who had struck quickly. An answering pulse of fresh heat and arousal pumped through him, and his hand closed with convulsive intensity on her squirming body. Between the explorations and the feeding, they were both lost in a heady high of sensation.

Damien and Syreena suddenly slid down the wall, landing in a twisted combination of hands and bodies. Syreena snaked herself around him in every way she could manage, and it was almost all Damien could manage just to help her by holding on to her.

He had craved her for too long, wanted her so much. Now she was invading him both inside and out, working a wicked feminine magic that could never have a measure. Damien reached to free himself from his clothing, finding her hands helping him as he slid free of the restrictive slacks, eventually allowing him to kick them away.

She was on her back, beneath his weight, and welcoming him to lie heavily against her. She slid her legs around him, pulling him down onto the center of her body, scraping her fingers through his beard as she reached to caress his ears and neck and back. She reached for him with her mouth, finding him more than eager to comply with her demand for a kiss. He was burning up with heat now, all of it hers in one form or another, and he was reeling with the sear of it. He felt her with every inch of his being as he scorched her in return with a violently passionate kiss. She was gasping for air in breathless little bursts that hummed down his spine.

He let her breathe, sliding down her sinful form until his mouth was coasting over every inch of her lavender-scented skin. He laved shoulders and neck, the insides of both wrists and elbows, and a path across her delicious belly. He briefly nipped at her hips on each side, then traveled a voracious track back up her rolling stomach and the ledge of her rapidly heaving rib cage. He suddenly shot out to catch her nipple between his teeth, sucking her with a deep, new hunger that made her squirm in shocking delight.

His work at her breast bordered on savage. She felt the telltale scrape of super-sharp fangs, the swirl of his tongue teasing her against the exposed canines in an astoundingly sensual stroke. She cried out, her hands gripping his shoulders as she moved in wild response.

Hmm, someone's a little on the kinky side.

The thought flitting through her mind in his deep, speculative voice made her laugh in blind joy.

"Damien," she uttered hoarsely. "Forgive me. Please . . ."

Damien closed his eyes briefly, then kissed her breastbone up to the little hollow in her throat. He lifted his head and looked down into her eyes. They were a combination of great passion and great anxiety. He could smell the adrenaline on her, the scent heady under the lavender.

"And if I do not forgive you, Syreena?"

"Then just make love to me," she whispered, half in pain, half in pleading. "Even if it will ever be just this once. I don't care anymore. I just know what I want, and I want you."

"What part of me, sweetling?" he asked as he shifted forward against her, pushing so that he slid hot and hard through the slippery moisture just outside of the sanctuary that so impatiently awaited him. "This part?"

"Damien!" she gasped, the upward arch of her questing body returning his naughty caress measure for measure.

Damien clenched his teeth shut on a deep groan that shuddered violently out of him. He braced a hand on the floor, grasped her thigh firmly, and did the complete opposite of his intentions.

He meant to settle her down away from him, to give himself the space to hear the answers she still had not clarified for him. But he found that he could not do so. He could not leave her or remain outside of her any longer. He surged forward suddenly, sliding through a torrent of moisture and heat, pushing into devastating tightness of muscle made tighter by the unexpectedness of his breach of her body as she reacted to him. Syreena's neck arched wildly, her shoulders half lifting from the floor as he made his remarkable invasion. She realized how little she had known or imagined about the reality of this moment. There was no describing such a thing, now or ever.

For a man with no true circulation, it was amazing how he seemed to pulse inside her. He was crafted as if to suit her needs, making their fit together a stunning lesson in the truth of fate and being two halves of a perfect whole.

"Sweet Goddess, I must have been mad," she gasped as she writhed beneath him in blatantly honest pleasure.

Damien smiled at that, understanding the sentiment perfectly. She was precious and perfect for him, and nothing he did or felt would ever succeed in changing that.

He pushed a bit deeper into her, thrilling in both the way she felt and the way she reacted. The joining of their bodies was a bliss of perfection, and he almost could not bear to change it from exactly what it was.

Almost.

He covered her mouth, kissing her deeply and catching all the startled sounds she made as he moved in a full stroke within her. The honesty in the clutch of her hands and eager body was almost unbearable.

Almost.

Damien lost his sense of everything around him, save her and her wild little body squirming with very vocal pleasure beneath the magic he made within her. He slowly searched her for what would pleasure her the most, shifting a little higher on her when he realized it touched her just right that way.

In the beat of just three strokes, she went from unbelievable pleasure to utter ecstasy. What he was doing to her was nothing short of mysticism. Here, she thought numbly, was a true user of magic. Only he was not evil or an enemy. It was the magic of fairy stories and angels, good and sweet and clean.

And all the stronger for its purity.

Damien watched as her eyes closed and her face became a map of beautiful reaction to his every action. As his entire being locked off in cell after cell of blinding need, he knew he was about to have an experience unmeasured in his lifetime.

He loved her.

He loved her madly, and it made all the difference in the universe.

"Syreena," he rasped hoarsely, suddenly needing to say her name. "Sweet Syreena."

The deeper he moved into her, the more he felt like he was becoming a part of her. If someone could truly possess another person, she was doing so to him. Everything about her was blending into him, especially the unchecked squeaks and gasps of delight that came faster and faster from her. She was heading for an astonishing crescendo that he thought he could not even begin to understand. He would find out within moments that he was absolutely wrong in that assumption. They became like a single consciousness, feeling the mixture of their fervent bodies from all sides and all emotions.

Damien could no longer hold any part of himself in check. He made love to her with an untamed passion that bordered on brutality. She only encouraged him further, thrilling in the beautiful form of abuse they both needed with a zeal beyond reason and well beyond three-dimensional sanity.

Damien reached an unimaginable summit, the sudden theft of his sense and equilibrium leaving him without center or focus as he detonated into a powerful, pulsing climax. He was dimly aware of vocalizing ferociously, and of her matching exclamation as she imploded with ecstasy. She seemed to be a vortex, a Vampire in and of herself, drinking from him this time with her hungry, sucking body. He was her prey, and delightfully so. She could drain him dry for all he cared. Now and in the future. He had hardly known her when he knew he would lay down his life for her.

Damien finally fell against her with a disbelieving groan. Her power over him was complete. If he had not been lost before, he certainly was now. She panted hard and heavy beneath him, still floating somewhere between completion and consciousness. That familiar limpness wended up through her arms, and he felt her touch fall away as her overtaxed body swirled into a half-conscious state.

He recalled that he had no way of knowing what other ramifications there would be, so he took the opportunity to draw them both up from the floor. He smiled as she lolled against him with a sound of postcoital delight. He tucked her into his bed, sliding in after her immediately. He could not remember ever being this warm in all of his life, and he did not want to shed any of the heat too soon.

Damien turned her so her back was to him, and then drew her securely to his chest. He wrapped a tight, possessive arm across her waist. Not that he thought she would, but just in case, she would not be able to go anywhere without him knowing about it.

Chapter 10

Damien woke with a start, surprised to realize he had fallen asleep.

The first thing he noticed was that Syreena was no longer in his arms.

She was sprawled across him, and, to his amusement, had somehow managed to turn completely upside down in the bed so her foot was nestled snugly in the vicinity of his neck. He raised his head slightly to look at her, getting a rather stimulating view of her bare bottom, and realizing his feet and ankles were sheeted in her brown and gray hair. Somewhere between her back and his thighs, they were twisted up into the bedspread, tied together like an odd pair of Siamese twins.

Feeling extremely happy just because she was there, he turned his head and kissed the bottom of her nearby foot.

She jerked in her sleep, sliding against him for a moment, and then settled down into deep, even breaths again.

"Oh, you must be kidding," he whispered to the silent room, biting his lip hard to keep from laughing out loud.

He instantly reached for the same foot and drew a quick finger up the instep.

Damien had to dodge to keep from getting kicked in the head.

Syreena, heir to the Lycanthrope throne, was ticklish.

Unable to resist, he reached for her again.

"Touch my foot again and I will take your head off," came the sudden mumbled threat through the muffling of bedclothes.

"Too good to be tickled, Princess?" he teased, ignoring her warning and attacking her foot in earnest.

Syreena yelped, trying to kick him again, rolling over in her sudden wakefulness.

"I'm warning you!" she shouted. Her threat came out as a squeal, however, stealing its intended punch.

To escape him, she slithered right off the bed and onto the floor. Damien dared to look over the edge of the bed in search of her.

"Come now, pouting does not become a Princess."

"A black eye doesn't become a Prince," she countered tartly, tossing back her hair as she sat up. "You are not a very considerate bed partner," she accused.

"I heard no complaints last night," he mused, giving her the cocky combination of half a smile and a lifted eyebrow.

"Perhaps that is because you were snoring too loud to hear them." She laughed when his expression immediately altered to a frown. "What? Too good to snore, Prince?"

"Why is it that when you say Prince like that, I feel like a German shepherd?"

"If the breed fits . . ."

She got to her feet and shook her hair back into place with a primp worthy of her royal status. Then she settled back onto the bed, sitting to face him and studying his amused expression.

"You know, I never actually considered it before . . ." She

trailed off as if contemplating her thoughts. Damien was not fooled. He knew a setup when he saw one.

He indulged her, however.

"Considered what?"

"I never thought you might actually be *fun*. Here I was thinking sex was going to be my only entertainment."

"I see. I guess you have to consider yourself fortunate then. I, however . . ."

Syreena smirked as he teased her with her own verbal trick. "However?" she prompted dutifully.

"I think I am the more fortunate one."

The answer was surprisingly serious, taking her a little off guard.

"How do you see that?" she asked, looking away from him to smooth absent fingers over the sheet beneath her.

"Because no one has ever been in the position to tell me that I snore before, and I find I am quite delighted to hear it."

Syreena looked immediately taken aback by the comment. "How is that possible?"

"Because I have never been in the habit of sleeping in the presence of others. Call it a Vampiric trust issue."

Syreena felt the impact of the remark quite keenly. In an instant, it rewrote over a dozen suppositions she had made that were in error. "I never thought about that before."

"I always have to think about it. I find I like my head securely attached to my shoulders. I would have lost it long ago if I were easily able to trust."

"But Jasmine . . . ?"

"Jasmine?" He chuckled. "Jasmine would rather run naked in daylight than sleep near the likes of me. She is much smarter than you are."

"I am getting that impression." She leaned forward, lying over his chest until they were practically bumping noses. "Can I ask you something without you getting bent out of shape?"

"You practically accused me of carnal intentions with another woman less than a minute ago. If that does not disturb me, I do not see what can."

"Can I have it back?"

Damien blinked questioningly for a second, and then came that slow smile of comprehension. "I did not think you had noticed."

She laughed at him and held out her hand.

He slid his hand beneath his pillow and then reached to give her what she wanted.

Gold and moonstones fell into a glittering pile in her upturned palm.

Jasmine was sitting in the main parlor with one leg slung over the arm of the sofa, the other braced on a coffee table, as she slowly leafed through a slightly mildewed volume that was wider than her lap and thicker than the width of both her hands laid end to end.

She leafed through the pages slowly, reading with interest.

"Is that from the Library?"

Jasmine looked up when Syreena addressed her, giving the Princess a long, disapproving appraisal. The Lycanthrope female was wearing one of Damien's silk shirts, the extra fabric hanging to her knees. She was not very big, Jasmine thought. She could not see how Syreena could ever prevail in a fight, yet she was supposed to be some kind of an expert at Lycanthrope battle techniques.

Jasmine was unimpressed. Considering the fact that the Lycanthropes had been on the losing side the entire three hundred years of war with the Demons, it was not saying very much.

The female Vampire had been aware of Syreena's presence in the house immediately upon her return from her most recent foray into the Nightwalker Library. Judging by the clothing she wore and the loud laughter coming from the vicinity of Damien's bedroom earlier, she imagined that they had found a way to reconcile. This was also unimpressive. Jasmine was glad Damien was happy now, but the memory of his despair was too keen to be easily forgiven.

"Yes, it is. Your sister assigned a librarian a couple of days ago so we might begin to take selective volumes with us. It is easier to study in familiar surroundings, without so many strangers around."

"She did? Whom did she choose?"

"A sexy little thing," Jasmine said with a smile. "Dark and pretty, beauty mark on her neck." Jasmine's smile grew with taunting mischief as she purposely noted the area her kind was notorious for exploiting.

"Jinaeri," Syreena said absently. "I see."

"If you do not mind, I was just getting into this."

Jasmine dismissed her without waiting for a polite response, turning a page in spite of the fact that she had not finished the previous one.

Syreena was not dense. She knew Jasmine did not like her. Normally, she wouldn't care. Jasmine was important to Damien, however, so she figured she had to care. There would be time to improve the situation later, so she left the other woman to her reading.

She continued to move through the enormous house that Damien called home. The windows were all tinted so dark they were nearly black, except those in the library and the kitchen, which were stained glass. She understood the kitchen, because they had little to no use for it, so the colored light coming through was weak enough in case someone had to enter the room, yet able to add enough light to add appeal to the otherwise darkened hallways just off it.

Damien had warned her not to enter the library before she had even left the bedroom. Although the windows were stained, the balcony doors leading into the upper level of the room were not. They only used that room at night, which was why Jasmine was using the parlor to study.

The Princess touched absent fingers to her collar. Unlike her sister, she knew the secret to putting hers back on. She wasn't supposed to know it until after she was wed, but she had picked it up covertly from an instructive manual they thought they had sufficiently hidden from her. She did not know how to take it off. Now, however, all she needed to do was ask Damien to do so.

She had thought she would feel enormous relief at the proof of the removal of the necklace, but she had not. Not because she was not reassured, because she supposed that she was. She had not felt relief because she had already given way to her convictions. She supposed Damien had known this, and that was why he had removed it from her as she slept. He had waited until it became an issue that had nothing to do with their decisions to choose one another.

Well, her choice was most definitely made. There was no turning back for her now. Though there were additional ceremonies to formalize such things, the minute Damien had breached her maidenhead, he had become wed to her soul.

As if the sexual act had anything to actually do with it, she mused with humor. His soul had captured hers long before that. That and his wisdom and perfect words. His gentleness of touch and his understanding. How she had ever resisted, *why* she had ever resisted, was now completely beyond her understanding.

She sighed, looking around the kitchen for something to eat, having little hope of actually finding anything considering it was the home of a Vampire.

He was exhausting.

Granted, she was working on a reduced blood supply after she had fed his hunger the night before, but he had also proven his stamina and appetite to be worthy of his legend. He had woken her repeatedly through the dark hours, making fine love to her body, always with the same intensity as the first time. Though he had experienced no pain the last time he had taken her blood, he had not taken it again. She had mistakenly thought that it was a major part of lovemaking with a Vampire, one that she could very easily get used to because of its powerful aphrodisiacal abilities and its blatant eroticism. His passion, however, reached the same extraordinary heights no matter what he did or did not do to her. She had never realized the body could be manipulated to pleasure in so many ways.

Lessons on sex and sexuality paled in comparison to the actuality of it.

Especially the part they neglected to mention about how sore it left one. It was a physically demanding workout, one that taxed even her athletic and well-trained body.

She realized that there was not even a refrigerator in the kitchen. Not so much as an icebox. She made a sound of consternation.

"Hungry, pet?"

She turned with a start. Now at full power, Damien could once again use the little tricks of stealth and strength that were seemingly an automatic part of his makeup. He had crept up behind her without raising so much as a hackle on the back of her neck.

"You need to teach me how you do that," she said with envy as he moved to wrap a single muscular arm around the slight circumference of her waist. He drew her tightly to himself, swinging her slightly as he leaned in to kiss her collarbone where the gaping of his shirt in front left it exposed.

"It is a trick of the mind. I would be very interested to see if you could accomplish it one day. I would not put it past you."

"Neither would I," she agreed smugly, making him laugh at her.

His laughter vibrated over her skin, giving her a shiver as he moved his mouth in a line of slow, moist kisses up her throat and neck. She giggled when his whiskers coasted over her damp skin, and she squirmed out of immediate reach of his mouth.

"I warned you about that!" she scolded him, pushing at his chest when he would not allow her to wriggle free.

"So you are not ticklish there only if I am biting you?" he concluded in delight with a flash of mischief going off in his eyes.

"Some Vampire you are. Ooh. Watch out! The Prince of Vampires might tickle you to a horrible death!" She threw the back of her hand up to her mouth and went as wide-eyed as a serial heroine. "Somebody save me!"

"Did anyone ever tell you that you are a troublemaker?" he asked dryly, reaching to pull down the obnoxious hand blocking her lips from his.

He ended the entire repartee by kissing her into obedient silence. The kiss was just as stimulating to her now as it had been from the start. The only improvement was in her skill, she felt. She was learning the ways of his mouth and his kisses, just as she would learn the topography she used to fly from point A to point B when she was the falcon. Every crest and every valley was a marker, his clean, masculine taste and the dominant sweep of his tongue like road signs and landmarks to guide her.

Within the span of a minute, Damien had her body melting against his, as if she were made of a soft, pliable clay he could mold perfectly to the bend of his body. She became very aggressive with her kiss, in spite of the relaxation of the rest of her. Syreena knew best what would please him. A lick. A nip. Unmatchable appetite for him that always floored him in its intensity and abandon. He could bend her over backward, as he was almost doing now, with the ardor of his kiss, and she would gladly accept it. More than acceptance. Encouragement. She had a way of making attractive, compelling sounds of delight and invitation.

When he finally was able to make himself withdraw from her hot little mouth, he did not go very far. She was clinging to him like a second skin, a leg snaked around him, arms wound over his back and shoulders, and her entire torso clinging to his like a magnet.

"Syreena," he said with soft relief as he pulled her sweet face into the curve of his neck.

Syreena knew every nonverbal sentiment that came with the action. She felt it just the same.

"I am very fortunate," she whispered into his ear. "I know that now. From this moment on, I will always find my way back to you, Damien. I will know that your kiss, your touch, and your warm sensitivity will always be waiting patiently for me, just as I will always make my heart your home, so you always have a place to come back to." She kissed his neck with a sweetness that rang like a poignant bell through his spirit. "If you ever did hurt me—and believe me, I know I am well deserving of it after what you went through—but if we had a misunderstanding, I would find you or wait for you or anything I had to do to make it better."

Damien swallowed as emotion rose like tight fingers under his skin. She was making a confession that could potentially make her weak to him and give him the power to make a slave of her emotions and promises. It was a measure of trust from her that he had not expected. Time would bring more depth like it; time and familiarity. There was no arguing that they were still learning about each other and, given their varied lifestyles, a great deal of understanding would need to come.

It was clear to him that when Syreena defeated an enemy, she did it entirely or not at all. All or nothing. Independent woman who made choices for herself, or automaton at everyone else's command. It was a bemusing trait for a woman who played the role of a royal advisor, someone who had to exploit the gray areas of a situation at every turn. He could see the benefits of decisive thinking, of course. Syreena was the one who would agree or disagree with a monarch who might one day wish to go to war.

There were very few gray areas in war.

She had always had a strong opinion, always fearlessly expressing it. She had just never expressed her opinions about what she wanted. Now that she had, now that he was what she wanted, he knew he would never be able to do anything to change it. He was already irrevocably attached to her, his shadow sewn to her feet, in a manner of speaking, and he could not imagine taking himself away from her and managing to survive the segregation.

It would only grow stronger over time. However, if he did try to walk away from her, he had no doubt that she would hunt him down and force him to keep every verbal and nonverbal promise they had made to one another these past few days.

"I would not punish you on purpose," he said to her in quiet admonishment. "I am not capable of being that petty."

"I know that. I only said I would deserve it. I cannot imagine that we will never argue. I know that one day we will have a disagreement. Possibly a very bad one. If I thought this was all going to be sunshine and glorious sex, I would be a naïve and silly female."

"You are neither of those," he assured her with a chuckle. "Glorious, hmm?"

She giggled, nipping at his sensitive neck in punishment. "As if your ego requires any stroking," she remarked.

"I was not thinking about my ego, actually . . ." he murmured suggestively, reaching for her hips and rear, sliding his hands with clear appetite and sensuality over them.

"Damien," she scolded, squirming against his body. "Damien, I'm hungry," she complained. His hand continued to run the intimate curve of her backside, his fingers slipping beneath the bottom of the shirt so he could reach her bare skin.

His hands and wickedly adept fingers, she decided, were lethal. The grace with which he always seemed to move made for a flow in his touch that seemed perfectly uninterrupted. It was mesmerizing and easily addicting. It took a dizzying five minutes of standing under the enchantment of his touch before she remembered to protest again. Her skin was numb or tingling in slow paths that swirled her entire body, everywhere his clever caress had swept over her. She had to drag herself out from under his weighted spell in order to speak.

"Damien . . ."

He chose that moment to slide both of his hands up over her belly, under her shirt. His fingers splayed over the heat and softness of her skin as he slowly slid them over her breasts, her peaked nipples being burned by the continuing stroke as he continued to let them flow without stopping over her skin until they reached her shoulders, then her neck, then her hair.

By the time he reversed the route, she was moaning softly, her breath rasping out of her so hard that she began to feel the dizzy rush of hyperventilation. All she could do was cling to his shoulders, feeling muscles shift beneath her fingertips as his arms moved to access her heated body.

"I am hungry, too," he whispered, pausing to toy with her earlobe and the entire sensitive circumference of her ear. "I believe my appetite for your delicacies will prove to be insatiable, sweetling."

"I am getting that idea," she responded breathlessly.

When his hands reached her bottom again, they gripped her tightly and pulled her up his body. He turned toward a nearby countertop, bracing them against it as he slid forward between her knees. He drew her up tight and close so she could only look into his face and his darkly intent eyes. His hands still crept over her, but this time he moved down her belly, over her navel, and on to the softest, silkiest skin he could ever imagine. She gave a little wriggle of momentary protest, but he had her locked up tight around him.

His fingers slid into honeyed heat, intimate places flushed with arousal and nerves that were sensitive and very susceptible to his skills. Syreena gasped, a pleasured sound that made him smile with knowing confidence.

"There now, let's ease your hunger, Princess," he mocked her in sexy playfulness.

She laughed at him, a sound crossed between her amusement at his delight in mischievousness, and the incredible response she was having to his manipulation of her pleasure centers.

"Not working?" he asked. "We can try mind over matter, then."

His free hand closed around the back of her neck, holding her head in a locked grip so she could not look away from his deep eyes. Syreena's pupils widened as she felt him passing into her thoughts and perceptions. It felt, for a moment, as if he was crowding her inside her own head. But within half a minute, his consciousness had spooned itself against hers, catching on to the rhythm of her thoughts and functions.

Instantly, Damien gave her a new understanding of being touched everywhere at once. This time, she truly did feel him all over her skin, not a single inch of it deprived of an encompassing stroking sensation. She shuddered hard and groaned with unmanageable pleasure. Damien's mouth fell over hers, muffling her intensifying cries with the play of tastes and tongues. He manipulated her as if he were sculpting art, running with intimacy over every place he had come to know so well. He blended the mastery of touch, kiss, and thoughts together, whipping her up into something light enough to defy gravity. He did not even skip a beat as he freed himself of his clothing and brought himself smoothly inside the trembling trap of her hot body.

His sudden invasion sent her spiking off into uncharted sensations of explosive pleasure. She screamed into the seal of his mouth, clutching him tightly enough for her nails to pierce his skin. He refused to release her from that peak, conning her systems into believing they could maintain the brutal crest the entire time he made fast and fierce love to her. Her wild, gasping reactions and the pulsing hold of her pulled at him like a merciless whirlpool, drawing everything violently toward it without prejudice. He groaned deeply, the cadence of the sound matching the maddening tempo of his thrusts into her.

Syreena couldn't even breathe anymore to scream. She was arched back into a silent whipcord shriek of blinded bliss. In a sudden frenzy of movement, as if he could not seat himself deep enough within her to ever give his soul satisfaction, he reached the ferocious culmination he was seeking so aggressively.

In a moment, Syreena was able to catch the breath she needed in order to cry out as he finally released her from that mental crest of fulfillment. Her entire body seized fitfully in his grip, and he held her tightly in order to absorb it into himself. She was slick with perspiration, so it was not an easy task. Luckily, she soon settled down with a sudden increase of weight, dropping forward against him. She was gasping for breath, her struggle for air punctuated by the occasional disbelieving giggle.

She laughed even harder when he drew their entwined bodies away from the counter and dropped with obvious weakness onto a nearby bench in the breakfast nook.

"Nice nook," she chuckled.

"Nice cranny," he rejoined, wiggling his eyebrows lecherously.

Syreena laughed so hard that she nearly fell out of his lap.

In the hallway, leaning against the wall just outside the entrance to the kitchen, stood Jasmine. She had turned away from the scene a moment before Damien's turn in position would have revealed her. He was so wrapped up in his new toy, literally, that he had not noticed her observation for even a second.

Jasmine was beginning to realize that she was going to end up paying a heavy price for her monarch's happiness. Maybe not right away, but sometime very soon, she would be forced to leave his household. The truth of the matter was, she was far too selfish for her happiness for him to ever outweigh her own self-interests. The Lycanthrope had breezed into their life and changed everything in the matter of a heartbeat.

A heartbeat, compared to five hundred years of friendship.

And the heartbeat was clearly going to win.

Jasmine wished she had the guts to stick it out, but again her feelings for Damien interfered. If she stayed, she would end up in a confrontation with Syreena, and it would probably be a very bad one. Damien loved Jasmine, but he was clearly *in* love with the little Lycanthrope tart. That meant that anything the two women did to hurt one another would end up hurting him instead.

That was an unacceptable consequence.

Jasmine reached up to brush away the single hot tear that had escaped her control.

Whatever would she do without him?

Damien walked through the quiet house looking for Jasmine. Syreena had left in search of something to eat, promising to return soon. He had passed Jas in the parlor earlier, but a glance told him she was no longer there. He followed his senses to the cellar. Blasted out of solid rock, the cellar was a vault of safety in the event that they felt the need to protect themselves as they slept. There was only one entrance, and it was invisible to human eyes. It also required great strength to remove and replace the stone portal leading to it.

He was disappointed to realize Jasmine had chosen to sleep behind it. He understood it was probably because she did not trust the new presence in their household, and he knew he would have been very likely to do the same thing had the tables been turned.

Still, he could not help his moment of dejection. It passed quickly, however, and he decided to let her rest in peace. They would have plenty of opportunity to talk about the situation later.

Meanwhile, he returned to the ground floor, resealing the hidden entrance to the stairways leading down to the cellar. California homes did not often have basements. It was impractical when there were fault lines rocking and rolling every chance they got. No one would even think to look for such a place, never mind a hidden one. That, plus the heavy bolts on the opposite side, made it virtually impossible to discover.

Damien moved back into the parlor and sat down in the seat Jasmine had been in earlier. Sitting on the table across from him was the volume she was currently studying. With all that had happened, he had practically forgotten about the Library. It occurred to him that he had not had the chance to pick up even a single book from the vast hidden Nightwalker vault.

Amused with himself as he recalled exactly what his distractions were, he stood up and left the book untouched. His desire to shower and change before Syreena returned was stronger.

Jasmine waited until Damien was in the shower.

She moved to the book Damien had left untouched and swept it up in protective arms.

The volume was three times as old as Damien was and it held the explanations to a lot of elusive questions. Yes, these questions were probably answered repetitively in the other books in the Nightwalker Library, but the difference was that Damien was not likely to appear there anytime soon. He no longer seemed interested in such information, no longer seemed to need it, so she had no motivation to share it. If he asked her directly, that would be another story. For the moment, she would be more protective of the old compendium.

What Damien did not know, hopefully would not hurt him.

Chapter 11

It was mid-dusk, so it was safe for Syreena to travel.

She was not familiar with the area, but it was easy enough to follow the human roads to the rather large town several miles down the shoreline.

It would have taken less time if she had not been forced to walk.

Damien's marvelous ability to transform, like the Mistrals', allowed his clothing to take shape with him or whatever it was exactly that allowed that to happen. Since Lycanthropes were not so fortunate, walking was Syreena's only alternative unless she wanted to end up shopping in the nude. She did not wish to attract that kind of attention, of course. As it was, Damien had forced her to borrow something of Jasmine's. The female Vampire apparently did not believe in wearing dresses. Syreena felt a bit confined in the silk blouse and kid breeches, not to mention the fact that Jasmine was quite a bit taller than she was.

With her health returned to her, including the additional bounce in her step, the Princess made fast work of the trip. Shortly after arriving at the booming seaside town, however, she recalled the reason why she avoided human dwellings and metropolises.

There were too damn many of them.

It was always overwhelming to her. That was probably because she had not moved about in an area of this type very often, so she did not get the chance to get used to it. Were she a Mistral, she would probably have a heart attack from fear on the spot. To a species who felt, literally, that three was a crowd, this would be a nightmare.

Considering how the human population had grown so rapidly in just her lifetime, Syreena could not fathom how any Nightwalkers were going to manage to remain in perfect isolation for much longer. Even the wild areas humans put aside for conservation efforts were swarming with scientists and tourists. The Monks had always believed that nature would find a way to create balance, but they had never been able to satisfy her points about extinction. Siena was more practical, as were Noah and Damien, she suspected. Siena had made certain the forest land the village and the majority of the royal Lycanthrope territory was situated upon had been purchased a long time ago. What they did not own belonged to communal parks or the government.

What will keep the Nightwalkers from going the way of those species now lost to the planet forever? she wondered. At least in Russia, politics and inhospitable winters had kept the tundra and other lands undeveloped. Even so, species like the Siberian tiger were fast fading from their lands. If something as beautiful as that subspecies of tiger could be so easily disrespected and senselessly murdered, what would prevent the same from happening to Nightwalkers humans deemed dangerous or somehow unworthy?

Humans obviously did not have the same regard for Nightwalkers as Nightwalkers had for humans. The hunters that plagued Damien's and Syreena's people were an example of that. The only defense Nightwalkers had were their enormous powers. Unfortunately, that was balanced with a weak-

ness to daylight that could be too easily exploited. That was
worsened by the centuries of folklore about them in human
mythos. There were grains of truth in every one of those
weird and wild tales, as Damien had once pointed out to her.
Enough truth to do terrible damage.

Why she was worrying about such things escaped her for
a moment. As she entered the market, she realized it was because, for the very first time, she was considering what would
happen in her personal future. Her world of concern had always been limited to what others wished of her. That circle
had widened only slightly to include Siena's interests and
well-being fifteen years ago. In spite of helping Siena run
their populace, she did not have the passion for it that her
sister had. She used logic to best decide on things for Lycanthrope welfare as a whole. Siena used that *and* her vehement
heart. Syreena had always been convinced that this was why
she could never be the queen her sister was.

Now Damien and, she had to admit, others were making
their mark on her and this was broadening her concerns. Because they were making themselves indelible parts of her
emotions and psyche, how could she not begin to feel passion for things that would concern their safety? She was not
a cold person as many thought; she was merely inexperienced with certain feelings.

Something she seemed to be making up for at a double-
timed pace, she thought with a smile.

Syreena scooped up a small handheld basket and walked
the happy convenience of the market. The electricity and the
refrigeration units were something she had grown to miss
over the past years. Lycanthropes loved modern comforts
and conveniences, even if they did live in caves, but ever
since ambassadors from the Vampire and Demon courts had
begun to stay in the Lycanthrope court, Siena had ordered
everything be retrograded back to the gas lighting systems
and other nontechnological conveniences. The chemistry of
those two groups of Nightwalkers did not agree with tech-

nology on any level, really. Things had a way of blowing up, shorting out, or otherwise malfunctioning. Now that the Demon Elijah was a permanent fixture at the court, and considering that her new mate was a Vampire, Syreena supposed this was the closest she would get to electricity.

She made some quick choices, so ravenous for so many reasons that she had eaten two apples out of the pre-weighted bag before she even reached the register.

Money was an interesting concept to her. She was used to a royal lifestyle where everything was provided for her and money was just numbers on sheets of paper that listed household expenses and such. She handed over what Damien had given her and got strange looks when she actually laughed at the feel of cold coins in her palm. She was still inspecting their shape and design as she walked out of the market.

She had barely cleared the parking lot when all of her senses suddenly flared with alert.

Someone was tracking her.

She wasn't immediately alarmed. It was not Ruth's way to track someone of her ilk, giving her prey the opportunity to become aware of her presence behind them. Syreena was suspicious, however, because she sensed that it was not a human who was slipping from shadow to shadow behind her.

Neither was it Damien. She would have known that immediately. He was fast becoming an extension of herself, so it would be like not knowing where her left hand was.

She dropped her coins into her shopping bag and absently ran a nervous finger along the waistband of the snug breeches. Fleeing from a loose dress was one thing; escaping these clothes if she needed to change rapidly was close to impossible.

So be it, she thought firmly to herself. She was no slouch at hand to hand, in spite of her failures with Ruth. She was not the first Nightwalker to have been harmed or even defeated by that Demon's wicked power, and some of those who had met defeat at Ruth's hands had been the most powerful creatures on the planet.

She let her pursuer follow her as far as he was going to. The closer she got to Damien's territory, the better off she would be.

Just in case.

She felt him closing in on her—and it was definitely a male—just before she reached the borders of Damien's property. Though it was still some distance into the acreage to the house, she marked the fact that she was being confronted before she could reach that specific border. It told her that whoever was behind her was aware of its significance.

She stopped short and turned to face her stalker. "I know you are there."

He stepped out of the shadows instantly. He was tall and slim, pale and redheaded. Wild curling hair had been forced into a tail very much like Damien's, only not as sleek or neat as the Prince managed. He was giving her a smile, holding out his palms in a neutral gesture.

"No harm intended. I was just watching out for you."

A Vampire. She had never met him before, but she knew he was by his lack of heat and his classic Vampiric features. Plus, he had no discernable pulse.

"Damien sent you?" she asked calmly.

"Well, after a fashion. He would not tell me to do that, because I am certain you would take a bit of offense to the idea."

"You would be correct. So you took it upon yourself to offend me?"

"Not intentionally," he assured her. "I am just doing what any friend of the Prince would do when it comes to the protection of his . . . other friends."

Syreena knew what he meant by "other friends." Her brow furrowed in momentary consternation. Since no one but Damien and Jasmine knew about her relationship with the Prince—no one from his world that she knew of, at least—

that would mean that Damien had run out and sent someone to tail her the moment she had left his home . . . or that Jasmine had done something similar.

Since Jasmine seemed to be a bit too cold toward her to care, Syreena was forced to assume Damien was responsible. It disturbed her to think that he did not trust her to take care of herself. Was that the impression she had given him? Granted, he had been forced to rescue her and she hadn't given the impression that she was very good at making the best choices for herself, but she thought he knew her just a little better than that.

"Who are you?"

"Nicodemous. But everyone calls me Nico."

"Well, Nico, I was curious as to just how far we were going to carry this charade," she asked, watching him with a neutral expression, betraying nothing of her feelings of the moment.

He became instantly uncomfortable. "Charade?" he echoed.

"Yes. Do we walk up to the house boldly together, or do we pretend my Prince has succeeded in guarding me without my knowledge?"

"Your . . ." He relaxed, smiled boyishly and chuckled. "Your Prince would be a bit put out if he saw us walking up to the manse together."

"Then I suppose you should get back to your skulking," she said, giving him a dismissing wave as she turned to continue her journey.

"But!" he said quickly, reaching for her arm to pull her to a stop. "But I would not wish to lie to him."

Syreena turned to face him slightly, looking down at his fingers with an expression of warning disdain that came with genetic royal birthright. He did not seem to get the hint, his hold around her bicep growing firmer. She smiled disarmingly, turned full around to face him, and smacked him in his nose with the heel of her palm so hard that she could hear it break. She dropped her bag, using the arm he held to wrap it around the one still clinging to her. She snagged him like a merciless python, twisting bone and muscle into opposing directions until he cried out a curse and buckled to his knee. She followed through by kneeing him in the throat.

She couldn't make him gag for breath, and she had only won a slight show of blood from his nose, but she was quite satisfied when he fell back into the dirt. She stepped forward, putting her foot firmly on his neck and leaning at least half her weight forward onto it.

"Now," she said calmly. "Keeping in mind I can remove your head from your shoulders with a single shift in weight if I wanted to, I think I should like you to tell me what you are really doing following me."

"I already told y—"

She leaned forward onto her knee, cutting him off. She felt his hands closing around her ankle, but he was in for a surprise if he thought to overpower her.

"You just happen to be following the Vampire Prince's woman, who you just happen to know about when no one else does, and then just happen to stop her twenty or so yards from the border of the Prince's property and coincidentally putting me just out of range of his sense of telepathy? He could sense me, sense you, but not sense that you were endangering me. Not until I cross that little invisible line."

He was turning whiter than normal, but he still managed to glare at her. "You are not human!" he croaked.

"Well . . . duh!" she said dryly. The remark made her realize he was probably too young to have the experience to tell the difference between humans and Lycanthropes in infrared. Youth often came hand in hand with ambition, not to mention rash stupidity. "Thought the Prince was slumming, did you? I am curious, though, what did you hope to get from me? Not the throne, I would hope. What were you going to do, beat him over the head with me?"

Syreena snorted in disgust at the impetuous Vampire who

clearly had all ambition and no plan. "I am going to let you go in about ten seconds," she told him. "If I were you, I would take a few factors into consideration. First, I can run twenty yards faster than you can get up and chase me, even if you *are* a Vampire. Secondly, if you caught me, I would not be this nice a second time. And lastly, if I bruised a single apple in that bag, I am going to change my mind and take your head off after all. If I were you, I would fly away very, *very* fast."

She did as promised, lifting up her foot and letting him scramble away. He turned toward her as if he was going to say something and she reached pointedly for her bag.

He ran, and then flew away from her.

"Children. You cannot live with them, you cannot kill them until they are older."

Syreena whirled around at the deep-voiced comment, gasping a moment before a second Vampire reached out to seize her violently by the neck with a powerful hand. He was tall, taller than Damien even, and he was enormous. She knew because he lifted her feet off the ground as he raised her by her neck to his eye level. Syreena struggled, but she got the impression she was like a fly crawling over his skin that was merely an annoyance and hardly worth noticing.

This was no child. This was a well-matured Vampire of indescribable power and unfathomable age.

"You shall have to forgive my son," he said to her, his dark mouth twitching with amusement as she was forced to stare into eyes as black as a moonless night. "He has his father's ambition but is as weak as his mother was."

The Vampire took too long a moment to inspect her. If not for the fact that she could hold her breath for a very long time, Syreena could have easily lost consciousness in that time.

"Clever of him to use his father's name, however," her captor continued conversationally. "Then when he fouled up you would run and tell Damien it was Nicodemous. Damien would come after me while my son ran off and cowered somewhere." Syreena saw the flick of nictitating membranes for a second. "A Lycanthrope? Interesting choice for a mistress."

Nicodemous jerked her closer, her legs knocking against him like those of a rag doll. He turned her head, inspecting her closely.

"Well, well," he mused, "someone took a bite on the wild side."

Syreena felt her time running out. She had no leverage in the air and she could not beat his strength any more than his son could beat hers. She tried to fight off panic so she could think about what she had been taught, what she knew.

"Yes. Do tell. What do they teach a Lycanthrope about how to kill a Vampire?"

Syreena cursed herself in her head. How could she have forgotten that he could get into her mind? She had to be more careful. If he could divine her thoughts, then he could manipulate them. She would not know which end was up if he decided to confuse her in such ways.

"In case you were wondering, I do not plan to use you to beat him over the head," Nicodemous continued smoothly. "Only to lure him out of that house of his. Damien I can handle, Damien *and* Jasmine is an entirely different story. Unfortunately, every time I turn around, she is in his pocket. Either her or some Demon. I suppose I could have used Jasmine and spared you all of this, but she is hell in a bitch's body. She would be too hard a fight if I expect to take on Damien right afterward. Besides, she clearly likes to ride the royal pony, so I imagine one Prince is as good as the next for her. I would hate to waste such a luscious opportunity. I bet Damien takes that opportunity every chance he gets—between passing fancies such as yourself, that is."

Syreena wondered for a moment why it was that people loved to talk so much when they were trying to kill someone. Then she jerked both her feet up and used his chest as a push-off to walk herself into a back flip.

She took his strength out of the equation. No one with a fixed wrist could maintain a hold on a rotating object, unless they wanted to break their wrist. Since she was working against his function and not his force, her neck slipped easily out of his grasp. She landed on her feet, kicking up roadside dust as she finally drew in a breath. It took everything she could muster to keep from gagging as she sucked air through her swelling throat. If she succumbed to a coughing fit, she would be little protection to herself.

Since she had done him no damage, he was able to recover quickly from his surprise at her escape. She grabbed the nearest thing she could, her shopping bag, and spinning once around hard, cracked him in the head with the full force of five pounds of apples, minus two. It was like hitting him with a rudimentary mace, only no spiked extras included.

He staggered under the blow, clearly shocked by her speed and her strength if the look on his face was anything to judge by. The truth of the matter was that she had no hope of fighting him hand to hand if it came down to brute force, and less of a chance if he had the opportunity to play with her head.

So she ran.

She made sure to focus and use all of her speed. He could catch her easily once he recovered, but that would be fine so long as she kept in the right direction and avoided mental games that might send her elsewhere.

Just because she crossed into Damien's range of perception also did not guarantee that he would perceive her. This Vampire could be strong enough to cloak her presence from him, or there could be a dozen other factors that could affect the outcome of the next few minutes.

Her pursuer did not hesitate to light out after her. Syreena tore at her blouse as she ran into Damien's territory. She had no choice but to risk a change half clothed. She could feel Nicodemous reaching for her.

Her one advantage of skill was her ability to change on the fly, so to speak. There were few who could do so with the ease and speed she did. So when Nicodemous grabbed for her arm, all he caught was the tips of feathers. The Vampire stumbled in shock when his hands came up all but empty, but recovered fast and leapt into the air after the peregrine.

Being smaller and quicker, she gained air and distance in that short heartbeat of advantage. If he was as strong as she suspected, however, he would catch her soon enough.

Her right wing suddenly struck something, spinning her nearly out of the sky. Pain blossomed along the right side of the falcon's form. Syreena realized too late that she had hit a tree. The Vampire had tricked her into believing she had cleared the treetops, so she had flown flat-out into a hard, stinging branch. She plummeted toward the ground precariously, and then finally managed to catch air with her uninjured wing. She reeled, spiraling down in a braking decent.

Nicodemous was hot on her heels as she struck the ground on running feet. Off balance and injured, she crashed to the forest floor, dead leaves and brush her only cushion as she skidded to a stop. The Princess did not even have a second to get off her back before he was on her.

He was not going to let her get even the slightest advantage this time. He bored into her with the blanketing fear that he could mentally drill into his prey. Her sister had the same gift in the form of the cougar's scream, only even more intense than the natural fear that cry instilled. So did Syreena, but the chilling cry of the falcon had left with its form.

Syreena let the terror he was feeding her wash over her. She merely relaxed and gave in to it. Adrenaline and fear-response chemicals burst into her blood, blinding panic overcame her every thought.

Damien swung around so fast as Syreena's screaming presence of fright bombarded him that he sent a heavy statue crashing over. The marble immediately burst around his feet as his head blossomed with terror and pain so overwhelming he could not see straight for the first twenty seconds.

Realizing what was happening, he cursed himself for wasting those twenty seconds as he ran out of the house. He did not change form, his speed and skill as the raven still leaving too much to be desired. He did not need to. He was like a black streak of lightning as he crossed scrub and forestland in a matter of a minute.

What in the world had he been thinking? He had known they were out there!

He just had not thought they would bother Syreena since no one knew her significance to him. It was an underestimation Syreena was now paying for.

Damien plowed into the altercation powered by pitch-black rage.

He leapt over Syreena and drove the force of his body into the attacking Vampire. The two males tumbled clear of Syreena, which was Damien's intention. Nicodemous tore over the ground on his back, the Prince driving hard into his chest so that when they finally braked to a halt, Damien's knee crunched down into ribs and breastbone.

"Nico, you miserable bastard, I will kill you for touching her!" Damien snarled, his fangs flashing with a wild roar as he drove his fist into his enemy's throat. His intention was to rip off the other man's head with his bare hands, but Nico was too powerful to make it that easy. He threw off the Prince, sending him flying back a good ten feet into the trunk of a mighty tree. The crack of wood under stress filled the area, echoing off every distant point it could reach.

Nicodemous gained his feet and turned to advance on the Prince with his own mad gleam of huge, pointed teeth and a vicious vocalization to match. Before he could advance on the stunned Prince who was, in essence, the real focus of his intentions, he was railroaded by a speedball of gray and brown hair. Damien's female was strong for her size, but what was more, she was smart. She went for his knees from behind, knocking all the support out from under him. He hit the ground, tumbling back over her. He instantly reached through his rage for the only thing he could see of her.

Her streaked hair.

His hand came away empty, save maybe two strands. Frustrated and in a fine rage, Nico turned his attention to Damien. The Prince had easily gained his feet, his bitch giving him the time he had needed to regain his equilibrium.

The larger male reached into his boot for a dagger and flung it at the advancing Prince.

Damien's hand moved with imperceptible speed and snatched the dagger out of the air right before it would have pierced his throat. The blade cut his hand with the impact, but it was incidental damage.

Nico realized he had just very effectively armed the Prince. Hand to hand was one thing, but when weapons became visible, it usually meant that blood began to flow. Lose enough blood, and lose the fight. The aggressor had drawn the first blood, and he took satisfaction in that as Damien's fingers dripped precious red fluid.

Nico reached for his second dagger, moving at Damien with a speed faster than even preternatural vision.

Damien felt the puncture of the weapon in his lower left side, but he took the damage in stride. He allowed the attack so he could wrap a powerful arm around Nico's throat. The dagger drove deeper into his midsection as he used all the force of his body to pin Nicodemous to his injured side and plunged the other stiletto into his back. The blade glanced off solid ribs, then found a mark between two of them, slicing through muscle, lungs, and liver with the ease of a thrust through water.

Nico grunted in pain, but both Vampires broke apart with weapons in hand. Most people did not realize it, but the drawing out of a blade hurt more than the going in. It also did a hell of a lot more damage.

Damien felt his blood soaking through his shirt and the waistband of his black denim jeans. He ignored the wound, however. In a battle between Vampires, it often came down to which one gave in to the fear of losing too much blood. It was a distraction that disrupted battle skills, but it was also nearly impossible to resist.

Damien had not lived to be 974 years old because he easily gave in to such things. It was the uncanniest part of his power. He had no fear, no consideration, for the prospect of his death.

The Vampires clashed and passed again, both drawing blood before stepping away. Damien lowered his head as he crouched, his eerie blue eyes looking deeply into Nico's black gaze. Manipulating the mind of another Vampire was an incredible feat of command. It was nearly impossible to do because they were always aware of the possibility of the attempt. Normally, neither could succeed in tricking the perceptions of the other.

But Damien was no normal Vampire.

Nicodemous charged Damien, but the Prince disappeared before his eyes. Sensing a trick, he whirled around, trying to break the illusion so he could seek his enemy's true location. All he saw was that infernal Lycanthrope falcon flying above his head.

Nico suddenly felt his body exploding from back to front, unimaginable pain tearing through his chest wall and his heart. He looked down in shock as a ragged branch protruded with a burst of blood through his chest.

He whipped around, staggering as he yanked the opposite end of the limb out of the hands of his attacker. His eyes widened with astonishment when he saw the Lycanthrope bitch standing where he had just stood, his blood sprayed across her bare skin and remnants of bark falling from the arm she wasn't favoring.

Nico whipped his head around to find the bird he had seen earlier. The deception exposed, he saw it for the raven that it actually was. Damien had used the bird to make him think he knew the location of the female, so she could attack him from behind.

Realizing he was defeated and in peril of losing his life, Nico went for a hasty retreat. The branch spearing his body struck just about every other tree branch on the way up from the forest floor and into the air above the canopy, the pain of it indescribable. Nico did not give it much thought, however. Wherever Damien had disappeared to, Nico could bet he would not let him escape with his head if he caught him.

He need not have worried. Damien's first concern was what it always had been.

Syreena.

After a clumsy landing, Damien changed back into his natural form. Syreena watched him expand from the shape of the raven to the shape of a man kneeling at her feet. His hand went to the wound at his side automatically in an attempt to stanch the heavy flow of blood as he got to his feet and dragged Syreena up against his body.

"Are you okay? Did he hurt you?"

"Shh, yes, I'm okay . . . and yes, he hurt me. Not as bad as he hurt you, just a broken arm and few more lost feathers. I am so glad to see you!" She wrapped her uninjured arm around his neck, hugging him with all of her strength.

"Ditto," he said with relief, exhaling with it now that he had heard her talk and felt her warmth. He glanced up at the treetops and sky. "It's not safe here. It is not uncommon for a second Vampire to attack after he thinks the mark has been worn out by a first one. Let us return to the house so we can add Jasmine to our forces."

"Okay. I think, for once, I am actually going to be happy to see her!"

Damien chuckled at that. He scooped her up and flew up into the night sky with incredible speed.

"Lois Lane, eat your heart out," she sighed against his neck.

* * *

"Well, it is definitely broken."

Gideon, an Ancient Demon of the Body and a healer without measure, moved his fingers gingerly over Syreena's arm.

"As you know, I cannot yet heal Lycanthropes," he continued, "but I can set it and let your natural healing abilities take over from there."

"Damien, I am so glad you brought her home," Siena said gratefully, resting a hand on his shoulder.

"Well, with two out of three of us injured, I figured a change in venue was the best choice," Damien explained, wincing as he shifted position in the chair he had pulled up to Syreena's bedside.

"This is ridiculous. He's hurt ten times worse than I am," Syreena complained, trying to wave the Demon medic away as she sat up.

"And bled all the way from California to here," Jasmine chimed in.

"Gideon stopped the bleeding already. Syreena is more important at the moment."

"Damien, you need to hunt. Very soon," Jasmine argued. "You are cold as death and weak as well."

"After Gideon is done, we will have a hunt. I will not leave Syreena until then."

"Damien," she said in consternation. "She is not going to die if you leave her."

"That is enough, Jasmine."

Jasmine fell silent, clearly angry and put out by his behavior, which was so impractical and impossible for her to understand. The Princess had just staked one of Damien's strongest enemies, literally with one arm behind her back. Though the myth of staking fell short of the instant death it was reputed to have, once Nico removed it he could bleed to death very quickly. Syreena had very likely killed him. It was not as if she were some frail flower of a woman or anything. She could not be so. That kind of woman would have turned Damien's stomach in an instant.

Sacrificing his health to see to a mere broken arm was ridiculously illogical. For once, Jasmine was in agreement with the Lycanthrope.

"Very well, then. At least drink from me to sustain yourself," she said, sweeping back her ebony hair and moving closer to him.

"Jasmine."

Damien's warning tone came only a second before a threatening, predatory growl erupted from the woman he sat near. Jasmine's dark eyes snapped to the Princess, instantly reading the threat that had wired her entire body. She comprehended immediately that this was a territorial vocalization. If there was one thing she knew, it was the reaction of someone warning others off their property.

Her property.

How dare she interfere, Jasmine thought in outrage. *Who does she think she is? I have supported and sustained Damien all of my life!*

"Very well. Have it your way," she snapped at them. Then, with that supernatural speed all Vampires were blessed with, she tore out of the underground Lycanthrope castle.

Once she was gone, Syreena turned regretful eyes to her mate. "I'm sorry. I don't know why I did that."

"I think you do," Siena said consolingly. "I would do the same if a woman offered herself up to Elijah right in front of me. It was insensitive for her to do that."

"No. She was only being practical," Damien said quietly. "Jas is practical to a fault. You and she are more alike than you realize, Syreena. She sees me as someone worthy of protecting. She has been loyal to me all of her life, in the way that you would be loyal to your sister. Be patient with her. None of us understands the nature of what has happened between us, and it has been such a sudden thing." Damien waved off the serious topic, turning back to Gideon. "Are you certain she will heal properly, old friend?"

"It is broken, not shattered. The bruising looks bad, I know, but I assure you it will mend once it is set. If you doubt me, perhaps you should gain access to one of the healer Monks."

"I do not doubt you in the least," Damien returned surely. "It was a question I am certain you would ask yourself were you forced to put Magdelegna's health in someone else's hands. We Nightwalkers are just very protective of our wives."

Damien raised Syreena's healthy hand to his lips, so he missed the delighted look Siena shot to her husband, who was leaning back against the wall of the room with casual ease as he observed all the personal dynamics unfolding before him. Elijah knew Siena was soaring with joy for her sister having found such apparent happiness, especially after the days of worry Syreena had put her through recently. The Warrior Captain was, of course, glad to have his wife in good spirits again. However, he would reserve opinion on the rest of the matter. If the joining of a Lycanthrope and a Demon had been incredibly difficult, Elijah figured that a union between a Lycanthrope and a Vampire would be damn near impossible.

Obviously that did not include emotions or physicality, he realized as he watched Damien's intimacy with Syreena. For all their bangs and bruises, there was no mistaking their feelings and the tracks of themselves that each had left upon the other. That they were mated was unquestionable. That they were in love was also clear. But Elijah remembered the pause that had come after his similar experiences with Siena. The fact of the matter was that they were members of two completely differing societies, both with positions of great influence, responsibility, and obligations.

Elijah glanced back to his wife. He realized instantly that she was aware of his thoughts. Though she was pretending to remain focused on Gideon's manipulation of her sister's arm, her eyes were suddenly upset and disturbed. As were her thoughts.

She looked up at him briefly, her expression and thoughts feeding into him instantly.

Can our people ever accept two alien men as mates to their monarchs? They have barely begun to accept you, my love.

I know, kitten, he thought in return. *What is worse, Vampires may very well try to slaughter their ruler if he thinks to take a Lycanthrope bride.*

But Vampires hold no ill will toward us!

Vampires have very few rules in life, Siena, so those they do have are very seriously frowned upon if they are broken. For some reason, it is against their laws for Damien to feed from your sister. Add this to their greed for power and the position that Damien holds, and it bodes ill for their safety and well-being overall.

He could have tried to lie to her, to comfort and coddle her delusions of her sister's potential happiness, but he was a leader of warriors and she a queen. Both required the hard practicality of reality in order to be of any use in their positions and to those who depended on them. Even if Siena had not been able to read his thoughts, she always needed to face the blatant truth of things. There were no coddling fairytales for a queen . . . not for a good one.

And his wife was an exceptional one.

So if they stay here, they meet with censure and hostility. If they stay there, they meet the same or worse.

Elijah looked down at the stone floor for a second, his wife's anxiety almost too much to bear from across a crowded room where he could not get to her to comfort her without being terribly obvious to the objects of their concern.

If you touched me now, I would start to cry like a child, she told him.

I know. That is the only thing keeping me against this wall at the moment, kitten.

Siena turned her head, her golden lashes blinking rapidly as she felt the burn of tears anyway.

"Hey, babe, let's leave these two with the doctor." Elijah spoke up suddenly, moving across the room to fetch his wife from between Damien and Gideon with a single smooth pull. "Why watch the doctor when we can be playing it instead," he teased, giving Syreena a sly look of mischief.

The Princess laughed at him as he swept her sister into the corridor without another word. Once outside the door, he drew his mate to the comfort of his embrace and all the shoulder she would ever need to cry on.

Damien reached to place a gentle kiss of pure affection on Syreena's forehead. She was asleep, so the gesture went completely unnoticed. He was sitting on the bed next to her, or rather, half beneath her. She had fallen asleep in a semi-upright position, her back nestled to his chest. He touched her hair, the living tendrils shifting beneath his fingers, some moving away, and some wending lightly over them.

He realized that he had some hard choices ahead of him.

Jasmine, for one. He could not be the rope in a tug-of-war between the two women who meant the most to him. He needed to find a solution as soon as possible. He mostly wanted to talk to Jasmine and make sure she understood there was nothing for her to be so afraid of. He was not going to abandon her, and he was positive that Syreena would not wish for him to do so, either. Territorial was one thing, jealous even another, but demanding that he choose between the person he considered his most valued friend and her? She would never ask it.

Jasmine, unfortunately, was not above such a demand. That was the nature of Vampire selfishness. He knew that, and he suspected even Syreena knew that. What he could not understand was why Jasmine would feel threatened all of a sudden. They had walked the world together for five hundred years. What on earth did she think was going to make that change?

He had also realized exactly what kind of danger he was exposing Syreena to. Nico's aggressive actions against them had shown him that. Damien was used to battling for his throne. It was simply a fact of his life. However, he no longer had the luxury of being blasé about it. The possibility of meeting death had always been an incidental thought. He had always figured that it simply would not matter; that if it happened, it was meant to happen. It was the price he would pay for a millennium of life and for the privilege of being the longest surviving Prince in all of Vampire history.

Now he had other interests to consider.

Syreena's interests.

He had only just found her, so he was hardly eager to lose her or to have her lose him. He could not bear the idea of causing her that much pain.

And there would be unspeakable pain.

He knew, without a doubt, that Syreena loved him. She had not spoken of it yet, probably not even to herself. He could accept that, considering how quickly everything had come about for her. What really mattered was that she felt it. Though unacknowledged, it was in her thoughts and it was in her spirit. He would have known it to be the truth even if he had no insight into her mind. He had understood that the moment she had sacrificed herself to Nico in order to warn him of danger.

Damien knew she could have found escape if she had only run a couple of yards in the opposite direction. The cliffside at the point where she had met Nicodemous was only that far away. It would have been nothing for her to leap off it and down into the water below. Whether or not she could change into the dolphin, she had every water-born instinct in her human form she would need to survive the plunge and swim out of reach of Nico's grasp. He never would have followed her down such a treacherous fall. To him, it would have been suicidal; to her, it would have been like breathing.

Instead, she had run toward him. As promised, she had used every ounce of advantage and strength she had to try and return to him. In this case, to give him fair warning. Damien had fought Nico once before and, though it was a challenge, he would have defeated him with or without warning this time as well. Of course, she had no way of knowing that, really, so she had done what she thought she had to do to protect him.

Again, he was not used to others stepping in front of him in that kind of role, but he was beginning to become more tolerant of it, not insulted by it. Those actions, in and of themselves, only further proved to him that it was an act of deeply felt love for him.

The last thing to be considered was Siena.

He was telepathically sensitive himself, so he had known the basic nature of the exchange that had passed between the Queen and her mate. Siena feared for her sister's happiness. Parallel to that, she was afraid of the displeasure of her people. He did not have to think too hard to figure out why. He had known what the possible consequences could be if Syreena, Siena's only heir, chose an outlander for a mate. Syreena had known them as well. He had made certain that she did. Siena probably did not realize that this was the source of Syreena's deepest conflict in the entire situation. He understood that this was what had kept her thinking, in spite of horrific sadness, for nearly three days. She had put herself and him through indescribable hurt just so she could make her choice with complete consideration.

"And now, sweetling, I must hunt. I will return to you warmed and hopefully at a better peace," he whispered into her hair.

"No women," she murmured to him, the response so sleepy she was barely awake.

"None whatsoever. I promise."

Her only response was a sleepy sigh. He smiled against her and then gently eased himself from beneath her. He carefully arranged her and her injured arm so that pillows mostly took his place supporting her. He would not go far, nor would he be long. He could not manage it in his present condition in any event, and he wanted to be back by her side before she even noticed he was gone.

Every other concern was secondary to that.

Nicodemous kept up his flight for as long as he calculated he could. He realized soon enough that Damien was more interested in tending his harlot than chasing him, and he supposed he was grateful for that.

It did not keep him from being livid beyond reason.

If he ever got his hands on that devious, backstabbing little Lycanthrope whore, he would gut her with his best silver knife in an instant.

Unfortunately, he had to survive the removal of this cursed stick of wood first.

He landed awkwardly somewhere in the Nevada desert shortly after that thought. There was method to this particular place. It would hurt like being staked out in the sun, but sand was his quickest choice to fill the gaping wound the removal of the branch would cause him. At least within the area he had been forced to flee to. After packing the wound, he would find shelter out of the sun and the path of humans or animals and resign himself to torpor while his body healed.

It would help if he could hunt. He would never be able to in this condition, but fresh blood was always a Vampire's best resource when it came to speeding the healing process. Since he did not have a choice in the matter, he would settle for torpor. At least he would be able to sleep and mull over exactly what it was that had gone wrong. He couldn't put his finger on it, but Nico was positive something strange was going on.

A Vampire bedding a Lycanthrope was strange enough, but Damien, the so-called Lawful Prince, had drunk her Nightwalker blood. More than once, by the look of the marks. There were a great many Vampires who, if they had only known about that, would take serious umbrage to it. Perhaps this would be something he could exploit at a later date.

But there was something else besides all of that. There had to be. He was too old and too experienced to not know when strange things were afoot. Damien was the best at playing mind games, but there was something about the whole trick of the falcon and the raven that was grating on his intellect.

Nico lowered himself to his knees, bracing them far apart as he closed his hands around the branch.

This would be easier to do and survive if that worthless son of his had not turned tail and run off like a weeping woman, he thought angrily. He had known that Cyril was going to make an attempt at the woman, just as he had known Cyril was haunting the edges of Damien's territory for the past few days. The idiot child got grades for ambition, but that was just about all he had earned in his father's eyes. The rest had been sloppy and stupid and far outside of Cyril's capabilities. Nico had no idea what his son had been thinking, trying to find a way to take on Damien.

At least Nico was smart enough to admit that Damien had been the longest reigning Vampire Prince because he deserved it. The Prince was no slouching figurehead, that much was certain. But each battle taught Nico a little bit more. If he survived this one, he would be more than willing to gamble on his success at a third try.

"Do you need some help with that?"

Nico looked up with a start. He was in so much pain and so drained of essential fluids, he had not even heard the approach of the stranger who addressed him. He looked her over with sharp black eyes. She was tall, excessively so for a woman, and she had the longest blond hair he had seen in some time. She was young in appearance and extraordinarily beautiful. Her darkly tanned skin told him she was no Vampire, but her matter-of-fact attitude about finding a man stabbed through his heart and still alive in the middle of a desert told him that she was not unfamiliar with Nightwalkers.

She leaned forward, her hands braced on her knees as she looked at him with cold, clear blue eyes. He saw fierce intelligence there, as well as a palpable fearlessness that immediately piqued his interest. She was gowned in sheer lilac panels of something like silk or chiffon, but the moon easily backdropped her figure through the material so that, in shadow, she might as well have been naked.

"I can help you," she whispered to him, her eyes coasting over his wounded body with a sort of covetousness that, had he been a little healthier, would have delighted him no end.

"I expect you will want something in return," he countered. "I can manage by myself."

"I was not speaking only of this nonsense," she said shortly, waving off his crucial injury as if it were merely a splinter in his finger.

"Then tell me what you were speaking of, and make it quick, will you, woman? There is a time issue to be considered here."

"I meant that I could help you get what you want." She smiled prettily when he arched a sarcastic brow at her. She leaned even closer, and he could smell the scent of clover, musk, and frankincense. Strangely, he found the mixture extremely pleasing. "I meant," she purred softly as she touched his face with a hand as soft as kid gloves, "I can get you Damien's head on a pretty platter. A silver platter, with a Lycanthrope heart sitting right next to it."

Nico's eyes narrowed on her and he looked her over once again. "Who are you?"

"I am the one who knows how Damien defeated you. I am the one who knows how to make you stronger than you ever imagined. I am your one true angel, Nicodemous."

With that, she grasped the branch impaling him and jerked it clear of his body. Nico's scream could be heard by every desert creature for miles. In agony and rage, he reached for the woman and dragged her down to her knees before him. Blood poured from his wounds and, since it was very likely that he would die no matter what, he was going to at least give her a good thrashing for taking him off guard like that.

She laughed at him even as his blood splashed across her dress. For a moment, he thought she was completely mad.

Then she laid her slim fingers over his torn flesh and began to whisper softly under her breath. The words were a mixture of Latin and Arabic and about three other languages that he could immediately identify. The rest of it was gibberish to him.

Gibberish or not, whatever she was doing, it was helping. It was as if he could feel his flesh knitting together on the spot, starting with his damaged heart and working its way outward.

"You are a Demon," he accused her softly.

"Mmm," she affirmed, those huge blue eyes of hers beautifully spooky with their depths and emptiness.

"You are using magic. A Demon who casts spells? How is it you are not censured for such a thing?"

Her response was a half-smile and pointed lift to her brow.

"Ahh," he said with sudden clarity. "You would be censured . . . if they could catch you."

Nicodemous was positively sucked in by this interesting bit of fortune. He realized from what she had said so far that she had some sort of vendetta against Damien or the Lycanthrope female. She had probably seen their earlier battle and had followed him this far in search of an ally. Apparently she had had no luck catching up with her target on her own either.

Perhaps together though . . .

Between her inborn skills, this magic she had acquired, and his own power . . .

Nico was dizzy with the possibilities.

"It is very likely blood loss," she said dryly, responding to a thought he had not voiced aloud.

He chuckled. "I do not suppose hunting for blood would be another of your hidden talents, would it?"

"I have a better idea," she whispered eagerly as her blood-stained hands fell away from his repaired body. "Would you like to know how Damien was able to trick you before?"

"Can it wait until after I eat?"

The beautiful blond moved forward suddenly, her hands diving into his fiery-colored hair and her mouth pressing to his. Nico was startled at first, but she was quite a warm and luscious handful of woman, so it did not take him long to get over it. He kissed the forward wench soundly, making damn sure she was gasping for breath by the time he finally released her. She pushed back into another kiss aggressively, her warm body wrapping around him with sinuous sensuality.

It was clear she knew her way around a man. It radiated in the way she moved against him, the way her hands roamed boldly over him. She was also assertive and brazen, which Nico very much liked in a woman.

"Okay, you win," he growled at her, pulling her off his mouth by her hair. He wrapped a fistful of it around his hand and held her perfectly still while he appraised her face. "How did he do it?"

"Would you like to find out?" she asked breathlessly.

"I just said so, didn't I?"

"Good."

She reached to push back the remainder of her hair, baring her slender, appetizing neck to his starving eyes and craving body.

"Bon appetit," Ruth murmured with a wicked smile.

Jasmine rubbed her chill arms absently as she walked around her room for the third time.

She was not one for material goods, so even though there was a small bag half filled with her clothing, she realized there was nothing else she truly wanted to take with her.

Beside the bag on her bed was the old book she had borrowed from the Nightwalker Library. She moved closer to it, touching its leather cover and the obscure title across its bottom.

It was in Vampyr, their most ancient language, and it simply said: *Reasoning*.

So modest a title for so profound a topic, she thought with more than a little dejection. She had done nothing but examine and reexamine her reasoning these past forty-eight hours. No matter what she did, she seemed to think herself into circles, logic seeming illogical after a while and everything sounding whiny and emotional in her head if she thought on it long enough. Half the time she felt like a child throwing a tantrum because another child had stolen her favorite toy, and some adult somewhere looming above her was lecturing her on the reasons why she should share.

Share, or have it taken away from you forever. If you cannot share, you cannot play.

Jasmine stomped a foot against the floorboards, even if it did perpetuate the metaphorical image in her mind. She had shared Damien with his women before. Why was she having so much difficulty this time?

"Because she is not Vampire and she does not understand our ways," she complained to the silent manse.

Did a Lycanthrope understand the way Vampires compensated for solitude and boredom with an intimacy of touch that had nothing to do with sex? What of the way Syreena had threatened her when all she had been doing was helping the male Syreena professed to care about? Would the little Princess be upset if Jasmine and Damien spent the entire day behind closed doors merely talking, as they often had before? Vampires were not insulted by being shut away from those who wanted privacy, just as they were not insulted when others behaved with explicitness in the presence of others.

Jasmine could imagine Syreena pitching a fit the first time she strolled in on someone having sex in the common room or saw someone walking naked through the house. The female Vampire was too angry to take into consideration that she had lived in the Lycanthrope court a few weeks here and there over the centuries, and it was a culture almost exactly like her own in that respect. Between the communal baths and the hot springs dotted through the castle, public nudity and sex were often just as frequent, if not more so.

After a few moments, Jasmine reconciled her irrational thinking. She turned and sat next to the compendium on her bed with a deep, dejected sigh.

Whose problem was this anyway? she wondered.

She looked down at her bag and then the book again, taking measure of both. If she packed the rest of her bag and left, who would that be hurting? Only Damien and herself. Syreena could not comprehend the depth of drama in such a change in the household dynamic, so how could it hurt her in any way? Unless she hurt because Damien would hurt. Which would mean she truly did have a serious concern for him.

Which Jasmine did not want to accept.

Jasmine groaned pitifully as she came full circle in her own mind yet again. She flopped back onto her mattress with a bounce. Her hand fell on the book again, bringing immediately to mind her second dilemma of action and consequence. Within the book lay the proof Damien had asked her to seek: the reasoning and consequences behind Vampires feeding on, or rather being inherently *against* feeding on, other Nightwalkers. Some of what she had read supported everything Damien had suspected and concurred with everything he wanted to hear. It would bind him all the tighter to the Lycanthrope, if such a thing were possible.

Some of it was also frighteningly deadly in consequence and, in her opinion, conveyed very supportable logic for why feeding on other Nightwalkers had evolved into the taboo it now was. In truth, it was such a cold and deadly piece of logic that it had the potential to drive Damien away from his supposed love and, with any luck, back into their normal, quiet routine.

Jasmine, however, was forced to remind herself how much she hated normalcy and quiet routine. A couple of weeks ago she had been ready to lie down in the ground for a century. Today, she was reeling with thoughts and choices and, she had to admit, the potential for adventure and the future risk of existence that so many Vampires like herself thrived on. But should she risk Damien's well-being, possibly his life, for the sake of entertaining herself? Not that the danger was a definite. If it were, she would not hesitate to act. Because however she felt, whatever happened, she knew she would always put Damien first.

She would die for him.

These long-buried truths and dangerous consequences could die as well, Jasmine considered. Say, for instance, if the Library were to suddenly burn to the ground, the cursed book on her bed included. Was it so far-fetched an idea that a torch might come too close to one book, accelerating a catastrophic obliteration of all these secrets that should have stayed in their musty tomb? What would they really be missing out on if such a thing happened? They had survived this long . . .

Merely survived.

Jasmine never would have thought herself capable of it,

but she could not turn her back on the tempting idea that this volume, so full of information, could lead to something so much more vital and beautiful than bare survival alone could ever compare to.

Bang. She was back at the beginning again. Circle complete.

Jasmine took her hand off the book so she could slap herself on her aching forehead. This was ridiculous! For all her age, wisdom, and experience, she could not sort out what to do with a stupid book and one short woman? If Damien married Syreena, she would become Jasmine's *Queen*! Jasmine would become the subject of a twit who had no clue as to what benefited the Vampire race!

And, if Damien did marry her, he would need Jasmine more than ever. Leaving him would make him domestically vulnerable. Stephan, head of Damien's organized fighting forces, was fine when it came to dealing with other races and human hunters, but Jasmine didn't think he had what it took to kill his own en masse should a civil war break out. And even if they managed to avoid internal strife of that magnitude, it would still invite a wave of challengers to his throne. There was no way Damien could ever survive such an onslaught. Not alone. Not without someone who did not care who she killed for the sake of protecting him.

Someone who would not get their little twiggy arm broken at the first flick of an enemy finger, then lie around crying about it. If Jasmine stayed, though, it would mean she would have to give them both her support, including Miss Twiggy.

She would rather run across a desert naked at noon on a bright, sunny day.

And once more, back to her own start she went.

Why was this so hard? Why couldn't she just kill the bitch and end it all?

It was just then that Jasmine felt an acute, throbbing sparkle skip across her senses so suddenly that her head and sinuses flared with sharp pain. She sat up quickly, gaining her feet and becoming instantly alert to the fact that there was an intruder in the house.

It was no one she knew, and not a Vampire. She would have felt a Vampire coming the moment they crossed into the territory, no matter how distracted by her own thoughts she had been. Besides, Damien was the one who attracted that sort of trouble, not her. Anyone who wanted to challenge the Prince would not want to come up against her first. The wisest thing would be to wait until Damien was on the premises without her being present.

Jasmine turned toward the door just as the air pressure in the room snapped in violent displacement. She flinched as her sinuses were abused once again by the pressure change. By the time Ruth turned to face her, however, Jasmine was flashing a serious set of fangs and hissing sharply in threat, crouching at the ready.

"Hmm, scary," Ruth remarked, giving Jasmine a theatrical shiver. "Down, girl," she ordered as if speaking to a dog, pointing a commanding finger to punctuate the insult. "I am not here to hurt you."

"Not that you could," Jasmine spat, her fingers curling slightly until they were hooked into ready claws.

"If you insist." Ruth waved the matter off, conceding as if it did not matter in the least. "I am only here to deliver the littlest bit of a message to your Prince, his bitch, and all the rest of the little dogs back where she comes from, *including* the warrior who murdered my child. You tell them that things are going to change from this moment on. If they thought I was trouble before, wait until they see what I can do now. My power will continue to grow, I promise you. Just as my rage and my thirst for vengeance grows. Truly, Jasmine, it is quite an extraordinary thing. But you would know all about that now, would you not?"

The Mind Demon appraised Jasmine for a moment and then suddenly exploded into the Vampire's mind. Shocked,

Jasmine staggered under the force of it. She was powerful in her own right, but all of her barriers and resistances were like dust compared to the presence that stormed through her thoughts.

"I know your mind, poor, troubled girl," Ruth said softly. "Those shapechangers are quite the nuisance, are they not? But why struggle so? You know what you want to do in your heart. I can show you how to get him back, you know. No one would ever be the wiser. I could . . ."

Ruth suddenly looked down at the bed, her pale blue eyes widening.

"Where did you get that?" She spoke with awe as she reached for the volume with eager hands. Jasmine instantly went to stop her, but found she was rooted in place. Shocked that her body would fail to serve her, she became enraged. But it was Ruth who began to shout. "A Library? A Night-walker Library? *That was supposed to be* my *treasure!* All those months of digging in that frozen wasteland!" Ruth's head snapped up as she narrowed evil eyes on Jasmine. "You have seen the Black Tome. I knew we were close! I could feel it!"

Jasmine had a feeling she knew what Ruth was talking about. There was a book in the Library, a centerpiece set on its own pedestal, with black covers and page after page of magic spells in every language imaginable and, like the other books hidden within the Library, even some that were unimaginable.

Jasmine felt her stomach clutching with impotent anger; at Ruth, yes, but mostly at herself. Her mind had become a diamond mine for the Demon, and Ruth was excavating its priceless treasures with such ease, as if Jasmine were five, not five hundred. She should have been powerful enough to push away the intrusion of a Mind Demon.

"Ah, but I am no ordinary Demon. Or hadn't you heard? In fact, I think it is safe to say that I am not really a Demon anymore. And why would I want to be, I ask you? All that hypocrisy and holier-than-thou preaching they do . . . it turns my stomach. You know"—she turned back to Jasmine, brightly smiling—"I believe I have the answers you are looking for, Jasmine. Since you have been such a delightful resource, I don't see why I shouldn't share in return.

"So many questions spinning in your head, Vampire. You could have peace and have the exciting life you have always craved. I tell you, every day I learn something new. I see things you would not believe. The world is my oyster, and you could not possibly begin to consider what little pearls like this," she rubbed the leather of the volume as she hugged it to her chest, "can do. But the biggest pearl, the Black Tome, what we could do with that!

"I have grown wiser about magic, Jasmine. All along I kept looking for a human necromancer powerful enough to join with me and be an effective partner. Now I realize there is no such thing! That is why we always defeat the human necromancers. Magic was never meant to be theirs, it was meant for us! That is why they always turn evil. It is too much for them to manage. It was meant for Nightwalkers."

Ruth moved closer to Jasmine, reaching to touch the paralyzed woman's cheek as she looked deep into her stormy, dark eyes.

"I know how powerful you are. Even now, your struggles against me are wearing me out. But imagine your power tripled, or even raised to the tenth power. There are no limits. Not once you shed all these mortal limitations we all seem to have picked up. Come, Jasmine," she coaxed eagerly, "I already have my first, my right hand man, so to speak." She giggled like a girl with a crush. "But you can be my left hand. You can take my daughter's place. You would never want for anything at my side. I would never abandon you for another. I am not like a fickle male. I will not make you weak with pain. I will fill you with the strength of power! I know you are thinking about it. I feel you thinking about it. Come, let me show you the truths that make lies of everything you have been told to believe."

Jasmine could not speak. She was breathing hard with emotion, something she had not done in over a century. She closed her eyes, thinking of Damien and everything they had shared for the past five hundred years. Who would she be without him? Who *could* she be without him?

Jasmine was dismayed to realize she was trapped once more in another, never-ending circle.

Chapter 12

Syreena awoke to pain and bliss.

The former was caused by her arm, the splinted limb hurting more as it healed than it had originally. The latter was because she was surrounded by the warmth and arms of her mate. She turned toward him, sliding her body over his with a long sigh. He stirred instantly from his sleep, seeking for the softness of her face with his lips and the touch of graceful fingers.

Without opening his eyes, he traced the shape of her features, his fingertips moving slowly over her chin, cheeks, brows, and then soft eyelashes. By the time he touched her lips again, he could feel her gentle smile.

"I could get very used to this," she told him on a reverent whisper.

"I think you are going to have to," he rejoined with a low chuckle. "You will not be waking beside anyone else for the rest of your life."

"That is quite an extended promise, Prince Damien," she observed, her eyes flicking open to look up into his. She was also growing used to the magnificent depth in his midnight blue eyes. Sometimes, she felt as though he looked into parts of her even she could not see. Then he would say something that only reinforced that idea all the more.

"One I intend to keep, Princess Syreena," he said quietly, punctuating the solemn oath of his words with the lingering seal of his mouth.

Syreena tried to move more aggressively against him as the kiss changed and grew in intimacy and intensity, but he placed a restraining hand above her right breast and pushed her away gently.

"You need rest and healing, sweetling, not lovemaking," he tenderly scolded her.

"It doesn't hurt," she argued, capturing his mouth before he could formulate a further protest.

He pushed her away once more, giving her a look full of reprimand. "You are a liar," he accused her.

"Well, it doesn't hurt much, then," she edited impatiently. "Why don't you let me be the judge of my own capabilities?"

"Because the idea of causing you pain is detestable, Syreena. I might add that pitting my good intentions against my overwhelming need for you is terribly unfair and inconsiderate of you."

Syreena sighed and her bottom lip plumped out in a little pout of dejection. "I suppose so, if you look at it that way. Forgive me?"

"Always," he assured her, giving her another kiss to make it official. "Especially when I must move on to more difficult topics than making love to you."

"Such as?"

"I hardly know where to start." He sighed with brutal honesty as he settled back again. He ran an absent hand over his whiskers, his entire expression morphing into the seriousness he had promised.

"Then may I?"

Damien arched an eyebrow in curious invitation.

"Let us begin with Jasmine," she said.

"Yes. Jasmine." Damien reached to flick a finger down her cheek. "What can I do that will satisfy you both? I am at a loss for a solution at present."

"I can only tell you what I would prefer you not do with her," Syreena answered. "Do not feed from her ever again. I could never bear her scent permeating you like that. I am not certain I could be held accountable for my actions if I were faced with such a thing. I never thought I would be jealous, but I suppose I am."

"No more or less than I would be. I have no intention of feeding off another female again, unless it is some kind of dire emergency. It would be like you allowing another Vampire to drink from you. I am positive my reaction would be possessive and probably violent."

"Well, we seem to be agreed on these things so far. What exactly do you wish me to tell you about Jasmine? I will not tell you to stop being friends with her. I understand that would be like asking my sister to renounce her friendship with Anya. They grew up together. They are like sisters. I understand that it is similar between you and Jasmine."

"Except Anya is gracious in her acceptance of your arrival in Siena's life and your elevation to a position above her in importance and perhaps even love as well as loyalty. Jasmine . . . I think Jasmine is incapable of that generosity."

"Because she feels threatened. We will have to find a way to make her understand that it is not my intention to cast her to the wolves."

"No," Damien said, shaking his head. "It can have nothing to do with you. She would be insulted if she felt you were deigning to tolerate her presence. The friendship will remain, but it will have to be Jas's decision whether she stays under my roof or not. I would hate to lose her. She is a skilled hunter. Second only to me, I believe."

"You could use her skills to protect our territory," Syreena agreed. "I have a feeling we will need a great deal of protection."

"I will need to recall my entourage shortly. We will have encapsulated privacy in our suite, of course, but the household will be much different in dynamic than you have seen it to be once they all return."

"How many?"

"Six, besides us. Two household servants, two guards, Jasmine, who is to me what you are to Siena, and Stephan, who loosely serves as my Commander in times of war. Mostly he is a friend. Of course, Horatio, who is Jasmine's brother, by the way, and Kelsey are always welcome when their diplomatic duties release them from the foreign courts. These are my most trusted friends. My family, if you will. We have traveled centuries together."

"Well, I suppose we will not be making love in the kitchen again anytime soon." She chuckled.

"I am certain they couldn't care less if we do." Damien laughed in return. "Come to think of it, you may find things a tad too liberal for your tastes. You are rather conservative, for a Lycanthrope."

"Then there will have to be adjustments on both our parts, I imagine. We will find a way to make this work. So long as I can be accepted, the rest is minor details."

"Agreed." Damien was silent for a long moment. "As for acceptance, I believe those who are loyal to me will find their way. Those who oppose me just for the sake of argument will kick up a fuss, but it will die down. It is those who resent my power or covet it who concern me. I am not comfortable with the idea of you mending from broken bones on a regular basis."

"It will be less likely as I learn what to expect, who to trust, and how to sense the tricks your people use for deception. In my studies I have learned that any advantage can be circumvented with learning, time, and skill."

"Am I to hope you do not get killed in the meantime?" Damien queried, a bit more harshly than he had intended.

"Now who is it who has not considered the results of his

actions before making his choice?" she asked, sitting up and looking down at him. "Are you regretting me already?"

"I am regretting my position, Syreena, nothing more," he assured her. "I have held this mantle for a very long time, and as a dominant male with no family or dependents to consider, it was a much easier choice to take the risks involved. And no," he interrupted when he saw the cloud that crossed her features, "I do not consider you dependent, nor do I regret my choices. I am merely considering the changes in my path as it lies before me. I once walked it alone. It makes sense to move aside slightly to share it with you by my side from this point on. By doing so, my view changes or I walk a different edge, but I would much rather have the company. One can go mad with none but themselves for company on such a very long road, Syreena."

That was a concept Syreena understood. However, she also realized he was trying to tell her something else with the metaphor.

"You are considering abdication, aren't you?" she asked bluntly.

Damien was silent as he toyed absently with her hair and his inner thoughts.

"Damien, your people have thrived under your rule. You are used to being a leader. Can you honestly live in a society where you will have little to no say in how it evolves? You have known nothing else for over six hundred years. You were the youngest Vampire ever to attain a throne. You are the longest surviving monarch in all Vampiric history. You have also managed to keep peace not only within your people, but with most of the Nightwalkers as well."

"With a few arrogant exceptions," he corrected with a chuckle.

"It seems Noah has forgiven your war with his people, and I think everyone gets into scuffles with Shadowdwellers. They are impossible to understand."

"So were we all, once upon a time," he reminded her. He

looked deeply into her bicolored eyes for a very long time. "So you wish me to maintain my throne? I think you just enjoy being a Princess."

"I think I am used to being one. I think I know what it means to rule and," she gave him a wink, "co-rule a species."

"And if you come to rule with me, my love, what becomes of your sister's heiress?"

"She is the one who abdicates. Damien, Lycanthropes will never accept this. Siena thinks I have not realized that, but I do. They will not accept two foreign males married onto their soil and into the monarchy. One is the limit of their tolerance. This has been my home for fifteen years, but it will never mean to me what it does to Siena. I will not risk her throne with the potential for rebellion. If I marry into foreign soil, it can be used as . . . as a sort of propaganda. Marry off royal blood of one clan to the royal blood of another for the sake of never-ending peace. Something like that. So long as you do not have one foot on their throne, they will find it easy to celebrate our . . . to celebrate us."

"You can say it, you know," he told her softly, those ceaseless fingers roaming the length of her cheek slowly. "Our marriage. You may speak of it as a foregone conclusion, Syreena, because we both know that it is."

"Vampires do not marry," she reminded him.

"Vampires do not marry *now*," he corrected. "We did once. Our ceremonies are much like other Nightwalker ceremonies, actually. We have only grown too spoiled and whimsical in our selfishness to find it of much use or meaning. For me, I have found both use *and* meaning. In you, beloved."

"Beloved," she repeated softly. "You are my beloved, Damien. I have not told you that, but I feel it with all of my heart."

"I already know. I have felt your heart in our every kiss and touch. I would be foolish to mistake it."

"Mmm, I wish I had your confidence." She sighed, snuggling up to him tightly. "I do not mean about us. I have come to see the source you see when you see the inevitability in us. However, I have not been easy or forthcoming in my expression of my feelings. Yet you believe in them so absolutely. You seem to know them even before I do."

"It is only because in my lifetime I have learned how to divine truth from confusion. You will, too, one day, when you have lived so long." He hesitated a moment, then turned to kiss her forehead. "You did not say if you wished to wed me, Syreena."

To his discomfort, she laughed at him. Her humor was hard and rollicking, even to the point of kicking out her heels, and grasping her injured arm as the vibration of her giggles caused her pain.

"So much for Mr. Confidence." She snickered with delight. "What happened to 'you may speak of it as a foregone conclusion'?" As she quoted him, she mocked the depth of his voice and the common gestures in his airs. She was laughing so hard that she made him chuckle as she reached to dash tears from her brimming eyes.

"You are an ungrateful little brat," he admonished her.

"Because I dare to laugh at you, my Prince? Such are the things you will suffer if you think to marry a Princess who knows not to be so very impressed by title alone." She eased off her humor at his expense. "You make impressions and impacts in other ways, my love. I would not worry overmuch."

His reaction to her words was an instantaneous smile. He snuggled down with her again in immediate satisfaction.

"Say that again," he demanded in a whisper against her ear. "If you only knew the delight it gives me . . ."

"My love," she repeated softly, allowing herself the warmth of a blush. "My love. My lord, if you wish it. I would have no future if it did not include you, Damien. I knew that when I came to you. Probably long before I acknowledged it. I will always remember your surety, though. It will never leave me."

"Just as I have learned to appreciate your care of thought.

You waited for certainty so you would not cause anyone more injury than you had to. I understand that now."

She raised her chin to his deeply affectionate kiss, smiling against his lips just before he parted from her.

"Is there anything further you wished to discuss?" she asked him. "Is there anything that troubles you still?"

"Actually, there are two further issues. We will need to mark these as our first joint decisions as rulers."

"It sounds serious."

"Only partly. First, I wish to find a way to repay Windsong and Lyric for all they have done for us both. Normally I would suggest a fashionable gathering, but it would not be something they would enjoy."

"So make it a friendly gathering. In a very large place, but only with those Nightwalkers they would feel safe and familiar around. Make it a very specific honor, and yet give them the opportunity to accept or decline without any fear of insult."

"Perhaps a wedding?" he suggested, seeing where she was headed immediately.

"Yes. Take the focus off them. They would be self-conscious if it was a gathering centered around them. So we shall center it around us. To be invited to the Vampire Prince's marriage will be an astounding honor to them."

"Perhaps with Noah as host, in his home. It is certainly large and familiar surroundings. It is an organized and safe environment which the Demon King has complete control of. It is an advantage which, I am afraid to say, my home will lack once news of this marriage gets about."

"With only our immediate family attending. And I do include Jasmine in that, of course."

"I know you do."

"And the second matter?" she prompted. "The more serious one, I take it. The first was rather benign."

"It is. The second matter is Ruth. She escaped from her infractions against you as she has escaped repeatedly over these many instances of pain and even death. She must be found and punished, if not stopped entirely. She only grows more powerful the longer she remains out there. I think it is time she was hunted in earnest, a joint effort, like the Nightwalker Library. It concerns us all and we all have a responsibility to it."

"I have long been in agreement with that. Each of us uses our own resources in the effort, but rarely do we consider joining them in a permanent effort to capture her once and for all. She is mad. You can see it in her eyes and feel it with every ounce of your being. Mad and evil are the worst of combinations."

"Add to it intelligence and great power and you have the reason why she has slipped through our fingers time and again."

"I believe she is the larger threat," Damien said as he paced slowly across the Great Room of the castle of the Demon King. "If we split amongst ourselves searching for her, and then split again our focus between her and the magic-users, we weaken ourselves and leave ourselves terribly vulnerable. I think this is why we have been failing to stop her all of this time. She has crossed over, taking on dual cultures, and now has twice the access to power because of it. We too must combine cultures."

Damien paused to look at the circle of Nightwalker leaders sitting around him, listening intently as he voiced his opinion. The gathering was unprecedented. Every known Nightwalker species in the world was represented, and it had only take twenty-four hours to gather them.

Then again, it had taken thousands of years.

There was Siena and Elijah, Queen and Consort of the Lycanthropes; Noah, King of all Demons; Hawk, a Mistral Bard, and Windsong the Mistral Siren, who were among the eldest and most respected of their kind; Isabella, the first of the Druids to emerge from dormancy; and, much to everyone's surprise, Malaya and Tristan, the two High Chancellors of the Shadowdwellers.

Though the Shadowdwellers were often extended overtures of peace and social invitation, Damien could not recall them ever responding before. They were the reason why the room was so dim, only the fire in the fireplace and a few selectively placed candles set about. Their sensitivity to light of any kind was well known. They were the most singular curiosity of all the visiting dignitaries. They were a striking, medium-skinned people, their features a breathtaking combination of Middle Eastern exotic and American Indian strength. Both of them had capes of straight black hair that gleamed like polished onyx and stunning eyes to match.

To Syreena, they had a level of sophistication in their air that she had not been expecting. The male moved with the same careless grace that Damien always did. He wore long, loose clothing over a surprisingly fit and tall body structure. She could tell he was lean and athletic for a purpose, that he had been specifically crafted for flexibility and speed of movement. She did not know how she knew, but she felt it with every instinct she owned.

The female also was built with long grace, like a prima ballerina whose figure was cut to accent the length of her legs, arms, and neck. She was adorned in the simple elegance of a black sari with black embroidery, in addition to a snug, midriff-baring shirt of a blue so dark it almost matched Damien's eyes. There were simple pieces of gold jewelry that included a thin ring around her pinkie, a superfine chain holding an onyx pendant around her neck, and a delicate piercing through her nose that led back to a matching clasp in her ear with a gentle sweep of an even thinner chain. The arc of that chain accented the lower curve of her highly defined cheek, and heavy lines of kohl enhanced the frames of both her eyes in such a way that they seemed to leap out with penetrating beauty.

They were nothing like Syreena had expected in both looks and manners. Perhaps this unexpected aura of culture and class was what allowed them to position themselves for the mischief they were reputable for, but she could not imagine how anyone could have all of the appearance of something, and none of the actuality. That was probably naïve of her, she thought as she looked back to the man who was going to be counting on her wisdom in the coming future. She could not afford the luxury of such naïveté.

"We too must combine cultures," Damien repeated softly as he thought out loud before them. "Not just one or two, but all of them. Every Nightwalker here is now in danger from Ruth's plotting, I am convinced of it. She has attacked Demon, Druid, and Lycanthrope already and now has been seen in Mistral territory."

"And yesterday she struck Vampire territory."

Damien and every dignitary in the room turned toward Jasmine when she made the damning statement. The Prince was immediately concerned. He had thought her safe at their home. He could tell by her appearance, however, that her safety had been in question.

"Jasmine, what happened?"

Damien ignored the others in the room and hurried over to her. She looked like she was ready to pass out. It was a state of weakness Damien was not used to seeing in her and it was enough to rattle him. He immediately began to search her for any other signs of damage.

"No, no, I am fine," she said, though she took his arm for support. "Merely tired, as well as being in desperate need of a hunt. Luckily I ran into Horatio outside and did not have to sneak in. I honestly do not think I would have had it in me."

"I take it you saw Ruth."

Jasmine looked up at the Demon King after he addressed her. As usual, he got right to the point. She did not blame him. Ruth was by far the most serious kind of business.

"I just spent the better part of the night in her company.

She arrived around eleven and left an hour after dawn. I believe her departure time was planned so she would be assured that I could not follow her."

"Oh, my God," the Druid Isabella exclaimed. Isabella knew firsthand what five minutes in Ruth's company could do to a person. She couldn't conceive what could be done to a body when it spent as much time in threat as Jasmine had just laid claim to.

But although there were a variety of such reactions going through those who knew Ruth best, the only one that made a real impact on Jasmine was Syreena's. Out of the corner of her eye, she could see that the Princess had gone pale, but other than that the Lycanthrope remained still and quiet.

If it had not been already too late, Jasmine might have had time to respect that quiet stoicism.

But it *was* too late.

None of them knew it, however.

At least, not yet.

"Jasmine, have a seat and explain this to us," Damien encouraged her, looking her over yet again for signs of injury. He was puzzled. How could she have met with Ruth and escaped her relatively unharmed? He was grateful that she had, but he had seen what Ruth had done to Syreena with only a few hours of time on her hands. To spend nearly eight hours with Ruth and survive untouched? It was nothing short of miraculous.

"Let me start by saying that everything you told me about Ruth is basically a lie, Damien. At least, it is now," she added when she saw his reactive expression. "She is ten times more powerful than you warned me about. She kept me imprisoned all of that time with nothing but the force of her mind. I have never felt anything like it. Everything I know, she now knows." She looked to the Lycanthrope Queen. "That includes the location of the Library, I am afraid."

"Sweet Goddess! *Jinaeri*! If it is as you say, she is woefully underprotected! There are only a few guards and which-ever Nightwalkers are there . . ."

"That is why I rushed to your territory as fast as I could. You can relax, Siena," Jasmine eased her, holding up a weary hand and gesturing back to her seat. "I found Anya, the General of your Elite army, and she is handling it. She is the one who told me where to find you all." Jasmine looked up at Damien. "I do not know what happened after that. If Ruth can travel in daylight or teleport that entire distance, it is likely to be much too late."

"There is nothing any of us can do about it now." Elijah spoke up softly, his hand going to his wife's shoulder and easing her back into her seat. "Ruth had the entire day to do her damage. I believe she is more than strong enough to fight off the lethargy that affects us during daytime, but she cannot possibly resist it for long. Let's hope she waited until dusk to cause trouble. Either way, it's already over by now."

"Elijah, I cannot just sit here and—"

"Running pell-mell to the Library could very well be exactly what Ruth wants, Siena." Elijah made her sharply aware of that, trying to keep his serious tone from sounding like he was scolding her. It would not be right to chastise her in such a way before so many dignitaries. "She let Jasmine go, relatively unharmed by the look of it, for a reason. That reason could be so that she raises an alarm that sends us all into one of her traps."

"I do not understand." Malaya spoke up for the first time. It had the impact of getting everyone's immediate attention, especially Jasmine, who had not even taken note of their remarkable presence. "Forgive me," the Shadowdweller apologized in an exotic, dulcet accent. "I do not mean to interrupt this thing of great importance. However, I do not understand why a Demon renegade is attacking Vampires. Or Lycanthropes, for that matter."

Noah's sigh was the beginning of the necessary response.

"Malaya . . . that is a long story that involves the disjointed reasoning of a madwoman."

"No, Noah, it does not." Jasmine cleared her throat. "It is a mistake to think there is no method to Ruth's madness. When she spoke to me, though there was that affectation of madness, her logic and her intellect were frighteningly intact. Maybe previously she boasted with half-empty threats, but now . . . now it is clear she has a plan of great depth and detail and she has been methodically carrying it out for some time."

"Jasmine is correct," Elijah added with dawning understanding. "We have been bumping into her accidentally over the past few months in the least expected places, at the least expected times, doing things we have no explanation for. However, if you put all of this together . . ."

"She is in search of something." Syreena sighed softly. "We knew she was looking for the Library when we found it purely by luck after finding her in Lycanthrope territory doing what looked like an archaeological excavation."

"The Black Tome. She was after that enormous black magic-user's compendium in the Library," Jasmine agreed. "She said it herself."

"Which she very likely has by now! Sweet Goddess," Syreena uttered with fear and outrage, "you were right, Noah, we should have burned it!"

"Mmm," Noah speculated, his green-gray eyes flicking over to the distraught and horrified expression on Isabella's face. She had been the one to argue against that, and no doubt she was feeling extremely guilty for it.

But Noah took immediate mercy on her. "We can do so now if we like," he said calmly. "It is downstairs."

"It's where?"

That response and similar exclamations battered him from all around.

"In the Demon library," he clarified. "Siena and I discussed it a long time ago and decided it should be in a much safer place once the Library was going to open. Especially because Ruth was sniffing about for it. I made haste to do so as soon as possible, especially after what happened to you, Syreena."

"But I saw it there just a couple of days ago," Jasmine argued.

"Of course you did. It would not be wise to tell frequent visitors to the Library what had happened to it, just in case Ruth found the place and started scanning their minds. I know my enemy, Jasmine. I replaced it with a black compendium exactly like it, except that one is full of"—he lifted one corner of his mouth in a grin—"I believe I will call them Demon limericks."

Jasmine's mouth fell open in surprise, Isabella gasped and choked on a laugh of relief, but most of all, the Shadow-dwellers began to chuckle in earnest. Syreena looked at them, saw their dark eyes sparkling in ready delight and their white smiles flashing wildly. It was clear they were perfectly delighted by Noah's mischief against his enemy. It was worthy of even their admiration.

"Well played. Well played indeed," the male pronounced, his deep voice projecting his humor around the entire Great Hall. "So this Ruth has likely stolen a volume of naughty rhymes instead of the powerful book she intended."

"I only hope she realizes it *after* she has absconded with it, and not before," Noah said, his smile fading. "I would hate to think of her becoming angry and taking it out on those she might have left alive otherwise."

"Elijah is right, Noah, you cannot change what Ruth has done or be responsible for what she will do from now until the time we find the way to stop her," Damien said. "It is a waste of time and a destruction of very necessary morale to dwell on what we do not have the power to stop just now."

"Meanwhile, the important thing is your actions managed to keep the cursed volume out of her hands," Jasmine said thoughtfully. "She believes the use of it by herself and other

Nightwalkers is the way it should be, that magic destroyed humans or faltered in their hands because they were too weak to manage it. She thinks Nightwalkers can manage it without losing control of it, without becoming evil."

"Bullshit," Elijah barked shortly. "Has she taken a whiff of herself lately? She smells like a garbage scow. That is the way all evil persons smell to us, especially those tainted by magic."

"She is one of them now, so she does not notice it as we do," Siena said.

"There is more," Jasmine interjected quietly. "There is someone else."

"Someone else?" Noah asked sharply, his head turning with a snap to look at her. "What the hell does that mean?"

"It means that she told me, when she offered me a place in her growing party of mayhem makers, that she already has 'a right-hand man'. It was clear what she meant. She has turned another Nightwalker to her perspective. I do not know who or how, but it sounded like a very serious development."

"I should think so! Damn her straight to hell!" Elijah growled ferociously. "*Two* of them! And if she turns one, then she will be looking for others."

"She will," Jasmine agreed. "She realizes humans are too weak to defeat you, that she needs Nightwalkers on her side. Nightwalkers using magic that makes them more powerful. That is why she let me go, Damien. She wanted me to tell you this. She wanted you all to know you were no longer going to succeed at defeating her followers with such ease."

"It's a mental ploy," Noah agreed with a grim nod. "She is trying to make us afraid. Fear will undermine our strength."

"It's working," Isabella said with a shudder.

The discussion continued, but Jasmine turned to tug Damien closer and whispered into his ear. The Prince excused himself momentarily and led Jasmine away by her arm. Syreena watched them go and tried not to feel slighted by the clearly secretive manner of their departure. She had told herself she would not do things like that, that she would allow him to carry out his friendship with Jasmine in any way he saw fit, save the small conditions she had already discussed with him.

She kept telling herself that as she watched them walk out into the garden.

Chapter 13

Damien led Jasmine out of doors where they could be assured of a private discussion, which Jasmine had requested.

"Damien, I have a terrible confession to make to you, one that may make you very angry with me, and justly so. But I have to tell you because there is so much at stake now."

"Very well," he agreed, sitting halfway on a stone wall that lined the courtyard they had entered.

"Ruth took the compendium I was reading with her when she left."

"I see. But she will have just as much access to all the others in the Library, if Anya does not stop her beforehand."

"The difference is, I am ignorant of their importance. I have been aware of the importance of this volume for quite some time now and I cannot ignore the damage it can cause."

"Explain," he encouraged her quietly.

"You set me to the task of finding a precedent for your relationship with that—with Syreena," she corrected herself in time, smiling sheepishly when he lifted a brow at the obvious self-omission. "Well, I found it within the pages of that book."

"How long ago?" he asked, his tone still level, and thereby far more unnerving than anger might have been.

"Days. Since Jinaeri became librarian. But you had already reconciled with the—with Syreena." Jasmine exhaled in frustration. "I told myself you no longer needed the information, but it was wrong of me no matter how you look at it. There are things, terrible and wonderful both, that you should know."

"Let us get to the heart of them, then, shall we?" he said directly.

"Very well. There is precedent for this relationship. In fact, there are ceremonies within this book strictly for the marriage of Vampires to foreign Nightwalkers. Apparently, thousands of years ago, it was a commonplace occurrence. As you suspected, this is where those myths of Vampires changing into different forms originate, because they are the truth. If a Vampire and, for immediate example, a Lycanthrope are attracted to one another and are compatible in their souls, they can engage in a practice called the Exchange. The Exchange is the first step in a ceremony called the Bonding. A wedding, in other words. The Exchange is exactly that. The Vampire feeds from his intended mate. By doing so, he absorbs an aspect of that mate into his makeup forever."

"The raven, in my case."

"Yes. But there is more to it than that. It is a full circle. She must drink of you to complete it. Once that circle is complete, she absorbs an aspect of you. I do not know which one, but it is something that our ancestors were impressed by enough to be more than a little nervous about it." She waved her thoughts off. "I get ahead of myself. I also found out that there is a very good reasoning behind the taboos we have inherited over the ages. While there can only be one Bonding between a Vampire and Nightwalker, there can be a dozen Exchanges. Thousands of them. Do you understand? Your heart will be Bonded to this woman for all eternity once you let her feed from you. Nothing, no force on the earth can change that, save death. The same is reciprocated for her. She is Bonded to you, till death.

"But the terror comes from the Vampire, Damien. The Vampire who feeds on Nightwalkers can gather their powers like a child gathers toys, adding to his inventory over and over again, taking on aspects of them all until he finally holds them all like a complete collection. Do you understand," she breathed fiercely, "what I am saying? A Vampire can become indestructible. Nothing, no power on all the earth, could ever stop him if he decided to obtain all of that power. The choice to stay away from feeding on Nightwalkers was a moral one. Our ancestors gathered together and swore to teach their children to be terrified of taking the blood of Nightwalkers. They made fables and stories and scared them out of their wits. They controlled future generations because they had seen what had happened when it was allowed to be common knowledge."

"Damn," Damien uttered hoarsely, shock clearly written over his shadowed features. She heard the striking apprehension in that single word, and knew the feeling well.

"It was a sacrifice, Damien, with ramifications. Yes, they succeeded in what they wanted, but I have come to realize that this is why we are the way we are. When they took away that special joining from us, they robbed us of the love and depth of emotion that comes with it. They bred out of us the opportunity to have what I see you now have with this woman you have chosen. This is what saddens us, Damien. This is why we cannot stay aboveground for unbearable loneliness; this is why we do not wed. We eliminated our mating pool, threw away the switches that would turn on our greatest emotions. A sacrifice made to keep us from destroying innocents and others if we decided to become monsters of power.

"This is why we have so few children. It takes great depth of love and desire to want to raise children. We have children, but we never raise them. They just . . . sort of grow up.

We have sex, but no love. No true pleasure, though we seek it constantly with indiscriminant sensuality. We seek, we yearn, we want, but never knew what we longed for all of these centuries. We"—she swallowed painfully—"we threw away our happiness right along with our fear."

"Just like the Demons did when they destroyed the Druids," Damien murmured.

"Except they did not know what they were consigning themselves to. I think our forbearers did. I am not certain," she added when he looked at her for clarification. "There were a lot of couched euphemisms. They wrote down the history, however, with the hopes that one day we would be mature enough as a species to handle the responsibilities again. To mate without opening up the opportunity to criminal exploitation. You did this thing, the Exchange, by accident. Can you imagine if others knew what they could do on purpose?"

"Jas, do you know what you are asking me to do here?" he demanded roughly. "You are asking me to make an impossible decision!"

"I know that! Why do you think I kept this to myself for so long? I did not want to do this to you! But now that Ruth has that book, I have no choice. If she reads it . . ."

"If she finds a Vampire she can lure to her side," he added painfully.

"Then we will have much more to deal with than an insane Demon who uses magic. And then there is the matter of the rest of the information at stake."

"Yes, I know," he snapped bitterly. "Do I watch my people continue to walk this world suffering the trouble and pain of hearts that can feel loneliness and agony and desperate need without the relief of love and joy and satisfaction? Do I give them the freedom to know the love I have been blessed with? How can any one man be allowed the right to make that kind of choice? How can I decide the fates of so many?"

"That is your duty as Prince," Jasmine said.

"No, it is not! A government has no right to dictate the

pursuit of happiness to anyone! And this is not just my people we are talking about anymore, Jasmine. The people of those leaders in that room we just left are affected as well. How many times have we heard about the loneliness and solitude of those Nightwalker species outside of our own? What if that dreadful, despairing condition is because they are deserving of Vampire mates who will not come anywhere near them?"

"Demon mates who will not come near them," she added thoughtfully, clearly thinking of Elijah and Siena.

"Jasmine."

Damien could say nothing more for a moment, just her strangled name. The ramifications of these findings were endless and extraordinary. This was not the first hint they had gotten that the separate races of the Nightwalkers had once, long ago, belonged together as one. The Library was the largest hint of all. A combined effort between clans that had been notorious for collaborating on nothing. Then he thought about the Shadowdwellers behind them, the leaders of a race that they had believed to have no political structure to speak of, sitting in representation.

"Jas . . . do you realize . . ." He paused to swallow in nervous reflex. "Do you realize this is the first time in all of my life that none of the Nightwalkers have been at war? There was always something. Someone always fighting someone else. Since Siena was crowned, the only war we could claim was a cold war between all the races and the Shadowdwellers. There has not been an overt hostile action from them that I can remember in several decades, but we all have suspected them of this and that, of covert mischief and tactics. But I look at their Chancellors and I realize that they may have been scapegoats for too many things. Too many other explanations that were too hard to figure out when so easy an explanation was available."

"Do not jump so far ahead," Jasmine scolded gently. "What is your point?"

"That maybe it is time we stopped making things Vampire business, Demon business, and Lycanthrope business, and started making things Nightwalker business." He looked at her with serious eyes. "This thing you have told me is not Vampire business, Jasmine. It is Nightwalker business. It affects all of them, as well as us."

"Damien!" she whispered harshly. "You cannot be thinking of walking in there and telling them something like this! They could see us all as a potential threat when you tell them of the part about the Exchange and the power we can get!"

"Perhaps. And perhaps they would be right to do so. Just as they have the right to see if we are hiding the hearts of desperately needed and sought-for mates, Jas. I know you couldn't care less, that you find all of this emotional stuff to be a bother and a weakness, but I promise you, it is not. It is a strength. It is a mighty power to be loved and to love."

"I see. A mighty power that makes you want to toast yourself in the sun like a Pop-Tart?" she said with bitter sarcasm.

"Or drink poison in the family crypt, or betray the King of Camelot, or trade feet for fins and watch your love marry another. Yes, Jasmine, all of those terrible things and more. But when it works, when it is given the chance to be completed, you get the Imprinting, you get the Bonding, and you get marriages that last from one life to the next. Partnership, friendship, laughter and tickling and lovemaking." He had reached for her hand with the passion of his speech. "You get to stay above the ground, Jasmine, and learn something new each and every day so that it never gets boring. You are able to protect and care for something so much more than yourself, and so much more worthy, too. Would you never want to know what that is like?"

"I would never again want to know the pain I have experienced this past week when I knew I was losing you, Damien! Can you imagine if I had to suffer being in love and going through that? I cannot bear the thought!"

But there was something about the way he spoke about his newfound love, the passion and the truth and the confidence he exuded, that made her long to know what he was speaking of. She suddenly wished to know what it was that she was missing.

No.

Not suddenly.

Always. Every day of her life she had known something was missing. She more than others, more sensitive than so many others, falling into that dark despair over and over again and never knowing why.

What if this was why? She had said so earlier, but she had not truly considered what it would mean. She had not realized what could be gained. She had been too afraid of it as she had watched Damien move away from her.

What was more, she had been jealous of it.

"Damn you, Damien," she whispered, throwing off his hand and moving away.

The Prince watched her back for a moment, knowing what her conflicts were. He had run that gauntlet himself several times this past week. There was only one truth to all of this, as far as he was concerned, one thing that it all came down to.

He would go to the ends of the earth to see Jasmine as happy as he was now.

He would risk everything for that.

"I would risk Syreena if it meant you would be happy," he said softly.

Jasmine turned quickly at that, her arms folding defensively beneath her breasts as she faced him. "No, you would not. You would die before seeing anything happen to her."

"It would not be the risk you are talking about, Jasmine. I meant, I would risk going public with her. I would dare to set her on my throne beside me for everyone to see, making an example of her, taking on every threat in our world and others, if it meant giving you and the others I am responsible for the happiness that I now know. I mean that there is no choice here, Jasmine. I was right the first time. I have no right to choose for others: All I can do is speak the truth and let others decide for themselves what will happen next." He took a breath. "My responsibility will be to check those who would do evil with this knowledge. I will have to set the precedent among us that the Demons have set for themselves. I will have to select someone to enforce those who would abuse the privilege of the Exchange."

"Damien, that is an impossible task!"

"Not for the right person," he argued. "Not for someone with the right senses, the proper skills."

"Jacob and Isabella were born with the senses needed to constantly monitor their own. We have no one like that."

"We all have that. We have the skill to sense those of us who have power," he countered.

"Hunting after the fact. After an Exchange has already taken place? That is deadly work."

"I never said it would be easy. Between that, however, and education, perhaps this will be conceivable."

"It is madness," she muttered, "but . . ."

"But?" he encouraged.

"Perhaps," she said thoughtfully, "if it was not just one of us. Not an Enforcer per se. There should be a leader; however, it should be like . . . like Stephan," she said suddenly, the idea forming quickly. "Damien, Stephan has an entire army of us at his disposal. Since we are no longer at war with anyone, perhaps we should give them a new purpose. Or a dual purpose."

"Go on."

"We cannot leave ourselves without an army, just in case this peace thing you are so gung-ho over does not work out. However, since peace has prevailed, they have languished with nothing but training on their schedules for decades. For centuries, really. Frankly, I think they have gotten lazy. Giving them domestic duties might just give them something to do. Something that will also keep more of them out of trouble. You know the best Vampire is an occupied Vampire. Stephan has always chosen his soldiers very carefully. Dedicated, honest, excellent fighters. If we spread them out over selected territories, Vampire, Nightwalker, and human, it would be like . . . like . . ."

"A sensor net," he supplied for her. "A monitoring system spread out to catch unlawful Vampires before they go too far."

"Better than that. Unlawful Nightwalkers in general. Of course, we would not want to harm foreigners, but we could alert their homeland government."

"You see? This is what I am talking about. If all six Nightwalker species brainstormed like this, together, we could easily protect ourselves and each other from the Ruths of our worlds. Frankly, there is probably a version of Ruth, or several of them, from each one of our societies. The one who always manages to stay out of range of our usual policing methods."

"Like Nico. You were fortunate, Damien, that he was the one killed in that fight." She smiled slowly, her eyes lighting softly in the moonlight. "Keeping these warriors around you domestically might not be such a bad idea, either. I realize you have always been capable of taking care of yourself, and that it is not our way to keep an official court, but perhaps it is overdue. This game of King of the Mountain we play for your throne is due for a change. Maybe you should keep a court, with all the appropriate protections, discouraging those who would harm you . . . and Syreena, for that matter. They will use her to get to you."

"I know. They will be in for a surprise, because she does not lie down easily. But I would prefer to eliminate exposing her to that kind of grief. Especially if . . ." He broke off and looked at the ground, kicking at a stone as he smiled sheepishly. "Especially if we wish to start the family I know she longs for." He looked up at Jasmine, his pleasure and gratitude very clear in his eyes. "Which I now believe is possible, thanks to you, Jasmine. I would hardly think weddings outside of the species would have been as acceptable as you claim they were if children were not possible."

"That had not occurred to me," she admitted, a smile of her own appearing. "But then again, I do not have the motivation you do to consider these things. You surprise me, Damien. You have never had children."

"Neither have you," he pointed out.

"We were not the parental type. I still am not."

"So long as you allow the opportunity for that to change, Jasmine."

"Pregnancy?" Jasmine shuddered theatrically. "Perish the thought. Save it for yourself. Or rather, her who will play dam to your sire."

"And what of falling in love?"

"Again, for you and the poets, not for me." She paused a beat before relenting. "At least, not soon. I have an enormous task ahead of me, if you recall. I have to help Stephan set up a police force, and I have to coordinate efforts with our ambassadors. Then I have to help advise you on ambassadors for the Shadowdwellers court, as I know you are thinking of sending one. That will leave us with choosing someone to live among the Mistrals. Someone mentally strong enough to overcome the charm of their voices, perhaps musical so they will enjoy their post, but quiet and demure. Well-behaved and shy. Someone who says little, but when they speak has much to say."

"I am glad I am getting a domestic security in place. I think someone is vying for my throne," he teased her, reaching up to chuck her under the chin. "Does this mean you will stay with us, Jas?"

"I will stay at a court," she corrected. "I think you should seat yourself in Romania, Damien. Our homeland. Your holdings there are more than large enough to expand your household in the way you must, and yet has enough distant wings to afford privacy to yourself, me, and any guests you might have. Besides, it is closer to your future bride's homeland. She could fly home for a visit very often that way."

Damien laughed at her sly smile when she made it clear that the more often Syreena flew off, the better it would suit her.

"Promise me one thing?"

"That depends," she responded in true Vampire fashion.

"That if Syreena should prove herself to be adequate to sit by my throne, you will afford her the respect she deserves?"

Jasmine thought about it for only a short moment.

"I will promise you this much. In public, I will always treat her as you wish me to. In my own head, however, I will very likely continue to think of her as a twiggy little twit. It is the best I can do."

"Very well." He chuckled.

"And I have never been shy about arguing my opinion, whether anyone liked it or not."

"I would expect you to continue to do so. An advisor is no good to me if she cannot contradict me."

"Or your Princess. But I will contradict her with great respect," she said with magnanimous charm and a flourishing bow.

Damien laughed at her, then opened an arm and gestured her forward with the flick of two beckoning fingers. Jasmine submitted to the show of affection he wished to give her, and stepped into his hug. She sighed with great relief in spite of herself when she felt him stroke his fingers through her hair just as he always had, as if nothing between them had changed, as if nothing ever would.

It was two hours before dawn when they finally received word of what had happened at the Library. The time passed with unbearable sluggishness for Siena, in spite of the fact that they had been sharing an overwhelming influx of information and ideas thanks to Damien's revelations about the Vampires' history and possible future. Siena did not know if she would have been so readily forthcoming about her domestic problems, but she was quickly understanding why Damien had felt it necessary. The Vampires had always been the first to break ground in issues of peace; at least, once Damien had decided war simply bored him to death. Offering an ambassador for the Shadowdweller court was an astounding risk, but what was more astounding was that they accepted. Siena was just beginning to realize that Malaya and Tristan would be a very interesting pair to get to know, when the airborne messenger from Anya arrived.

Her name was Nita, and Siena recognized her instantly as she transformed from her form of an owl to the pretty, rounded figure of Anya's most favored lieutenant.

She sketched a courteous bow to her Queen, and then again to all the other dignitaries, never once blinking an eye at the remarkable nature of the collection of Nightwalkers before her.

"My Queen," she began immediately, "I have news of the Library."

"You may tell it now." Siena gave leave impatiently, though grateful Nita had given her the opportunity to choose whether she would have preferred to hear it in private.

"By the time we arrived, it had been completely ransacked. Jinaeri reports that—"

"Jinaeri lives?" Siena asked abruptly. She had been tormenting herself for hours for putting such a close friend in such terrible danger.

"She was the lone survivor," Nita admitted regretfully. "It was her form of the lemur that saved her. She could climb to a safe place where she hid herself. She is not a fighter, as you know, so it made sense for her to stay out of the way. The Monks, however, and the others were not so lucky."

"Kelsey?" Damien asked sharply.

"Dead. I am sorry," Nita said softly. "There were four guards, three Monks, and a Mistral besides. I am so sorry for you all."

She waited for several moments as the silence of grief fell over the room.

"Jinaeri tells us that Ruth was not alone. There was a—"

"A male," Jasmine interjected bitterly.

"A Vampire male," Nita corrected.

"*A what?*" Damien exploded, his calm vanishing completely as he lurched to his feet. "How does she know?"

"Because he overcame the Mistral and tore open her throat, leaving her to bleed to death. Only a powerful Vampire could overcome the Mistral's song and then display fangs in such a usage. They teleported in, attacked, and then ransacked the Library. There was no trail we could follow. That is all we know."

"I can follow her. I am going to kill that—"

"No, Damien. You could not stand up to Ruth alone, never mind Ruth and a Vampire. It is as you said just a few hours ago," Noah argued, "this is something we must handle in a joint effort."

"Ruth and a Vampire is a deadly combination," Jasmine reminded them all. "The more time they have, the worse it will be."

"It is a risk we have to take," Noah said grimly. "This knowledge is too new for any of us to use against her. We have no preparations or skills in place. If we go forward without taking the time we need, we will only be consigning more of us to death. I will sacrifice no more of my people on that psychotic woman. And it is my people who will be in danger from this Vampire the most, if what you say is true. Yes, we are all at risk, but Demons hold the variety of powers the Vampire would desire. The further away we stay, for now, the better. Our time is better spent getting the warning out to each and every member of all our societies. We are so disparate and so dispersed that it will be like lambs to the slaughter to leave them out there with no warning."

"Agreed," Siena said quietly. "My people are easier to contact because we live in groups in dens and packs, but not until hibernation is ended."

" 'Dwellers still tend to live in clans as well, but they also love to bicker and it will take some time to get them to agree on actions," Tristan said.

"Common danger has a way of bringing such people together," Jasmine noted.

"One can hope," Elijah said. "Noah is right, we have so many personal upheavals within our own species to handle on top of this threat. And the Mistrals are the most vulnerable. Windsong, your people depend on the stun of your voices to protect you, but this is a Mind Demon and a Vampire, and they are both able to defeat that protection."

"Depending on the skill of the Mistral, yes." Siena spoke up for Windsong, knowing that was what she would wish to get across if she could speak without stunning most of the room into a daze. In the future, they would have to set up a telepathic interpreter for the Bard and the Siren so they could communicate better without risking putting everyone into limbo. "There are very few of us who can defeat the charm of someone of Windsong's skill. Damien . . . maybe Jasmine, though I do not know her skill level as a telepath."

Damien began to pace the room in uncharacteristic impatience as they spoke, drawing Syreena's worried gaze along with him over his repetitive path around the backs of their chairs.

"I cannot tolerate inaction for the amount of time you are speaking of," Damien said suddenly. "It would be unconscionable to let this opportunity slip away when she can be traced, now . . . today."

"Traced and then what? Battle her immeasurable power as well as that of an unknown Vampire? A power that just murdered seven Nightwalkers in one sitting, four of whom we know were excellent fighters?" Siena made a sound of equal impatience. "I feel as you do, Damien, but I have lost too many good people to this sick bitch just as Noah has, and I am learning quickly that chasing after her on impulse never gets us anywhere."

"It got rid of Mary last time," Syreena said.

"Almost at the cost of your life not a week ago, Syreena," her sister retorted. "Personally, my vote is for Damien's original idea. Cast out a well-trained net of people. She is not a subtle creature. She will trip over us eventually."

"Hopefully before she gains enough power to slaughter us by the hundreds," Damien said sarcastically. "Or a larger following. My idea was meant for future occurrences, not for ignoring the present." He stopped suddenly, a single brow lifting in sudden thought. "But let us say for a moment that we wish this sort of collaboration to work in the future. What better way to prove it to our followers than if we, all in this room and those who are most powerful that we know, go now to take care of Ruth once and for all?"

"And risk the one group of leaders in several millennia to manage to find peace with one another? If any one of us dies, Damien, the ramifications will ripple back through an entire people, and I hate to say so, but this calm is too young, too immature to survive that right now."

Damien looked at Syreena with cold eyes as the sound argument came past her lips. It had been a knee-jerk reaction for her to say what she was thinking no matter how it might be received. She had gotten into the habit of speaking her mind against even Siena's authority. It wasn't until she was on the receiving end of his displeasure that she realized how he might take such a thing from someone he hoped to get support from. But she could not bring herself to rescind any part of the remark, not even for love of him. There was too much at stake, and she had faith that even he would know that eventually.

At some future time when he was not feeling the death of Kelsey and the defection of another so keenly.

"Meanwhile," she continued more gently, "we should take the other actions we discussed, as well as a few others. The Library must be relocated, what is left of it. It is a trove in which there is sure to be treasures we still do not know anything about. Ruth was looking for only one book, but in her usual shortsightedness left thousands of others behind that may mean just as much, if not more. That is how we must protect ourselves right now. We must guard that knowledge for the sake of our future generations who may one day have as great a need for it as we are learning we have."

"So we have an agenda," Malaya said firmly. "A very large one. First, we must all learn to perfectly police our own to the best of our ability. I speak, of course, for the Vampires and us 'Dwellers mostly. We are the ones who fall short there."

"Second," Tristan picked up, "a full ambassadorial exchange in all courts so we learn about one another. The truth. Not speculation or prejudice."

"Third, the protection of the Library," Syreena said. "A communal place, so it will be a location where it can be shared with ease and peace, but one that is a hundred times better protected by all of us."

"Fourth," Damien said at last, his resignation all too evident as he conceded to the majority, "the alert of all our members to the threats we face, and the formation of the multicultural net based on Jasmine's idea of domestic Vampire policing. A Nightwalker version of the United Nations, I suppose you could call it."

"Policing, preparation, protection, and peacefulness," Syreena alliterated with a small smile.

"Let us add 'propaganda' to that," Noah suggested. "A regular gathering of this very kind every month, in the open, well publicized, so that those who follow us understand what our goals are. This time, I intend to do everything I can to see that Nightwalkers remain on speaking terms all around."

"Agreed," Siena said quickly.

"Agreed," Tristan and Malaya echoed.

All the others agreed at exactly the same time, and it was vibrated into them by the musical pitches of the Mistrals' voices.

Syreena walked slowly down the empty hallway of the old Romanian compound. Damien's homeland holdings were enormous, by aboveground standards. There were catacombs as well, which only added to the maze of stone, both natural and built up, rather reminiscent of Siena's holdings in their turning and twisting confusion of pathways.

Jasmine had gone back to the California manse and would return the next night. Damien had left to hunt quickly before dawn arrived. He had first guided Syreena to this place and told her to wait within the walls, that she would be safe there.

She was, unless she could be threatened by cobwebs, of which there were plenty. The main house, a cross between a castle and some kind of institutional rectangle of endless rooms, was not in any disrepair. It was clear that Damien did not neglect his property, even when he spent decades away from it. Still, it had not had a two-legged visitor for quite some time, by the look of it. If not for her still-healing arm, she would have turned into the falcon and flown the centers of the looping hallways, under and over the webbing that seemed to reach out and cling to her from everywhere at once.

The arm would be perfectly healed in another day or so, and a few cobwebs were not going to hurt her. Besides, she would never admit that the things just gave her the willies.

She had an image to uphold, after all.

"Oh yuck," she complained as she ran face first into one of the silken traps. She pulled it from her face and hair, frantically trying to shake it from her fingers.

"I think you have a spider in your hair."

Syreena gasped, reaching for her hair as she spun around to face Damien. "Where?"

"Right behind that part of your head that likes to contradict me in front of half a dozen or more visiting dignitaries," he said dryly.

"Damien!" She slapped his shoulder, very hard, forcing him to take a step back for balance as he chuckled at her. "That is not funny!"

"The big bad former Monk trained to kill with her bare hands being afraid of spiders?" His smirk told her he thought otherwise.

"It is my job to contradict overinflated royal egos, especially when they want to run off and get their heads chopped off," she retorted tartly.

"I never realized you had so little faith in my abilities," he said.

"Yes, actually, you did. You told me yourself that you would never take on Ruth by yourself."

"When did I say that?" he demanded.

"The minute you rescued me," she pointed out.

"Explain that, if you please. I seem to recall you being unconscious at the time."

"Answer me this, then," she countered. "Why didn't you face down Ruth then and there? You had opportunity, time, strength, and all of your power. Why not take care of her once and for all?"

"Because I was busy saving your impertinent, ungrateful backside!"

"One life in trade of the dozens of others you would have been saving?"

"One very important life," he argued, although a bit more gently. "Very important to me."

"Good. Remember that the next time I contradict you in front of half a dozen visiting dignitaries."

Damien sighed deeply, reaching to rub at his temples. "Remember, or regret?" he asked blandly.

"Ha. Ha. Ha."

He smiled at her, unable to help himself. Even when he was angry with her, she delighted him.

"I have a feeling," he said, reaching out to brush a remnant of webbing off her hair, "that this thing we have might actually work out in the long run."

"I am glad *you* think so," she said, giving him an impish grin.

"Provided I do not kill you before then."

"Good provision," she agreed.

Damien was silent for a moment, and then he grasped her wrist, using it to tug her closer to him.

"Will you be happy here?" he asked as they mutually settled her against the fresh warmth of his body. "Will you be happy away from your home?"

"Goddess, yes," she breathed, as if with relief. "I have outgrown the Monks, and Siena does not need me any longer. Perhaps my absence will help her get over her fear of having children, when people start looking at her even more closely in search of an heir."

"Siena is afraid of children?"

"Terrified. She just does not realize it yet. She thinks she is doing it for convenience or because her marriage is too new. Lucky for her, her husband is pretty much a huge chicken about fatherhood, too. Though I suspect he might come around faster than she will."

"Elijah as a father," he mused, his humor at the thought evident. "He is used to getting them from someone else, fostering them as *Siddah* after the age of eighteen or so. He will not have a clue what to do with a baby."

"I know," she giggled. "Come to think of it, I am quite glad I will not be there for this. They would exhaust me."

"Their children?"

"No, the parents!"

He laughed. "And what of our children, sweetling?"

She tilted her head and looked up at him with arched brows. "Do you want children, Damien?"

"It is one of those more important questions we have not gotten to yet, is it not?"

"Yes. It very much is. I am not certain if you know this, but I have always wanted to have a lot of children. To fill the house."

"Not this house, I hope," he chuckled.

"No. Definitely not enough to fill this house." She flashed a grin. "I guess we'll have to get a bigger house when the time comes."

"Very cute," he said, reaching around to pinch her bottom in punishment.

"Stop that!"

"Then be serious. Tell me what you really want." His tone became serious to make her understand it was important to him that she put her taunts aside for a moment. "I want to know what you want."

"I want to be happy," she said simply. "One day at a time. One discussion at a time. One baby at a time. Life is too volatile to plan too far ahead. Especially now."

"I understand your point. But at the same time, I do not want us putting our lives on hold because of fear of what Ruth will do next."

"No? But we can run off at the drop of a hat and risk our lives? That is okay?"

"Syreena . . ."

"I'm serious, Damien. I do not understand your distinction. Safe some of the time, reckless others? You want me and children, yet an hour ago you were contemplating something tantamount to suicide." She shuddered. "I don't expect either of us to sit idly by while others risk themselves for us, but I do expect you to remember you are not the only one you have to consider anymore. Don't you know that you take my heart with you everywhere you go?"

"Just as you take mine," he assured her softly, bending to kiss her forehead gently, his eyes sliding closed. "You are right, and I am sorry. I promise I will take more care for your feelings and thoughts in these matters in the future. I was upset earlier. I am still adjusting to this new depth of emotion I find myself privy to all of a sudden."

"You have always felt strongly. You could not be the leader you are if you did not."

"Yes. But now it is even stronger still."

"Damien, do you trust me?"

"What kind of a question is that?" he asked abruptly, pulling her head back so he could look down into her odd-colored eyes.

"I was just wondering if you were ever going to complete the Exchange with me," she said directly.

"Why would I not?"

"Because it is daunting, to give away a part of yourself without knowing what it will be." She reached to stroke warm fingers over his cheek. "I did not know what I was doing when you first received the part of me that makes you the raven. I did not have a choice to make."

"Do you regret that?"

"Actually, I don't. I am glad things happened like they did. I might have been too hung up to make the choice myself. Remember, I was not very good at deciding things for myself then. I still am not."

"But you are improving," he noted.

"Yes, I know," she laughed.

"Do you want to complete the Exchange, Syreena?"

She hesitated a moment, knowing his expectant gaze was on her face the entire time she considered the question. She had only known about this thing for a couple of hours, and the information on it had come from Jasmine, a source that had proven to be untrustworthy when it came to complete disclosure. It was not that Syreena was squeamish about the act of drinking blood, either. She was mostly an animal, when it came right down to it. She had dined on an omnivorous selection all of her life. The main concern was what an added power might do to one of her design.

Then again, what was she if not a guinea pig? Her entire existence was the result of an experimentation in the combination of Nightwalker abilities. When she had been ill as a child, Windsong had Spirit-sung Syreena back to life, sharing her spirit with Siena's and Syreena's own spirits. Syreena now suspected that this was where her avian half had come from. Mistrals only became birds. It could not be a coincidence that one of her forms was a falcon. With all of those spirits in her at once in that moment of near death, anything could have caused her to become the combined soup she was, the split being that she was.

Now a whole because of Damien's spirit linking it all together at last.

It would only be fitting to truly add his blood to hers in such a way, also adding whatever part of himself that seemed to belong mixed in with the rest of her soup.

"You make it sound like minestrone," he teased her softly.

"Would you rather I used a mixed-nuts metaphor? With you being the biggest nut of all? Stop nosing around in my head."

"Sorry. I could not resist. You looked like you were working so hard at your thoughts. Curiosity got the better of me."

"So now you know my answer."

"I do."

"Yes. I do."

Chapter 14

Damien reached to pull her close, grasping her beneath her knees to slide her toward him. She slid easily over the sheets until her hips touched the insides of both his thighs and he was leading her legs around his back. They sat facing one another, so close now that her thighs rested atop his and they each had their ankles linked behind the other's back. Damien's hands slid up her beautifully shaped legs until they rested lightly on her waist. Their foreheads touched, their noses rubbing gently together as he reached to kiss her several times. The tips of her naked breasts brushed lightly against his equally bare chest, and he liked the reaction that immediately followed.

"I love the way you feel," he said softly against her swelling lips.

Syreena smiled briefly before he kissed it away, exchanging that pleasure with another and then another as he slowly searched the taste and moisture of her mouth, feeding her the same from his own. Her hands slid around his rib cage to his back, the warmth and smoothness of his taut skin such a sensual delight that she spread her fingers far apart to cover even more of it. She liked how his muscles contracted in little twitches every time she moved her palms and fingertips to new places. If nothing else did, this would tell her how much pleasure he took in the exploration of her hands.

Damien's hands moved into her hair, making the living strands curl happily around them, trapping them to the warmth of her head so it could constrict his fingers and wrists like a hungry nest of boas. Within moments, he was wrapped up to his elbows in it, his forearms snugly held in its pulsing shafts.

She kissed him as her hands continued to move over his skin. She forgot about the dust and barrenness of the enormous household around the master suite he had taken them to, even though every breath she drew seemed to echo into every near corridor. The must and cobwebs around them seemed to disappear, replaced solely by his masculine scent in combination with hers as they wafted together around the small world they had created between their close bodies.

They were both completely nude, save for the bandage and hard splint still dressing her right arm. But even that small restriction could not interfere with the total access they desired for this moment. Syreena felt as though it had been ages since they had touched one another, in spite of the fact that she knew she had never been touched by another being in her lifetime as much as Damien touched her. It seemed as though he could even caress her from a distance, with only his eyes and the very obvious desires within them that always took away any and all space between them.

"Let go of my hands," he said with humor as he gave a curl of her hair a tug.

"Why should I?" she asked, her thoughtfulness and mischief coming through loud and clear.

"Because I know you want me to touch you," he said with the assuredness of a telepath.

She could not argue with him, so she relaxed, releasing the stranglehold her hair had on him. Once he had slipped free of the loving snarl, he stroked his fingers over her face, down her throat and shoulders and arms. He started over the pulses in her neck, working his way down the path of the pounding arteries all the way to her fingertips.

Damien laced his fingers with hers, giving them a momentary squeeze. He released her almost as quickly, so he could stroke the backs of his knuckles down her chest, starting at the hollow in her throat. He followed a straight path over her collarbone and breasts. After briefly slipping his caressing fingers past her erect nipples, he turned his hands so he could cup the full weight of her within his palms.

For Syreena, every moment of the searching caresses was a slow beat that thrummed like a bass drum through her body. She closed her eyes, drawing in a deep breath as his hands flexed around her, their heat somehow more than the steady temperature that was normal for him. Perhaps it was her own hot skin that made it so, the eddy of it warming him incredibly, but if that were the case, how would she note the difference?

"Damien, I love the way you touch me," she murmured against the rub of his lips.

"I know," he told her before catching up her mouth with a depth that transcended the physical capabilities of their meshing lips and tongues.

His right hand released its loving hold on her breast so it could skim over her side and hip. He grasped her firmly and drew her completely up his thighs and into his lap, seating her with incredible intimacy against him. It was contradictory for him to be so blunt and bold when he had been so patient and tender until then. She made a gasping sound of surprise as iron hardness and heat swam through the exterior dampness of her body, but surprise immediately gave way to pleasure, and the gasp turned to a long, sweetly pained moan.

"I have missed you," he said suddenly, pulling her ear to his lips so she could hear and feel the heat of his whispered words. "It cannot be more than a day since I was last here, close to your body, wrapped in your heat, but still I missed you."

"You are not yet wrapped in my heat," she argued, her entire being squirming against him in clear frustration over that fact.

She felt him smile against her ear.

"You seem impatient, sweetness," he teased her, his teeth scraping over her earlobe and then releasing the sensitive flesh so he could blow a gentle breath over the dampness his mouth had left behind. She shivered as goose bumps raced along her spine and a fresh wash of liquid invitation flowed from her body and onto his.

"Tell me you are not," she demanded, punctuating the request with an artful tilt of her hips, teasing him right back with a perfect seat that was the prelude to an even better one.

Damien made a rough, masculine sound as he felt the welcoming pulse of her inner body beckoning him from that intimate perch on the edge of the haven she was for him.

"I am," he agreed hotly, finding her mouth again as his hands fell to her hips and held her with tight possessiveness.

He drew her forward onto himself even as she arched her hips and body to take him inside herself. There was always something so breathtaking about the initial joining of their bodies. It was a moment that could last forever in a heartbeat, their focus nowhere but on the blending fit of their heated sexes. He inhaled the shuddering groan of pleasure that she exhaled. Then her kiss seemed to come alive in tempo and intensity, twisting over and inside his mouth as if she intended to devour him.

She was steadily becoming bolder and more aggressive during their lovemaking, but she also was learning how to give herself over to him, allowing him to lead her to pleasurable places. It was all an issue of trust. In these moments, he knew she trusted him implicitly. She had to. It was an act of pure exposure and vulnerability.

It made him feel a power that went beyond his gifts of Vampirism.

Syreena put a hand against him, firmly pushing him several inches away from her chest and mouth. He pulled back, blinking his deep blue eyes at her.

Then, as her other hand slid away over the bedsheets, he remembered why they had come there.

Syreena picked up the steel poniard, the metal glinting fiercely in the candlelight, the emerald embedded in its hilt winking its fire-green facets at them. She held it between their breastbones for a moment, looking down at the haft of the razor-sharp blade. There was an inscription in Vampyr on the hilt, wending in a spiral around the decorative swirl of crafted metal.

"*I will break thee in any heart counter to my own,*" she said softy, impressing him with her ability to read his native tongue.

"Family motto," he explained with half a smile.

"Very emotionally passionate for a Vampiric saying," she mused in a whisper.

Syreena touched the cold blade to his chest, lengthwise, scraping it with delicate concentration over his skin. Considering the hone of it, he was amazed it did not cut him. It was her skill alone that made it so, he realized.

"Tell me where," she asked, her breath catching nervously in spite of how excited she was on other levels.

"Anywhere. It is your choice, Syreena."

Her choice.

The basis of their entire relationship, in two syllables.

But she would not vacillate this time. She had already been through her debates and her decisions. Now, with their bodies conjoined so perfectly and his trust as naked between them as the blade, there was no need for choice.

She moved so quickly, it was more like a twitch. Damien did not even feel the bite of the blade as it nicked his throat. Her aim was remarkable for the speed she had used, the breach of his skin under an inch wide in the lower left space just off center of his Adam's apple. Instantly, a scarlet bead of blood welled out of the wound, quickly filling and break-ing, running down his chest, over his pectoral muscle and onto the ridges of his abdomen. The thin stream of his life's essence continued on until it disappeared where their bodies connected.

Syreena flicked up her bicolored gaze to his as she dropped the poniard over the edge of the mattress and onto the floor. She did not even notice the clatter of the metal against the stone as she leaned toward his neck.

The minute her lips sealed over his skin, Damien felt the balance of the world spin away from them. He groaned sav-agely as she swept her tongue over him slowly, her deft little mouth burning him like a brand, and then began to suck softly against him. He gripped her tightly as she did this, his head falling back to increase her access. His fangs made a violent appearance as the groan turned to a rolling growl of pleasure.

Syreena felt the effect she was having on him from the center of her body outward. He swelled within her, heated intensely, the increasing hardness of him pulsing with wicked life inside her. His taste was not what she had expected. It was somehow different from the rust and salt tang that she had anticipated. His flavor was bold and nearly sweet. As the warm fluid slid over her palate and down her throat, she began to get a hint of what it had been like for him the very first time he had tasted of her.

There was power in his blood. All Nightwalker blood held the power of its owner, but this was like nothing she could have ever expected. There was so much of herself within him, and so much of a combination of Nightwalker power from within herself. The addition of his essence was numb-ing and erotic and pleasurable beyond words. She was not prepared for the fire that flowed from her belly and into all of her limbs. If it could, it would have exploded out of her fingertips, toes, and the ends of her hair, that was how violently it burst through her.

She pulled back from the place where she fed as her entire body locked in a delicious spasm of delight. Damien felt the convulsion as it passed through her, constricting her around him so tightly he thought he might lose his mind with the intensity of the recoil of pleasure that followed. He knew what she was experiencing, if it was anything like the experiences he had had. The very idea of it was as thrilling as the feel of it.

Damien slipped his hands down over her bottom, fitting her to his palms so he could lift her against himself, drawing himself slowly out of the incredible clutch she had on him. Syreena's hands reached out to grab his shoulders suddenly, her strength remarkable as she did so. She cried out roughly as he relaxed his hands and allowed her to slide back down over him, fitting him like a spandex glove made solely to his dimensions. Her arms slid over his shoulders, wrapping around his neck and head as he repeated the motion again and again.

Syreena closed her eyes because she could not have focused on anything, and it was making her dizzy to watch the room spin and move. She was so lost to the tearing eroticism flowing through herself that she could do little more than let him manipulate her as he wished. Without the intercourse of their bodies, she would still have felt that way. With it, she was beyond feeling any one coherent emotion or sensation.

Her shoulder nudged up against Damien's lips, exposing it to the scrape of his teeth.

He could smell her.

Lavender, sex, sweetness, all blended into the pulse that flowed over her collarbone. He closed his eyes, rubbing his lips and his face over her skin, trying to remember that he had hunted that night already, only a short while ago, in fact.

Until she lowered her head back to the cut she had made on him and put her lips to him again.

He swore in Vampyr, a vicious growl of impatience and

lustful intensity. He timed the thrust of his teeth into her shoulder with the thrust of his body. Her warmth flowed over his lips and tongue and the ever-hardening shaft surrounded so tightly by her all at once. Damien understood in that moment why this thing between them was meant to be the way that it was. This was the spice of true life. It flowed over him in liquid and emotional form and he knew that he could live twenty millennia and never grow tired of the sensation. It could have been the newfound acuteness to his feelings that made him wax so poetic in his thoughts, but he did not think that was so. This went beyond all of that. This was the blending of souls, the joining of spirits and blood and body.

It was everything.

She was everything.

"I love you," she gasped beneath his ear, gripping him frantically as she spoke the words brewing behind his own lips. He sealed the punctures he had made in her body and pulled back to look into her eyes.

"I love you," she repeated for him once she could see the blue of his eyes. She sobbed sharply, tears welling in her eyes as she cried with both emotion and pleasure. Her sobs and gasps mingled with one another as their movements together grew rapid and frantic.

Damien had never known the sting of tears, the rending of emotion that spiked and sparkled within the entire body right before they made an appearance. He turned his face into the blessed curve of her neck, dampness clinging to his lashes in answer to her honesty of feeling.

When she climaxed, it was as if she were thrown into a seizure. Her entire body seemed to jerk and spasm in time with the sobbing she could control no more than she could the orgasm itself.

Damien felt as if she were tearing him out of the sane world. He could barely hold her as her body writhed in his hands, wrenching at him in demand that he follow her into her bliss. For all his strength and power, he could never have

denied her or himself the inevitable release she stole from
him. No force on the planet could ever be that strong.

The Vampire Prince fell back onto the pillows and Syreena
fell with him, sprawling weakly over his chest. She could not
breathe, yet was breathing too hard. She could not silence herself as she continued to weep against the column of his neck.
She felt his hands weave into her lax hair, holding her against
him with that masculine gentleness of touch only his hands
could ever convey. Damien did not try to console her in any
way other than that fitting of his hands against her hot scalp.
He was busy enough trying to settle back into his own body,
trying to figure out how so much fullness of feeling could
ever fit back within the limited confines of his skin.

She had told him she loved him. He had known that, but
hearing it in the traditional phrase had affected him in new
and blinding ways.

Ways that made him believe he could do anything.

Anything she needed or wanted him to do.

Because her loving him meant so much more than him
loving her.

Syreena felt as though she were completely paralyzed.

She could not move, even quite some time after she had
calmed down from her emotional and sexual roller coaster
of feelings.

So she simply lay still, sprawled over her lover as if she
had been doing so for years, not days. She could feel his fingers drifting up and down the length of her spine, the sensation soothing and sweet in the aftermath of such tumultuous
feedback.

She thought she wanted to sleep, everything she had been
through recently both mentally and physically exhausting.
At the same time she was far too wired to ever succeed at
rest, even though it was certainly past sunrise.

Syreena sighed, feeling safe as well as content. Sunlight had always been such a fearful thing for her people, the sun poisoning they could suffer a terrible thing to experience. Now, however, the sun meant such different things to her. It meant the likelihood of enemies disturbing them was reduced to nearly nothing. It meant that neither of them would go beyond the walls of their living space again until dusk. There was something about being locked in with Damien that made it seem like they were cocooned together. He could not leave her, and she could not leave him. Of course, they did not need such things to keep them together, but still it provided an added sense of togetherness and security.

"I can hear those abstract thoughts of yours even without trying," he murmured close to her ear.

She smiled.

Syreena realized she had never smiled much in her lifetime. She had always been such a seriously centered person. She'd really only first discovered the ability to be lighthearted when she had become a part of Siena's household fifteen years earlier. Her sister was known for her mischief and humor and had a way of getting to everyone's funny bone. She had taught Syreena the pleasure to be found in joking and teasing.

But it was Damien who had sparked one irresistible grin after another this past week in a way that she had always thought to be beyond her, just out of reach of her understanding. She knew now it was because she was becoming comfortable with herself for truly the first time in her life. One needed self-comfort in order to find ease in humor and happiness.

"Are you always going to be this philosophical after we make love?"

Syreena giggled, raising her head to look at him and finding she was glad to actually be able to do so. She looked down into those eyes that seemed as deep as the deepest ocean.

"I hope it's telepathy, this part of you I am supposedly getting. I would very much enjoy snooping around in your head in return."

"Sweetling, I would love it if you did. It would save me a lot of foreplay."

"Mmm, sure it would," she said, her disbelief all too apparent. "I think you'd be very upset if we subtracted the neck nibbling from this whole affair."

"Too true," he agreed with a laugh. His grin lingered as he reached to rub a thumb over his latest brand on her. "I am sorry if I get carried away. I cannot seem to help myself."

"Do not apologize, Damien. It always seems natural when it happens. It is an enhancement, not an intrusion."

"I can believe that," he said, reaching to touch the wound on his throat that was already beginning to heal. "I have never felt anything like this before. You make a very good Vampire."

"Thank you."

Syreena found she had regained strength in her arms, and using her healthy arm, she levered herself up into a sitting position over him. She paused midway, making a sound of discomfort as parts of her body protested fiercely at the movement.

"Hurting?" he asked.

"A little. I feel . . . I feel like . . ."

"You have been turned inside out?" he supplied.

"Yes. Of course, you would know that."

"Yes, though I believe it was a bit more violent for me."

"I beg to differ. I would definitely claim violence on this end." Syreena groaned as she moved a little too far in a sore direction.

She felt his hands reach up to help support her efforts, but then he went distinctly still. She watched as his chin tilted down and he acted as though he were listening to something. Her heartbeat picked up momentarily, her sensation of security bleeding away suddenly as she tried to sense what had caught his attention.

"What is it?"

He looked at her as if surprised by the question. "Nothing. No, that is not true. It is nothing bad. Relax, sweetheart, we are safe here."

"How do you know that?"

"Trust me. We are surrounded by Vampires, Syreena. They know I have returned. They would never let anything make it this far inside our county."

"I thought Vampires did not congregate in the same areas."

"Romania is the homeland. It is different here. The Vampires of this county have been affiliated with my bloodlines for generations. You may not think so, but even we honor certain loyalties. This is why Jasmine wanted me to come here. She knew it would protect us from all threats to surround myself with known allies."

"So then, what were you listening for?"

"To. I was listening to a telepathic message. Forgive me, I did not mean to get distracted."

"Never mind that." She waved him off. "What kind of message? Must I ask you for everything? You are so stingy with information sometimes."

"I suppose I am. I am not used to . . . well, never mind. It was just a greeting of sorts. A very old-fashioned one. It actually has no linguistic equivalent." He paused to think about how to best explain it. "It is our version of a call-out. An 'all's well,' so to speak. I have not heard it in so long, I almost forgot it existed. It heralds the dawn, marks the time when all should be accounted for and safe. If anyone answers, it means something is wrong. Out of habit and respect, you listen in case there is an answer."

"That is very . . . well, it's like a pack cry. It's very Lycanthropic."

"We are not so different as we sometimes think, our two peoples."

"I am learning that. I—"

She broke off as the room spun out from under her suddenly. She made a sickly noise and instantly lay back down over him. His hand went into her hair, the other against her cheek with concern.

"What is it?"

"Just a little dizzy," she said as lightly as she could, considering the turning of her stomach. "There you go, this is the part of you I am doomed to get. The off-balance part."

"Do not joke when you are seriously not feeling well," he scolded her gently. "I hope we have not been reckless, doing this Exchange with so little knowledge."

"We have been," she admitted, resting her cheek on his chest and trying to focus on the candle on the bedside table. Closing her eyes only seemed to make it worse. "But I knew that before we did it. I was prepared to accept the con—"

She broke off again, this time with a shudder that flowed over her entire body.

"Syreena?"

Damien sat up with her still clinging to him. There was a helplessness in her grasp that troubled him. He gingerly turned her in his hold so that he was cradling her in his lap. He braced her forehead to his chin, hoping it would help the dizziness that was clearly not getting any better.

"It will pass," she murmured, though less with conviction so much as with hopefulness.

"You know, it occurs to me you have not eaten much since you have been dwelling with those of us who do not eat. That could be why."

"Yes. You are right. Of course."

She took a breath, and then passed out cold in his arms.

Damien was trapped.

The sun was up and he was in a barren household with no assistance, no supplies, and no way of obtaining any of the above. Syreena was still breathing, but in soft, shallow bursts that were more unnerving than they were reassuring. He had laid her out on the bed, succeeding in finding a reasonably clean sheet in a nearby cedar trunk in order to cover her. He could feel she was losing body heat, but could find no explanation for it other than the one he dreaded.

He had survived his part of the Exchange, but it had been a fairly close dance with the beyond, as he recalled. Though Jasmine had told him that there was proof of it being a regular success between breeds in the past, Syreena was nothing like an ordinary Nightwalker. What if her mutations had made this a deadly choice for her? Damien did not think he could bear to live if anything happened to her because of this.

"Okay, relax," he said aloud to himself.

She was going through what could be termed a catastrophic change in her physical makeup, just as he had done. It would simply take a little time for her to recover. It had only taken him a day to overcome the same effect. Perhaps that was all he needed to do, remain patient for a gathering of hours.

The reassurance helped to keep him from panicking, but it did little to relax him.

Damien spent the remaining daylight hours keeping vigil over her, watching her very closely, to the point where he knew exactly how many breaths she would take in an hour. He recovered his pants from their discarded clothing and searched the household, but he had been right to assume nothing of any usefulness would be found there. Unsuccessful in that venture, he took to pacing the room.

About five hours into the ordeal, she began to breathe a little easier and seemed to slip more into a form of sleep than a state of unconsciousness.

This was what finally relaxed him a little, enough so that he could settle down beside her instead of circuiting the room helplessly. He gathered her up against him, cocooning her body with his in every way he could manage.

The Prince closed his eyes, but he did not sleep. He simply listened to the way she breathed.

About three hours before dusk, she began to get restless. It started with a few nervous twitches, but then her central nervous system seemed to take over. She twisted and turned as if she were having a brutal nightmare. She made low noises deep in her throat like a small wounded animal. He bore this torture for nearly an hour, cursing himself the entire time for putting her through such a terrible experience. It gave him no comfort when he recalled that she had made the choice willingly.

In the later part of that hour, he wished Jasmine had never told him about the Exchange. This was because the restlessness gave way to petite seizures, and then escalated to worse ones until he thought her delicate spine would snap in two from the arching of her body.

Nothing signifying love and bonding should be so painful, he thought with anger.

He forgot that he had not minded so much in the aftermath of his own painful process. All he could think about, all he could see, was the woman he loved suffering.

At last, an hour before dusk, she fell into a deep sleep. So deep that he could not even sense her dreaming. Her body temperature returned to normal; so did her breathing. The perspiration that had coated her and soaked the first sheet had evaporated by the time he tucked her beneath a second one.

He rested beside her again, and again he did not sleep.

Damien closed his eyes as he settled back against the headboard of the huge bed. He acted as Syreena's pillow, her back in a reclining repose against his chest and her head nestled securely beneath his chin. He could feel the soft movements of her hair against his skin as the restless ends seemed to seek a comfortable position.

Damien did not notice that the gray stubble that fuzzed over her altered hairline was growing, at quite a rapid pace. The cool gray hair darkened as it lengthened, the living strands spilling over Syreena's cheek. Then, with every delicate pulsation of blood that circuited through her hair, the brown side deepened in color as well. For the first time since recovering from her illness as a young girl, her hair came as close to having a uniform color as it had ever had. In the end, however, it was all a marvelous charcoal color, not quite the pitch black of Damien's hair, but nearly so. The distinction that remained, however, was the clear streaks of dark gray, dark brown, and pure black, that plumed back from her hairline just above her forehead, then fountained in three separate directions down the full length of her hair.

When Syreena opened her eyes at last, it was with the overwhelming sense that it was past dusk. All Nightwalkers could sense that on one level or another, but it seemed somehow sharper to her than usual. She did not feel well rested, but neither did she feel the exhaustion she probably should have. She took a moment, resting contentedly against Damien, ridiculously happy to find herself waking with his arms around her.

All traces of the dizziness that had plagued her earlier were gone, and it was a relief. The soreness had faded with her healing time, though she suspected once she moved she would find a few tender spots that would still be under reconstruction.

She had no idea how accurate her metaphor would turn out to be.

Damien felt her busy thoughts bumping around his extrasensory awareness before she even moved, opening his eyes quickly to look down at her. The change and growth in her hair was dramatic, and it took him several beats to absorb the impact of it. He was barely recovered from it enough to tell her about it when she looked up at him, exposing her eyes.

Her eyes. Eyes which had become the uniform color of charcoal, peppered with gray, brown, and deeper blackness. It was like looking down into intricate Italian marble.

It was, for a moment, like looking into the eyes of a stranger.

But then she smiled up at him, and she was instantly all

Syreena. Changes notwithstanding, she was the same sharp, beautiful, tenacious woman he had fallen in love with.

And she was smiling.

He did not realize what a relief it was until he actually exhaled in release.

"I think I might have an idea of what you are going to get from me," he told her wryly.

"Oh? Care to share?"

"Well . . ."

He thought for a moment, and then lifted her with himself as he leaned to the side and looked over the edge of the bed. She snickered as he tilted her to reach for something. When he came back to an upright position, it was with the poniard in his hand. He held the knife up for her, turning the flat of the blade toward her face. She gave him a puzzled look.

"Look into the blade."

She did, and saw her slightly distorted reflection.

Syreena gasped, grasping his wrist to better angle the makeshift mirror. She could see the darkness of her hair in patches and pieces, but her eyes were quite clear.

"I match!"

It was a very childlike exclamation of clear delight, and he was more than a little bemused by it. He had thought she might be disturbed to see herself further altered. It had not occurred to him that the new uniformity of color might be pleasing to her. As he thought about it, however, he realized why it would be. Though it was all still very unique in coloring, there was nothing about it that marked her as a stand-apart being, not like the harlequin looks she had sported most of her life had done.

She kept tilting and retilting the knife, thrusting the inadequate mirror into all sorts of positions so she could see various parts of her new look.

"I wonder what it means," she said softly.

"What it means?"

"The black, Damien. Remember? Lycanthrope hair colors to signify the form they take."

"A raven?"

"Unlikely. I gave that to you. Seems a hard chance that you could give it back." She sat up away from him further, scrambling for the edge of the bed, her feet hitting the dusty floor for only a second before his hand closed around her upper arm and pulled her back into the bed with him.

"You have just gone through a radical physical transformation that kept me up all day terrified for your health and safety, and you think I am going to let you trot around like nothing happened?"

"Damien, I am not the type to lie in bed all weak and moaning. I feel fine, and I want to . . ."

She broke off, reaching for the splint and bandages on her arm. After an all too brief touch test for pain, she tore the restriction away, throwing the shreds down onto the floor. She flexed her fingers and her arm, turning a brilliant smile on him.

"I want to fly!"

"Syreena!"

But she had escaped his grasp and was rushing across the suite, entering their private sitting room and running to the window, which she immediately levered open. Damien flew off the bed after her.

"Syreena! What if you have lost the falcon for some reason?"

"I haven't. I would know."

For a terrifying, breathless second, she ran at the window and dove out of it in human form. They were many stories up, so Damien's heart seemed to leap out of his chest after her. He ran to the window, gripping the frame, almost afraid to look. But he had not gotten where he was in life by being cowed by new and dangerous things, so he looked after her immediately.

Her streamlined body sprang outward in an arc, passing

the top of it as she formed an arrow out of herself. She began to plummet toward the ground, diving toward it as if it were water and not mountainous rock, her long, marblized hair fluttered in sheeted snaps as she finally spread her arms wide.

It took only a blink of time before she flashed into the form that resembled a harpy, although the way she caught wind in her dark wings and buoyant feathers made her swoop elegantly from her death dive in a graceful sweep that was reminiscent of an angel instead of that mythical creature of hostility. She reeled, climbing upward now, using the powerful draw of her wings to skim back up the stone of the wall she had leapt from. Damien had to jerk back sharply to avoid cracking heads with her as she speared past the window.

Moonlight glinted off sleek, gray-black feathers as she whipped past. He grinned widely as he leaned back into the window frame to watch her take to the night sky. Her fly-by not withstanding, she clearly took to the air as naturally as she breathed. He envied her that ease for a moment, then tossed aside the sense of limitation and snapped himself into the form of the raven so he could join her.

Just as the raven cleared the building, his partner changed form once again, into the falcon that was so familiar to her. Only instead of the multifeathered brown they were used to seeing, she was the colors of her new hair tinting. Her back was striped black, her underbelly a soft, dark gray, and all the rest of her that dusty charcoal color.

The raven and the falcon dipped and turned in that eerie way birds had of perfect synchronization. She led, he followed. It would take quite some time for him to match her skill, but he was learning quickly enough to keep up with her.

Syreena swooped back down toward the ground, catching an updraft off the mountainside Damien's holdings were built into. She was heading for the lake just beyond a ledge of rough-grown stone. Damien anticipated her, catching wind in his wings to brake his speed as she dove recklessly for the water just as heedlessly as she had leapt out of the window.

Again, she transformed on the fly.

She had missed the ripple of rubbery skin that immediately coated her distorting body. Even more, she had missed the artwork of the streamlined form of the dolphin. She hit the water at top speed, but the cut of her body made not a single splash. The dolphin skimmed beneath the surface like a flashing light of dark gray, the speed of the movement so quick, it was impossible to track while on the fly.

Damien settled onto the edge of the lake, mutating back to his most natural form until he was crouched low with one hand bracing his balance upon the ground. He watched her with more ease then, until she disappeared into the depths of the water.

She returned shortly, surfacing as the woman he was used to seeing, her exultant laugh making him smile wide.

"It has been so long!" she declared. "Only a week, but still too long!"

"So is there anything different? Beside the coloring, obviously."

"I am sure there is, but I am not aware of it yet."

"Are you sure you do not know what I am thinking?" he asked in such a way that he got a smile out of her to match her jubilant laugh.

"Yes, I do, but it has nothing to do with telepathy." Syreena raised a hand out of the water and beckoned to him flirtatiously.

"Mmm, same result either way, so I do not particularly care how it was managed," he told her as he rose up briefly and pushed off from the edge of the water.

His dive was clean and well-practiced.

When he surfaced, it was with a sputtered gasp.

"That's right," she said with an obvious snap of her fingertips. "It is wintertime, isn't it?"

Damien was not amused. He swam to her in earnest, snagging her by a slick arm easily when she spent more effort in giggling than she did in trying to escape him.

"Let me guess, you do not feel the temperature of the water."

"Not much," she agreed, letting him drag her warm body through the water until she was sealed close to his. "But I did owe you for the attack of cold hands."

"How is it you can feel that, but not this glacial cold?" he demanded.

"Because I was prepared. A flip of a mental switch, so to speak, and the fact that I am not entirely in human form."

He felt her slap her legs against his, only to realize it was a finned tail and not legs at all.

"Well, well, if it isn't the little mermaid," he mused, running a curious hand down her back and backside, noting the point where skin blended away and became the smooth coldness of her tail.

"Don't expect me to sing for you. I cannot carry a tune."

"Not even with a partial spirit of a Siren within you? I find that hard to believe."

He kissed her before she could retort.

"I thought I heard complaints about the frigidness of the water," she purred as she snuggled against his immersed body a moment later.

"Yes, but as the heat leaves my body, it is easier to take. You cannot claim the same, I imagine. I am wondering about the way you will react to my cold appendages this time."

She laughed, pushing away from him, splashing water at him.

"The joke is on you, Prince Damien," she taunted him. "You would have to catch me first."

She dove under the water, leaving him with an impertinent flip of her tail that sent a wave of water over him.

"The joke is on you, Princess," he muttered, "because I can hold my breath longer."

He did not bother to chase her, waiting instead for the inevitable call of oxygen to strike her.

When she did come up, he was going to see to it she warmed him up for her penance.

Chapter 15

Jasmine entered the old Romanian stronghold slowly by using the convention of the door rather than one of the numerous balconies that dotted the edifice. The very first thing she did was to seek out the powerful signature of Damien's presence.

She had known he was on the property, but had expected him to be within the building. She was surprised to realize he was actually outside, some yards distant from it. She was not surprised to note that his new shadow was also quite close to him. She sighed with a little impatience. Did the woman never leave him alone?

Jasmine put aside the thought the moment she entertained it. She was just going to have to get used to this. It was clear that Damien intended to keep the Lycanthrope female as one might keep any pet. Apropos, considering she was more animal than anything else.

Jasmine took a long moment to survey the grand room she had just stepped into, looking over the cobweb-streamed ceiling with its domed roof and fresco paintings. When it was cleaned up, it would be restored to its former brilliance of color as well as the gleam of gold inlay that graced the moldings and latticework.

There was obvious pride in her appraisal of what she could see of the dim work. Her brother, Horatio, had done them during the Renaissance when it had been a fashionable way of doing artwork. He had always been the artistic, creative soul of their family. They had made a complementary match, she the student, he the artist. That is, until he took the diplomatic post in Noah's court many decades ago, taking what was to be permanent leave of their already dwindling clan.

One would think that, over so much time, the one constant someone like her should have gotten used to was that nothing remained constant. Things changed. Always. Considering how hard it was to entertain oneself after the first century or two, that was probably supposed to be a good thing.

But the absence of her brother had been as welcome to her as the arrival of the Lycanthrope Princess. In both cases, she had had no say in the matter. Which, of course, was how it should be.

That did not mean she had to be pleased about it.

But she would adapt, as she always did, in one way or another. She took solace in the volatility of the time that approached them so rapidly. At least she would not be bored. On the other hand, there were bound to be casualties that would be unwelcome.

And Damien carried the highest probability of being on the early list.

She had made her choices, however. Ruth had tempted her with all manner of choices, a feast of selections that had held so much appeal in so many aspects, and unconscionable results in others.

She would stay here, in this place, with this man who was like a brother and a father to her. She would tolerate the annoying consequence of a steprelative that Syreena would become as a result of that. Damien needed her help, and she would not abandon him at this dangerous time. She could at the very least give Syreena the credit of being capable of the same goal. It was very likely the one thing they would ever manage to have in common.

Though they had made the choice to settle back and play a waiting game with their enemies, Jasmine had made a decision of her own. She agreed that they needed time and effort to properly approach the situation, but there was something that could and should be done almost immediately.

After thinking it over all day, she had decided to include Damien in her plans. He had voiced his opinions on the situation in such a way that she was forearmed with the great potential that he could be swayed to her way of thinking.

Provided his little tart did not have the opportunity to object. If she did, she could sway him away from Jasmine's desires.

Something she seemed to do with frustrating frequency.

The real trick was going to be separating the two of them long enough to win Damien over to her way of thinking. Of course, she had a plan for that, one that was already set into motion. In a short while, brethren would begin to arrive and they would start to organize and revitalize the castle. They would be her key piece of bait for the little Princess.

Jasmine made her way through the household to her rooms, the ones she always stayed in when they resided in the homeland. They were too close to Damien's quarters now, so she would be choosing others in the wing farthest from the happy homemakers.

She began to relocate her stored belongings to that section of the house while she waited for others to arrive, including Damien.

Damien raised his head from the pleasurable task of nuzzling Syreena's stomach and looked back toward the castle they had abandoned. He sat up quickly, tugging her with him so that she settled high against his chest, her legs and bottom drawn up into his lap as he kept her secured to his body.

"We have company," he informed her when she looked at him with clear curiosity.

"Let me guess . . ." She trailed off with a meaningful up-cast of her eyes.

"Yes, it is Jasmine." He chuckled. "But I would hardly be concerned about that. There are Vampires moving in this direction. Several of them. I imagine it is our new household."

"Remind me to thank her," Syreena said, not sounding thankful at all. But Damien knew it was born mostly out of her disappointment of having their private tryst interrupted. He was beginning to know her better, and knew that she worried that they would have little to no opportunity for such private intimacies in a full court. She had spent fifteen years in that fishbowl, with everyone watching her so closely. She had probably looked forward to escaping a little of it.

"She is not fully responsible. They sensed my arrival. It is a combination of tradition and curiosity that draws them here."

Damien also knew she understood that this was for the best, even though it was potentially dangerous in its own right. This was the minute where their private affairs would become fodder for public opinion and reaction. She probably worried too much about it. Vampires were very unlike Lycanthropes in that respect. Those who dissented over the idea of their relationship would not make it well known, in order to suit their own purposes. The majority, however, would lose interest in the whole situation relatively quickly, if indeed it interested them to start with.

This was one situation where Vampire capriciousness would come in handy.

Syreena and Damien returned to their new home together, dressing in preparation to meet those who would soon arrive. The Princess left Damien's rooms first, since dressing for her was no more complicated than slipping her light dress back on. As she exited, she literally bumped into Jasmine.

The female Vampire made a momentary effort to excuse her part of the collision, but it halted almost immediately as she got a good look at the Princess's altered hair and eyes. Syreena did not begrudge the other woman her stunned shock. She imagined it must be a fairly startling change. Jasmine was obvious in her silence, her expression inscrutable, save for the sensation Syreena had that the Vampire was not quite pleased to see the transformation.

"I see you have completed the Exchange," she said at last. "I congratulate you and Damien. You are the first in thousands of years to do so. Let me know if I can assist you in the remainder of the Bonding ceremony."

"We will," Syreena said, more than a little taken back by the other woman's unusual graciousness. "Damien says the household is arriving."

"They are. I am sure it will be something for you to look forward to."

Again, Syreena had that sense that Jasmine was concealing something that gave her private pleasure in a seemingly banal statement.

"In what way?"

"You are mistress of this household now, Princess. You will be chatelaine, expected to organize and run it smoothly. I have performed the role in the past, but it is your place now."

"I see. It is a familiar role. I ran my sister's household in this manner."

Jasmine just gave her a smile in return as response. It would be amusing to watch the Lycanthrope try to give orders to a Vampire staff.

"Then I suggest you go to greet your arrivals. They are at the door." Jasmine reached to take Syreena's arm and guide her in the right direction. "They will continue to arrive throughout the night. You will easily be able to tell the domestics apart from the higher-ranking guests, I am sure. Sybil, the woman we use as head housekeeper, will be the first to show herself, if I know her, and she will make an excellent assistant for you."

Damien leaned back against a wall, his arms folded over the expanse of his chest, his dark eyes following his mate while she busily took charge of organizing the household staff. By turn, she greeted other guests politely and then promptly sent them back away. The house, she explained, would be in order in a few nights, and at that time she would extend a nationwide greeting to all who wished to pay homage to Damien. She disarmed the potentially insulting nature of the refusal of their company with a graciousness and a gregarious smile that was pure diplomacy.

No one who was not looking for it would ever think she was not a Vampire, he realized. First, it was an inconceivable idea that Damien would set up a household with a female not of their kind, so there was no reason to expect it. Those who found it curious that she did not evoke that natural sense that alerted Vampires to each other's presence did not mention it outside of a curious wrinkling of a brow. If anyone evaluated the strange female with those heat-sensing membranes of their eyes, they would know the truth immediately as she flared hot and red in their vision.

It was the latter that would likely provoke a response, so Damien watched them all very closely for it and any adverse reactions that might follow.

Soon the balance of those who would come to work and reside in the household reached the point where Damien could finally relax. These were the people most loyal to him, who had protected and defended this household near to their deaths in the past. From butler to scullery maid, their families had served his for eons and considered it a mark of pride that they were allowed to do so. It did not matter to him that they were the least powerful of his species, which limited them to their rank in Vampire culture. There was a power in these seemingly subordinate people that far outranked those Damien associated with in his personal entourage.

It was the power of contentment, loyalty, and satisfaction, all those things that were so elusive to those who held greater abilities. He had never quite understood it until now. Now, he realized, it was because they did not have to worry every moment that someone might stab them in the back or take off their heads at the first opportunity. They had remained limited to the same land, the same clan, the same relationships all of their lives. Yet it gave them security, not boredom.

It fascinated Damien to watch it.

At least, it did now. Now that he was finding contentment himself. He had avoided this land and these people for quite a long time now, because they had disturbed him and frustrated him with their seemingly simplistic pleasures of life. He had not understood it then the way he understood it now.

He could tell by the jubilant atmosphere that they were very happy he had returned to the homeland at last. That they had missed the presence of their Prince. *If only those of more elevated rank would be so welcoming*, he thought dryly. But he would deal with that as it came.

Once the main hall was filled with at least ten domestic Vampires that he knew, Damien finally pushed away from his wall. No one would dare be stupid enough to give Syreena any trouble now that so many knew she had his approval to be in charge of who came and who went. Those who now surrounded her would also see to her protection if anyone was stupid enough to challenge her. It was clear that she was the Prince's woman, and she would be respected and protected as much as the Prince himself.

So Damien took the opportunity to seek out Jasmine, who had requested a private audience with him at his earliest convenience. Since he wanted to give special care to making

Jasmine feel she was still important to him and that he valued her input and opinion, it was high in his mind to attend to her summons. It was very true that he felt that way; he only needed to make certain Jasmine felt it.

Jasmine was instructing a petite girl named Lucia on how she desired her room to be kept and where her things were to be best organized, when Damien found her.

It was not lost on him that Jasmine had chosen new quarters as far away from his as possible, whereas she had always done the opposite these past five centuries. It put a sadness on his heart to see this passive resistance to the changes in his life, but he had done all he could for her, and she was doing all she could to accommodate him. Perhaps over time this would better resolve itself.

"You requested an audience, madam?" he greeted her, his voice echoing in the large chamber.

Lucia gave a terrible start, and Damien had to work at not being amused when she looked at him with eyes that nearly popped out of her head. She could not be more than a couple of decades old, and she certainly had never seen the Vampire Prince before. Between his mere presence and the stories and rumors she had no doubt been raised on, Damien figured she had cause to be intimidated.

"Damien," Jasmine greeted him with a warm smile. She set down the bottle of perfume she had been inspecting and moved to embrace him. Her slim body leaned against his with warm affection, her lips pressing to his cheek with fondness. "I am glad you have come. I wish to discuss something with you."

She linked her arm through his, giving her gawking maid a shooing wave back to her work as she led the Prince out into the hallway. She chose a nearby door and led him into a heavily dusted, abandoned storeroom.

"You are plotting something," he said immediately after the door was closed behind her back.

"I admit it, I am. While I agree with most of what has already been discussed about this situation with the Nightwalker renegades, I believe we have a course of action that must be taken."

"Jasmine, you are looking for trouble," he warned her.

"Exactly," she breathed in earnest. "And so should you! Damien, you are Prince and I am your most trusted advisor. I have always been in charge of domestic troubles, and you have always entrusted them to me." She moved to grasp him by both shoulders, making sure he looked down into her serious eyes. "Since when do we allow others to manage our domestic problems? We have a responsibility here that must be attended to immediately. The rogue Vampire. His identity must be discovered. We must know who among us is a traitor, lest we find ourselves giving information away where we do not want to."

Damien looked at her, searching for her motivations in her expression and body language. What she said made very good sense, but he could not escape the instinctive feeling he had that there were ulterior motives behind her logic.

Then again, Jasmine always had ulterior motives to everything she said or did.

"It is very likely one of those whom we would not trust to begin with," he told her, unconcerned with her reasoning.

"And if it is not?" She sighed in frustration. "It is not like you to ignore potential threats."

"I am not happy to do so, Jasmine," he said darkly, "but I am not about to run off and confront a Vampire who is backed by someone like Ruth . . . and quite possibly black arts as well. Whoever he is, he has killed an innocent. There is no coming back from that. It will change him forever."

"And you and I have both seen what a Vampire who crosses that line can become. In the past, you and I would not rest until we stopped such a being. Why do you hesitate now?"

"Because I no longer have only myself to think about, Jasmine."

"You mean you are afraid of upsetting your fragile little mate?" she taunted him.

"I mean," he snapped, "that I have a people to run and I am responsible for leading them into this era of peace even you have seen the wisdom of. If I should die now, who knows what manner of Vampire will supersede me?"

"It would very likely be me," she said cockily. "Do you have so little faith in my upholding your ideals?"

"You?" He laughed harshly, purposely provoking her indignant emotions. "Jas, you cannot manage to stay aboveground more than a century at a time. You would be deposed the moment your first melancholy struck."

"That is not fair!"

"It is, or you would not be so upset by it," he pointed out, being a little more gentle with her now. "You do not have the patience to rule, dearest. I love you and I depend on you very much, but I know you. In your heart, you know it, too. My death, which would be necessary for you to reign, would by itself send you into a tailspin of pain and depression."

"You think far too much of your importance to me," she said, but they both knew it was pure bravado. "Anyway, I am not asking you to engage in battle. I think we should do some recon, however. Tell me you do not burn to know who would betray our people in such a way and I will promise you never to suggest it again."

As usual, Jasmine knew him too well, so she called him on his bluff perfectly.

"I suppose you have a proposition on how we should go about discovering this?" he asked, ignoring the triumph that lit her eyes.

"We should start at the Library. Perhaps we will find a clue there. If we are lucky, Ruth's trail will not be too cold to follow."

"Jasmine . . ."

"Just to follow," she said quickly. "Only we would have the power to sneak up close without detection from her."

"And what if the Vampire is powerful enough to detect us?"

"Powerful enough to circumvent your cloaking abilities? Even I cannot do that."

Damien went silent for a long minute, trying to make himself think clearly, rather than act on impulse. He wanted to do this; more than anything, he wanted to find out who would do such a thing. Unless punishing that person counted separately. That was one thing he wanted to do with an even greater passion. If they could determine who their traitor was, then they would have an advantage over him. He would think he could still move among them, with others none the wiser for his duplicitousness. Perhaps that would give them the advantage to separate the Vampire from the Demon, making each more vulnerable, to the point where Damien could take care of punishing his own, as he had always done. If there was ever going to be a time when that was possible, it would be now, before Ruth had the opportunity to exploit her knowledge of the Exchange or before the Vampire started to pick up the Demon female's black magic tricks.

"Very well," he said at last. "Just give me a few minutes with Syreena—"

"You do not have the time, Damien. Already there must be Lycanthropes tromping over and over our only trail as they start to empty the Library."

"But I cannot just leave her alone with a house full of Vampires who do not realize who and what she is," he argued.

"Is she as fragile as that? After killing Nico, I would think her more than capable of keeping a group of mere servants in line."

Jasmine had a point. He was being a little overprotective. Syreena was a lot tougher than he gave her credit for, and she was very used to running a household full of strangers.

There was no one who could really do her any harm. If she could defeat Nico's son on her own as easily as she had, then she could certainly stand her ground against any one of the domestics.

Damien's desire to know who the rogue Vampire was won out over all other concerns.

He left his Romanian holdings quickly, with Jasmine at his side.

It was over an hour before Syreena realized that Damien had completely left the property. In that time, she had been busy settling small squabbles, sorting out duties, and ignoring suspicious glances from more and more corners of the rooms she walked through. The Vampire staff was quickly beginning to realize she was not one of them. She could tell because it was getting increasingly difficult to get them to respond to her requests.

She did not want to go crying to Damien, so she tried very hard to handle it all herself, but she had not a single ally, and it was taking its toll on her ability to be efficient. Jasmine, of course, had been hoping for just such a thing to happen. That was no doubt why she was nowhere to be found.

Syreena expected that, but she had not expected Damien to leave her alone in such hostile conditions. On the other hand, she was glad he had moved out of the way and let her try to take care of everything without him hovering over her shoulder.

"Well, Syreena, you can't have it both ways," she muttered to herself under her breath.

He had probably just gone hunting for the night. With or without Jasmine, Syreena couldn't care less. She did wish him a speedy return, however, as she saw a maid who was supposed to be sweeping out the fireplaces wandering the halls for the third time.

Syreena had had enough by then.

She marched up to the maid just as she entered the main parlor, where four other workers were trying to put it all in order. Syreena gave a glance at the already cleaned fireplace and then let her temper simmer over.

"Oria!"

The chatter in the room ceased abruptly as the girl jumped in her own skin at the way the Princess called her name, the cut of it slicing across raw nerves.

"Yes?" the indolent girl asked, clearly returning to her smirking, uncaring attitude.

"The fireplace in this room has already been swept," Syreena informed her.

"So?"

Syreena glanced at the avid interest of the four others who were in the room.

"So unless you want to start washing down the lavatories," Syreena said with pseudocharm, "I suggest you get back to the ones that need cleaning."

The girl's hands immediately shot to her hips, her spine straightening in indignation as she worked up a retort.

"And if you sass me," Syreena interjected in a warning tone, "you will never return to this house again after you get kicked out of it, do you understand me?"

"You can't do that. You aren't anybody. Next month Damien will be tossing some other girl around in his bed and you won't mean a thing!"

There were muffled chuckles from the others in the room.

For about three seconds.

That was how long it took for Syreena to grab the smart-mouthed girl around her throat and rush her up against the nearest stone wall with a smack that sounded frighteningly damaging. The maid made a gurgle of protest, her hands reaching to claw at the iron wrist that held her pinned to the wall. The Vampire girl was too young to have learned how to do without oxygen, so she struggled to catch even the smallest portion of a breath.

When the others moved to come to her aid, Syreena turned on them with a snarl of warning that froze them mid-step.

"Anyone who thinks to touch me will find out exactly how much I mean to your Prince," she threatened with cold surety. "I assure you, he will do far worse to you than banish you from his home."

Her confidence was unnerving to them. Enough to make them step back and watch her with wary eyes as they rethought their actions. She turned back to the chit she had clasped between her fingers.

"Yours will be the lesson that the others learn, girl. I do not like to repeat myself, and I only warn someone once. I am a Lycanthrope Princess, and I am used to being obeyed without question. I will accept no less in my mate's household."

And with that one statement, the Vampire grapevine was satisfied and forewarned. The four in the room would quickly tell who and what she was, and that her easy-going nature hid a very short fuse that probably should not be lit.

"Leave this house under your own power, or you will leave it under mine. And remember, you only get one warning."

Syreena let go of Oria, letting her slide unprepared to the floor. Ignoring the crumpled heap of girl at her feet, she turned to smile at the others.

"You are doing an excellent job in this room. When you are done, do not forget to go to Sybil for new directions. Remember, her voice is the same as mine, just as my voice is the same as Damien's. I expect you will behave for Sybil far better than this baggage has behaved for me."

She cast a look of disdain down at Oria, then turned so she could find Damien.

After Syreena had left, the indignant female Vampire got to her feet in fury. She marched up to the others.

"Do you believe the nerve of that foreigner? Who does she think she is? Mate? Damien's mate? Damien would never bind himself to a non-Vampire!"

"Shut up, Oria," one of the men snapped impatiently. "What do you know of Damien? The Prince has been gone for a very long time, certainly longer than you have been alive."

"You better leave, girl, if you know what's good for you," a second worker said. "If she's telling the truth, Damien will have your head for mouthing off to her."

Outnumbered now, Oria suddenly realized she no longer had a choice in the matter. The shapechanger had won, she had lost, and there was very little she could do about it.

So with a flounce of outrage, she left the compound.

When Damien still had not returned after an hour, Syreena began to question where he might have gone to. She did not know his habits all that well, but he had not struck her as the sort to dawdle over a hunt when he had so many things to do. Jasmine had not returned, either, and that only served to treble the Princess's concerns. She left the main halls and rooms, leaving them to a measurably subdued household staff. After the incident with Oria, they were more agreeable and inclined to do as she asked, so she did not worry about leaving them to complete their tasks without cracking a whip over them every minute.

Syreena made her way to Jasmine's new quarters. Perhaps they would reveal a clue as to where they had both disappeared to.

What she found upon opening the door was a very young Vampire girl, carefully folding and hanging clothes in Jasmine's wardrobe. The small girl, just barely a woman by her looks, went wide-eyed when she saw Syreena. She sketched an immediate curtsy to the Princess, which made her smile. It was the first act of respect from any of her new staff.

"Hello, young one," Syreena greeted her gently. "Do you know where your mistress is?"

"Standing before me, miss," the girl answered instantly.

Syreena smiled at her eagerness to please and not offend.

"Perhaps. I suspect that Jasmine will expect you to be loyal to her over me, however, and I will not hold that against you if you are in conflict. What is your name?"

"Lucia."

"Lucia, have you seen my . . . your Prince?"

"Yes, miss. He left with my mistress a couple of hours past."

"Do you know where he has gone?"

Now Lucia hesitated, the contest in her thoughts clear in her expression.

"Lucia, I only wish to know because . . . because I am concerned that they have not yet returned. If my concerns are unfounded, merely say so and I will believe you."

"I cannot say so," Lucia breathed softly. "I am not supposed to know where they have gone, but I do."

"Would you care to explain that?" Syreena asked as patiently as she could.

"I was in the hall and overheard my mistress—Jasmine, I mean, speaking in another room to the Prince. They have gone to discover the identity of a Vampire they were calling a traitor."

Syreena felt as though her heart had suddenly stopped beating. She knew instantly what Lucia was speaking of, even if the girl herself did not.

"I thank you for your directness, Lucia."

"And I thank you, miss," the girl returned quickly. "The others will never say so, but they have longed for Damien to return to the homeland. If you are the reason why that has been possible, then we all owe you thanks. I know so many who have missed his attentiveness to this region."

Syreena nodded in a combination of acknowledgment and farewell. She backed out of the room, her thoughts full of emotion and racing speculation.

Oddly enough, she focused on the more inane portion of information first. She had not realized that Damien had not been home in so long. Even though she had been faced with the layers of dust coating all the surfaces of his dwelling, it appeared that this had occurred over a much longer time than she had originally assumed. From what Lucia said, it had been long enough for Vampires to feel neglected, something that would probably take a great deal of time to occur in a species who marked time in large increments. She wondered why that was, and what had driven or kept Damien away until he'd had no real choice but to return.

And then the more serious reality and realization struck her. Damien and Jasmine had gone off to do exactly what he had promised her only hours ago that he would not do. He had claimed to understand how irrational an act it would be to risk himself in such a way, and had sworn to think about her needs and feelings before making such reckless choices ever again.

Syreena felt a sense of betrayal on top of a deeply driven fear. She wanted to believe that he and Jasmine could care for themselves, but how could she trust that when she could not even trust him to keep his word on so important a promise? How could she live the rest of her life with someone who double-talked her, then waited until her back was turned before doing exactly what he wished anyway? How could she securely believe anything he said if these were the things he would do?

It hurt to think he would do something like this. She had so wanted to believe him, had found it so easy to do so once she had made up her mind about where she belonged. Had she so misjudged his character? Had they all? Was her judgment so poor all of a sudden?

No. She had to try not to be that hard on herself and on

him. Damien was passionately disturbed by the idea of a traitor amongst his people. He was used to them being somewhat untrustworthy, but only in certain matters and up to a certain point. Anything beyond that certain point, well, it was clear that he took such a betrayal very personally. Syreena knew Siena's reaction would very likely be quite similar in passion and strength had this sort of thing occurred in her court.

However, Syreena would have advised caution to her sister, and her sister would have listened to her and obeyed, trusting her wisdom on the matter, or she would have put her foot down without giving opportunity for arguments. Siena would not have made a pretense of agreeing with the Princess, and then snuck out behind her back like a naughty child dodging curfew.

Syreena would be damned if she was going to let Damien think he could be this capricious with his promises to her. She could accept his Vampiric ways, from boredom to the need for strange relationships and amusements, but she would never accept duplicitousness.

It only took her a few minutes to conclude where they would have started the kind of hunt they were on. She ran through the stone rooms until she found one with a window that opened outward into the cold night.

She leapt over the sill instantly.

Chapter 16

Syreena winged her way toward the cavern Library with all speed. They had a good head start on her. She had no idea what she was going to do when she caught up with them, if she was even able to do so, but she was working on an impetuous flood of emotion and determination that dictated her actions. She would take this journey one leg at a time, deciding her actions on the fly.

Syreena's sister was the huntress of the family, and as such was the more skilled tracker. The Princess's forms were more for speed and visual acuity needed once a target was already achieved. Syreena was debating whether to recruit her sister into this venture even as she alit outside of the entrance to the Library.

She immediately became aware of the silence and the mess scattered from the interior room into the outer caverns. The Library was lit by little more than a single smoldering torch, and from what she could see, it had been hastily excavated of all the rest of its inventory, the furnishings as well. What had once been ancient orderliness and craftsmanship marred only by touches of must and mildew was now torn and tattered chaos.

She could smell blood, all kinds, all of it bearing great power even in its spillage. She hesitated on the threshold of that place now that it had seen such violent death. It was not because she was squeamish, but because it felt as though it should be treated with respect. There was a feeling like the place had been raided, a tomb pilfered by grave robbers.

Of course, that was not truly the case. It was little more than her imagination and the remnants of the battle that had stolen precious lives.

Outside of the taint of the dead and the awesome amount of variety left by the Lycanthropes that had plundered the Library, there was the fresh scent of Vampires.

One of whose aroma was as familiar to her senses now as her own was.

Damien.

She had almost been hoping Lucia had been mistaken, hoping she would not find any trace of them having been there, but of course it had been a foolish pipe dream to think so. Damien was passionate about his people, apparently even more than he was passionate about her.

She pushed aside her disappointment and crouched down in the darkness to seek out his path.

She was not looking for anything with actual use of her eyes; it was more like a visualization of a trail made by the collection of small pieces of data through her varied senses. Syreena discarded the extraneous information, including Jasmine's notable trail, and focused on her mate.

They had walked out of the caverns together.

That was all well and good, but would she be able to track them in flight?

It was the strength of Damien's trail that made her believe that she could. Either he was making absolutely no effort to conceal his actions, or she was developing a knack for sensing where he had been. Add that to her natural affinity for detecting things while airborne, and she might very well be in luck.

She quickly set out after him.

* * *

It turned out that tracing Damien and Jasmine was far easier than she would have ever expected it to be. Of course, they really had no reason to hide their trail even if Ruth or one of her cohorts decided to backtrack them for some reason. But then Syreena realized that if Ruth backtracked them, it would mean she was the victor in whatever contest was taking place, and it was quickly an unbearable thought. It made her fly all the faster after him.

Syreena's advantage was that she was following a fresh trail, unlike Damien and Jasmine, who were tracking one nearly twenty-four hours old. It made her able to travel much faster than they had. She prayed it was enough to get her to them before they got themselves into any trouble.

Her heart began to pound with anxiety as she realized they were once again heading toward France and Mistral territories. It was understandable that she was apprehensive, she reasoned with herself, because she had experienced so much pain and trauma the last time she had been in the area. However, her self-psychoanalysis did little to soothe her frantic heart or her mind. The idea of Damien exposing himself to the dangers of that psychotic woman was near devastating.

Syreena watched more carefully now, flying low to the ground, skimming over and under treetops in whatever manner would keep her best concealed. She knew she was nearing Brise Lumineuse. She also realized the trail would end very soon. Ruth had a recent motivation, whatever it was, for skulking around in Mistral lands, and it was very likely she was still there in pursuit of her purposes.

That is, provided the information in the text she had stolen from Jasmine had not redirected her passions. Ruth had already recruited a Vampire and been to Vampire territory. What was to say that she would not end up there again, quite soon, pressing for more Nightwalkers as followers?

Syreena was making herself sick and a little bit light-headed with such thoughts. She lighted onto a branch for a moment, nervously shaking out feathers and rearranging them while she gathered a couple of breaths and some new fortitude.

She was close now, she could tell that. Very close.

Syreena was suddenly afraid to move any closer to the two she tracked. She was not stupid, after all. Jasmine and Damien had mental abilities that would protect them from Ruth's detection. If she flew into that situation and the Vampires were hiding or using stealth for some reason, she would give them away by her thoughts alone.

She realized then that she was just as guilty as Damien was for not thinking this through. It served to make her even angrier with him. If he needed assistance, how would she know? How would she be of any help to him like this? If they made it out of this situation in one piece, she would kill him herself.

She closed her eyes and tried to calm her thoughts and her breathing. If she kept on as she was, she would broadcast her presence to anyone skilled enough to sense her. Of course, as the falcon she was impossible to discern from other animals, unless anyone got close enough to see the collar around her neck that was half hidden in feathers.

When she was quite a bit calmer, she was able to use logic and her own refined senses to make the most of her vantage point. She peered through the darkness in the direction of the Vampire duo's paths. She took off from one branch and glided through the shadows and leaves until her talons caught another. The change in position was perfectly noiseless, and the bare branch of her roost was hardly disturbed by her careful landing.

Her silence of movement was what allowed her to hear the unmistakable sound of wings pushing through air. The little heart in the falcon's breast picked up in tempo immediately and she used her sharp sight to pick through the trees, branches, and night sky. The glide of black wings in relief against the glow of the moon was perhaps one of the most valuable sights she could ever remember seeing.

The raven spiked down from the sky, diving toward her with impressive speed and markedly increased accuracy. One day soon he would attain a level of skill that would make him indiscernible from Lycanthropes or Mistrals who were partly birds for all of their lives. However, the slight wobble to his glide as he aimed for the same roost she sat upon told her that there was no mistaking the inexperienced Vampire.

He buzzed her, wing tips flapping over her beak and eyes in clear pique and admonishment. She jumped off the branch, winging down to the forest floor, half-human by the time her feet touched the ground, and fully so before he had even alit beside her.

Damien's form unfurled from the raven's and she was immediately relieved to see him in his usual perfect health and strength.

"Are you mad?" he demanded.

"I was about to ask you the same question! What in the Goddess's name are you doing here, Damien?"

"Later," he barked sharply, silencing her with a sharp hand gesture. "You are too close to Ruth. If I can sense you, she most certainly can. You need to leave before—"

"Before I get to watch her break your idiot neck?" she cut in with a snap. "Before I really lose my temper and kill you for her?"

"This is neither the time or the place for this, Syreena!"

"Precisely my point! But if you truly agreed with me on that, you would not have come here after we purposely discussed how stupid and foolhardy it would be to go after her!"

"I am only here trying to find out who the traitor from my people is. I have no intention of getting into a battle with Ruth, but if you do not leave now I may be forced to do that very thing!"

"Don't you dare blame this on me! You made a promise to me, Damien, and now I find you breaking it! You are a liar and an inconsiderate ass!"

"Damien, shut her up or I will do it myself!"

The feminine hiss from the darkness of the trees was all too familiar to Syreena. Her face flared with heat and color as outrage roared through her. Her small hands clenched into fists and her teeth ground as she clenched her jaws together tightly. Her multicolored eyes flickered with the violence of her emotion as Damien's cool blue gaze remained on hers with dispassionate wintriness.

"I am unaccustomed to reporting my actions to someone as if I were a child, Syreena, and I am sorry if that disturbs you but, as I have said repetitively, this is neither the time or place for an argument about it."

"Very well," she said. "Go and skulk about in dangerous territory with that troublemaking woman if it pleases you to do so, but if you think to find me waiting in supplicant domestication for you when you return, you are sadly mistaken!"

Syreena moved to pass him, but he grabbed her about the upper arm and forced her back around with a whirl of her own momentum.

"Think before you threaten and act in haste, Syreena," he warned her on a heated whisper.

"Oh, you mean like you have done?" she shot back. "Do as I say and not as I do? What are you mistaking me for, Damien? A child? A puppy in need of training so you may bring me obediently to heel? You craved my independence of thought and action all this while, but now when they run counter to your own, it is undesirable? I will not be brought to heel by you or anyone else ever again!" She shook him off her arm with impressive violence of strength. "I came to you for my freedom, and you offered it to me with blessings and pretty words, on an imaginary silver platter. I will be your equal and your respected companion, honored and trusted and given nothing less than full disclosure and truth where it matters most, or I will be nothing at all to you, do you understand?"

Syreena whirled around sharply, surprising Jasmine, who had been coming up behind her. "If you touch me, Vampire, I will rip out your treacherous heart with my bare hands, I promise you!"

"If you do not shut that shrewish mouth of yours, I will be happy to test your abilities, Princess, but it will be up against Ruth and her partners that you will be forced to do so. Can you get that through your head before she pops up in the middle of all this?"

"Let her come! At least she is honest in her motivations!"

"I thank you for the compliment, Princess."

Syreena felt both Vampires jerk when Ruth spoke just off to the right of them, but she was surprisingly calm as she turned with a single step, bracing her feet apart. Her small hands curled into tight fists as her heart began to pound.

"I owe you," she whispered softly to the Demon, who was smiling at them as if they were guests at a party.

"I imagine you do. Come, girl, and get your pound of flesh if you dare."

"Syreena!"

Damien's shout and grasp were both completely useless as the Lycanthrope Princess lunged for the Demon necromancer. Syreena changed form midleap, wings and talons of human dimensions sprouting out with awesome speed. Ruth had not battled either of the Princess's Wereforms before, and seeing the harpy streaking toward her with a vengeful fury of speed was startling enough to give Syreena the advantage.

With disruption of concentration, Ruth could not teleport. However, she could still react and move like the warrior she had once been. Nonetheless, in spite of a skillful dodge, the blond Demon still caught the brunt of large talons across her left shoulder, clothing and skin ripping audibly under the rend of them.

Damien and Jasmine moved to react, but were brought up short by an explosion of thick, black smoke that appeared between them and the two fighting women. The smoke billowed up in clouds with all speed, immediately revealing a figure in the center.

"Nico," Damien hissed.

"It figures," Jasmine added a little more dispassionately.

"In the flesh, so to speak," Nico agreed. He spoke a single phrase, rapid and sharp, a flick of palm and fingers gesturing toward his enemies.

Jasmine and Damien both made sounds of surprise when the forest floor suddenly came alive beneath their feet. Tree roots burst out of the soil, slapping around the Vampires' ankles and calves, effectively tying them to the spot.

Damien's solution was quick. The raven came with speed, making him small enough to slip free of the magical trap. Jasmine was less delicate and artful about it. She reached down with bare hands and a growl, grabbing at the restraints with a violent ripping motion. The flesh and pulp of the roots went flying everywhere as she tore into them like a vicious little animal on the attack.

Damien flew at Nico's head, and then purposely changed form mid-momentum. He used his clumsiness to his advantage as his full body weight plowed into the traitorous Vampire. Both men drove down into the rotting litter on the forest floor, but when they skidded to a stop, Damien was on top, his hands clutching the other Vampire's clothing across his chest as he showed fangs and snarled in his enemy's face.

"Here it is, Nico. The moment you have been waiting for. Let's see who deserves my throne."

Jasmine finally freed herself, stumbling away from the fresh uprooting of tendrils that the continuing spell sent after her as she escaped. She flew up into the air far enough to remain out of reach of the snare, and far enough to give her a rounded view of the struggles below her. Damien could handle Nicodemous for the immediate moment, and she was not worried about him. At first glance, the Princess had made her mark, having an upper hand over the Demon female as well. However, Jasmine knew that surprise had been her advantage, and from that point on the Princess was going to be seriously outgunned.

Jasmine streaked toward the battling women just as Ruth turned on Syreena with a cry of enormous fury. Syreena had struck first blood, and it seriously affected Ruth's self-image of invulnerability. Ruth screamed out a spell, fueled by the power of her rage, and the entire forest exploded with a blast of percussion that centered from the Demon's position. Syreena was struck full-on by the blast, as was Jasmine, and both women were catapulted back through the air before they slammed into trees. Too stunned to get her wings under her, Syreena plummeted to the forest floor with a mighty crash and a kickback of debris that clouded around her for a few fluttering moments.

Jasmine, however, did not need wings to keep buoyant. She recovered quickly because she had no breath to get knocked out of her. Stunning pain could be put aside for the moment, even though she was certain she had cracked a couple of ribs at impact.

Her immediate problem was how to shut Ruth up. As long as she could speak, they would never gain an upper hand. Her spells were too unfamiliar, unexpected and indefensible. *But*, Jasmine thought wickedly, *she cannot cast spells if she gets her tongue ripped out.*

Logically, she knew she would never get that close. She had to come up with an alternative.

Meanwhile, Damien and Nico had also been thrown by the magical blast, sending them rolling and skidding across the ground, each getting torn, punctured, and battered along the way. This time, Nico managed to gain the upper position over Damien. He pinned the monarch to the ground with the sheer power of his enormous weight, strong legs, and the deadly grip of his hand over the Prince's throat. He reached for his dagger now that he had a better target. But as he stabbed for Damien's heart, the Prince threw a forearm up and there was a clang as metal clashed with metal.

Nico tried to press through to Damien's flesh, through the leather of the jacket he wore, but it was as though the Prince's skin were made of steel. It was when he withdrew for a second strike, the action slicing away a strip of leather, that the gleam of the poniard up the Prince's sleeve showed itself.

"Tricky, tricky," Nico said breathlessly.

Nico realized that hand to hand was not going to give him an advantage over Damien, especially since the Prince had concealed weapons on his person.

The traitorous Vampire had not had much time to learn spells, not the way Ruth knew them, but there were some like the ensnarement spell that he had focused on because of their tactical usefulness in a fight. Since the Prince was on the ground, it made sense to use the advantage to try again. Now that Nico was on top of him, changing form would be too dangerous for the Prince.

Nico went to speak the spell that would trap Damien helplessly beneath him and his ready blade.

Syreena could not breathe for a long moment. Her lungs simply would not work as she knelt on her hands and knees on the forest floor. Finally she coughed and inhaled, her lungs expanding against bruised and battered ribs. She struggled to gain her feet, whipping around to try and seek her enemy even before she could straighten up completely.

What she could see was Jasmine. The Vampire was streaking toward a target. From her position, Syreena could not see what it was. On impact, she had reverted to human form.

She hesitated as she tried to decide which winged creature would be best for the moment, when a loud clang of metal rang from just behind the grove of trees she had crashed into. She whirled and leaned around the nearest tree trunk. She saw Nico's blade gleam in the moonlight as he withdrew for a second attempt at her mate's heart. Then he thought better of it and she heard him utter a singular phrase in a language foreign even to her.

Roots sprang up from the ground around Damien, whipping out to lash him about the legs and throat, pinning and strangling him at once. Syreena felt immediate rage flood over her, and Ruth was completely forgotten. She flew with all speed from her hiding place as Nico reached back to plunge his dagger into her mate's exposed breast.

Damien felt her coming, a speedball of charcoal hair and violent protective instinct. She struck his enemy with the force of her full weight. It was enough to move even a mountain of a man such as Nico. She tackled him clean off Damien's body, and the two went tumbling off into leaf litter and underbrush. Damien immediately began to strain against his bonds of nature, using all of his strength as roots began to snap under the stress, one by one. Flat to the ground as he was, he felt like Gulliver, tied fast by thousands of Lilliputian ropes. When enough snapped loose to free a limb, the spell immediately revived and lashed him back down again. The trees around him began to list dangerously in his direction as their root system was torn away, altered and pulled out from under them.

Meanwhile, Nico was learning the true definition of a well-trained Monk of The Pride. As she had struck him, Syreena had reached for his blade and neatly disarmed him as her surprise strike tumbled them away from Damien. Without preamble, the moment they slid to a stop with Syreena pressing a knee into the Vampire's throat on one side and groin on the other, she reached with both hands to commit to her strike.

The Vampire's dagger sank into his flesh, cracked explosively through bone and through his heart.

Nico roared with pain and outrage as she once again stabbed him through that vital organ. The Vampire could not believe she had gotten him a second time. This time, however, it was much worse. She was able to withdraw the blade, unplugging the hole she had made, her updrawn arc spraying his blood across her thighs, breasts, and face. Before he could react, she was plunging into him again. Her eyes were wide and wild, her lips curled into a feminine snarl of wrath, and her hair swung in a dark gray cloud with her movements. She withdrew again, coming away with even more blood this time as the force of her weight, strike, and his contortions sent it spurting up over her.

It was all Nico could do to finally stop the chopping descent of her hands before she struck him yet again. She slammed into the catch of his hands instead of his chest, and it seemed to only infuriate her further. She struggled against his strength, which, in spite of his deadly injuries, was still quite enough to overpower her. He threw her off him with a powerful pivot of his body, sending her tumbling over. He tried to seal the gushing wounds on his chest with his palm as he scrambled to his knees and lunged after her. She had rolled up onto her feet, the bloody dagger still clutched in her small but clearly capable hand.

Jasmine diverted away from Ruth, perplexing the Demon for a moment. Then the Mind Demon realized that Jasmine's nature was far too much like her own for Damien's good. As long as Ruth did not threaten her directly, the Vampire would not be likely to risk her own neck for any purpose that was not solely her own. It was clear how much Jasmine hated Damien's new mate. Why would she come to the Princess's rescue?

Ruth teleported, appearing by Damien's side. Seeing that the struggling Prince was no threat at the moment, and not wanting to risk Jasmine's focus, she popped out and in again, this time appearing beside her injured partner and the Lycanthrope who had seriously wounded him.

"At least I will have you," the Demon murmured with eager delight and intent.

As Nico was lunging for the Lycanthrope, Ruth reached to grab her by the hair that was as great a weakness, as it was her one true strength.

To the shock of both enemies, they passed through their intended targets, crashing hard against each other instead in a tangle of clothing and limbs. Ruth cursed Nico; Nico cursed Ruth, shoving her violently away as he tried to find the quick little minx who had somehow managed to elude them both.

When Ruth and Nico both finally located Syreena, they were shocked to see her standing side by side with the Vampire Prince, not ten feet away from them.

"Impossible!" Ruth hissed.

"It's a trick! An illusion," Nico growled.

"*Impossible*!" the Mind Demon insisted.

"Clearly not," Damien remarked dryly.

Ruth struggled to her feet, making to lunge for the couple that had outfoxed even her considerable mental powers. She had barely managed to make it to her full height when her hair was grabbed violently from behind, tearing out in painful clumps, her head jerked back so hard it nearly sent her back to the ground.

Ruth screamed in pain.

Jasmine slapped her other hand over Ruth's mouth, the thick handful of pasty mud she had mined from the nearest puddle filling the orifice thickly, sealing off all sound and ability to speak.

Damien reached for the poniard up his sleeve, and he and Syreena advanced on Nico with clear menace. Realizing he was outnumbered and too wounded to make an impact if he continued fighting, Nico closed his eyes and promptly disappeared in a roiling cloud of smoke.

"Damn him!"

"Teleportation!"

"Apparently, Ruth figured out how to share her power with him," Jasmine said dryly. "Did you not, dearest?" she asked, jerking the suffocating woman back against her body by her hair. "You would not want to tell me where my book is, would you?"

Jasmine looked up at Damien and Syreena with a flashing smile that was brilliant and surprisingly pretty. "Oops. That's right. Speak no evil." Jasmine wiggled one of the fingers sealed over Ruth's mouth, forcing her to keep the paste of mud within her lips.

"Do we kill her, or take her to Noah?" Damien asked.

"Kill her. Kill her before she can—"

Jasmine's words and figure were lost in a sudden explosion of thick black smoke. The cloud roiled up from between her arms as Ruth disappeared from her grasp. Damien and Syreena heard the Vampire woman scream with outrage and frustration as the smoke cleared to show her stomping her foot in fury, her hands empty of her prisoner.

Damien and Syreena exchanged a look and a sigh.

"Nico," they said in unison.

For the most part, the mission had been a victorious one, even though Jasmine was still grousing over losing her captive. Syreena, however, knew that they had been the first in a long time to best Ruth to the point of nearly capturing her. And that was with the added threat of Nico included. It was something to feel very proud of, in spite of the undesirable outcome. She sensed clearly that Damien felt the same way. That did not change the fact that they were about to have a very difficult discussion.

Syreena sat on the bed where they had completed the Exchange only the night before. Damien walked into the room with a clean bowl of water, clean cloths, and bandaging materials.

"Scoot."

Syreena obeyed, sliding aside so he could sit beside her. He placed the bowl on the night table, then, after wetting a cloth, turned to face her. He reached to cleanse one of the many cuts on her back, urging her to turn so he could better see.

He was silent for several long minutes before speaking.

"You have every right to be angry with me. In spite of everything I said, I do know that," he said quietly. "I let Jasmine convince me too easily into doing what we did. I was itching for a fight because of Kelsey's death and the idea of a Vampire joining ranks with Ruth. I am not an idiot, but I suppose to you, I was acting like one."

She felt him lean forward and give her bare shoulder what felt like an apologetic kiss. "I don't care if you are an idiot, Damien. I do care that you broke a promise only a few hours old. I have given you my complete trust in so many things and asked little in return, and the first time—"

"I know. I know," he interrupted her with a fierce whisper. "It was bad of me. And worse to place fault in your lap. I was just taken off guard and I was afraid for your safety. Jas and I could go undetected, but I knew the minute I sensed that you were close . . ."

"And that, perhaps, was bad of me. It was certainly foolish. I know I could have gotten us all killed."

There was quiet again as he gently cleansed her wounds. They were superficial, and she would heal by the next evening, but he wanted to tend to her in this way. It was part apology, part concern, and even a part gratitude. She had proven herself valiantly against enemies who had both bested her once before and had been a great source of fear and rattled confidence since. She was quite possibly the bravest creature he had ever met, and it made him quite proud to have her next to him.

When he finally set aside the cloth he had used on her, she immediately reached for another and turned toward him with expectant intent. He obediently shrugged out of his jacket and loosened his shirt. When he peeled back the dark blue fabric, he exposed numerous bleeding lacerations, but more importantly, ring after ring of livid bruising.

"Damien," she breathed in obvious despair as she reached to touch light fingertips to the discoloration. The ensnarement spell had been powerful, and the roots of the trees had strangled him from head to toe. The damage looked profound and probably felt worse. "I am so sorry."

"It will heal in a day or two." He smiled at her. "It is worth it, because I now know who the Vampire is. I could not tell from a distance. In a way, you helped us find out exactly what we wanted to. You lured them out into the open."

"Yes, well, I have come up with better plans."

"Yet they were probably less effective," he chuckled.

"It is not very funny," she said, reaching to cleanse a particularly nasty abrasion on his shoulder. "It was a mess and we were lucky to get out relatively unscathed."

"About that," he said suddenly, reaching to stop her ministrations by catching her wrist. "Would you mind telling me how you managed to trick Nico and Ruth into thinking you were somewhere you were not?"

"I . . ." She gave a distinct blink of her dark eyes. "I don't really know. I just had this instinct . . ."

"An instinct to cast an illusion of yourself while you escaped his target area." Damien let a corner of his mouth curl into a smile. "Well, well. I think we can stop guessing what part of me you are going to achieve. I must say, it was a pretty powerful trick to play on two people of such mental skill. Especially for an amateur."

"But you are not an amateur," she reminded him.

"Yes, but you are a very skilled shapechanger and it is clear that I did not inherit that from you intrinsically."

"Actually, perhaps you have. Not every detail, mind you, but it does take several decades before a shapechanger can change with the ease you showed only a day or so after discovering you could do so. You are quite good at the changing skill, even doing it on the fly tonight, which very few can do. Behaving true to avian form, that is an entirely different skill."

"So perhaps you can project powerful illusions, but you may need a great deal of time and practice before you can see through them yourself."

"Exactly! Oh . . . really?" she asked, sounding instantly dejected. "They are two different skills?"

"I am afraid so, sweetling." He chuckled. "But if you teach me how to land, I think I can teach you how to see through some pretty strong illusions."

She smiled at that, taking her wrist from his hands and going back to her task as she grinned happily. "I think I will like this ability. For a while, I was worried I might sprout fangs."

"Worried? I was hoping," he countered, giving her a sideways look and a mischievous lift to his eyebrows.

"Pervert," she chuckled. "Do you ever think about anything besides sex?"

"With you sitting this close to me naked? I hardly think it is possible."

"Stop it," she scolded him, slapping away the hand he started to slide up her thigh. "I am covered in blood and battle, not to mention the fact that I may very well still be mad at you. I have not decided yet."

"What part of being covered in blood is supposed to make you unattractive to a Vampire?" he asked teasingly.

"The part where it's the blood of a corrupted Vampire using black magic," she reminded him.

"Ah. Excellent point."

Then he shoved aside her hands and in a single movement scooped her into his arms and rose off the bed. He carried her into the adjoining bath, ignoring her protests about his high-handed treatment of her.

"You are arguing as if you do not want to take a bath," he pointed out, "when I know that you do."

"Why do you always make it sound like you have divined some great mystery of my mind? I pretty much just said as much," she said dryly, pushing away from him slightly when he set her on her feet and leaned over to start the water in the old claw-footed tub.

"Unfortunately, the water will be cold. The heating systems are in need of repair, I am told," he warned her. "Though I imagine it will bother me far more than it will you."

"I can have water boiled and brought up for you," she said simply, stepping into the tub lightly, giving herself a moment to adjust herself to the promised chill once her toes had taken its measure. Syreena sat down and stretched out, allowing the clean water to creep up over her skin slowly as the bath filled.

Instead of leaving her, Damien knelt down beside her on the tiled floor, folding his arms across the near lip of the iron tub and bringing his gaze level to hers. The sound of the water splashing into itself was strong for a few minutes, and then he broke it.

"I am truly sorry if I worried you."

Syreena sighed softly, drawing a lip between nibbling teeth for a moment as she thought a little before responding. Her habitual care in all her responses had become charming to him, and a strong reflection of who she was, so an inner smile blossomed beneath his skin as he watched her.

"That is not the point, Damien," she said softly. "You broke a promise to me. That is what upsets me most. And I feel I need to remind you that I only asked you not to do something reckless, not that you could not approach me and tell me if you had an entirely new argument and purpose. I would not have been happy about letting you and Jasmine go, but I would have preferred to know than not. It would have saved all of us this trouble tonight if you had merely told me where you were going and why. You promised to consider my feelings, and all you considered was that if we discussed it, I would countermand your desires and attempt to keep you from doing what you wanted to do.

"In truth, Damien, I would have seen the logic behind it as well as the risk. I have always been able to see both sides of an issue. I do wish you would have thought, even for a moment, to give me credit for that. Instead, you snuck off behind my back."

"As I said, I am not accustomed to answering to another," he said quietly.

"It is not answering to me," she said sharply, then reigned in her flash of temper with a breath. "I am not out to curb you or leash you into obedience, Damien. That would destroy the very essences of what attracts me to you, of what holds my heart captive. I only want this to be a fully reciprocal partnership. I know you are capable of it. I see it every time you and Jasmine bend your heads together. I also know it will take time for us to reach the same level of familiarity and comfort you share with her, but I expected you to at least remember the principle of trying from one hour to the next." Syreena sighed, running damp hands back through her hair. "This is sounding like a lecture, like I am scolding a child, and I do not mean to make it that way."

"I imagine that is because we are still learning how to communicate with one another, Syreena. I am taking no offense. You have a right to your frustration with me. You do not make an unreasonable request here. I know you would have shown me far more consideration than I showed you. And you are right; it took the breadth of a day before I acted against the decision we had made together. I owe you an apology for that as well."

"And there is fault with me here as well," she said, waving off the apology with an acceptance that would do the least damage to his pride. "I flew off half-cocked myself, giving in to my temper, heedless of the danger I was causing, just so I could say my piece."

"That is very true," he agreed with readiness that clearly bordered on humorous.

"Oh, hush up and help me wash this stuff off of me."

She softened the command with a kiss on his nearby lips, smiling halfway through the exchange until she had to break off a giggle.

"You know, I may have created a monster," he mused, reaching out to push back a strand of hair straggling over her nose. "You are beginning to get quite bossy about what you want."

"Well, I am afraid you will have to live with that," she informed him.

"I think I can manage that, sweetling," he promised her.

"Then I think you are right, Damien. I think we may actually be able to make this work after all."

Epilogue

Jasmine sat off in the shadows, not necessarily sulking, but not exactly joining in with the festive actions going on a short distance away from where she stood.

Damien had actually done it.

He had wed himself to the Lycanthrope Princess.

Now Princess of the Vampires, her other throne put on the back burner, a promise of abdication given to her people on the event of the birth of Siena's first child. It had been a gesture meant to placate them for marrying into another race, but the lack of Lycanthropic attendance spoke volumes about how well the match was being accepted.

There were even those whom Damien considered reasonably close comrades who had not deigned to attend the marriage. This did not really surprise any of those who had decided to wish the union of the two Nightwalker houses of royalty well. It was a breach of too many deeply engrained taboos, buried in Vampire psyche for generation upon generation. The only thing that saved them from a civil war or an uprising of protest was the writings from the Library they had found to confirm Jasmine's previous claims about the ritual that was older than those taboos.

Even so, the couple had waited until spring to join, waiting until their domestic policing system had reached beyond its initial organization stages. A wise choice, really. The timing had been selected carefully so that the information justifying the wedding would come after the security network meant to keep Vampire behavior in check was firmly in place. There had been clues before then, of course, because Damien and Syreena had kept house together publicly in the increasingly growing court. However, any reactions from *that* had been Jasmine's and Stephan's job to handle.

Jasmine smiled at the thought.

It had certainly kept her from being bored. It was strange how something she felt so little agreement with personally could actually give her a sudden feeling of fulfillment and satisfaction of purpose. Court intrigues of the Vampire variety were definitely keeping her on her toes. Not to mention the ripples that were flowing outward into all Nightwalker communities as the entire political atmosphere began to change with dramatic publicity.

Needless to say, it was making for a busy, volatile time.

That pleased her.

What did not please her as much was the silence from the realm of the traitors. There was no sign of them, as usual. Not even as the security net expanded over the continents. There was no way of knowing if Nico was alive or dead. There was no clue as to what Ruth's next tactic was going to be. They still had no idea what she had been up to in the first place, and Jasmine suspected that the Demon female was only going to become more careful even as she became more powerful. Jasmine had exploited her weaknesses, and in doing so had set her on guard to them. In the end, it could very well have made things much worse.

However, even if Nico had managed once again to survive, it would take a long time in a state of torpor before he would be able to rise again and cause further trouble with Ruth. Jasmine suspected they might get lucky and have the time they needed to grow stronger themselves before they would have to face the duo as a real threat once again. She had to give that much to the Lycanthrope Princess. Her actions and battle skills could very well have bought them some valuable time.

"If the wedding displeases you so, why have you come?"

Jasmine roused from her inner thoughts to look at the female who had addressed her. She dismissed her immediate surprise at being found in the stealth of the shadows when she realized it was Malaya, the Shadowdweller Chancellor. Her breed lived in the shadows even more than Vampires did, so it made sense that she would be able to detect Jasmine in spite of her best skulking abilities.

"I have gotten over my initial displeasure," Jasmine said with a simple shrug as Malaya joined her in the shadows. "I cannot affect jubilance, however. Although, I will admit to being glad that Damien is happy."

"I have tried to place myself in your perspective," the Chancellor said with soft thoughtfulness. "How would I feel if my brother, co-ruler of our species, were to wed outside of our breed?"

"And have you had much success with this?" Jasmine queried.

"Yes. I have realized that we are not Vampires, therefore I cannot begin to put myself in your place even if it were to come true."

Jasmine chuckled at her wry wisdom. She saw her smile flash in the dark.

"I know even less about your people than you do mine," Jasmine admitted, "so I would have equal lack of luck."

"I do know a perfect match when I see one, however," she countered. "To battle against such a thing would be like holding out your hand to ward off a tidal wave. It is a battle against the inevitable, and a foolish position to take."

"Very true," Jasmine agreed. "And so, you have answered your own initial question."

"I suppose I have," she said after a moment of thought. "I have met the new child of Demon prophecy. The newborn of the King's sister. It is believed by them that he will bring new power to the Demons."

"Which means a lifetime of being closely protected. Ruth knows of the prophecy as well as any Demon, and she will seek ways of getting it for herself if she can. The little boy *and* his counterpart, the girl child who was born to the Enforcers will both learn to walk on a fine line of danger. Why anyone would give birth in such volatile times, exposing their young to such peril, is completely beyond me."

"Apparently your ruler does not agree with your assessments."

Jasmine lifted a brow in surprise. "What do you mean by that?"

"I mean the Princess is clearly in a breeding cycle, and your Prince does not behave like a mate who will be keeping from her bed the next couple of weeks."

Jasmine's gaze instantly flashed to the newly wedded couple that Malaya had indicated with a nod of her head. Damien was, quite literally, all over his new bride. His hands were roaming her figure with public hunger, his mouth leaned close to her ear and was saying or doing something that had her in squirms and giggles. Syreena was not behaving within her usual conservative borders, either. From the placement of her hands and the insinuating rubbing of her body against the Prince's, it was clear what she had on her mind, and damn the fact that there were clusters of witnesses all around.

"It is Beltane," she argued softly. "And they are newly wed. Everyone gets a little . . . freer than usual on this night."

"You are looking with your eyes, Vampire. I am looking with much deeper senses. I promise you, she is in heat, and if they head along this path very often these next weeks, there will be a child soon. The first of its kind, too. At least, the first in many millennia. The child of a Vampire and a Ly-canthrope. One has to wonder . . ."

"Please," she held up a hand to ward off her speculations. "My stomach is already turning. Do not make it any worse!"

"You do not like children?"

"I hated being a child. I dislike the complications a child of theirs will cause, also. But it is a waste to speculate over the future. Nothing is ever certain. It may be that time has erased the compatibility required to bring offspring between the races."

Jasmine sighed. "Do not be discouraged," the Chancellor murmured gently near her ear. "Your life promises to be one of excitement and fulfillment, whether Damien is a part of it or not."

Jasmine turned her head to look at her again, laughing with a short, clear burst of sarcasm. "You clearly do not know me very well."

"No, but I know the future in ways other Nightwalkers never can."

Jasmine's eyes widened with shock and surprise, but the Chancellor silenced her surging queries and demands with a single finger to her lips.

"This is not information we share with outsiders, but I share it with you for a reason. Your sadness of the past is rooted further in history than you realize, and your future happiness will depend greatly on the extreme despair of an-other as well. But yours is a special destiny, and it begins here, today, with this ceremony. I have no specifics, so do not ask me. I just thought it would make you look more kindly on your present situation if you knew that Damien and Syreena will one day be directly responsible for the life you will one day come to know."

Jasmine was speechless. All she could do was blink blankly as she watched the other woman move away from her with a smooth, gliding grace that reminded her so much of the way Damien moved.

After a minute, she allowed herself to look back at the deliriously happy and overtly affectionate couple whom she had lived with the past few months. They had managed to learn to live with each other, even learning to respect each other's contributions.

Perhaps, just perhaps, they might begin to find something more than that as well one day.

Of course, that was entirely up to Jasmine, and she rather preferred to cause just a little more trouble for the woman who had stolen away the best man she knew before she would give in to her inclinations to grudgingly like her.

Try Jacquelyn Frank's NIGHTWALKERS series
from the beginning!
The journey starts with JACOB,
available now from Zebra . . .

It was daylight once more when Jacob floated down through Noah's manor until he was in the vault, one moment dust dancing through the incandescent light, the next coming to rest lightly on his feet. He looked around the well-lit catacomb, seeking his prey. He heard a rustling sound from the nearest stacks and moved toward it.

There was a soft curse, a grunt, and the sudden slam of something hitting the floor. Jacob came around just in time to find Isabella dangling from one of the many shelves, her feet swaying about ten feet above the floor as she searched with her toes for a foothold. On the ground below her was a rather ancient looking tome, the splattered pattern of the dust that had shaken off of it indicating it had been the object he had heard fall. Far to her left was the ladder she had apparently been using.

With a low sigh of exasperation, Jacob altered gravity for himself and floated himself up behind her. "You are going to break your neck."

Isabella was not expecting a voice at her ear, considering her peculiar circumstances, and she started with a little scream.

One hand lost hold and she swung right into the hard wall of his chest. He gathered her up against himself, his arm slipping beneath her knees so she was safely cradled, his warmth infusing her with a sense of safety and comfort as he brought her down to the floor effortlessly. In spite of herself, she pressed her cheek to his chest.

"Must you sneak up on me in mid-air like that? It's very unnerving."

She had meant to sound angry, but the soft, breathless accusation was anything but. Anyway, how angry would he think her to be if she was snuggling up to him like a kitten? Damn it, Demon or not, he was still a sinfully good-looking man. Jacob was elegant to a fault, his movements and manner centered around an efficiency of actions that drew the eye. He was dressed again in well-tailored black slacks, and this time a midnight blue dress shirt with his cuffs turned back. She could feel the rich quality of the silk beneath her cheek, and when she breathed in, Jacob smelled like the rich, heady Earth he claimed his abilities from.

Besides all the outwardly alluring physicality, Isabella knew that he was extremely sensitive about all his interactions with others. She could feel his moral imperatives tingling through her mind whenever he was near. His heart, she knew, was made of incredibly honorable stuff. How could she find it in herself to be afraid of that? Especially when he had never once hurt her, even though there had been plenty of influences compelling him to.

"Shall I put you back and let you plummet to your death?" he asked, releasing her legs and letting her body slide slowly down his until her feet touched the floor.

The whisper of the friction of their clothes hummed across Jacob's skin, and he felt his senses focusing in on every nuance of sensation she provided for him. The swishing silk of her hair even in its present tangled state, the sweet warmth of her breath and body, the ivory perfection of her skin. He reached to wipe a smudge of dust from her delectable little

nose. She was a mess. There was no arguing that. Head to toe
covered in dust and grime and she smelled like an old book,
but those earthy scents would never be something unappeal-
ing to one of his kind. Jacob breathed deeply as the usual
heat she inspired stirred in his cool blood. It was stronger
with each passing moment, with each progressive day, and
he never once became unaware of that fact. He tried to tell
himself it was merely the effects of the growing moon, but
that reasoning did not satisfy him. Hallowed madness would
not allow for the unexpected compulsion toward tenderness
he kept experiencing whenever he looked down into her an-
gelic face. It would never allow him to enjoy these simple
yet significant stirrings of his awareness without forcing him
into overdrive. True, he was holding onto his control with a
powerful leash of determination. He was tamping down the
surges of want and lust that gripped him so hard sometimes
it was nearly crippling, but somehow it was still different.

Then he had to also acknowledge the melding of their
thoughts as something truly unique. Perhaps a human could
initiate such a contact if they were a medium or psychic of
noteworthy ability, but she made no claims to such special
talents. Every day the images of her mind became clearer to
him. She had even taken to consciously sending him pic-
turesque impressions in response to some discussion they
were having with Noah, Elijah, and Legna. He believed that,
if things continued to progress in this manner, he and Bella
would soon be engaging in actual discussions with each
other without ever opening their mouths. He didn't have fact
to base that assumption on, but it seemed the natural evolu-
tion to the growing silent communication between them.

He had seen Legna staring at them curiously on several
occasions. Luckily, because she was a female Mind Demon,
she was not a full telepath. If she had been a male she would
have been privy to some pretty private exchanges between
him and Isabella. Nothing racy, actually, but he found Isa-

bella had such an irreverent sense of humor, that he wasn't sure others would understand it as he seemed to.

It was a privacy of exchange he found himself coveting. It was the one way they could be together without Legna or Noah interfering. It was bad enough that the empath was constantly sniffing at his emotions, making sure he kept in careful control of his baser side. Since the King was not able to subject him the usual punishment that was meted out for those who had crossed the line as he had with Isabella, his monarch had been forced to be a little more creative. Setting Legna the empathic bloodhound on him had done the trick. It was also seriously pissing him off. He knew she was always there, and it burned his pride like nuclear fire.

What was more, he couldn't keep his mind away from Isabella. And since even the smallest thought of her had a way of sparking an onslaught of fantasies that brought his body to physical readiness . . . well, it was the very last thing he wanted an audience for.

It had taken quite a bit of planning, and the deceptive use of herbal tea mixtures, in order to slip out from under Legna's observation so he could sneak away to the vault. The empath slept as soundly as the dead, and she would stay that way until this evening.

"I wouldn't have fallen to my death," Bella was arguing, her stubborn streak prickling. "At the most, I would have fallen to my broken leg or my concussion or something. Boy, you Demons have this way of making everything seem so intense and pivotal."

"We are a very intense people, Bella."

"Tell me about it." She wriggled out of his embrace, putting distance between them with a single step back. Jacob was well aware of it being a very purposeful act. "I've been reading books and scrolls as far back as 700 years ago. You were just a gleam in your daddy's eye then, I imagine."

"Demons may have long gestation periods for their young, but not seventy-eight years' worth."

"Yes. I read about that. Is it true it takes thirteen months for a female to carry and give birth?"

"Minimum." He said it with such casual dismissal that Bella laughed.

"That's easy for you to say. You don't have to lug the kid around inside of you all that time. You, just like your human counterparts, have the fun part over with like that." She snapped her fingers in front of his face.

His dark eyes narrowed and he reached to enclose her hand in his, pulling her wrist up to the slow, purposeful brush of his lips even as he maintained a sensual eye contact that was far too full of promises. Isabella caught her breath as an insidious sensation of heated pins and needles stitched their way up her arm.

"I promise you, Bella, a male Demon's part in a mating is never over like this." He mimicked her snap, making her jump in time to her kick-starting heartbeat.

"Well," she cleared her throat, "I guess I'll have to take your word on that." Jacob did not respond in agreement, and that unnerved her even further. Instinctively, she changed tack. "So, what brings you down into the dusty atmosphere of the great Demon library?" she asked, knowing she sounded like a brightly animated cartoon.

"You."

Oh, how that singular word was pregnant with meaning, intent and devastatingly blatant honesty. Isabella was forced to remind herself of the whole Demon-human mating taboo as the forbidden response of heat continued to writhe around beneath her skin, growing exponentially in intensity every moment he hovered close. She tried to picture all kinds of scary things that could happen if she did not quit egging him on like she was. How she was, she didn't know, but she was always certain she was egging him on.

"Why did you want to see me?" she asked, breaking away from him and bending to retrieve the book she had dropped. It was huge and heavy and she grunted softly under the weight of it. It landed with a slam and another puff of dust on the table she had made into her own private study station.

"Because, I cannot seem to help myself, lovely little Bella."

Can't get enough Jacquelyn Frank?
Don't miss GIDEON: THE NIGHTWALKERS,
in stores now from Zebra.

Gideon wore the habits of his lifetime like an unapologetic statement, and he wore them very well. He blended the male fashions of the millennium in a way that was nothing less than a perfect reflection of who he was and how he had lived. This only served to beautify his distinctive and powerful presence with his incidental confidence.

"Gideon," she said evenly, inclining her head in sparse respect. "What brings you to my chambers, so close to dawn?"

The riveting male before her remained silent, his silver eyes flicking over her slowly. Her heart nearly stopped with her sudden fear, and immediately she threw up every mental and physical barrier she could to prevent an unwelcome scan and analysis of her health.

"I would not scan you without your permission, Magdelegna. Body Demons who become healers have codes of ethics as well as any others."

"Funny," she remarked, "I would have thought you to believe yourself above such a trivial matter as permission."

His mercury gaze narrowed slightly, making Legna wish that she had the courage to dare a piratical scan of her own.

She was quite talented at masking her travels through the emotions and psyches of others, but Gideon was like no other. She was barely a fledgling to one such as he.

Gideon had noted her more recent acerbic tendencies aloud once before, irritating the young female even more than usual, so he resisted the urge in that moment to scold her again and let her attitude pass.

"I have come to check on your well-being, Magdelegna. I am concerned."

Legna cocked a brow, twisting her lips into a cold, mocking little smile, hiding the sudden, anxious beating of her heart.

"And what would give you the impression that you need be concerned for me?" she asked haughtily.

Gideon once more took his time before responding, giving her one more of those implacable perusals in the interim. Legna exhaled with annoyance, crossing her arms beneath her breasts and coming just shy of tapping her foot in irritation.

"You are not at peace, young one," Gideon explained softly, the deep timbre of his voice resonating through her, once again giving her the feeling that she was but fragile crystal, awaiting the moment when he would strike the note of discord that would shatter her. Legna's breathing altered, quickening in spite of her effort to maintain an even keel. She did not want to give him the satisfaction of being right.

"You presume too much, Gideon. I have no need for your concern, nor have I ever solicited it. Now, if you do not mind, I should like to go to bed."

"For what purpose?"

Legna laughed, short and harsh.

"To sleep, why else?"

"You have not slept for many days together, Legna. Why do you assume you might have success today?"

Legna turned around sharply, driving her gaze and attention back out of the window, trying to use the sprawling lawn as a slate to fill her mind with. Mind Demon he was not, but she knew he was capable of seeing far enough into her emotional state by just monitoring her physiological reactions to his observations. Legna bit her lip hard, furious that she should feel like the child he always referred to her as in their conversations. Young one, indeed. How would he like it if she referred to him as a decrepit old buzzard?

The thought gave her a small, petty satisfaction. It did not matter that Gideon looked as vital and vibrant as any Demon male from thirty years to a thousand would look. Nor did it matter that his stunning coloring gave him a unique attractiveness and aura of power that no one else could equal. All that mattered was that he would never view her as an equal, and therefore, in her perspective, she had no responsibility to do so for him.

Gideon watched the young woman across from him closely, trying to make sense of the physiological changes that flashed through her rapidly, each as puzzling as the one before it. What was it about her, he wondered, that always kept him off his mark? She never reacted the way he logically expected her to, yet he knew her to be extraordinarily intelligent. She always treated him with a barely repressed contempt, though she never had a harsh word for anyone else. He had almost gotten used to that since their original falling out, but this was different, far more complex than hard feelings. Gideon had not encountered a puzzle in a great many centuries, and perhaps that was why he was continually fascinated by her in spite of her marked disdain.

"It is not unusual," she said at last, "to have periods of insomnia in one's life. Surely that is not what has you rushing into my boudoir, oozing your high-handed version of concern."

"Magdelegna, I am continually puzzled by your insistence in treating me with hostility. Did Lucas teach you nothing about respecting your elders?"

Legna whirled around suddenly, outrage flaring off of her

so violently that Gideon felt the eddy of it push at him through the still air.

"Do not ever mention Lucas in such a disrespectful manner ever again! Do you understand me, Gideon? I will not tolerate it!" She moved to stand toe to toe with the medic, her emotions practically beating him back in their intensity. "You say respect my elders, but what you mean is respecting my betters, is that not right? Are you so full of your own arrogance that you need me to bow and kowtow to you like some throwback fledgling? Or perhaps we should reinstate the role of concubines in our society. Then you may have the pleasure of claiming me and forcing me to fall to my knees, bowing low in respect of your masculine eminence!"

Gideon watched as she did just that, her gown billowing around her as she gracefully kneeled before him, so close to him that her knees touched the tips of his boots. She swept her hands to her sides, bowing her head until her forehead brushed the leather, her hair spilling like reams of heavy silk around his ankles.

The Ancient found himself unusually speechless, the strangest sensation creeping through him as he looked down at the exposed nape of her neck; the elegant line of her back. Unable to curb the impulse, Gideon lowered himself into a crouch, reaching beneath the cloak of coffee-colored hair to touch her flushed cheek. The heat of her anger radiated against his touch and he recognized it long before she turned her face up to him.

"Does this satisfy you, my lord Gideon?" she whispered fiercely, her eyes flashing like flinted steel and hard jade.

Gideon found himself searching her face intently, his eyes roaming over the high, aristocratic curves of her cheekbones, the amazingly full sculpture of her lips; the wide, accusing eyes that lay behind extraordinarily thick lashes. He cupped her chin between the thumb and forefinger of his left hand, his fingertips fanning softly over her angrily flushed cheek.

"You do enjoy mocking me," he murmured softly to her, the breath of his words close enough to skim across her face.

"No more than you seem to enjoy condescending to me," she replied, her clipped words coming out on quick, heated breaths.

Gideon absorbed the latest venom directed toward him with a blink of lengthy black lashes. They kept their gazes locked, each seemingly waiting for the other to look away.

"You have never forgiven me," he said suddenly, softly.

"Forgiven you?" She laughed bitterly. "Gideon, you are not important enough to earn my forgiveness."

"Is your ego so fragile, Legna, that a small slight to it is irreparable?"

"Stop talking to me as if I were a temperamental child!" Legna hissed, moving to jerk her head back, but finding his grip quite secure. "There was nothing slight about the way you treated me. I will never forget it, and I most certainly will never forgive it!"

Keep the magic going with ELIJAH,
in stores now from Zebra . . .

The cold of another breeze rushed up from behind her, blowing at the brief skirt of her dress and whipping through her hair. It surrounded her, engulfed her, forcing her to come to a halt just as muscled arms appeared around her waist.

Siena sucked in a startled breath as the cold vanished, replaced by the warmth, the heat, of a familiar male body. She was drawn back against his chest, his hands splaying out over her flat belly and pushing her deeper into the planes of his hard body.

"Elijah," she whispered, her eyes closing as a sensation of remarkable relief flooded through her entire body. Every nerve and hormone in her body surged to life just to be held in his embrace, and she was light-headed with the power of it all.

He put hands on her hips, using them to spin her full around to face him. The warrior dragged her back to his body, seizing her mouth with savage hunger just as she was reaching for his kiss. She could not have helped herself. Not after the deprivation of all these days. But still, the weakness stung her painfully, leaving frustrated tears in her eyes.

It was all just as she remembered it. The vividness of the memories of their touches and kisses had never once faded to less than what it truly was. It was all heat and musk and the delicious flavor of his bold, demanding mouth. His hands were on her backside, drawing her up into his body with movement she could only label as desperation.

Elijah had not meant to attack her in this manner, but the moment he had sensed her nearness, smelled the perfume of her skin and hair, he could not do anything else. He devoured the cinnamon taste of her mouth relentlessly, groaning with relief and pleasure as her hands curled around the fabric of his shirt and her incredible body molded to his with perfection. He pulled her hips directly to his own, leaving no question about how hard and fast her effect on him was. He felt her swinging perfectly with the onslaught of his pressing body and adamant kisses.

Everything was perfection. Top to bottom, beginning to end, and he had been starving without her. He also knew she had been just as famished without him.

She was the first to put any distance between them, by breaking away from his mouth, letting her head fall back as far as it could as she drew for breath hard and quick.

"Oh no," she groaned huskily, shaking her head so her hair brushed over the arms around her waist.

Even those strands betrayed her, reaching eagerly to coil around his wrists and forearms, trapping him around her effectively, just in case of the outrageous scenario that he might want to move away from her. She lifted her head and opened her eyes, their golden depths full of her desire, and her anguish.

"I did not want this," she whispered to him, her forehead dropping onto his chest when the heat in his eyes proved too intense for her to bear. "Why will you not let me go?"

"Because I can't," he said, disentangling one hand from her hair so he could take her chin in hand and force her to look at him. "No more than you can."

"I hate this," she said painfully, her eyes blinking rapidly as they smarted with tears of frustration. "I hate not being able to control my own body. My own will. If this is what it means to be Imprinted, it is a weakness I will abhor with my last breath."

Then she pushed away, defying every nerve in her body that screamed at her to step back into his embrace. She could only backtrack a couple of steps, however, because her hair remained locked tight around his upraised wrist, pulling him along with her . . . as if he wouldn't have followed her anyway.

When she realized her back was to a window, she felt a moment of panic. However, she realized no one was likely to see them, because they were over three stories up from the houses and people below.

"You call it weakness, and yet as affected as I am by it myself, I choose to call it strength."

His rich baritone voice echoed around her, making her heart leap in alarm. She grabbed his wrist and pulled him farther down the hallway, the dark shadows enclosing them as they reduced the potential for echoes.

"Why are you here? And do not blame it on a holy day that will not arrive for two days."

"I do not intend to 'blame' anything. I don't believe I need an excuse to see you, Siena." He reached for her face, but she jerked back and dodged him. "And it is because of that holy day two nights from now that I am here. We need a little bit of resolution between us before that night comes, Siena."

"I am not in need of resolution. If you are, you must come to it on your own."

She turned to walk away from him, but she forgot he was just as quick as she was. No one could outrun the wind. His hand closed easily around her forearm, pulling her back . . . and snapping the temper and pain she had been holding in tenuous control for days.

She released the cry of a wounded animal and flew at him. He saw the flash of claws and felt the sharp sting of their cut as they scored his face. Shocked by the attack for all of a second, Elijah reacted on instinct. He had her by her hair in a heartbeat, wrapping it around his fist in a single motion, turning her around so her back was to him and her claws pointed in a safer direction. She grunted softly and then screamed in frustration as she found herself trapped face first against the stonecutter's art.

His enormous body was immediately flush against her back, securing her to the unforgiving stone as he caught one hand and pushed it against the stone as well.

"Let go of me!" She struggled in vain, unable to move a micron in any direction. "You'll have hands full of a spitting-mad cougar if you do not release me this instant!"

"I highly doubt that," he purred easily into her ear, his mouth brushing over the lobe of it in a way that made her shiver involuntarily.

And here's a sneak peek at NOAH,
coming in September from Zebra . . .

"Noah."

He felt Corrine's hands on his back, her empathy all too apparent in the tenderness of her touch. Noah could not bear the comfort. He did not want to be comforted. He shrugged her off hard enough to make her stumble backwards away from him.

"She's dead," he said, his voice far rougher with his unspeakable emotion than he would have liked. He ran cold fingers down his soiled face, focusing straight ahead until the detail of the velveteen fabric before him came more and more into visual clarity. The truths of his words were devastating to him, and on so many levels. He laughed mirthlessly at the capricious nature of fate. "Now I know why I have not dreamed of her in a week. Those dreams are . . ." He swallowed hard, trying to tamp down emotion far too violent to express in front of gentle friends. "They were a connection that needed both sides to be completed. And now I just stood here and let it happen again!" He turned sharply to look down at the red-headed Druid. "You were right. I was so stupid to wait. I wasted six months. If I had come to you when this started, she would have been safe under my protection!"

Corrine closed her eyes, fighting back her sympathetic tears.

"I don't understand any of this myself, Noah. You can't be sure—"

"I am damn sure, Corrine. Did you look out the windows? The sky went from noon to dawn, moving time backward to the moment this thing occurred. Backward to what I am guessing was a week ago. And do not tell me there was nothing I could do to change it. I felt that carpet beneath my foot! I could have . . . I should have done something! I could smell the difference between this room and that one. I felt the energy of an entire city. For that moment, that place in time was as real as this place is right now."

The monarch finally took a good look at the tall redhead who, in spite of a sordid layer of soiling, seemed to emanate with power. She had done a potent and amazing thing, a feat beyond all expectations of her abilities, and the aftermath showed in over-bright, forest green eyes and an aura that glowed like a Christmas tree.

"Consider," he said, this time more gently. "How would Kane feel if Isabella had found you too late, Corrine? I have a right to grieve a loss of such magnitude." Noah said this in that way he had that promptly ended any open avenues of discussion on a matter. The room vibrated with pain and tension, the silent noise punctuated with the occasional cough of Corrine's niece.

"Yuck," the child declared. She licked her hand and rubbed it on her clothes in an attempt to clean the soiled palm. Leah was fastidious about cleanliness, though clearly not as much so about the nature of germs.

Wordlessly, Noah crossed to Kane and plucked his charge out of her blood uncle's hands, carrying her across the room. He held the child to his chest with one massive hand, and she instantly hooked her small, skinny legs around his waist, her head dropping onto his shoulder with contentment and the security that her Uncle Noah would help her. The way he held her, however, grabbed at Corrine's heart somehow. She was hooked around him as if she were some sort of bulletproof vest, protecting his all too vulnerable heart.

Kane moved to hold his distraught wife when her thoughts and emotions impacted him fully. He followed her gaze, which was affixed on the door to the room as if Noah were standing on its threshold, instead of having already passed through it.

"Shh, sweetness," he soothed softly, leaning to kiss a dirt streaked cheek sympathetically. "You will see. He will be fine in time. Like any death, this will be grieved and then it will be put aside."

"I wish I could believe that," Corrine whispered to him on a fast, nervous breath. "The last time someone learned of the death of her potential Druid mate, it drove the girl mad."

"Mary? *Ruth* drove Mary mad, Corrine. From the minute that child was born she was spoiled, sheltered and held far more above her station by Ruth than was warranted. The mother was to blame for her daughter's actions because of her carelessness in Mary's upbringing. That can never happen to Noah. Noah comes from a upbringing that defies explanation and a place I couldn't even begin to put in plain words for you." Kane shook his head when he felt her puzzled expression. "Not a physical place. A metaphysical one. Noah was born with something none of the rest of us could ever lay claim to. It is why he, above all others, is King."

"That's why he, above all others, deserved a complimentary Queen," Corrine sighed.

Noah knew on some level of instinct that it was the child he was now watching play contentedly before his fire who was responsible for what had happened.

The Prophecy had been clear and unmistakable. The Enforcers would give life to the child who would be the very first of their kind to have the power to manipulate the element of Time. Though she was only a little over two years old, Leah clearly had shown her first evidence of her ability. An astounding development even had it been a known element. Even his power had not come to him this early.

Of course, she had no idea what she had done and no clue as to the significance of the part she had played. Suddenly certain things began to make sense to him. Noah spent enormous amounts of time with this special child. Though she'd had no conscious control of what she was doing, somehow Leah had formed the conduit through time for him. Perhaps it was simply a child's desire to please that had triggered the subconscious ability. Leah loved her Uncle Noah with incredible devotion. She strived to do things that would please him. Combine this with the power of his and Corrine's wills, their need to be successful in their hunt, and it had made the perfect catalyst for a child with an untried power who wanted nothing more but to give him what he wanted. What he needed.

And for a terrible moment, Noah wanted to use her for exactly that reason. The King was a scholar, so he full well knew what all the infinite implications to altering time, and a person's presence in time, could theoretically mean. However, he could not bring himself to care for that long second of self-indulgent thought.

Noah stood up abruptly, pacing over the playing toddler in order to lean close against the mantle. Normally the proximity to such intense heat would comfort him, but this time it did not.

He wanted to burn. Oh, yes, he was impervious to any and every form of flame or molten fire that the natural world could offer up; but this was not what he meant. In his dreams, *she* had made him burn. Kestra Irons. He laughed with the dry irony of her last name. The metal iron was toxic to Demonkind. It burned on contact. Just like Kestra.

The fire of passion was no stranger to him; he manipulated it well and with arrogant skill, and he had more than one lover in his history who would attest to that with a longing sigh of remembrance. This thing with the woman who had pervaded his sleeping world was out of reach of all of that. It was lacking cohesion and transient, and yet somehow all the more real. Now made unreal and inescapably out of reach for all the rest of time as he knew it.

Unless . . .

Noah shivered. He was unused to selfish thought. He was a man who lived every moment of his existence with the well-being of so many others as his first priority. Family. When not family, Council. When not family or Council, the multitude of his subjects. If none of them, then the races of others with which they associated. That was the essence of a good monarch. Everyone else must come first, especially those you loved best.

In that moment, all he wanted was to put himself first.

Whatever the cost.

No matter who paid the price.